THE SORCERER'S APPRENTICE

THE
Sorcerer's
Apprentice

AN ANTHOLOGY *of* MAGICAL TALES

EDITED BY

Jack Zipes

ILLUSTRATED BY NATALIE FRANK

PRINCETON UNIVERSITY PRESS
Princeton & Oxford

Grateful acknowledgment is made for permission to
reprint the following material:

"The Do-All Ax," from *Terrapin's Pot of Sense*
by Harold Courlander. Copyright 1957, 1985 by
Harold Courlander. Reprinted by permission
of The Emma Courlander Trust.

"The Guru and His Disciple," from *A Flowering
Tree and Other Oral Tales from India*, by A. K.
Ramanujan, with a Preface by Stuart Blackburn
and Alan Dundes (Berkeley: University of
California Press, 1997). Copyright © 1997 by the
Regents of the University of California.

"The High Sheriff and His Servant," from *Dog
Ghosts and Other Texas Negro Folk Tales*, by J.
Mason Brewer (Austin: University of Texas Press,
1958), pp. 20–21. Copyright © 1958, renewed 1986.

"Krabat," from *Sorbische Volkserzählungen*, edited
by Jerzy Slizinski (Berlin: Akademie-Verlag,
1964), pp. 45–50. Copyright © DeGruyter.

"The Magician's Apprentice" by Farīd al-Dīn
ʿAttār, from *The Ocean of the Soul: Man, the World
and God in the Stories of Farīd al-Dīn ʿAttār*, by
Hellmut Ritter, trans. John O'Kane with Bernd
Ratke (Leiden: Brill, 2003), pp. 640–41.

"The Man and His Son" by Corinne Saucier,
from *Folk Tales from Louisiana* (Baton Rouge, LA:
Claitor's Publisher, 1962).

"The Mojo," from *Negro Folktales in Michigan*,
collected and edited by Richard M. Dorson
(Cambridge, MA: Harvard University Press,
1956). Copyright © 1956 by the President and
Fellows of Harvard College.

The Sorcerer's Apprentice, by Richard Rostron,
illustr. Frank Lieberman (New York: William
Morrow, 1941).

"The Two Magicians," from *Tales from the French
Folklore of Missouri*, by Joseph Médard Carrière
(Evanston, IL: Northwestern University Press,
1937), pp. 91–96.

Published by Princeton University Press,
41 William Street, Princeton, New Jersey 08540

In the United Kingdom: Princeton University
Press, 6 Oxford Street, Woodstock, Oxfordshire
OX20 1TR

press.princeton.edu

Jacket illustration by Natalie Frank
Jacket and book design by Chris Ferrante

All Rights Reserved

ISBN 978-0-691-17265-1

British Library Cataloging-in-Publication Data
is available

This book has been composed in Adobe Jenson
with Latimer for display

Printed on acid-free paper. ∞

Printed in the United States of America

10 9 8 7 6 5 4 3 2 1

Contents

PART II. THE REBELLIOUS APPRENTICE TALES

Early Tales

Nineteenth-Century Tales

Twentieth-Century Tales

PART III. KRABAT TALES

List of Figures

Preface

I BEGAN GATHERING, translating, and writing about tales concerned with "The Sorcerer's Apprentice" six years ago, and as I was developing this project, it gradually became clear to me why I had become infatuated with these tales: they have given me some signs of hope when it seemed that we were living in hopeless times. The more I dug into the "Sorcerer's Apprentice" tradition, the more I discovered examples of opposition and resistance to wicked sorcerers of all kinds, who exploit magic for their own gain, and of the ways magic can enlighten readers about oppressive conditions under which they live. It is this hope that has prompted me to publish the tales in this book.

Though many of the diverse tales about sorcerer's apprentices are quite old, they still speak to contemporary problems of mentorship, child abuse, and exploitation as well as the misuse of cultural and political power. For example, during the past thirty years there has been a worldwide crisis that involves the maltreatment of young people by sorcerers, the degeneration of public education, slave labor, child abandonment, poverty, and violence. The renowned scholar Elisabeth Young-Bruehl, in her book *Childism*, has demonstrated how adults treat young people unconsciously and consciously as possessions and slaves, seeking to mold them in their image or in the normative image of accepted success and achievement in economic, cultural, and political institutions and networks.

If childism, as Young-Bruehl argues, spread throughout the world very early in history, and if magic played a prominent role in most societies as a positive force of supernaturalism, it makes sense that all sorts of magical tales would emerge—about conflicts between children and parents, apprentices and masters, troubled families and bureaucratic and hierarchical governments, and devout and humble followers of various religions and orthodox authoritarian leaders—and that these tales spread across borders and boundaries. Stories took shape from these conflicts before people knew how to write and read, preserved through oral traditions and gradually through modern technologies such as writing and printing. These tales of wish fulfillment and magical transformation articulated the human desire for social justice, autonomy, and knowledge—and still do.

No matter what the culture or society, magic represents "mana"—a supernatural sense of knowledge and impersonal spiritual power. According to the scholars Bernd-Christian Otto and Michael Stausberg,

> "Magic" belongs to the conceptual legacy of fifth-century Greece (BCE). Etymologically the term is apparently derived from contact with the main political enemy of that period, the Persians, and "magic" has ever since served as a marker of alterity, dangerous, foreign, illicit, suspicious but potentially powerful things done by others (and/or done differently). From referring to concrete objects and practices, "magic" eventually turned into a rather abstract category . . ."magic" has been a term with an extremely versatile and ambivalent semantics: it is the art of the devil or a path to the gods, it is of natural or supernatural origin, a testimony to human folly or the crowning achievement of scientific audacity, a sin or a virtue, harmful or beneficent, overpowering or empowering, and an act of othering or of self-assertion.[1]

For a variety of reasons throughout the centuries, people have sought knowledge and power through magic. Tales about the desire for magic, which have evolved from words, fragments, and sentences, are not only wish-fulfillment tales but also blunt expressions of emotions that reveal what the people who tell, write, and listen to the tales lack, and what they want. Most people in the world believe in some kind of magic, whether religious or secular, and want to control "magic," or "mana," to escape enslavement and determine the path of their lives. According to the French sociologist Pierre Bourdieu, all people are stamped by what he calls our "habitus"—the beliefs, values, and customs that mark and shape our thoughts, values, and behavior from birth. To know ourselves and to free ourselves, Bourdieu writes, we must continually confront masters, who, if they do not learn from their slaves, will ultimately have to die in order for the slaves to gain release and freedom. Our knowledge of ourselves and the world is attained through experiencing "slavery" and knowing what being in slavery entails. This means that we are all involved in what the philosopher Georg Wilhelm Friedrich Hegel, in *Phenomenology of Spirit*, calls a dialectical bloody battle to death that underlies all types of the "Sorcerer's Apprentice" tales.

In most of the oral tales and many of the literary tales about sorcerer's apprentices, the narrative perspective is what I call the "slave's perspective," a voice and view from below, no matter who the collector, mediator, or publisher of the tale may have been. This view is what makes the tales so striking. Though it may be difficult to explore and explain how people, defined and treated as slaves, contributed to the formation of culture from below, it can be done, as Sara Forsdyke has demonstrated in her book *Slaves Tell Tales and Other Episodes in the Politics of Popular Culture in Ancient Greece*.[2] Even before her study was published, the renowned American folklorist Richard Dorson drew important historical connections in his collection *Negro Folktales in Michigan* in dealing with American master-slave tales told by African Americans.

> Seemingly these unified and highly localized Old Marster tales grew on Southern soil from American Negro experience, but actually they come from the ends of the earth. By the mysterious selective process of folklore, jousts between masters and servants recounted centuries ago in Europe or West Africa have found their way into slave traditions. . . . From India comes the wonderful tale of the Sorcerer's Apprentice, with its magical transformation combat between the wizard and his pupil, to surface in Michigan in a unique text brilliantly adjusted to Negro slave life, with Old Marster out-hoodoing John at each successive step.[3]

The "Sorcerer's Apprentice" tales do not provide a solution to the master-slave conflict; they are not prescriptions or formulas for ending this conflict. What I have tried to demonstrate through collecting tales from various periods, and from different European, Asian, African, and American countries, is how these stories play out essential conflicts whose resolutions determine the nature of what it is to be human and humane. As Ernst Bloch, the German philosopher of utopian thinking, once wrote, "The fairy tale narrates a wish-fulfillment that is not bound by its own time, and the apparel of its contents. In contrast to the legend, which is always tied to a particular locale, the fairy tale remains unbound. Not only does the fairy tale remain as fresh as longing and love, but the demonically evil, which is abundant in the fairy tale, is still seen at work here in the present, and the happiness of 'once upon a time' which is even more abundant, still affects our visions of the future."[4]

In the introduction to this book I point to the contemporary relevance of the "Sorcerer's Apprentice" tale type in the worldwide popularity of

J. K. Rowling's Harry Potter novels, which are part of this tale type's long and varied tradition. In these novels and all the "Sorcerer's Apprentice" tales, magic is essential for the fashioning of the self. I then argue that the tale type actually forms a hybrid, or what I call a "memeplex" of two major tale types, the "Humiliated Apprentice" and the "Rebellious Apprentice." Tales often form pools of relevant information that become cultural replicators, or what I call "memes." As they evolve and change, tale types act like memes with bits of significant information, which take hold historically in the cultural memory of a society. We spread them, and they spread themselves by latching onto our cultural memories. They are both optimistic and pernicious: I discuss why the "Humiliated Apprentice" tale type fosters authoritarianism and enslavement, while the "Rebellious Apprentice" tale type engenders notions of empowerment and self-awareness. The two "ancient" tale types still stand in opposition to one another today, and their endless conflict, which reflects different perspectives on childism and master-slave relations and conditions, is the reason the tales endure and continue to spread.

To illustrate this point, I study the evolution of a particular set of tales that arose in a specific region in Central Europe called Sorbia, or Lusatia, during the latter part of the eighteenth century. These "Krabat" tales, in which a poor, wandering young worker learns magic and overcomes a tyrannical sorcerer, have become intrinsically woven into Sorbian, and, to a certain extent, into German culture. Since technological advances throughout the world have altered the ways in which relevant tale types are diffused, I conclude the introduction by showing how films have dealt with Krabat and other tales of magical transformation, and analyze how the "Sorcerer's Apprentice" tales have played a major role in the stories and novels disseminated and published in contemporary English-speaking countries.

Four premises guide my interpretations and analyses:

1. The belief in magic as "mana" has existed for thousands of years and continues to delineate religion and science while forging a crucial critique of secularization in the modern world. As Randall Styers, one of the foremost scholars of magic and religion, has remarked:

> Magic and supernaturalism of all sorts pervade modernity, eagerly adapting modern modes of knowledge and technology and actively engaging the anxieties and discontents of the modern world. Indeed,

modernity has depended on its own specific forms of mystification—commodification, mass entertainment, celebrity culture, and much more. The desire to suppress or expel magic has been such a formative component of efforts to produce the modern that it becomes impossible to grasp the nature of modernity without acknowledging the active magical undercurrents that pervade the contemporary world.[5]

2. While Styers and other scholars, such as Bernd-Christian Otto and Michael Stausberg,[6] have thoroughly studied the immense research on the theoretical meaning of magic, they have overlooked the great number of tale types that reveal how deeply rooted the belief in magic is throughout the world. The "Sorcerer's Apprentice" tales are highly significant because they present magic primarily as a stable value of transformation that allows for self-consciousness and self-fashioning. The "Sorcerer's Apprentice" tales counter the defamation of magic by religion, science, and the state, and challenge the status quo through the interrogation of the master-slave dialectic.

3. Most people tend to believe that the ideal, if not definitive, version of "The Sorcerer's Apprentice" is the Disney cinematic and literary tale produced as part of the film *Fantasia* in 1940. This is a misconception, and our unquestioning acceptance of the Disney version has ramifications for the abusive way children are treated throughout the world. In fact, the transformation of ancient "Humiliated Apprentice" tales into children's tales is one of the ways in which mass-mediated and commodified children's literature ideologically warps, if not perverts, folklore to induct children into authoritarian civilizing processes.

4. In contrast to a few misguided scholars who believe that common people were not imaginative and intelligent enough to create and retain their own stories, I believe that the oral traditions of anonymous storytelling serve as the basis for literary tales. This does not mean that oral tales are pivotal in the evolution of every tale type. In fact, literature often spawns oral storytelling. What it means is that, given the hundreds of thousands of years in which printing did not exist, tales were told and sung by all sorts of people, remembered, and altered as social and cultural conditions changed. The recollection of similar tale types enabled later-day writers to conceive literary tales. As R. G. Collingwood has convincingly noted in his short essay on "The Authorship of Fairy Tales":

To distinguish the folktale as a traditional narrative, passively transmitted by a process from which creative imagination is absent, from
the literary as the creation of an individual artist, is therefore to deal
in shadows, and to frustrate in advance any attempt to construct a rational theory of fairy tales. The folktale and the literary fairy tale are in
this respect on the same footing. Each of them uses traditional themes
and handles them by traditional methods; in each, the teller or writer
modifies both the themes and the methods in the course of his work,
sometimes for the better, sometimes for the worse; in neither case does
he leave them exactly as he found them.[7]

Clearly, it is foolish to conceive of the evolution of fairy tales in such
dichotomies as oral versus literary. Stories, storytellers, and writers look for
the most fitting and artistic way to articulate views about life and the world.
In the formation of what I call a memetic tradition of folk-tale types and fairy
tales, a communal expression of themes formed tales remembered for their
relevance. Many of the themes are connected to beliefs in magic and magical
transformation. Indeed, the pursuit of magic often underlies the patterns of
folk and fairy tales. In this regard, the themes found in folk and fairy tales
are organically connected with the customs and beliefs of people who engen-
dered them, and they form never-ending cultural traditions. As Collingwood
writes, "tradition is a creative process, in which the transmitter is more than
a medium through which the story conserves itself (or, if it be a distorting
medium, fails to conserve itself and suffers degradation); he is a sharer in the
work of invention. This is the only conception of tradition which will fit the
known facts of human history; if the science of folklore has failed to attain
it, that may be partly serve to explain why the science of folklore occupies so
unsatisfactory a place among the historical sciences."[8]

In this regard, I have framed this anthology of "Sorcerer's Apprentice" tales
to represent the two major strains of the "Sorcerer's Apprentice" tradition
and their historical development. It begins with tales of the "Humiliated
Apprentice," followed by the "Rebellious Apprentice" stories and "Krabat"
tales. The majority of the tales I collected stem from the "Rebellious Apprentice" tale type. This larger number, compared to the smaller quantity of the
"Humiliated Apprentice" tale type, does not reflect my prejudices but simply
the fact that I did not find as many "Humiliated Apprentice" tales in my vast
research as I did "Rebellious Apprentice" tales. The disparity speaks for itself.

It is only fitting, I think, to end this preface with a magical tale that reveals the reverence that magic demands not only in the tales that I have selected for this anthology, but also in our lives, which we are always seeking to transform. This tale was collected around 1070 from an oral tradition, adapted, and written down in Sanskrit by the Hindu poet Somadeva in his superb *Kathāsaritsagāra*, usually translated into English as *The Ocean of Story*. It is called "The Youth Who Went through the Proper Ceremonies. Why Did He Fail to Win the Magic Spell?" The renowned Sanskrit scholar Arthur Ryder included it in his book *Twenty-two Goblins* (1917), which is a part of *The Ocean of Story* and set in a frame narrative about the brave king Vikram. This king is mysteriously honored by a sham monk, who gives him gifts of fruit with jewels inside, and consequently, the king promises to assist the monk in completing a magic ritual. The monk, who is actually a sorcerer, tells the king that he will gain more than earthly riches if he goes some distance to a *sissoo*, or fig tree, cuts down a dead body hanging from it, and brings the body to him. However, inside the corpse is a *vetāla*, a ghost or goblin, and the king is not to speak to this creature, otherwise, the corpse will return to the tree. Since the king is curious and compassionate, the ghost/goblin manages to divert him with stories and questions so that he is never able to fulfill his task. The king instead learns, through the ghost/goblin and his twenty-two tales,[9] how much magic matters, and how he can improve himself by answering riddles. Here is one of the goblin's most important stories that sheds light on the significance of magic in the "Sorcerer's Apprentice" tales.

There is a city called Ujjain, whose people delight in noble happiness, and feel no longing for heaven. In that city there is real darkness at night, real intelligence in poetry, real madness in elephants, real coolness in pearls, sandal, and moonlight.

There lived a king named Moonshine. He had as counsellor a famous Brahman named Heaven-lord, rich in money, rich in piety, rich in learning. And the counsellor had a son named Moon-lord.

This son went one day to a great resort of gamblers to play. There the dice, beautiful as the eyes of gazelles, were being thrown constantly. And Calamity seemed to be looking on, thinking: "Whom shall I embrace?" And the loud shouts of angry gamblers seemed to suggest the question: "Who is there that would not be fleeced here, were he the god of wealth himself?"

This hall the youth entered, and played with dice. He staked his clothes and everything else, and the gamblers won it all. Then he wagered money he did not have, and lost that. And when they asked him to pay, he could not. So the gambling-master caught him and beat him with clubs.

When he was bruised all over by the clubs, the Brahman youth became motionless like a stone, and pretended to be dead, and waited. After he had lain thus for two or three days, the heartless gambling-master said to the gamblers: "He lies like a stone. Take him somewhere and throw him into a blind well. I will pay you the money he owes."

So the gamblers picked Moon-lord up and went far into the forest, looking for a well. Then one old gambler said to the others: "He is as good as dead. What is the use of throwing him into a well now? We will leave him here and go back and say we have left him in a well." And all the rest agreed, and left him there, and went back.

When they were gone, Moon-lord rose and entered a deserted temple to Shiva. When he had rested a little there, he thought in great anguish: "Ah, I trusted the rascally gamblers, and they cheated me. Where shall I go now, naked and dusty as I am? What would my father say if he saw me now, or any relative, or any friend? I will stay here for the present, and at night I will go out and try to find food somehow to appease my hunger."

While he reflected in weariness and nakedness, the sun grew less hot and disappeared. Then a terrible hermit named Stake came there, and he had smeared his body with ashes. When he had seen Moon-lord and asked who he was and heard his story, he said, as the youth bent low before him: "Sir, you have come to my hermitage, a guest fainting with hunger. Rise, bathe, and partake of the meal I have gained by begging."

Then Moon-lord said to him: "Holy sir, I am a Brahman. How can I partake of such a meal?"

Then the hermit-magician went into his hut and out of tenderness to his guest he thought of a magic spell which grants all desires. And the spell appeared in bodily form, and said: "What shall I do?" And the hermit said: "Treat that man as an honoured guest."

Then Moon-lord was astonished to see a golden palace rise before him and a grove with women in it. They came to him from the palace and said: "Sir, rise, come, bathe, eat, and meet our mistress." So they led him in and gave him a chance to bathe and anoint himself and dress. Then they led him to another room.

There the youth saw a woman of wonderful beauty, whom the Creator must have made to see what he could do. She rose and offered him half of her seat. And he ate heavenly food and various fruits and chewed betel leaves and sat happily with her on the couch.

In the morning he awoke and saw the temple to Shiva, but the heavenly creature was gone, and the palace, and the women in it. So he went out in distress, and the hermit in his hut smiled and asked him how he had spent the night. And he said: "Holy sir, through your kindness I spent a happy night, but I shall die without that heavenly creature."

Then the hermit laughed and said: "Stay here. You shall have the same happiness again to-night." So Moon-lord enjoyed those delights every night through the favour of the hermit.

Finally Moon-lord came to see what a mighty spell that was. So, driven on by his fate, he respectfully begged the hermit: "Holy sir, if you really feel pity for a poor suppliant like me, teach me that spell which has such power."

And when he insisted, the hermit said: "You could never win the spell. One has to stand in the water to win it. And it weaves a net of magic to bewilder the man who is repeating the words, so that he cannot win it. For as he mumbles it, he seems to lead another life, first a baby, then a boy, then a youth, then a husband, then a father. And he falsely imagines that such and such people are his friends, such and such his enemies. He forgets his real life and his desire to win the spell. But if a man mumbles it constantly for twenty-four years, and remembers his own life, and is not deceived by the network of magic, and then at the end burns himself alive, he comes out of the water, and has real magic power. It comes only to a good pupil, and if a teacher tries to teach it to a bad pupil, the teacher loses it too. Now you have the real benefit through my magic power. Why insist on more? If I lost my powers, then your happiness would go too."

But Moon-lord said: "I can do anything. Do not fear, holy sir." And the hermit promised to teach him the spell. What will holy men not do out of regard to those who seek aid?

So the hermit went to the river bank, and said: "My son, mumble the words of the spell. And while you are leading an imaginary life, you will at last be awakened by my magic. Then plunge into the magic fire which you will see. I will stand here on the bank while you mumble it."

So he purified himself and purified Moon-lord and made him sip water, and then he taught him the magic spell. And Moon-lord bowed to his teacher on the bank, and plunged into the river.

And as he mumbled the words of the spell in the water, he was bewildered by its magic. He forgot all about his past life, and went through another life. He was born in another city as the son of a Brahman. Then he grew up, was consecrated, and went to school. Then he took a wife, and after many experiences half pleasant, half painful, he found himself the father of a family. Then he lived for some years with his parents and his relatives, devoted to wife and children, and interested in many things.

While he was experiencing all these labours of another life, the hermit took pity on him and repeated magic words to enlighten him. And Moon-lord was enlightened in the midst of his new life. He remembered himself and his teacher, and saw that the other life was a network of magic. So he prepared to enter the fire in order to win magic power.

But older people and reliable people and his parents and his relatives tried to prevent him. In spite of them he hankered after heavenly pleasures, and went to the bank of a river where a funeral pile had been made ready. And his relatives went with him. But when he got there he saw that his old parents and his wife and his little children were weeping.

And he was perplexed, and thought: "Alas! If I enter the fire, all these my own people will die. And I do not know whether my teacher's promise will come true or not. Shall I go into the fire, or go home? No, no. How could a teacher with such powers promise falsely? Indeed, I must enter the fire." And he did.

And he was astonished to feel the fire as cool as snow, and lost his fear of it. Then he came out of the water of the river, and found himself on the bank. He saw his teacher standing there, and fell at his feet, and told him the whole story, ending with the blazing funeral pile.

Then his teacher said: "My son, I think you must have made some mistake. Otherwise, why did the fire seem cool to you? That never happens in the winning of this magic spell."

And Moon-lord said: "Holy sir, I do not remember making any mistake." Then his teacher was eager to know about it, so he tried to remember the spell himself. But it would not come to him or to his pupil. So they went away sad, having lost their magic.

When the goblin had told this story, he asked the king: "O King, explain the matter to me. Why did they lose their magic, when everything had been done according to precept?"

Then the king said: "O magic creature, I see that you are only trying to waste my time. Still, I will tell you. Magic powers do not come to a man because he does things that are hard, but because he does things with a pure heart. The Brahman youth was defective at that point. He hesitated even when his mind was enlightened. Therefore he failed to win the magic. And the teacher lost his magic because he taught it to an unworthy pupil."

Then the goblin went back to his home. And the king ran to find him, never hesitating.[10]

NOTES

1. Bernd-Christian Otto and Michael Stausberg, eds. *Defining Magic: A Reader* (Sheffield, UK: Equinox Publishing, 2013): 3. For a mammoth study of the term "magic," see Bernd-Christian Otto, *Magie: Rezeptions- und diskursgeschichtliche Analysen von der Antike bis zur Neuzeit* (Berlin: Walter de Gruyter, 2011). See also Ernesto de Martino, *Primitive Magic: The Psychic Powers of Shamans and Sorcerers* (Bridport, Dorset: Prism Press, 1988). He writes: "But we now know, as a result of our study, that the main interest of the magic world is not to bring about particular forms of spiritual life, but to master and consolidate the elementary being-within-the-world or presence of the individual. We are now aware that the ideology, praxis and institutions of the magic world cannot be understood unless one considers them as the expression of one problem: the wish to defend, master and regulate the threatened being-in-the-world (and, at the same time, establish and maintain world order that is also threatened with disintegration). . . . But if we see magic as a movement, as the expression of the dramatic wish to establish oneself and to maintain oneself as a guaranteed presence in a world of clearly-defined things and events then all its drama is revealed" (150–51).

2. Sara Forsdyke, *Slaves Tell Tales and Other Episodes in the Politics of Popular Culture in Ancient Greece* (Princeton, NJ: Princeton University Press, 2012). See also Peter Burke, *Popular Culture in Early Modern Europe* (New York: Harper & Row, 1978).

3. Richard Dorson, *Negro Folktales in Michigan* (Cambridge, MA: Harvard University Press, 1956): 50.

4. Ernst Bloch, *The Utopian Function of Art and Literature: Selected Essays*, trans. Jack Zipes and Frank Mecklenburg (Boston: MIT Press, 1988): 163.

5. Randall Styers, "Magic," in *Vocabulary for the Study of Religion*, ed. Robert Segal and Koku von Stuckrad (Leiden: Brill, 2015); http://referenceworks.brillonline.com/entries /vocabulary-for-the-study-of religion/magic-COM_00000154. See also Randall Styers, *Making Magic: Religion, Magic, and Sciences in the Modern World* (Oxford: Oxford University Press, 2004).

6. See Bernd-Christian Otto and Michael Stausberg, eds., *Defining Magic: A Reader* (Sheffield, UK: Equinox Publishing, 2013).

7. R. G. Collingwood, "The Authorship of Fairy Tales," in *The Philosophy of Enchantment: Studies in Folktale, Cultural Criticism, and Anthropology*, ed. David Boucher, Wendy James, and Philip Smallwood (Oxford: Clarendon Press, 2005): 266. Collingwood, a renowned British philosopher, gave a series of highly significant talks to the Folklore Society in London during the 1930s. They have been published for the first time in *The Philosophy of Enchantment*, and Smallwood's essay, "The Re-Enactment of Self: Perspectives from Literature, Criticism, and Culture," in this volume (pp. xxiii–lv) is an excellent analysis of Collingwood's views on the history of folk and fairy tales.

8. Ibid., 271.

9. In the Tawney/Penzer major edition there are twenty-five Vetāla tales. See volumes VI and VII of Charles Henry Tawney, trans., *The Ocean of Story*, ed. N. M. Penzer, 10 vols. (London: Chas. J. Sawyer, 1924).

10. Arthur Ryder, trans., *Twenty-two Goblins* (London: J. M. Dent & Sons, 1917). For other translations, see Richard Burton, trans., *Vikram and the Vampire: or, Tales of Hindu Devilry* (London: Longmans, Green, 1870); Charles Henry Tawney, trans., *The Ocean of Story* (Somadeva's *Kathā Sarti Sāgara*) (London: Asiatic Society of Bengal, 1880–84); and Tawney, *The Ocean of Story*, ed. N. M. Penzer, 10 vols. (London: Chas. J. Sawyer, 1924). There are also strong parallels to Somadeva's tale in Rachel Harriette Busk, ed. and trans., "The Saga of the Well-and-Wise-Walking Khan," *Sagas from the Far East; or, Kalmouk and Mongolian Traditionary Tales* (London: Griffith and Farran, 1873); and Charles Swynnerton, ed. and trans., "The Story of the Merchant and the Brahmin," *Indian Nights' Entertainment, or, Folk-Tales from the Upper Indus* (London: Elliot Stock, 1892). Both these tales are included in this anthology.

Notes and Acknowledgments

UNLESS OTHERWISE INDICATED, all the translations from German, Italian, and French are mine. I credit other translators and editors of particular tales in the footnotes and the biographies at the end of the book. I am most grateful to Marcie Fehr, my research assistant at the University of Winnipeg, who was a great sleuth and helped me find numerous tales. I have received important advice and help from Cristina Bacchilega, Simon Bronner, Pauline Greenhill, Donald Haase, Ulrich Marzolph, Sadhana Naithani, and Jennifer Schacker. In addition, I have benefited very much from scholarly studies written by Graham Anderson, D. L. Ashliman, Donald Beecher, Susanne Hose, and Raffaella Riva. Throughout my work, Anne Savarese has been a great mainstay and perceptive critic. I am deeply grateful to her for her editorial work. As usual, Sara Lerner has supervised the entire production of the book with great care and diligence, and Jennifer Harris has provided meticulous and helpful copyediting. Finally I should like to acknowledge the support I received from the Social Sciences and Humanities Research Council of Canada Partnership Development Grant 890-2013-17, Fairy Tale Cultures and Media Today.

My goal in collecting the stories about the "Sorcerer's Apprentice" in this book was to include a large selection of the variants stemming from the tale types ATU 325 and ATU 325*, which have become popular in different cultures and have been disseminated throughout the world. Many of the other texts I have chosen are from nineteenth- and early twentieth-century English translations. The style and language of these works can sound somewhat quaint, but I believe that these unusual tales will provide readers with a sense of how the different tales were read, perceived, and transmitted in the course of the nineteenth and twentieth centuries. I have lightly edited the tales to correct errors, avoid antiquated grammar, provide clarity, and create smooth transitions. I have not made any substantial changes.

During my research I became aware that there are hundreds, if not thousands, of tales linked to the humiliated and rebellious sorcerer's apprentice.

To avoid redundancy and repetition, I selected narratives that best represent the different memetic strains, or that are most unusual in shedding light on the master-slave conflict. I have also included a selected and chronological list of "Sorcerer's Apprentice" tales, many of which are not in this anthology, so that readers can see how widespread the tale types are and why I have referred to them as memes. All the slight changes and adaptations in the telling and printing of the "Sorcerer's Apprentice" tales are fascinating, and they need further study so that their particularity in the sociohistorical context in which they appeared can be appreciated. My hope is that other scholars and critics will use my research to continue to explore the "magic" not only in the "Sorcerer's Apprentice" tales but also in tale types that are rooted in our cultural memories.

THE SORCERER'S APPRENTICE

The Sorcerer's Apprentice, Harry Potter, and Why Magic Matters

It is now widely admitted by anthropologists that magic is based on power. A rite which has efficacy *in se* is exactly analogous to a word of power. It is by his power or *mana* that the sorcerer or medicine-man works his will. But it is important to notice in the lower culture the sorcerer's power differs not so much in kind as in degree from that of the ordinary man. Everyone has some power, some personality.

—W. R. HALLIDAY, "THE FORCE OF INITIATIVE IN MAGICAL CONFLICT"[1]

The central problem, for anyone who wishes to use fairy tales as historical material, lies here. The common characteristic of such tales is their magical character. To understand them means understanding magic: understanding why people behaved in the ways for which we use magic as a general term. Now, if magical behaviour is irrational behaviour, this cannot be done. . . . In order to understand fairy tales, therefore, we must give an account of magic which will show that in its essence it is a thing familiar to ourselves, not as a spectacle, but as an experience: something which we habitually do, something which plays a part in our social and personal life, not as a mere survival of savagery, but as an essential feature of civilisation. If we can do this, we shall have reached a point of view from which, in principle at least, the magical elements in fairy tales become comprehensible; and we can go on to the strictly historical question of which of them can be understood, not only abstractly and in principle, but in detail, as manifestations of a particular historical stage of human development.

—R. G. COLLINGWOOD, *THE PHILOSOPHY OF ENCHANTMENT*[2]

FOR THE PAST FIFTEEN YEARS, I have wondered why a conventional series of fantasy novels such as the Harry Potter books has had such phenomenal success. I had tentatively proposed an answer to my own puzzlement in 2000, when I published *Sticks and Stones: The Troublesome Success of Children's Literature from Slovenly Peter to Harry Potter*. I claimed that there is something wonderfully paradoxical about the phenomena surrounding the phenomenon of the Harry Potter books. For anything to become a phenomenon in Western society, it must first be recognized as unusual, extraordinary, remarkable, and outstanding. In other words, it must be popularly accepted, praised, or condemned, worthy of everyone's attention; it must conform to the standards of exception set by the mass media and promoted by the culture industry in general. To be phenomenal means that a person or commodity must conform to the tastes of hegemonic groups that determine what makes for a phenomenon. In short, it is impossible to be phenomenal without conforming to conventionality.[3]

I am not about to recant this critique. In fact, I could even elaborate and deepen it by discussing how the network of publicity and promotion forms and determines meanings in contemporary cultures throughout the world, and by demonstrating that the Harry Potter novels do not have an inherent meaning, but meaning bestowed on them by a massive web of fanzines, mass-mediated publicity, merchandising, films, and the creation of "myths" about the author, J. K. Rowling, and the origin of her novels, which are, to be sure, well-written and readily accessible to the common reader. But Rowling complies, and has had to comply, with the conventions of the culture industry. After all, popular culture is no longer made popular by the *popolo*, or the common people, but by forces that influence and manipulate how the *popolo* will receive and react to commodified forms of culture. The *popolo* is to be enchanted by the magic of commodification.

That said, something significant escaped my attention when I first tried to explain why the Harry Potter novels had such a mammoth success, and I want to attempt now to take a much different approach that has, I believe, ramifications for understanding the deep roots of fairy tales, magic, children's literature, and popular culture. The Harry Potter novels hark back to stories about magicians and their apprentices, told and written down during and before the Common Era in Europe, Asia, and the Middle East. Such great dissemination was noted already in the nineteenth century by the great British folklorist, William Alexander Clouston, when he wrote:

The stem of what Mr. Baring-Gould terms the "Magical Conflict Root" has spread its branches far and wide in the shape of popular fictions in which two or more persons possessing nearly equal powers of changing themselves into whatever forms they please, engage in a life-or-death struggle. It seems to me that popular belief in men capable of acquiring such powers should sufficiently account for the universal prevalence of stories of this class, without seeking for their origin in primitive conceptions of the phenomena of physical nature, such as sunrise, sunset, clouds, lightning, and so forth.[4]

Indeed, these tales were widely disseminated over centuries by word of mouth and script until they became memetic, forming a memeplex, a pool of similar tale types, in Western cultural memory, expressing and touching upon core human dispositions and desires for self-knowledge, knowledge, and power that are related to the adaptation and survival of the human species. Underlying my thesis is the notion that "black" and "white" magic are opposite sides of erudite supernatural knowledge gained from an intense scientific study of the material universe. The "knowers" of the basic elements of our world—the magicians, sorcerers, wizards, witches, inventors, shamans, scientists, medicine men, priests/priestesses, gurus, generals, and politicians—use "black" and "white" magic to transform themselves and their environments in ways that most people cannot. In seeking omniscience and immortality sorcerers reveal that their success depends ethically on whether they will share their magic (knowledge or mana) to benefit the majority of the people or whether they will use their magic (knowledge or mana) to dominate the people of the world. These sorcerers are omnipotent shape-shifters, and they represent what we all want but cannot obtain unless we live in the wish-fulfillment of fairy tales that we project. The appeal and significance of magic in fairy tales stems from the manner in which it is contested. Magic is differentiated in the hundreds of tales about sorcerers and their apprentices, but one thing is clear: none of the protagonists and antagonists doubt the existence of magic, and they all realize that this mana can be used for good or evil purposes.

So to understand how and why we use magic in life-and-death struggles recorded as fairy tales, I want to first focus on the Harry Potter novels as a fairy tale,[5] for in doing so we can see their relationship to the tale type "The Magician and His Pupil," as classified by Hans-Jörg Uther in *The Types of International Folktales*,[6] a catalogue that enables researchers to trace the origins and dissemination of tales with similar plots. Then I shall discuss how deeply the tale type of "The Magician and His Pupil" is historically rooted and how widely it spread in Asian, Middle Eastern, European, and American folklore since at least the fourth century BCE, and how it became a staple of

children's literature much later—during the late nineteenth century, thanks
to the transformation of the Grimms' tales as stories for children, and during
the twentieth century, thanks to Disney's 1940 film *Fantasia* and book version
of *The Sorcerer's Apprentice*. Then I shall discuss how Georg Wilhelm Friedrich Hegel's notions of "The Master-Slave Dialectic" in *Phenomenology of
the Spirit* (1807) are crucial for understanding the conflicts in the "Sorcerer's
Apprentice" tales. This discussion is followed by a brief analysis of why and
how the tale type of the "Sorcerer's Apprentice" as meme is so deeply rooted
and disseminated in all cultural memories throughout the world, from transformations of cultural legends into magical fairy tales, as in the Krabat tales
of Central Europe, to contemporary cinematic and narrative adaptations of
sorcerer's apprentice tales in English-speaking countries.

   We can only manage to know ourselves in life-and-death struggles played
out metaphorically in tales we tell and write. The "Sorcerer's Apprentice" tales
concern not only past magical conflicts related to problematic apprenticeships
but also contemporary ways society teaches and "civilizes" young people either
to conform to contradictory values and norms that expose hypocrisies, or to
question and reform them so that magical knowledge can benefit the common good. It is precisely because the "Sorcerer's Apprentice" tales deal with
problems of attaining awareness of the self and of the world that they have
obtained great relevance and have become memetic in various forms. A "childist" world[7] hinders most children from gaining critical knowledge of their
societies and environments, or denies them the freedom to express themselves
and develop talents that will enable them to make decisions about knowledge
and power. Whatever magic they may attain is used for self-survival, but the
question remains: Is self-survival enough to guarantee the transformation of
the world into a haven where children can flourish and develop their talents
through peaceful cooperation? Is self-survival enough, then, to guarantee the
survival of the world?

THE HARRY POTTER NOVELS AS FAIRY TALE

Critics have proposed various theories about Harry Potter as a male Cinder-
ella or Little Tom Thumb, the odd little fellow who uses his wits to outsmart
ogres and predators.[8] He is the little guy who always triumphs despite the
odds against him. To my knowledge, however, no one has associated these
novels with the tale type ATU 325, "The Magician and His Pupil," which is

the classification number and title used by Hans-Jörg Uther in *The Types of International Folktales* (2004)[9] to identify narratives in which a young man seeks to obtain magic against the wishes of a sorcerer. If we were to undertake this task—to make a compact fairy tale out of the seven novels associated with ATU 325, "The Magician and His Pupil"—here is a summary of how they would read:

Once upon a time there was an eleven-year-old boy named Harry Potter. He was an orphan and lived in a boring town with his philistine relatives, the crude commoners known as the Dursleys, who treated him badly. They were insensitive Muggles, and Harry wanted to escape them and the town. One day he received a visit from the half-giant Hagrid, who informed him that he was a wizard and had been chosen to study magic at Hogwarts School, an enchanted place, a short train ride from London. When Harry traveled to Hogwarts, he made friends with Ron Weasley and Hermione Granger, who helped him in various struggles for survival. Indeed, Harry, anointed as "the boy who lived" after the murder of his parents by Lord Voldemort, the most evil and powerful wizard in dark history, had many battles with Voldemort in seven long years at Hogwarts. So he needed all the helpers he could find, such as the owl Hedwig and the wise Professor Dumbledore. In one of his first trials he learned to use the cloak of invisibility to protect the philosopher's stone of immortality from Voldemort. Numerous friends and foes were shape-shifters, and part of Harry's learning at Hogwarts demanded that he distinguish between true professors of the Defense against the Dark Arts and those who supported the evil of Voldemort. However, despite Harry's ability to use white magic, Voldemort's power kept mounting, and Harry was left to his own resources when Professor Dumbledore, his spiritual guide, was killed. By the time Harry turned eighteen, he developed into an adroit, powerful, and cunning wizard, and in a grand gesture of sacrifice, he allowed Voldemort to kill him because Harry contained a horcrux within him that was a fragment of Voldemort's evil soul. However, Harry learned from the spirit of Dumbledore in limbo that Voldemort himself had accidentally already killed the horcrux in him with a killing curse so that Harry could return to life and slay Voldemort with a disarming charm. In the happy ending Harry marries well and sends his children off to study magic at the exclusive boarding school at Hogwarts, just as many well-to-do British and American families send their children to elite private schools today.

In short the structure of Rowling's fairy tale resembles the folklore tale type ATU 325, which has the following plot functions: (1) A poor father apprentices his son to a magician/sorcerer to study magic for one or three years at a mysterious place/school. The son as pupil can be released only after he spends the designated time in the magician's school and only if his father or mother recognizes him in a transformed condition, usually as a bird (dove, raven). Important here is that the sorcerer more or less enslaves the boy and wants to keep him as slave. (2) The son secretly flies home and indicates to his father/mother how he or she can recognize him, or the father and mother are helped by a mysterious stranger who advises them on how to recognize their son. (3) Once liberated, the son, who has learned and gained just as much knowledge of magic as his master, can shape-shift, and he uses this magic power to transform himself into an animal so that his father can sell him for a good deal of money as an ox, a cow, a dog (often a greyhound), or a horse at country markets or fairs. Then, after he is sold, the son returns to his human form and escapes the buyer. The son can only return to his human form if the father keeps the leash/bridle/halter that binds him. Son and father become wealthy. (4) The magician seeks revenge at a fair/market, buys his former apprentice when transformed into a horse, and manages to keep the bridle/halter. (5) The magician imprisons the pupil as horse and punishes him through torture and with the intention to kill him. (6) The pupil uses his cunning and knowledge of magic to escape, and the magician pursues him in a battle of shape-shifting. They transform themselves into birds, fish, rabbits, rings, apples, precious stones, and grains of corn or barley. In one final major battle the magician becomes a rooster/hen, and the pupil becomes a fox and bites off his head or devours him. There is always a bloody battle to death. (7) Sometimes the pupil returns to his father; sometimes he marries a princess or maiden who has helped him. There is no indication how he will use his magic power in the future. There is no apparent reason for him to use it for malevolent purposes, because his life is no longer in danger and he does not seek to exploit other people.

In my opinion, the Harry Potter novels owe their popularity to the rich worldwide tradition of "Sorcerer's Apprentice" tales, which are ever-present as memetic stories in cultural memories. It is not necessary to trace just how the novels have stemmed from a particular literary or oral tradition. What matters is that they evince a deep belief in the power of magic/mana as a supernatural means to "fashion" or "create" one's life as one personally desires and to triumph over nefarious forces that seek to hinder self-development. What matters is that we recognize how the "Sorcerer's Apprentice" tales inform our lives more than we realize. They are historically and culturally prominent in our cultural memories. They make us aware that magic matters, no matter what its substance may be, no matter what form it takes.

To understand just how informed and formed we are by the "Sorcerer's Apprentice" tales, we must also consider an important variant of tale type ATU 325, among some other hundreds if not thousands of minor offshoots. This other tale type, ATU 325*—often called "The Apprentice and the Ghosts" or, misleadingly, "The Sorcerer's Apprentice"—involves a foolish apprentice who reads a forbidden book of magic. This occurs when the master magician leaves the house of magic. Sometimes, the curious and ambitious apprentice does not read a book but instead overhears the magician pronouncing spells, and tries to imitate the magician. In short, the apprentice wants to use magic to gain recognition and become the magician's equal. Since he does not fully grasp the power of the magic, the apprentice calls forth demons or ghosts, who cause chaos until the magician returns and brings everything back to order. In the end the apprentice learns a lesson about not using language and knowledge until he is capable and mature enough to control what he conjures. The magician reprimands, scolds, or punishes the apprentice and then vanishes. Sometimes the magician brings about the apprentice's death. In more recent stories or books for children, the apprentice is generally portrayed as a "blockhead" or bumbling ignoramus.

By studying the complex or memeplex of tale type ATU 325 (the major tale type, "The Magician and His Pupil") and ATU 325* ("The Apprentice and the Ghosts"), we can see how relevant the "Sorcerer's Apprentice" tales are in contemporary cultures throughout the world. In the development of a tale type as meme—and not all fairy tales become memes—one basic text or tale type becomes stable and more fit to survive under all social and cultural conditions than other memetic tales as it is adapted or adapts itself through diverse modalities. In the process it spawns variant memes that surround the stable type to form a memeplex.[10] The variants stand in dialogue with one another or are in opposition to one another. Though they have different plots and patterns, they are part of a whole—that is, part of the memeplex. Clearly, the tale type of "The Apprentice and the Ghosts," in which a young man is humiliated, is an oppositional version of "The Magician and His Pupil," in which a young man defeats a tyrannical and demonic master by using the magician's own magic.

Both tale types have roots in ancient India, Mongolia, Egypt, Siberia, Turkey, Greece, and Italy, and may share the same sources. Since the stories in these two oral and literary traditions listed as the same tale type are often referred to by the same title, "The Sorcerer's Apprentice," which can cause confusion, I will categorize the tales in "The Magician and His Pupil" tradition as part of the tale type "The Sorcerer's Rebellious Apprentice," and the tales in "The Apprentice and the Ghosts" tradition as part of "The Sorcerer's Humiliated Apprentice." Indeed, I am doing this because many catalogue designations in *The Types of International Folktales* are confusing or too general, and the titles and tales are not sufficiently distinguished from one another. This ambivalence is especially the case in "The Magician and His Pupil," which does not tell us anything about two distinct tale types that are in an antagonistic relationship with one another. Ideologically speaking, the one tale type, which I shall simply call "The Rebellious Apprentice Tale," challenges the basic assumptions of the other tale type, which I shall call "The Humiliated Apprentice Tale." Their antagonistic differences continue to play out historically and culturally in contemporary societies throughout the world, with diverse consequences. So we must return to the past to grasp why apprentices rebel against or comply with the holders of supernatural magical knowledge and power.

With this crucial distinction in mind I shall discuss the evolution of the conservative and conventional tale type, the "Humiliated Apprentice," and its more radical tale type, the "Rebellious Apprentice," with regard to the master-slave conflict, which is at the center of the memeplex. But before I do this, I want to mention that there are some significant variants from other genres that also contribute to the memeplex. One of the most significant tale types, "The Magic Flight," ATU 313, forms the basis of European folk ballads that can be traced back to many songs of the late medieval period. In his pioneer study *The English and Scottish Popular Ballads* (5 volumes, 1882–98), Francis James Child indicates in his analysis of "The Two Magicians" that there were and are hundreds of European ballads related to the tale type of the "Sorcerer's Apprentice."[11] One of them demonstrates a clear connection:

> *About a Godless Sorcerer and the Miraculous Redemption of*
> *His Innocent Children (Von einem gottlosen Zauberer und*
> *seiner unschuldigen Kindlein wunderbarer Erlösung)*

Once there were two innocent children	Es waren zwei zarte Kindlein,
a boy and girl without care or sin.	Ein Knabe und ein Mädchen;
But their father was a godless rake,	Ihr Vater war ein gottloser Bub'.

Who swore to the devil they were his to take.	Er schwor die Kinder dem Teufel zu
Oh, praise be the Lord in Heaven!	O höchster Gott im Himmelreich!
The children lived in a foreign land in an unknown cave filled with sand.	In einer Höhlen unbekannt, Da lebten die Kinder im fremden Land.
The sorcerer had a magic book which pleased him with each look he took.	Der Zauberer hatt' ein Zauberbuch Daran er groß Gefallen trug.
The boy, too, liked to read this book, Whenever the sorcerer was away.	Der Knabe las in dem Buch so gern, Wenn oft der böse Zauberer fern.
He cleverly learned magic from this book,	Lernt' zaubern wohl aus dieser Schrift.
And just how one made magic work.	Und wie man einen Zauber trifft.
"Sister, the wicked one's wandering about.	O Schwesterlein, der Böse ist aus,
Let's go now into the world! We must set out!"	Wir wollen nun in die Welt hinaus!
So the two rushed off as fast as they could	Die zwei, sie eilten den lieben Tag,
and wandered as far as they possibly could.	So viel nur einer wandern mag.
And when it soon became late at night,	Und als es war am Abend spät,
The evil spirit came all too near.	Der böse Geist hinter ihnen naht:
"Oh, brother, we are lost and can't stay here,	O Bruder, jetzt sind wir verloren hier.
For the wicked spirit is very near."	Der böse Geist ist nahe schier!
The young man uttered a powerful spell	Der Jüngling sprach einen argen Spruch
Learned from the book he had studied so well.	Den er gelernt aus dem Buch.
So his sister became a pond which he wished,	Das Mägdlein ward ein großer Teich.

10   INTRODUCTION

While he changed himself right
    into a fish.

The wicked man walked around the
    water,
But he couldn't catch the fish he
    sought.
So he ran back to his cave in a rage,
To see if he could fetch some nets
    and a cage.

The two rushed off as fast as they
    could
And wandered as far as they
    possibly could.
"Oh, brother we are lost and can't
    stay here.
For the wicked one is very near."

The young boy now uttered a
    powerful spell,
Learned from the book he had
    studied so well.
So the girl was turned into a holy
    chapel,
Her brother became an image on
    the altar.

The wicked man walked around the
    church,
But failed to snatch the image as he
    lurked.
So he went back to his cave in a
    rage
To see if he could fetch some fire or
    a cage.

On the third day they fled, as fast as
    they could,

Der Jüngling einem Fische gleich.

Der böse gieng um das Wasser
    rund,
Den Fisch er da nicht fangen konnt',

Da lief er zornig nach seiner Höhl'.
Ob er sich Netze holen könnt'.

Die zwei, die eilten einen Tag,

So viel nur einer wandern mag;

O Bruder, jetzt sind wir verloren
    hier,
Der böse Geist ist nahe schier!

Der Jüngling sprach einen argen
    Spruch,
Den er gelernt aus dem Buch.

Das Mädchen ward da eine Kapell',

Der Knab' ein Bild auf dem Altar.

Der Böse ging um das Kirchlein
    rund,
Das Bild er da nicht kriegen kunnt",

Da lief er zornig nach seiner Höhl',

Ob er sich Feuer holen möcht.

Die zwei, die eilten den dritten Tag,

And wandered as far as they possibly could.	So viel nur einer wandern mag;
"Oh, brother, we are lost and can't stay here,	O Bruder, jetzt sind wir verloren hier,
For the wicked spirit is very near."	Der böse Geist ist hinter dir!
The young boy now uttered a powerful spell,	Der Knabe sprach einen argen Spruch,
Learned from the book he had studied so well.	Den er gelernt aus dem Buch:
The girl became a barnyard floor.	Das Mägdlein ward eine Tenne fest,
The boy changed into barley corn.	Der Knab' lag drauf, ein Körnlein Gerst'.
The wicked man walked around the floor.	Der Böse gieng wohl um die Tenn',
He uttered a spell and became a hen.	Er sprach ein Wort, er ward eine Henn',
He wanted to swallow the corn on the floor.	Er wollte schlingen die Gerste hinein.
Oh, the boy's lost and won't live much more.	Der Knab' sollt' schon verloren sein
But the boy now uttered a powerful spell.	Der Knabe sprach einen argen Spruch,
Learned from the book he had studied so well.	Den er gelernt aus dem Buch;
And taking his time he became a fox,	Er ward ein Fuchs da wiederum,
That twisted the hen's neck until it was dead.	Und drehte der Henne, den Hals herum.
Oh, praise be the Lord in Heaven!	O höchster Gott im Himmelreich![12]

Child writes: "There can be little doubt that these ballads are derived, or take their hint, from popular tales, in which (1) a youth and maid, pursued by a sorcerer, fiend, giant, ogre, are transformed by the magical powers of one or the other into such shapes as enable them to elude, and finally to escape, apprehension; or (2) a young fellow, who has been apprenticed to a sorcerer, fiend, etc., and has acquired the black art by surreptitious reading in his master's books, being pursued as before, assumes a variety of forms, and his master others, adapted to the destruction of his intended victim, until the tables are turned by the fugitive's taking on the stronger figure and dispatching his adversary."[13]

"The Godless Sorcerer," collected and published in 1843 by Guido Görres, includes key motifs of the "Sorcerer's Apprentice" tradition such as the magic book, the clever boy who learns how to use magic better than the magician, transformation of humans into animals, barley corn, and a fox that kills a chicken or rooster. So, it is in other genres and art forms that the "Rebellious Apprentice" and the "Humiliated Apprentice" tales were disseminated and took hold of people of all classes. These tales had to mean something; they had to be relevant for so many variants to have been spread in many different societies for over four thousand years. They began with bits and pieces in stories and were cobbled together by anonymous storytellers and singers. The only reason we absorb them today is that they still speak to us more than ever.

THE HUMILIATED APPRENTICE

In two excellent studies, Graham Anderson's *Fairytale in the Ancient World* (2000) and William Hansen's *Ariadne's Thread* (2002), the authors both cite Lucian's comic *Philopseudes* (*The Lover of Lies*, ca. 150 CE) as one of the main sources of "The Humiliated Apprentice," which they believe has much older variants and stems from an oral tradition. Anderson summarizes the tale as follows:

> A young Greek called Eucrates is touring Egypt and in the course of a trip on the Nile encounters Pancrates, an amazing magician, to whom he is apprenticed; the latter does not require any domestic servant, but instead enchants household objects, a broom and a pestle, to undertake domestic tasks on their own. Eucrates overhears the spell and in the sorcerer's absence is able to activate the magical servant. Unfortunately he is also unable to stop its activities once started, having only overheard the first half of the spell; splitting the animated pestle with an axe only divides it into two servants instead of one. Only the returned sorcerer can put a stop to the now three magical servants, and having done so he disappears. Eucrates still knows his half of the spell, but dare not use it for fear of the

consequences. Thereafter, he travels on to Memphis, and the great stone colossi of Memnon delivers him an oracle.[14]

It is impossible to determine how this short satirical tale spread over the next several centuries either through oral tradition or print.[15] But spread it did. In fact, several similar Greek and Egyptian tales were circulating before and about the same time that Lucian wrote his version. In his important book *In Search of the Sorcerer's Apprentice*, Daniel Ogden outlines a schema of the motif-set of this tale type, which I have summarized here and which can be readily discerned in the other Greek and Egyptian tales and in most of the "Humiliated Apprentice" tales up through the twenty-first century:

1. An Egyptian setting. (The setting changes after the Hellenistic period according to the country in which the tale is told or printed.)
2. A keen and studious but prematurely ambitious young man apprenticed to a priest-magician.
3. A desperate desire to master a technology, but despite the young man's best efforts, he is unable to discover the knowledge that is key to the control of that technology.
4. A magical book or books supporting the technology that the young man tries to use or steal.
5. A venerable priest-magician who is the young man's master.
6. The young man's gradual working of his way into the confidence and friendship of the priest-magician.
7. The young man's beseeching of the priest-magician for an all-important specific revelation.
8. Failure of the young man's endeavors to use and control magic.
9. Revelation of or initiation into the key and essential knowledge in an underground cavern or crypt and/or punishment of the young man for overreaching.[16]

In discussing the history of both the "Humiliated Apprentice" and the "Rebellious Apprentice" tales during the Hellenistic period, we must bear in mind what Fritz Graf has to say about magic:

The practice of magic was omnipresent in classical antiquity. The contemporaries of Plato and Socrates placed voodoo dolls on graves and thresholds (some of these dolls can be found in modern museums). Cicero smiled upon a colleague who said that he had lost his memory under the influence of a spell, and the Elder Pliny declared that everybody was afraid to fall victim to binding spells. The citizens of classical Teos cursed with spells whoever attacked the city; the Twelve Tables legislated against magical transfers of crops from one field to another; and the imperial law books contain extensive sanctions against all sorts of magical procedures—with the sole exception of love spells and weather magic. . . . Ancient magic lived on: Greek spells from Egyptian papyrus books reappear in Latin Guise in astrological manuscripts at the time of Christopher Columbus; the story of the sorcerer's apprentice, told in Lucian, is famous in European literature and music, and the image of the modern witch is unthinkable without Greek and Roman antecedents. Magic, in a certain sense, belongs to antiquity and its heritage, like temples, hexameters, and marble statues.[17]

An example of one of the more interesting tales that indicates the prevalence of magic and the tale type of the "Humiliated Apprentice," discussed and summarized by Ogden, is the Demotic Egyptian romance, *Setne*, which was probably composed during the reign of Ptolemy Philadelphus (283–246 BCE). Here a wise man and scribe named Naneferkapah wanders through the desert of Memphis and encounters a priest, who tells him that he is wasting his time reading inscriptions on tombs. Instead, the priest directs him to a magical book written by the god Thoth that will teach him to understand the language of all the world's creatures and other things as well. Naneferkapah pays him and finds the book concealed within multiple chests and guarded by six miles of snakes and scorpions in the waters of Coptos. After he takes the book, Thoth is angry and obtains permission from the god Pre to destroy Naneferkapah and his family. After Thoth drowns Naneferkapah's son and wife, he buries them in Coptos. Then he drowns Naneferkapah in the Nile and buries him in Memphis along with his magical book. Now Prince Setne sneaks into Naneferkapah's tomb and steals the book despite the warnings of the ghosts of Naneferkapah and his wife, who then torture him with hallucinations until he returns the book. In the end Prince Setne is compelled to bring about the reunion of the bodies of Naneferkapah, his wife, and son. The chief of police builds a house over their resting place in Memphis.[18]

Lucian may or may not have known this and other similar tales. What is important is that numerous stories about magic and magicians were told and written down during the Hellenistic period and assumed cultural relevance.[19] Ogden even argues that Apuleius's *The Golden Ass* bears resemblance to the tale type of the "Humiliated Apprentice" tales. Interestingly, the Greek version of *The Lover of Lies* was not translated into Latin until approximately the fifteenth century, and it was not translated into European vernacular languages until the late eighteenth and nineteenth centuries. It does not seem to have been very popular, but some indication that it was being disseminated and told can be seen in Franz Anton von Schiefner's "The Magician's Pupil" from the *Kangyur* (ca. 13th century) and from François Pétis de la Croix's "The Story of the Brahmin Padmanaba and the Young Hassan" (1707). In von Schiefner's tale the pupil is deprived of magic power, while Hassan, his father, and stepmother are all killed by monsters because they betray the Brahmin Padmanaba.

By the time some version of Lucian's "Eucrates and Pancrates" had reached the great German writer Johann Wolfgang von Goethe, he decided to write a brief poem called "Der Zauberlehrling" ("The Sorcerer's Apprentice," 1797), which is a simplistic imitation of Lucian's more comical story. Here the apprentice is the speaker of the poem, which deals with his desperation and frustration when he calls forth ghosts who flood the sorcerer's house while the sorcerer is absent. Once the sorcerer returns, he calmly banishes the ghosts. This poem, which is not particularly interesting, was translated into English a few times in the nineteenth and twentieth centuries and was somewhat popular in Germany and the rest of Europe, where other similar prose versions were disseminated.[20] Such "popularity" can only be attributed to the fame of Goethe.

During the nineteenth century few oral folk or literary fairy tales were based on the plot of the "Humiliated Apprentice" tale type. However, mention should be made of a short ballad by the famous romantic poet Robert Southey. His "Cornelius Agrippa's Bloody Book" (1801) is a devastating depiction of what happens to a young man when his curiosity gets the better of him. Other notable short variants include tales by Sir Walter Scott ("The Last Exorciser," 1838); Bernhard Baader ("Magic Book," 1851); Sabine Baring-Gould ("The Master and His Pupil," 1866); John Naaké ("The Book of Magic," 1874); Alfred Fryer ("The Master and His Pupil," 1884); Sheykh-Zāda ("The Lady's Fifth Story," 1886); and Edith Hodgetts ("The Blacksmith and the Devil," 1890). In all these tales from Europe and Egypt the apprentice never achieves his goal even when, in one instance, the young pupil seeks to kill his master. Moreover, the sorcerers, even when they are the devil, are not depicted as evil. Rather they are powerful holders of magical knowledge.

Indeed, throughout history, sorcerers or holders of power are to be venerated. They inspire awe.

In 1896–97, Goethe's short work was transformed into a symphonic poem by the French composer Paul Dukas with the title *The Sorcerer's Apprentice* and the subtitle "Scherzo Based on a Ballad by Goethe." This adaptation was highly significant because Walt Disney used Dukas's music in his animated version of "The Sorcerer's Apprentice" in 1940. (Incidentally, Disney and his collaborators seemingly copied many incidents and motifs from a 1930 film directed by Sidney Levee and produced by William Carmen Menzies. They were the first to make use of Dukas's music to accompany their remarkable narrative, which is much more interesting than Disney's version.)[21] Disney included "The Sorcerer's Apprentice" in the film *Fantasia* as part of an effort to resurrect the popularity of Mickey Mouse, whose "fame" had declined during the 1930s. Mickey had always been drawn as scrawny and mawkish. In this film, which soon became a popular picture book in the 1940s, Mickey is portrayed with softer, more cuddly features and speaks in a little boy's sweet voice. As a servant to a powerful wizard he must do menial tasks like sweeping floors, chopping wood, and carrying water from the well to scrub the floors. When the sorcerer has to leave the house Mickey takes his wizard's cone cap and puts it on his head. He soon begins to command the broom to do all his chores. At one point he rests, falls asleep, and dreams that he is the greatest sorcerer in the world; meanwhile, the broom keeps carrying water from the well and floods the house. In desperation Mickey tries to stop the broom by chopping it with an axe. However, he only creates more brooms and a huge flood. When the sorcerer returns, he immediately restores everything with one command. Angrily he swats Mickey with the broom and sends him off to work. In the Disney picture book, the ending is slightly different; the magician frowns and says, "Don't start what you can't finish." Then Mickey trudges off to work like a slave.

The Disney film and book are significant in the oral and written tradition of the "Humiliated Apprentice" because they "infantilize" the tale type. By this I mean the original storytelling, which had been primarily intended for adults, including Goethe's poem, was transformed into a children's warning story about power and a young person's place in the world. The ideological message, already apparent in Lucian's story, is reinforced by Disney's version: young people are to obey omnipotent people, and if they try to use the knowl-edge and power of their mentors before they have been fully formed by these magicians, they will bring demons into the world and create chaos. From this point onward in Western culture, the meme of the "Humiliated Apprentice" assumes an importance and relevance that may be due to its response to the times. When the film was produced, dictators ruled Germany, Italy, Russia, and Japan, and the early years of World War II demanded strong leaders in allied countries. It is not by chance that a memetic tale type expands and rises in response to changing social and political conditions. The leader who can work magic, or who uses magic to entrance people, continues to have an appeal through all forms of mass-mediated culture. Magical charisma is necessary for any world leader to attain and retain power.

The favorable presentation of the omnipotent sorcerer in children's literature that followed the Disney film and Disney picture books in 1940 can be seen in three banal picture books for young readers: Richard Rostron's *The Sorcerer's Apprentice* (1941), illustrated by Frank Lieberman; Marianna Mayer's *The Sorcerer's Apprentice: A Greek Fable* (1989), illustrated by David Wiesner; and Nancy Willard's *The Sorcerer's Apprentice* (1993), illustrated by Leo and Diane Dillon. Moreover, in numerous other books such as Nicholas Stuart Gray's *The Sorcerer's Apprentices* and Barbara Hazen's *The Sorcerer's Apprentice* (1969), illustrated by Tomi Ungerer,[22] we find the same demeaning message for children who seek knowledge of magic and want to experiment with it: young boys need to be taught a lesson of obedience if they want to learn anything. In Rostron's version, evidently capitalizing on the popularity of the Disney film, the author sets the predictable action in Switzerland, and a bumbling apprentice named Fritzl causes chaos that has to be brought under control by the sorcerer, who screams at Fritzl in rage: "Get out of my sight, you blockhead! I've reached the end of my patience! Go on, get out! Go back where you came from!"[23] In Mayer's medieval tale, a boy by the name of Alec must learn that a little bit of knowledge can be a dangerous thing. Willard's version introduces a girl named Sylvia as the apprentice, and the author's rhymes describe how the red-headed girl upsets everything in the house of the great magician Tottibo while he is napping. At the end of the poem, when Tottibo comes to the rescue, he tells Sylvia with "a sneer" and a "tone and manner most severe" that she must learn to cast a spell and practice until she does it well.

While there is common sense in almost all the oral and written versions of this tale type, what is disturbing and questionable is the portrayal of the sorcerer as godlike, the possessor of absolute knowledge that only he possesses and knows how to use. Most of the tales depict male wizards, who "own" total knowledge of magic and whose power is unquestionable. They are to be obeyed without question, while the apprentices, mainly boys, are humiliated if they try to learn by themselves. (The tale type tends to be gender-specific.) The struggle between master and pupil is always won by the master in this tale type, but let us turn now to the other more prevalent tale type, the "Rebellious Apprentice," before we explore the ramifications of the two tale types and why they are so pertinent today.

THE REBELLIOUS APPRENTICE

The insightful scholar Donald Beecher has made some very astute comments about this tale type that can help us understand its historical significance. He cites Stith Thompson, one of the foremost American folklorists in the twentieth century, who found that "The Rebellious Apprentice" was known

> not only throughout Europe with a particular density of occurrences in the Balkans, but also in Turkey, Egypt, Siberia, India, North Africa, the Dutch East Indies, the Philippines, and even Missouri, where it was carried by the early French settlers. Clearly, as a narrative "meme" the story has invaded consciousnesses around the world on a competitive basis and has confirmed its survival in forms differing less from one another than is usually the case with orally transmitted materials. It has three parts that have remained firmly associated, namely, the circumstances leading to an apprenticeship, the boy's return home, where he shows his father how he can be sold for profit by transmitting himself into various costly animals, and the metamorphosis contest that arises as the master seeks to destroy his pupil.[24]

Though it is not entirely clear whether we can ever know the exact origin of this tale type and whether the Asian and Middle Eastern versions influenced the Western tales or vice versa, folklorists and scholars of classical Greek, Roman, Egyptian, and Asian literature have found and studied similar motifs in Hesiod's *Catalogue of Women*, Ovid's *Metamorphoses*, the ancient Mongolian *Siddhi-Kür*, the Turkish *History of the Forty Vezirs*, "The Second Kalendar's Story" in *The Arabian Nights*, and in Indian and Asian folklore of the early medieval period.[25]

The transformations in and of the sources and tales about sorcerer's apprentices are fascinating, for the major shape-shifters at the beginning of recorded tales seem to have been women, and the plots of the early Greek stories concern their desire to establish their own identity rather than to be married against their will, or raped. In addition, the tales reflect the social relations of their times and are somewhat influenced by religious rites and magic. Shapeshifting is possible among both males and females, particularly the gods, but women are always suspect in their ability to shape-shift, while men are rarely questioned when they transform themselves. In either case, shape-shifting was common for humans and mortals. As Elaine Fatham points out,

> Shapeshifters feature in the mythologies of many nations, but as Forbes
> Irving has argued in his recent study of Greek mythology, their capacity
> to move swiftly through a baffling series of transformations distinguishes
> them from either gods or mortals, who can merely transform or disguise
> themselves on occasions. What seems to have attracted Ovid to choose
> those figures for his narrative was the autonomy of the self-transformer,
> whose powers enabled him or her to shape his or her own tale.[26]

Much earlier than Ovid's *Metamorphoses*, Hesiod's version[27] of the Erysichthon and Mestra tale is a case in point. In this tale Erysichthon, who is king of Thessaly, is cursed with an insatiable appetite because he had offended the god Demeter. In order to obtain food, Erysichthon exhausts his wealth and then makes a plan to satisfy his hunger with the help of his daughter Mestra, whom Poseidon has given the power to transform herself into whatever she wishes. The clever Mestra allows herself to be sold repeatedly to various rich men, and each time, after she receives the money, Mestra transforms herself into some kind of animal and returns to her father, leaving the buyer perplexed. One of the first to be duped is Sisyphus, who wants his son Glaucus to marry Mestra. Sisyphus and Erysichthon quarrel, and the goddess Athena settles the dispute in Erysichthon's favor. Meanwhile, Poseidon takes Mestra away from her father to the island of Cos, where she gives birth to Eurypylus in her union with Poseidon. Eventually, Mestra returns to Athens to take care of her father. Indeed, she is her own woman.

The significance of this somewhat farcical tale, recorded sometime in the sixth century BCE, concerns its subversive and rebellious quality, which appears in a later version by Ovid and also in "The Second Kalendar's Story" (ca. 9th–14th century) in *The Arabian Nights*. In the latter, tragic tale a king's daughter, who has the ability to metamorphose as she wishes, engages an *ifrit*, or genie, in a vicious battle. She defeats the genie, but she also dies saving the life of a prince who had been transformed into an ape. Though there is no sorcerer-apprentice or master-slave conflict in this tale or in Hesiod's "Erysichthon and Mestra," the shape-shifting Mestra successfully rebels against a Greek god and retains her independence. In a superb scholarly study of the Erysichthon and Mestra tale, which places it in its sociocultural context, Kirk Ormand writes:

> The story of Mestra belongs to a set of myths about female shape-shifters, and like them, represents certain wide-ranging anxieties about women's sexual power in ancient Greece. Shape-shifting myths seem to be keyed to gender. Shape-shifting for males is not linked to a single moment or phase of their lives; for them it is a constant attribute, one that is present throughout their narratives, and it does not seem to be linked to any particular social structures. Female characters, by contrast, have and lose the ability in specific circumstances. Women have the ability to shape-shift only before marriage, and the stories about their shape-shifting always take place in the context of trying to avoid marriage. . . . The form of the Mestra narrative and her reasons for shape-shifting are different from other versions of this particular tale and from myths of other female shape-shifters. The trope of female instability is used in this story to reflect concerns about women's social mobility that are tied to the specific social milieu of archaic Athens and, in particular, to Athenian marriage laws.[28]

Of course, it is possible to study all the Mestra tales from other perspectives. For instance, Noel Robertson studies the ritual background of begging with regard to the Erysichthon and Mestra tales and similar stories.[29] But the themes of autonomy and self-consciousness tend to be prevalent in most. Other tales focus on the initiation of young men. Certainly, many of the "Rebellious Apprentice" tales that originated in other societies during the early medieval period adapt the motif of shape-shifting, change the gender of the tales' central character, and reveal a ritualistic background and pursuit of magic.[30]

In the introduction to the Mongolian *Siddhi-Kür*, for instance, which was derived from earlier Indian Sanskrit versions of the first century CE or even before,[31] a short, fascinating "ritualistic" tale serves as the frame for eleven other stories. It concerns the son of a khan, who steals the key to magic from seven magicians. His older brother had been sent to learn magic from the seven magicians, but he is not very good at it. When the young brother visits him with food, he peers into the house of magic and is able to learn all about the magic of the seven magicians almost instantly. Then he and his older brother depart, and he asks his jealous older brother to sell him as a horse in the country of the magicians and to return home with the money. He intends to change himself back into a human after his brother completes the sale. However, due to a mistake and jealousy, the brother sells him to the magicians, who want to slay him. Consequently, the young son of the khan changes himself into a fish, then a dove, and finally—with the help of Nâgârg'una, a wise Buddhist—into a bead, each time evading the seven magicians. Finally, when the seven magicians transform themselves into fowls to eat the beads that had become worms, the khan's son assumes his human form with a sword in his hand and chops off the heads of the fowls. In light of the fact that the khan's son has murdered the seven magicians, Nâgârg'una sends the khan's son to do penance on a quest to find and bring him the Siddhi-Kür (the enchanted corpse). The khan's son does this, and on his way back to Nâgârg'una, the Siddhi-Kür tells him eleven stories and then escapes.[32]

Here it is important to note that, according to Rachel Busk, "Nâgârg'una was the 15th Patriarch in the Buddhist succession, born in South India, and educated a Brahmin; he wrote a treatise in 100 chapters on the Wisdom of the Buddhist Theology, and died BC 212."[33] After his conversion to Buddhism, his school of thought played a major role in the conflict between Brahminism and Buddhism, and for many years after his death, Buddhist moral values were disseminated in tales and collections of tales such as the *Siddhi Kür*. Raffaella Riva maintains:

> Buddhism represents in fact the main factor of propaganda and transformation of the *Tales of the Bewitched Corpse*. The main direction of the migration has been northward, following the diffusion of Buddhism in Tibet, probably around the VII century A.D. . . . It is also important to stress the fact that tales easily circulate orally and the stories of the *vetāla* represented no exception. They travelled along with merchants caravans, with missionary monks or pilgrims crossing the Himalayan range. In this way they were taken over by Tibetan story-tellers and constituted the basis for the manifold written versions still circulating in Tibet.[34]

Throughout the Middle Ages and the early Renaissance in Europe there are signs that motifs of the tale type of the "Rebellious Apprentice" spread, took root, and defined the basic features that would make the tale more easily memorable and memetic. In his brilliant essay on the origins and history of this tale type,[35] Emmanuel Cosquin summarizes the numerous components of "The Rebellious Apprentice" that have been used and cultivated by storytellers, writers, and artists during the past two thousand years: (1) The hero is entrusted to a magician by his father or mother at a very young age; (2) father and son encounter a magician named Oh! or Ah! (or some other name) when either one of them breathes deeply and utters a sound that summons the magician; (3) sometimes the young man is promised to the sorcerer before his birth; (4) the young man alone searches for work and finds a position with the magician by himself; (5) during his time in the magician's mysterious or haunted house, the apprentice is helped or given advice by friends or by a young woman; (6) there are many different transformations of the master and the apprentice that take place inside the house in which the magician displays his powers by changing the young man into a bird, cow, snake, and so on; (7) there are also numerous transformations in the combat between magician and apprentice, both using magic to metamorphose themselves into diverse animals, fish, and fowls; (8) inevitably the apprentice who learns all he needs to know about magic frees himself from the sorcerer, and sometimes he steals the sorcerer's magic book; (9) the sorcerer seeks revenge and wants to kill the apprentice; and (10) kill or be killed, the apprentice uses his skill of transformation to defeat the sorcerer.

Cosquin makes it clear that there is no single source of the tale type of the "Rebellious Apprentice," and he took issue with his professor, Theodor Benfey, who asserted that the "Sorcerer's Apprentice" tales originated in India out of conflicts between Brahmins and Buddhists. In some cases this may be true, but Cosquin reveals that there are many different currents that one can trace in the Middle East, Asia, northern Africa, and Europe that have nothing to do with the Brahmin/Buddhist disputes, and all these other tales became prominent in the early Middle Ages, forming and informing one another to shape the meme of the "Rebellious Apprentice" tale type.

Motifs of rebellious apprentices, shape-shifting, magical duels, and fierce competition became widespread by the Renaissance period. The tale type is prevalent throughout Eastern Asia. Sometimes the competition is between two sorcerers or magicians, but for the most part, the Asian, Middle Eastern, and European oral and literary tales depict a poor young man who seeks to liberate himself from a master of magic who has taught him the art of transformation and stealing. The apprentice often receives some help from the magician's daughter, providing that he promises to take her away and marry her because she wants to escape her father's demonic powers. In more romantic versions, there is a princess or maiden who hides the apprentice as a jewel and helps him defeat his master. The basic components and motifs can be seen in such early "Rebellious Apprentice" tales as "Bhavašarman and the Two Witches" (1070) in *The Ocean of Story*; Farīd al-Dīn ʿAttār's "The Magician's Apprentice" (ca. 1220); and "The Deceiver Shall Be Deceived" (ca. 1700) in *The Dravidian Nights Entertainments*, a collection of tales that may have circulated before the seventeenth century.

The oral and literary dissemination of the tale type throughout Europe, the Middle East, and Asia led to Giovan Francesco Straparola's tale, "Maestro Lattantio and His Apprentice Dionigi," in *Le piacevoli notti* (*The Pleasant Nights*, 1550), which is the first known literary work that artfully combined all the different motifs of previous tales to form the groundwork for the prominent type of the "Rebellious Apprentice." Straparola's tale takes place in Messina, Sicily, and it concerns a poor man who places his son Dionigi as an apprentice in the home of Lattantio, who works as a tailor but is secretly a sorcerer. When Diogini discovers that Lattantio is a master of necromancy, he pretends to be a simpleton and is such a bad tailor's apprentice that Lattantio kicks him out of his home. Diogini's poor father pleads with Lattantio to take his son back, which he does, and Diogini acts so awkwardly and stupidly that Lattantio beats him and also feels free to practice his magic in front of the seemingly dumb boy. However, Diogini cunningly learns the art of necromancy so well that he becomes more skillful than his master. One day, his father visits him and sees that he has not made any progress as a tailor and takes him out of Lattantio's service. Soon thereafter Diogini tells his father that he is grateful to him for paying for his apprenticeship, and he wants to reward him by using the art of magic. So, he transforms himself into a beautiful horse and tells his father to sell him at the fair for a good deal of money, but he must keep the magic bridle so that his son can later change from horse to man and return to his father. However, Lattantio is at the fair, and once he recognizes the horse is really Diogini, he wants revenge. Consequently, he disguises himself as a merchant, outwits Diogini's father, buys Diogini as horse with the bridle, takes him back to his home, and beats the young man twice every day so that Diogini becomes a wreck. Then Lattantio's two daughters take pity on him when their father leaves the house. They lead him to the river, where they take off his bridle, and he changes into a fish. Immediately they run and tell Lattantio what has happened. So Lattantio pursues him as a vicious fish, but Diogini escapes, leaps to land, changes himself into a ruby ring, and accidentally falls into the basket of Violante, a princess, who becomes very fond of the ring. Eventually, Diogini reveals himself to the princess, who promises to keep his secret. But Lattantio, disguised as a doctor, cures the king from a malady and wants the ruby ring as his reward. As he is about to take it from the princess's finger, she throws the ring against the wall, and it becomes a pomegranate, which scatters its seeds on the ground. In turn, Lattantio changes himself into a chicken and begins pecking the seeds. But one seed escapes, allowing Diogini to turn himself into a fox and to kill the chicken. Then he devours it in front of the princess and the king. Of course, she weds Diogini in the end, and Diogini's father rises from poverty to become a rich man.

Straparola's version of the "Rebellious Apprentice" was composed at a time throughout Europe when more and more apprentices were engaged in learning processes that were often hard and demeaning.[36] In particular, young boys and men were often compelled to leave their families and become journeymen to support themselves. Often they joined guilds. Many were also forcefully recruited by armies. Depending on social class, the treatment of students of all kinds was patriarchal and authoritarian up through the twentieth century. If an apprentice could read or write, it was to his advantage. In all cases submission to the master determined whether the apprentice would have a successful career. The master-slave relationship was rampant throughout Europe. Willem de Blécourt, who has written a misleading and contentious history of the evolution of the "Sorcerer's Apprentice" memeplex, claims that Straparola's tale was essentially erotic and believes that the relationship of Lattantio and his apprentice is homoerotic: "The sexual symbolism has already been set in the figure of the tailor himself. The movement of the needle in sewing is a metaphor for the male sexual act. The secret craft, which the young man learns from his master is in a certain sense homosexuality with a submissive aspect. After he has fully spied the master's secrets, he knows how to be ridden. Moreover, Lattantios's speaking name 'Milk Giver' refers to a female attribute. It implies the bisexuality of the master with pedophile inclinations."[37] Though there may be an iota of truth to this ingenious interpretation, de Blécourt fails to take into consideration that the apprentice rejects sewing and recognizes the sadistic acts of the tailor/sorcerer as cruel ways to deny him autonomy and self-determination. The apprentice is more interested in knowledge than "learning about homosexuality" and sex.

Straparola's tale, which added a few new features such as the romantic episode with the princess and the emphasis on the poverty of the apprentice and his father, may have influenced Robert Armin, who wrote a verse version, "Phantasmos, or the Italian Taylor and His Boy" (1609), in which a tailor's apprentice suffers the same torture and persecution as Straparola's Diogini. Here, too, the young boy learns the sorcerer's magic and swallows the sorcerer as chicken at the end. Aside from having an impact on Armin, Straparola's story had a more direct influence on Eustache Le Noble's "L'apprenti magicien" ("The Magician's Apprentice," in *Le gage touché*, 1700), which followed the Italian narrative almost to a "T." The dissemination of the memetic tale type was now conducted through print and oral storytelling in Europe, the Middle East, Asia, and North Africa. There is a strong likelihood that the tale was transmitted by street singers, who played a prominent role in transforming tales into ballads, as we have already seen. In the case of Straparola he may have even learned about the tale through street singers who were common in Venice during the sixteenth century.[38]

It is clear from the numerous collections of folk and fairy tales in nine-teenth- century Europe and elsewhere that "The Rebellious Apprentice" was widespread, diverse, international, and written and told mainly for adults. The short and somewhat abrupt comic version of the Brothers Grimm was sent to them by Jenny von Droste-Hülshoff, who recorded it in a Münster dialect. It was published in this dialect in the second edition of *Children's and Household Tales* in 1819 and originally bore the title "Jan un sien Sohn," or "Jan and His Son." The Grimms changed it to read "Der Gaudeif un sien Meester," or "The Nimble Thief and His Master." They did not make major changes to this tale in the final edition of 1857, and it has aspects of a *Schwankmärchen*, or farce, though it should be remembered that the conflict between the apprentice and his master is a bitter one. In this brief pithy story a father named Jan is mocked by a sexton, who tricks him into believing that the Lord wants his son to learn all about thievery. Thinking that it is God's will, Jan places his son with a master thief, and his son learns enough to outwit the master. He then shape-shifts and makes money by becoming a greyhound and then a horse. As in other tales, the boy is captured and tortured, and then defeats the master by turning into a fox and biting off the sorcerer's head when he becomes a rooster.

Other variants that circulated in Scandinavia, Germany, France, Italy, and Eastern European countries can be found in most of the significant collections of the nineteenth century. The titles and plots might differ somewhat, but the tale type elements remain firm in the works of Kazimierz Wladyslaw Woycicki, "The Sorcerer and His Apprentice" (1839); Arthur and Albert Schott, "The Devil and His Pupil" (1845); Benjamin Thorpe, "The Magician's Pupil" (1853); Heinrich Pröhle, "Competition of Magic" (1854); Ludwig Bechstein, "The Magic Combat" (1857); Jón Arnason, "The Black School" (1864); Johann Georg von Hahn, "The Teacher and His Pupil" (1864); Giuseppe Pitrè, "The Tuft of Wild Beet" (1875); Adolpho Francisco Coelho, "The Magician's Servant" (1885); François-Marie Luzel, "The Magician and His Servant" (1885); George Webbe Dasent, "Farmer Weathersky" (1888); Charles Swynnerton, "The Story of the Merchant and the Brahmin" (1892); Robert Nisbet Bain, "Oh: The Tsar of the Forest" (1894); Marjory Wardrop, "Master and Pupil, or The Devil Outwitted" (1894). They share many similar features that reflect not only a generational struggle between old master and young learner but also a conflict that many young men experienced either as students, apprentices, or journeymen. The conditions throughout Europe under which boys worked in the eighteenth and nineteenth centuries were difficult and exploitative, and these tales indicate that learning a trade also meant learning how to survive. Most of these narratives focus on a peasant boy or a boy from an impoverished family. Interestingly, the family—mainly the father—is not averse to apprenticing the boy with a sorcerer. In other words, magic, or mana, is accepted or considered necessary as a means of survival for impoverished families, and the sorcerer's place is a school. Supernatural sorcery is necessary for poor or disadvantaged families to change their circumstances. Once the poor boy has spent a certain amount of years with a sorcerer and has become a young man, he is ready to assert himself but does not want to use dark pernicious magic to do harm. He simply wants to provide for his family. Another interesting aspect about all these tales, which stem primarily from the oral tradition, is that the female protagonist, generally a princess, is not afraid of forming an erotic relationship with a handsome peasant in her bedroom, and she plays an active role in saving him. She is, for the most part, the savior. Without her help, the peasant cannot outsmart the sorcerer.

The oral tradition of the "Rebellious Apprentice" tales remained strong in the twentieth century throughout the world, as can be seen in such examples, not all included in this volume, as Adolphe Orain, "The Transformations" (1901); Leo Wiener, "The Tale of the Sorcerer" (1902); Joseph Charles Mardrus, "The Twelfth Captain's Tale" (ca. 1904); Fletcher Gardner, "The Battle of the Enchanters" (1907); Peter Buchan, "The Black King of Morocco" (1908); Cecil Henry Bompas, "The Boy Who Learnt Magic" (1909); Achille Millien, "The Magician's Apprentice" (1909); Henry Parker, "The Teacher and His Pupil"(1910); John Francis Campbell of Islay/J. G. McKay, "The Wizard's Gillie" (1914); Claude-Marius Barbeau, "The Two Magicians" (1916); Adolf Dirr, "The Master and His Pupils" (1919); Dean Fansler, "The Mysterious Book" (1921); Elsie Clews Parsons, "The Battle of the Enchanters" (1923); Georg Goyert, "Jan the Sorcerer" (1925); Seumas MacManus, "The Mistress of Magic" (1926); Romuald Pramberger, "The Sorcerer's Apprentice" (1926); Helen Zinner, "The Two Witches" (1935); Joseph Médard Carrière, "The Two Magicians" (1937); Richard Dorson, "The Mojo" (1956); J. Mason Brewer, "The High Sheriff and His Servant" (1958); Corinne Saucier, "The Man and His Son" (1962); Katharine Briggs, *A Dictionary of British Folktales* (1970); and A. K. Ramanujan, "The Guru and His Disciple" (1997). These tales were collected in India, the Philippines, Europe, Egypt, Cape Verde, and North America. Not only do they demonstrate an incredible stability of plot and functions in the tale type of the "Rebellious Apprentice," but also a good deal of originality that emanated from cultural particularity. In some of the tales the sorcerer and apprentice are killed together, or the apprentice is persuaded not to kill the sorcerer. In one tale it is the princess who kills the sorcerer. A few are recorded in dialect. For instance the stories collected by Barbeau in Canada, Carrière in Missouri, and Saucier in Louisiana were all told in a local French dialect. The tales collected by Dorson and Brewer are in an African American dialect. There is almost no evidence that these tales were transmitted through books, but there is evidence that these tales became part of the cultural memory of individual societies.

The pervasive literary influence of "The Rebellious Apprentice" in the twentieth and twenty-first centuries can be seen in Hans Heinz Ewers's dark novel, *The Sorcerer's Apprentice* (1907); Edith Nesbit's comic parody, "The Magician's Heart" (1912); Hermann Hesse's extraordinary tale, "The Forest Dweller" (1917); Heywood Broun's bizarre "Red Magic" (1921); and Lord Dunsany's fantasy, *The Charwoman's Shadow* (1926). Also important are Otfried

Preußler's *Krabat* (1971); Charles Johnson's "The Sorcerer's Apprentice" (1986); Susanna Clarke's *Jonathan Strange & Mr. Norrell* (2004); Trudy Canavan's *The Magician's Apprentice* (2009); Lev Grossman's *The Magicians* (2009); and the short story collections *Alchemy and Academe* (1970), edited by Anne McCaffrey, and *Apprentice Fantastic* (2002), edited by Martin Greenberg and Russell Davis, not to mention the oral tales in Reidar Christiansen's *Folktales of Norway* (1964). Here and there one can find some versions of this tale type for young readers, such as Wanda Gág's *The Sorcerer's Apprentice* (1970), illustrated by Margaret Thomes, but for the most part the tale type of the "Humiliated Apprentice" became the more dominant tale type in the field of children's literature with the misleading title "The Sorcerer's Apprentice" that has circulated in Western countries since Disney's film *Fantasia* appeared in 1940 followed by massive publications of Disney's illustrated book, *The Sorcerer's Apprentice*, and imitations by other authors and publishers. Whether the general tale type of the "Sorcerer's Apprentice" takes the form of "The Rebellious Apprentice" or "The Humiliated Apprentice" will always depend on the sociocultural conditions in a particular country, the target audience, and marketing. What is significant is that the two antagonistic tale types form a memeplex and play out a crucial debate between masters and slaves that has existed since time immemorial. Philosophically speaking, in my opinion, the core of the appeal and attraction of all versions and variants of "The Sorcerer's Apprentice," disseminated through diverse modalities, is a life-and-death struggle to know ourselves, our desires, and our talents. The scheme of the narrative, based on patterns of "magicity," leads readers to grasp how difficult it is to become narrators of their own lives when neglected, enslaved, or abused, and how important it is to engage masters in a bloody battle.

HEGEL'S MASTER-SLAVE DIALECTIC

Taken together or even analyzed separately, the two currents of the tale type ATU 325 manifest a dialectical movement closely related to what Hegel discusses in his significant philosophical work, *Phenomenology of the Spirit* (1807),[39] precisely in the section called "Independence and Dependence of Self-Consciousness: Lordship and Bondage." This section has more commonly been referred to as "The Master-Slave Dialectic," and Hegel's astute cognitive approach to how the mind, what Hegel calls spirit or *Geist*, functions to determine self-consciousness and recognition of the ego ("I") will enable us, I believe, to understand not only the enormous response to the Harry Potter novels but to all the thousands of similar tale types that preceded them and also all the narratives, ballads, films, paintings, and artifacts that have succeeded them. Most of all understanding the political dimensions and implications of the Hegelian dialectic will help us understand childism and child abuse, why magic matters, and the struggles young people face in the process of individuation. In short the cognitive philosophical/critical[40] and memetic approaches to tale type ATU 325 are useful for demonstrating why the memeplex, or large pool, of the diverse "Sorcerer's Apprentice" tales have taken such deep root in most cultures throughout the world.

Stories in which the apprentice manages to defeat the magician and use supernatural mana (knowledge) to gain his freedom are essentially wish-fulfillment tales and embody voices from below: they oppose elite forces that dominate human society and spread a different kind of secularized magic. The rebellious apprentice's actions comprise resistance per se, not a solution. Symbolically, the apprentice as learner stands as permanent negation in a dialectic that leaves him, in most instances, no choice but to kill to save himself. In rare cases he avoids the role of killer when arbitration allows him to gain the recognition that he desires. In general full knowledge and individuation are not guaranteed, but the apprentice learns to use magic/mana to preserve himself and attain a modicum of self-consciousness, consciousness of the world, and happiness.

On the other hand the humiliated apprentice can never come to know himself because he submits to the power of the sorcerer: he will learn to use his knowledge only to conform to the demands of elite holders of magic and to uphold the systems of education and socialization that they establish to benefit themselves. He is the domesticated apprentice whose skills will be put to use in the socioeconomic network. Ultimately, in both versions of the tale type ATU 325, magic can be used for liberation only under conditions that allow for the democratic sharing of knowledge. Consequently, if magic is to have ethical and moral value, the struggle for it must become communal and universal. The dialectic of the "Sorcerer's Apprentice" tales *serves mainly to raise consciousness of the problem, not as a solution.* The ending of most narratives that feature a rebellious apprentice ends in resistance—perpetual resistance.

It is not by chance, in my opinion, that the "Sorcerer's Apprentice" tales and political revolutions, which were widespread during the nineteenth century, gave rise to Hegel's theories about masters and slaves. But just what is Hegel's master-slave dialectic, also called the lord-bondsman dialectic? Why did the brilliant German critic Theodor Adorno later call for negative dialectics in opposition to Hegel's conservative notion of dialectics? How does an understanding of dialectics help us grasp the phylogenetic evolution and memetic tendency of the memeplex ATU 325 and ATU 325*?

Hegel maintains that without understanding the *other*, that which is outside oneself and different, one cannot grasp oneself and come to self-consciousness. So we tend to think dialectically, and the goal of the dialectic is to move continually toward absolute knowledge, which includes knowledge of oneself. In Hegel's terms:

> self-consciousness is thus certain of itself only by superseding this other that presents itself to self-consciousness as an independent life; self-consciousness is Desire. Certain of the nothingness of this other, it explicitly affirms that this nothingness is *for* it the truth of the other; it destroys the independent object and thereby gives itself the certainty of itself as a *true* certainty, a certainty which has become explicit for self-consciousness itself *in an objective manner*. (109)

After outlining how the dialectic works, Hegel then discusses factors that can block self-consciousness in the minds of masters/lords/sorcerers and limit the self-consciousness of servants/slaves/apprentices. He writes: "the relation of the two self-conscious individuals is such that they prove themselves and each other through a life-and-death struggle. They must engage in this struggle, for they must raise their certainty of being *for themselves* to truth, both in the case of the other and in their own case" (113–14). If one independent individual kills or destroys the other, however, it will be impossible for the other to achieve and maintain the certainty of self-consciousness. It is, therefore, crucial to avoid annihilation of the other, because self-consciousness depends on the other. Thus, out of fear of death, one individual will generally acknowledge the other as master, resulting in a loss of authentic self-consciousness and mutual recognition on the part of both conscious individuals. What is left is the recognition of a master-slave relationship. Each recognizes the other in an unequal and one-sided acknowledgement.

Hegel demonstrates that the lord/master can never achieve the truth of himself by dominating another human being who is held in bondage and must labor for the lord. According to Hegel, the lord/master's truth is, in reality, the unessential consciousness and its unessential action. In short, the lord/master lives on in conflict with false consciousness because he loses touch with real conditions of living and working that are mediated by the slave/servant, who is compelled to work for the master. The threat of death and humiliation and the conformity to the lord's will do not enable the servant to provide the contrast to help the lord gain self-consciousness. On the other hand, the slave/servant develops a certain self-consciousness through his conditions of labor that enables him to gain independence. Hegel writes: "Through work, however, the bondsman becomes conscious of what he truly is. . . . Through this rediscovery of himself by himself, the bondsman realizes that it is precisely in his work wherein he seemed to have only an alienated existence that he acquires a mind of his own" (119). Being creative and productive and engaged with the material world, the servant obtains a sense of who he or she is. This self-consciousness allows the servant to find a measure of freedom not dependent on the lord, while the lord is dependent on the work carried out in servitude by the servant.

While it might seem that Hegel views dialectics as a critical mode of thinking and behavior that favors the oppressed and rebellion, this is not the case: in his later works, such as the *Philosophy of Right* (1821) and the *Philosophy of History* (1837), he was more concerned with demonstrating how the dialectics of thinking and action lead to a harmonious world order. Morally speaking, the individual must comply with the tenets of the world order or the state to fulfill his/her role in maintaining harmony. As Nicolas Laos has explained, "Hegel's historical and, hence, secular teleology implies that the universality of a civilization is equivalent to and stems from the total dominance of the state over society (in the same way that a more general concept 'dominates' over a less general one). . . . Hegel's political thought is concerned with the improvement of humanity, but, in contrast to classical Greek political thought, it ignores the improvement of man as a person, and, therefore, it legitimates absolutism and totalitarianism."[41]

Such nondialectical thinking on Hegel's part disturbed the German thinker Theodor Adorno, one of the founders of German critical theory, who escaped the Nazis and came to America in 1938. Throughout his life he sought to grasp the roots of fascism and authoritarianism, and in light of Auschwitz and the barbarianism of the Nazi period,[42] he wrote a scathing critique of Hegel in his book *Negative Dialectics* (1966). Above all what angered Adorno was Hegel's preference for the universal over the particular, which Adorno saw as the degradation of the individual in favor of a "mythological" world spirit and order to which all human beings should submit:

> Cognition aims at the particular, not at the universal. It seeks its true object in the possible determination of the difference of that particular— even from the universal, which it criticizes as nonetheless inalienable. But if the mediation of the universal by the particular is reduced to the abstract form of mediation as such, the particular has to pay the price, down to its authoritarian dismissal in the material parts of the Hegelian system.[43]
>
> If Hegel had carried the doctrine of the identity of universal farther, to a dialectic in the particular itself, the particular—which according to him is simply the mediated universal—would have been granted the same right as the universal. That he depreciates this right into a mere urge and psychologistically blackens the right of man as narcissism—like a father chiding his son, "Maybe you think you're something special"—this is not an individual lapse on the philosopher's part. Idealistically, there is no carrying out the dialectic of the particular which he envisions.[44]

For Adorno, who had already demonstrated with his friend and colleague Max Horkheimer in *Dialectic of the Enlightenment* (1944) that rationalism had become instrumentalized—that is, manipulated through seemingly reasonable laws and institutions—to favor the growing bourgeois interests in the nineteenth century, the domination of the universal cast such a powerful spell on human relations that reconciliation with the values and interests of the universal meant "enslavement" without a moral community that might justify conformity to the universal. Adorno argued that

> the universality that reproduces the preservation of life simultaneously imperils it in more and more menacing stages. The power of the self-realizing universal is not, as Hegel thought, identical with the nature of the individuals in themselves; it is always also contrary to that nature. The individuals are not only character masks, agents of value in a supposedly separate economic sphere. Even where they think they have escaped the primacy of economics—all the way into their psychology, the *maison tolérée* of uncomprehended individuality—they react under the compulsion of the universal. The more identical they are with it, the more unidentical with it are they as its helplessly obedient servants.[45]

The only way individuals can maintain themselves as self-conscious and critical-thinking individuals, according to Adorno, is through antagonism and resistance. Yet the universal world order is so powerful that these individuals do things that help maintain the universal, just to survive. It seems as though they reconcile themselves to the relations of master-slave while criticizing the world order, but in fact the world order obliges everyone to live according to illusions of harmony and denies the real conditions of work, education, and living.

Adorno claims that "history is the unity of continuity and discontinuity. Society stays alive, not despite its antagonism but by means of it. . . . This also implies the reconciling side of the irreconcilable; since nothing else permits men to live, not even a changed life would be possible without it."[46] In other words, while there is no purpose in our dialectical thinking, the purpose in keeping dialectical thinking alive and vibrant is its categorical imperative of negating what is not true. The essence of negative dialectics is the motor of history and knowledge without an end. It is also the principle of storytelling, for people tell stories for and against one another to determine what their relative truth values are. Adorno remarks that "if negative dialectics calls for the self-reflection of thinking, the tangible implication is that if thinking is to be true—if it is to be true today, in any case—it must also be a thinking against itself."[47]

In negative dialectical thinking we also reveal our own contradictions and the contradictions in the worlds in which we live. Nothing can be taken at face value, and the relations that form us, and that we form, are all changeable. They can be transformed. One of the most significant features of the "Sorcerer's Apprentice" memeplex is that—when we consider it historically—all the tales about the rebellious and humiliated apprentices focus on metamorphosis through antagonism. The alterity of magic matters. Whereas the tales concerned with the ideological conformity of the humiliated apprentice reinforce Hegel's notion of absolute knowledge and an absolute divinity, the tales concerned with the rebellious apprentice evince a tendency toward Adorno's negative dialectics. Antagonism is a historical necessity in the "Rebellious Apprentice" tales, and even though most of them end in the killing of the sorcerer, the apprentice preserves the categorical imperative to think and act to negate the absolute dictatorship of the sorcerer and the forces that cast harmful spells on people so that they cannot think for themselves. Without understanding Adorno's negative dialectics, we cannot understand the premises of storytelling.

There are, of course, numerous ways to interpret Hegel's dialectic and Adorno's negative dialectics. Some of the most significant thinkers of the nineteenth
and twentieth centuries, such as Karl Marx, Martin Buber, Alexandre Kojève,
Jean-Paul Sartre, Simone de Beauvoir, Maurice Merleau-Ponty, Jean Hyppo-
lite, Frantz Fanon, Herbert Marcuse, Ernest Mandel, and others, have written
extensively about Hegel's notions of the dialectic and the master-slave dialectic
in particular. Perhaps the most brilliant interpreter of the Hegelian dialectic,
in my opinion, is Alexandre Kojève. In his lectures during the 1930s he had a
profound influence on European intellectuals, and he provides an interesting
interpretation of the killing of the master dialectically in a more "utopian" light:

> Man can only free himself from the given World that does not satisfy him
> only if this world, in its totality, belongs properly to a (real or "sublimated")
> Master. Now, as long as the Master lives, he himself is always enslaved
> by the World of which he is the Master. Since the Master transcends
> the given World only in and by the risk of his life, it is only his death
> that "realizes" his freedom. As long as he lives, therefore, he never attains
> the freedom that would raise him above the given World. The Master can
> never detach himself from the World in which he lives, and if this World
> perishes, he perishes with it. Only the Slave can transcend the given World
> (which is subjugated by the Master) and not perish. Only the Slave can
> transform the World that forms him and fixes him in slavery and create
> the World that he has formed in which he will be free.[48]

For our purposes it is important to note that the universal struggle of
life and death that underlies the tale types of the "Sorcerer's Apprentice" can
be seen historically throughout all ages and in all societies. We only have to
think of familial relations (husband and wife, parents and children); school
(principal/superintendent and teachers, teachers and pupils, professors and
students); trades, such as carpentry, tailoring, weaving, sewing, shoemaking,
building (masters and apprentices/journeymen); the army, navy, and other
military organizations (commanders and common soldiers and sailors); cor-
porations (employees and bosses); farms and factories (owners and workers).
We all learn to live and develop self-consciousness in a dialectic relationship
with masters. There is virtually no domain of life that does not entail learning
within a master-slave dialectic.

No wonder that all kinds of tales, plays, novels, ballets, and other cultural
fields that reflect the master-slave dialectic—I am thinking of George Bernard

Shaw's *Pygmalion* as I write—have flourished worldwide in the past. There are too many to record and count. But sometimes a particular tale type gels, and is honed by storytellers over the years, and assumes memetic proportions so that it becomes readily accessible and representative of human struggles to move toward cooperation and mutual recognition through a dialectical relationship. The enormous number of variants indicates that these tales do not bring answers to the unequal and one-sided relationship in the master-slave dialectic. But the diverse tales raise pertinent questions about how to disperse knowledge democratically and use it to benefit a moral community.

MEMES, "MAGICITY," AND CULTURAL MEMORY

Secretly, we all know this. My heart leaps up when I behold
    A rainbow in the sky:
So was it when my life began;
So is it now I am a man;
So be it when I shall grow old,
    Or let me die!
The Child is father of the Man;
    I could wish my days to be
Bound each to each by natural piety.

—WILLIAM WORDSWORTH (1802)

Of course, today most people would say the child is mother and father of humankind, and in most human societies, people leave childhood and grow in civilizing processes that bind them to rules and regulations. Consequently, they become more and more aware that they will never be able to regain or retain that childhood wisdom, imagination, spontaneity, and ingenuity that they once had. Instead, adults eventually experience a fraught relationship with children that involves two contradictory impulses and drives: (1) adults want to nourish the individual talents of children and guide them to comprehend the complex social networks into which they are born, and protect them from adverse forces; or (2) adults seek to regulate and discipline children according to arbitrary rules of the civilizing process to which they are disciplined to comply—what Hegel, Kojève, and Adorno call the World Order, or some call the State—even though the adults might not understand the source and sense of the rules and do not even legislate them. In the process adults become envious of children's free spirit and unconsciously repress and oppress them to maintain power over them, for fear that they might expose adult hypocrisies and contradictions.

Now it is always difficult and dangerous to analyze how we as teachers/ mentors/masters/sorcerers treat children as pupils by using categorical dichotomies. It is wrong-headed to apply dichotomies to our study of children and how they were raised in past societies as apprentices, and how we continue to deal with them in a master-slave dialectical relationship. And it is not always helpful to use dichotomies to explain our own interrelationships with children in our roles of good and evil wizards. In fact, we often nourish and discipline at the same time. But we do this within patriarchal societies throughout the world and in societies that damage their children through civilizing processes, often religious, that withhold knowledge or use the magic of knowledge to manipulate children. Moreover, we are both victims and victimizers, often unrelentingly punishing children for what we may have suffered in our childhood. So, given the complex nature of how societies, childhood, and the education of children have evolved, dichotomies cannot provide the categories that we need to grasp the dynamics of the sorcerer-apprentice relationship, but I believe Elisabeth Young-Bruehl's theories in her book *Childism: Confronting Prejudice against Children* can offer a starting point to help us understand the ambiguities of our relations with children and their significance to sorcerer-apprentice stories. As she states: "People as individuals and in societies mistreat children in order to fulfill certain needs through them, to project internal conflicts and self-hatreds outward, or to assert themselves when they feel their authority has been questioned. But regardless of their individual motivations, they all rely upon a societal prejudice against children to justify themselves and legitimate their behavior."[49]

Young-Bruehl argues that children are a target group of a prejudice, which she calls childism. In order to understand how childism works, we must explore the various motivations of the victimizers. The foundation for prejudice against children can be traced back to ancient Greek civilization. To quote Young-Bruehl:

> Aristotle's assumptions about children—that they are possessions and lack reasoning ability—are childist. Nonetheless, they fit well with the common assumptions of the Greeks, and they were easily built into the European tradition after Aristotle, where they continued to intertwine

with sexism and justifications of slavery (which eventually became racist). The idea that children are by nature meant to be owned by their male parent and that they lack reason has justified treating them like slaves and like immature, unformed persons without the active qualities, the developmental thrust, the proto reasoning and choosing, and the individuality that contemporary developmentalists now recognize in them.[50]

Prejudice in general is a belief system, not a knowledge system about a particular group, and as a belief system, stereotypes of the targeted groups are formed based on some obvious distinguishing appearances, but more on activities and functions attributed to the group by way of fantasies. Young-Bruehl maintains that there are three elementary forms of fantasy, related to sexism, racism, and anti-Semitism, and childism can involve all three forms of fantasy, belief, and action: "1) fantasies about being able to self-reproduce and to own the self-reproduced offspring; 2) fantasies about being able to have slaves—usually sex slaves—who are not incest objects; and 3) fantasies about being able to eliminate something felt to be invidiously or secretly depleting one from within."[51] At the more fundamental motivational or fantasy level, Young-Bruehl explains that

> childism can be defined as a belief system that constructs its target group, "the child," as an immature being produced and owned by adults who use it to serve their own needs and fantasies. It is a belief system that reverses the biological and psychological order of nature, in which adults are responsible for meeting the irreducible needs of children (until the adults grow old and, naturally, reciprocally need support from children). Adults have needs of various kinds—and fantasies about those needs—that childist adults imagine children *could* and, further, *should* serve. The belief that children as children could serve adults needs is a denial that children develop; the belief that children should serve adult needs is a denial of children's developmental needs and rights.[52]

In the case of both the tale types, the "Rebellious Apprentice" and the "Humiliated Apprentice," we have fantasies that have taken the form of diverse fairy tales. The two tales form a whole narrative that allows us to grasp the myriad childist ways that young people are badgered and deprived of the knowledge of magic that might enable them to transform themselves as they wish—not just to survive. Even in those narratives in which the apprentice is successful in obtaining supernatural knowledge and power, he is often beaten, tortured, and demeaned in his struggle to become autonomous, or to avoid being murdered. The stories as fantastic projections stem from the actual lived experiences of storytellers whose tales about the childist maltreatment of apprentices are thousands of years old, and as they have been disseminated and honed, they have become memes that are relevant in almost every culture because they deal with the adaptation strategies and survival of young people and how they must deal with the prejudices of childism.

Though numerous scholars have dismissed the existence of memes or prefer another term to define a cultural replicator, meme has become a valuable concept in the twenty-first century for researchers in the field of cultural evolution studies,[53] and it is particularly useful in folklore and fairy-tale studies to explain the dissemination of tales, customs, rituals, and art. Unfortunately, very few scholars who study folklore, fairy tales, and children's literature have been drawn to study and analyze how significant memes are for the evolution of oral and written tales and how they form memeplexes that reinforce their position within cultural memory.[54] The tales related to the "Rebellious Apprentice" and to the "Humiliated Apprentice" form a memeplex that reflects positive and negative cultural attitudes about magic, power, and knowledge in most parts of the world. Memes proliferate only if they are relevant in the interactions of people and their experiences. They exist as long as people value them and use them to some extent to articulate their fears and hope. Here I want to focus on their roles in Europe and North America and why tale types play off one another in folklore and children's and adult literature. But first a word about memes and memeplexes.

In "Evolution of Culture, Memetics," Francis Heylighen and Klaas Chielens write:

> The concept of meme can be defined as an information pattern, held in an individual's memory, which is capable of being copied to another individual's memory. Memetics can then be defined as the theoretical and empirical science that studies the replication, spread and evolution of memes. Memes differ in their degree of fitness, i.e. adaptedness to the social-cultural environment in which they propagate. Fitter memes will be more successful in being communicated, "infecting" more individuals and thus spreading over a larger population. This biological analogy allows us to apply Darwinian concepts and theories to model cultural evolution.[55]

To grasp why and how numerous oral and literary tales become memes it is important to understand the power of words themselves. As Daniel Dennett, one of the most astute contemporary philosophers to pioneer the study of memetics, has written: "Words can be seen to be the foundational memes that permit the accumulation and transmission of ever more elaborate artifacts and practices."[56] Whereas the evolution of culture was first predicated on a vertical transmission of genes billions of years ago, this evolution was transformed as parents formed and informed their offspring. Dennett argues that

> once this path of vertical *cultural* transmission had been established and optimized, it could be invaded by "rogue cultural variants," horizontally or obliquely transmitted cultural items that do not have the same probability of being benign. . . . These rogue cultural variants are what Richard Dawkins (1976) calls *memes*, and although some of them are bound to be pernicious—parasites, not mutualists—others are profound enhancers of the native competences of the hosts they infect. One can acquire huge amounts of valuable information of which one's parents had no inkling, along with the junk and the scams.[57]

To understand how words as rogue memes have infiltrated our minds and play an important role in the evolution of culture as innovators and replicators, we have to take a memetic perspective. As he states:

> The best way to see how the concept of memes clarifies and extends our understanding of the role of culture in human evolution is to compare the meme's eye perspective to the traditional wisdom—"common sense"— according to which culture is composed of various valuable practices and artifacts, inherited treasures, in effect, that are recognized as such (for the most part) and transmitted deliberately (and for good reasons) from generation to generation. Cultural innovations that are intelligently designed are esteemed, protected, tinkered with, and passed on to the next generation, whereas accidental or inadvertent combinations of either action or material are discarded or ignored as junk.[58]

A good deal of oral folk tales and "kiddie literature" can be regarded as rogue memes, and as Dennett remarks, "Many of our most valuable cultural treasures have no identifiable author and almost certainly were cobbled together by many largely unwitting minds over periods of time. Nobody invented words or arithmetic or music or maps or money. . . . These excellent things acquired their effective designs the same way that plants and animals and viruses acquired theirs—they evolved by natural selection."[59]

Dennett concludes that "the key improvements, then of the memetic perspective are its recognition that 1) excellently designed cultural entities may, like highly efficient viruses, have no intelligent design at all in their ancestry. 2) Memes, like viruses and other symbionts, have their own fitness. Those that flourish will be those that better secure their own production, whether or not they do this by enhancing the reproductive success of their hosts by mutualist means."[60] Here it is important to add that memes often form memeplexes, groups of similar memes, which replicate together to reinforce each other's survival or compete with one another for survival. In the case of the two tale types, the "Rebellious Apprentice" and the "Humiliated Apprentice," which originated hundreds of years ago, we do not know what words were spoken, when, and where to generate tales about young men and women who learned how to transform themselves, young men and women who rebelled against their masters and sought to use magic words to enhance their knowledge and power, and tales about young men and women who were intimidated and humiliated by omnipotent sorcerers because they endeavored to use magic words to enhance their knowledge and power. Somehow, not by design, these tales became particularly relevant in the cultural memories of most countries throughout the world. They are particular because they have mutated according to changes in the civilizing processes in diverse countries and reflect different notions of childism, desire for self-consciousness and magic (mana) for self-transformation, class struggle, and competition for power.

In their informative reader, *Defining Magic*, Bernd-Christian Otto and Michael Stausberg develop the useful concept of "magicity," which, in many ways, helps explain why an understanding of the history of magic and how magic functions in the memeplex of the "Sorcerer's Apprentice" tales are key to grasping why we are drawn to these stories. They state:

> In physics, "magicity" refers to "The condition of a heavy isotype of having a *magic* number of protons and neutrons, and therefore of having particular stability" (http://en.Wiktionary.org/wiki/magicity). We have no ambition of emulating that model here in a quasi-scientist manner; but the point is the idea of some forms and conditions of structural stability. "Patterns of magicity" do not automatically involve "MAGIC" (as in the supreme meta-category, nor are they "magic" (as referring to ontological

features), but they are a way of dealing with cross-culturally attested observations. "Magicity" acknowledges the fact that they were traditionally assigned to the overall category "MAGIC" in which we have stopped believing. As we see it, based on a meta-analysis of definitions and theories of "magic," and the catalogue of objects to which that category is applied, future work should seek to model such patterns.[61]

In well over two thousand years, patterns of magicity have been formed in all types of narratives—a factor that most scholars of magic, religion, and science have astoundingly overlooked. As we have seen, certain tale types evolve and develop structural stability and enable us metaphorically to contend with acute social and political problems that involve our desires for magic of some kind. The discursive pattern of magicity, which is primarily apparent in most of the "Rebellious Apprentice" tales and lends them a structural stability that involves three basic features: (1) magic or mana is a positive force that a young man needs to survive and to gain recognition; (2) magic enables metamorphosis or miraculous transformation; and (3) without magic, a young man and his family will be destroyed by a tyrant who misuses magic.

What is fascinating about magicity in the memeplex of the "Sorcerer's Apprentice" is that the ambiguous magic, never fully explained, is the secular means through which humans manage to change themselves and their conditions. Moreover, people *continue* to believe in magic of this kind, and the tales about sorcerers and their apprentices *continue* to be told because people have never stopped believing in magic. Most religions testify to the belief in magic and cannot effectively disassociate their rituals and practices from magic, and cultural memories embrace magic.

When I speak of cultural memory, I am referring specifically to the work of Jan and Aleida Assmann.[62] In *Cultural Memory and Early Civilization*, Jan Assmann explains the basic principles that constitute cultural memory:

This book deals with the connection between these three themes of memory (or reference to the past), identity (or political imagination), and cultural continuity (or the formation of tradition). Every culture formulates something that might be called a connective structure. It has a binding effect that works on two levels—social and temporal. It binds people together by providing a "symbolic universe" . . .—a common area of experience, expectation, and action whose connecting force provides them with trust and with orientation. Early texts refer to this aspect of culture as justice. However, it also links yesterday with today by giving form and presence to influential experiences and memories, incorporating images and tales from another time into the background of the onward moving present, and bring with it hope and continuity. This connective structure is the aspect of culture that underlies myths and histories. Both the normative and the narrative elements of these—mixing instruction with storytelling—create a basis of belonging, of identity, so that the individual can then talk of "we." What binds him to this plural is the connective structure of common knowledge and characteristics—first through adherence to the same laws and values, and second through the memory of a shared past.[63]

Assmann stresses that repetition is the basic principle behind all the connective structures, and in the case of folk and fairy tales, I would contend that there are also elements in the narratives that are transcultural and account for the wide dissemination of similar tale types throughout the world. We can perhaps call them "global memes." They bind us in apparent and unapparent ways. They survive because they provide relevant information about conditions in contrived civilizing processes that further or impede the development of young people. They impel us to talk because they raise the question of what it means to fit into a world into which we were born not to fit.

In the case of the "Rebellious Apprentice" and the "Humiliated Apprentice," we are dealing with rogue positive and pernicious memes that form a memeplex as cultural replicators. Viewed ideologically and from a meme's-eye perspective, the tales that stem from the cultural memory of the "Rebellious Apprentice" continue to be relevant, in my opinion, because they expose the childist prejudices of authorities and parents and point to the necessity for young people to learn how to shape-shift, mutate, and transform so that they will not be sacrificed or killed by the insidious forces seeking to control them. The tales that have emanated from the cultural memory of the "Humiliated Apprentice" tend to reinforce the illusion of absolute omnipotence that metaphorically is associated with authorities and parents and some "mythological" notion of an absolute world order or divinity. According to these tales, young people are to be intimidated by and to comply with the power of authorities and parents. No questions are to be asked. In the global tradition of both tale types, words that form magical spells are essential to learn, whether they are part of the codes of black magic or white magic. It is through learning words that young people can attain a sense of themselves and the world around them. It is through pronouncing words that they can test themselves and the forces that have determined their *habitus*. It is through the retelling of tales that have spread like memes and question evil and good sorcerers that children and adults can learn to cultivate innovative strategies that bring about social justice and generate hope that the world can be transformed.

KRABAT, THE REBELLIOUS APPRENTICE IN LUSATIA AND CENTRAL EUROPE

It is not by chance that at one point in history a group of tales about sorcerers and apprentices formed an unusual cultural memeplex in a small region of Central Europe that has given rise to an exemplary rebellious figure depicted as a folk hero. Combining motifs and elements of the legend and fairy tale, a large number of oral and literary tales spread by word of mouth and by print throughout Lusatia from the early nineteenth century to the present that resonate with the hope of the negative dialectic—that is, with resistance to arbitrary domination. I am referring to the cycle of tales associated with the figure of Krabat and his transformation in Sorbian and German folk and fairy tales that emanated in Lusatia. But before I discuss the significance of the evolution and metamorphosis of the popular Krabat legend in light of the memetic dissemination of "Sorcerer's Apprentice" tales, a few words about the history of the Sorbs are necessary as a brief sociocultural background for understanding the tendentious nature of the Krabat tales.

Sorbs are a Western Slavic people of Central Europe, and they settled in regions of Eastern Germany, Poland, and Czechoslovakia that were called Lusatia in the sixth century. Two major languages, Upper Sorbian and Lower Sorbian, were developed and cultivated. These languages, also called Wendish and Lusatian, are still spoken today by well over 60,000 people. The languages and their dialects are basically Slavic, but due to the colonization of the Sorbs by the Germans, dialects mixed with German as well as a standard German are spoken throughout the region.

In 1635 the territory of Lusatia became a fiefdom of Saxon Electors. This was a dark period for the Sorbs because the Thirty Years War (1618–48) caused great devastation in all parts of Lusatia. Not only were the towns and villages pillaged and crops destroyed, but also peasants were recruited forcefully by German soldiers to serve in the war. By the beginning of the eighteenth century most of the land was owned or controlled by German Junkers or squires. Male and female peasants, day workers, craftsmen, and servants were badly treated. Later in 1815 the Congress of Vienna gave most of Upper Lusatia to Prussia and Lower Lusatia to Saxony, and the Sorbian language was banned along with Sorbian newspapers, magazines, schools, and customary practices. With the unification of Germany in 1871, Upper Lusatia became part of Prussia and Lower Lusatia, part of Saxony. Despite the "Germanization" of Lusatia, the Sorbs managed to maintain their different languages and dialects. The bans were gradually lifted toward the end of the nineteenth century, and during the first part of the twentieth century there was a revival of Slavic Sorbian culture that ended with the rise of Nazism in the 1930s. After World War II the Sorbs obtained linguistic and cultural autonomy in East Germany and Poland up through 1989, when political conditions continued to favor an even stronger sense of Sorbian customs and cultural identity.

Most important to note for comprehending how and why the Krabat legend took root in the early part of the nineteenth century, in my opinion, is that the Sorbs suffered greatly from exploitation and discrimination from 1600 through 1900. The Sorbs were colonized by their "masters," the Germans, and had to struggle to maintain their cultural identity. In fact, the master-slave dialectic was experienced bodily and spiritually by the majority of Sorbs, and while many were forced to conform to the "laws" of German rule and domination, they managed to keep their cultural heritage alive through language, stories, religious practice, and resistance to German prescriptions.

Resistance was and is particularly strong in Lusatia, and this can be seen in the storytelling of Sorbian folk tales. Susanne Hose, one of the foremost scholars of the Krabat stories, has remarked that

> storytelling is an essential activity of people. It belongs to the basic technologies that human beings have developed to share experiences and knowledge with one another and to pass on to other people. In the so-called folk tales such as legends, fairy tales, anecdotes, or jokes we encounter what many people have learned and what moves them. The tradition based on oral storytelling and later also written tales includes also the formation of a canon and censorship. . . . In contrast to other Sorbian folk tales, those about the Sorcerer Krabat have been recorded in a relatively continual way and by different writers since the nineteenth century.[64]

Hose, along with Paul Nedo, Marie-Luise Ehrhardt, and Martin Nowak-Neumann,[65] have shed light on how early oral storytelling in the eighteenth century transformed a mysterious, if not evil, squire named Johann Schadowitz, Lord of Särchen, from a demonic figure into a folk hero, who liberates himself from a satanic master and then supports the freedom of serfs and peasants. In an 1848 chronicle Franz Schneider recorded the following:

> 1704 d. May 29, Colonel Johann Schadowitz died in Särchen. He was 80 years old and was born in Agran, Croatia.
>
> He was buried in the parish church in Wittichenau below the Presbyterri at the bell. In 1795, when the reverend Georg Brückner was buried in this same place, the colonel's sword was found on this spot. This Croatian Schadowitz is the same man who was known in our region under the name of Krabat, for "Croat" had been changed in the vernacular to "Krabat." This Croat was rich—Lord of Särchen—and had the reputation of being a sorcerer. Accordingly he once—as the legend goes—threw a bunch of oats into the glazed cooking pot in the parish in Wittichenau and conjured up a regiment of soldiers who stood at attention in the courtyard of the church. The Croat formed a close friendship with Augustus I, the Elector of Saxony and King of Poland. It is said that he often lunched with the king at noon, and one time made the journey to Dresden through the air. During his flight he allegedly crashed into the church steeple at Kamenz and caused it to bend. One time it is said that he rescued the Elector from the Turks by using sorcery.—The book of obituaries at the parish church in Wittichenau did not record any other information.[66]

Throughout the nineteenth and twentieth centuries numerous oral and written tales about the amazing accomplishments of Colonel Johann Schadowitz, the lord of Särchen, were spread, adapted, and transformed. Moreover, films and plays were created to celebrate his deeds. At first they depicted him as an eccentric sorcerer/squire under the name Krabat, who often excited people with extraordinary magical exploits. At the same time they gradually portrayed him as a young man named Krabat from an impoverished family who goes to study magic in a so-called satan's mill and eventually learns enough magic to defeat an unnamed evil sorcerer. Many of these stories did not include the episode of Krabat studying magic at a mill. They often began with Krabat depicted as an extraordinary man who knew enough magic to astonish the folk and his king. Before he dies, he orders his book of magic to be destroyed so that nobody can use magic for evil purposes. The tales were told and printed in a Sorbian or Wendish dialect and in German depending on the region in which they were gathered and published. Some of the Slavic versions were translated, expanded in German, and printed in magazines and books. In the very first printed tale, which appeared in a 1837 German magazine, it is clear that the author Joachim Leopold Haupt viewed Krabat (unnamed in this version but obviously the Lord Johann Schadowitz) as a sorcerer who dabbles in magic. Moreover, it appears that Haupt had read either Lucian or Goethe's "The Sorcerer's Apprentice," for he introduces a coachman who vainly tries to imitate his master but fails. The master must come to his aid when the bungling coachman cannot turn the soldiers back into black oats.[67] Yet, what began as a legend about the humiliated apprentice quickly turned in subsequent stories into one about a rebel named Krabat from an impoverished family who attains folk-hero status.

Among the interesting tales important for our purposes are Michael Hornig's "Krabat: Sage aus dem Volksmund" ("Krabat: A Legend from Folklore," 1858); Georg Gustav Kubasch's "Krabat" (1865); Hendrich Jordan's "Der Zauberlehrling" ("The Sorcerer's Apprentice," 1879); Edmund Vecken-stedt's "Der Zauber Lehrling, I und II" ("The Sorcerer's Apprentice, I and II" 1880); and Georg Pilk's "Die wendische Faust-Sage" ("The Wendish Faust Legend," 1900). They reveal a trajectory in oral and written versions that favors the dominant rebellious apprentice in a memeplex that combines legends and fairy tales. The obsequiously submissive coachman disappears; the name Krabat becomes attached to a young peasant from a poor family who uses magic to assist a king; the focus shifts from the magical achievements of a sorcerer to a conflict between sorcerer and apprentice.

In Hornig's tale a young man named Krabat comes to Leipzig and falls into the hands of a sorcerer who always has twelve apprentices and teaches them magic. At the end of each year the evil magician demands the soul of one of his apprentices. Thanks to the help of his mother, Krabat escapes the sorcerer, whom he later defeats. Then he assists the Elector prince of Dresden in recruiting soldiers and receives a royal estate as a reward for his activities, or he flies in his coach toward Dresden.

In Kubasch's variant of 1865 Krabat is a herdsman from the poorest family in a village, and he is recruited by the devil's eleven apprentices to work in a nearby mill, where they study sorcery. Much to the dismay of the other envious apprentices, Krabat learns faster than they do and becomes the most adroit in the use of magic. Since he has learned so much after three years, the devil cannot kill him, and Krabat leaves the mill, demonstrates his command of necromantic arts to the people of the region, and becomes the squire of Groß-Särchen. Moreover, the king of Saxony takes a liking to him and invites him to dine with him in Dresden on every holiday. One time Krabat damages the church steeple in Kamenz as he flies there in his coach. Another time his coachman tries to use Krabat's magic but almost causes a catastrophe by forgetting the magic spell. Krabat must intervene to save him. He performs many other heroic deeds, and toward the end of his life, he knows exactly when he is going to die and orders his servant to destroy his book of magic even though the servant had wanted to keep it.

In Jordan's variant "Der Zauberlehrling" ("The Sorcerer's Apprentice," 1879), a poor peasant has his son apprenticed to a magician for three years. When the father recognizes the son after the apprenticeship, the son returns to him. Since the young man is now a shape-shifter, he transforms himself into different animals to help his father procure money until the sorcerer captures him. Then a young maiden helps him escape and defeat the magician in a shape-shifting battle. Of course, the young man marries the maiden in the end.

Veckenstedt provides two contrasting versions, both part of the "Sorcerer's Apprentice" memeplex. In the first, recorded by Hendrich Jordan, there is no mention of Krabat or the legend. Instead the tale concerns a smart farmer's son, who is apprenticed to a sorcerer, and when he manages to arrange with his father how he is to be recognized, he is set free after three years. Then the farmer's son transforms himself into various animals to be sold at a fair. Eventually the sorcerer hears about the transformations, captures the farmer's son, and mistreats him. But the farmer's son escapes and kills the sorcerer in magical combat. While this tale follows the "traditional" plot of "Rebellious Apprentice" tales, the second version, recorded by Alexander von Rabenau, is closer to the story of "The Humiliated Apprentice." Here, after a son survives a four-year apprenticeship, he escapes a powerful sorcerer, but the young man is recaptured and punished. Once again the young apprentice escapes and transforms himself into different animals. Unfortunately he changes himself into a mouse at the end, and the sorcerer as cat gobbles him up.

By the beginning of the twentieth century, the short legend about Colonel Schadowitz of Särchen had been transformed into a hybrid fairy tale with an emphasis on a poor young man, generally named Krabat, who is apprenticed to a sorcerer in a mysterious demonic mill and learns enough black magic to overcome the sorcerer and to use the art of necromancy to become a wealthy and somewhat eccentric lord. The pinnacle of the transformation of the Krabat legend into a major folk/fairy tale is Georg Pilk's "The Wendish Faust Legend" of 1900. Written under the influence of Goethe's *Faust*, stories told to him by his uncle Adolf Anders, and other tales that he collected or read, the proficient folklorist Pilk more or less defined the trajectory of the Krabat legend in the twentieth century. Hose writes:

> Pilk's version cannot be considered a legend or a fairy tale. It is a compilation of retellings based on written and possibly oral sources that must be ascribed to literature rather than folk stories. To be sure, it is indisputable that Pilk's version forms the starting point for all further adaptations and also provides the material for the research of Paul Nedos as well as for the literature and the mediation of the contemporary activities in the "Krabat" region [that is, Lusatia]. Pilk was the first to make the Krabat material known for a German speaking public. His "legend" appeared in popular magazines and in many collections.[68]

The notable features of the plot in Pilk's "Wendish Faust Legend" are: Krabat is a herdsman in an impoverished family; he is recruited by the demonic sorcerer of a mill to work there for one year; thanks to his mother, who must recognize him as a bird at the mill, he is able to flee and take the sorcerer's book of magic with him; Krabat changes himself into an ox to be sold at a cattle market to help his family and then a horse, but he is captured by the sorcerer; Krabat escapes the sorcerer at the blacksmith's shop and changes himself into a lark, then a fish, and a ring; finally, Krabat must transform himself into a barley corn and then a fox to defeat and devour the sorcerer; using magic, Krabat impresses King August the Strong and works at his castle for a while; then Krabat is recruited by the German soldiers to fight for the king of Dresden against the Turks; once again he uses magical means to save the king of Dresden and bring about the defeat of the Turks; the king awards Krabat an estate at Groß-Särchen; Krabat uses magic to improve the working and living conditions of the peasants in the region and bequeaths forty parcels of land to the peasants; before he dies, he has the book of magic destroyed; upon his death, he is revered by all the peasants and apparently has been transformed into a white swan.

Although many other versions about Krabat's life and deeds were published and told after 1900, it was Pilk's hybrid patriotic tale that stamped such diverse literary and filmic versions that followed in the twentieth century: Martin Nowak-Neumann's *Master Krabat* (*Meister Krabat*, 1954); Jerzy Slizinski's "Krabat" (1964); Jurij Brězan's *The Black Mill* (*Die schwarze Mühle*, 1968); and Otfried Preußler's *Krabat* (1971). The first three narratives were published during the communist period in East Germany, 1948–89, and the authors tended to sharpen the socialist ideology of the basic plot. For instance, Nowak-Neumann begins his narrative with a description of the Thirty Years War (1618–48) and relates how the ruthless German lords exploited the Sorbian peasants, while the priests merely placated the ruling forces. The hyperbolic ideological language focusing on social-class struggle that runs throughout the story gives rise in the very first chapter to a superman-like hero:

> Certainly nothing helped them [the peasants]. The lords were soon victorious, and the people were defeated and impoverished and had to slave away even harder than before. And they yearned for the sleeping heroes in Mount Kaponiza to awaken and to liberate the folk. And in their tales they told one another that one day a powerful hero with great strength and force would rise up from the folk, a magician, who knew the secret powers, knew the spells and words, had control of all kinds of sciences and was more powerful than the tyrants in their castles.[69]

The didactic and poorly written book for young readers seeks to transform a hybrid fairy tale into a Sorbian socialist legend and to transform Krabat into an exemplary champion of socialism. As in other tales Krabat is portrayed as the poor son of a herdsman who must go begging in the nearby region and then takes a job in the Kollmer mill because he wants to learn and to make something out of himself. However, he learns too much, and consequently, the sorcerer wants to kill him at the end of the year. Yet, because Krabat is so smart, he arranges a means for his mother to free him, and he also steals the sorcerer's magic book. Later he kills the sorcerer in a magical combat of transformations that is typical of most "Rebellious Sorcerer" tales. Thereafter, he wanders about the country, enlists in the war against the Turks, and is rewarded by the German king for aiding his cause. Once he returns to his home Krabat shares his property with the other peasants and uses the magic book to transform a swamp into fertile land. Up to his death Krabat behaves and performs magical deeds according to socialist moral principles and is honored by the Sorbian folk but not by the German squires.

Nowak-Neumann's "children's book" infantilizes Krabat as a folk hero, and he uses an intimate folk tone to offer a simplistic history of social-class struggle basically to align himself with the cultural dictates of the ruling government in East Germany of that time. In contrast Jerzy Slizinski took another approach, more aligned with scholarly folklore research. He collected a number of folk tales, recorded in Sorbian dialect and in German, and published them in *Sorbische Volkserzählungen*. They are essentially devoid of didactic politics, although the master-slave dialectic is still at the heart of this "authentic" tale from the folk. The storyteller is Hermann Bjenada, a tailor in the small town of Commerau in the district of Bautzen. While it is clear that Bjenada was familiar with Pilk's literary version, his simplistic language and awkward style reveal that his tale (and others) were still alive in the oral tradition in Lusatia. In other words the hybrid tale was spread by storytellers in Sorbian and German throughout the region that was once Lusatia. In this case the hero Krabat is a young worker from the lower classes, and like previous protagonists, he takes a position in the mill, escapes with a book of magic, engages in a life-and-death battle with the sorcerer, kills him, and then proceeds to gain fame by using his magic to help the king of Dresden in the war with the Turks. Then he continues to assist his fellow workers and peasants in Groß-Särchen until his death. In Bjenada's version the legendary nature of the fairy tale and the heroic actions of Krabat speak for themselves in a tersely spoken narrative. There are no frills to his story. There is no need for them.

In contrast the literary variants always tend to be florid, and this is the case with Jurij Brězan's *The Black Mill* (1968). Brězan, the foremost Sorbian writer of the twentieth century, had already translated Nowak-Neumann's children's book from Sorbian into German, and he was to write two extensive novels based on the Krabat material.[70] In *The Black Mill*, he manages to convey his most succinct interpretation of the master-slave dialectic, and it was this version that served as the basis for the East German TV film, *The Black Mill* (1975), directed by Celino Bleiweiß.[71] The focus of this novella for young readers is on the power of magic as knowledge. The motto "whoever knows can do anything" is repeated numerous times throughout the narrative that unfolds as though it were a shedding of ignorance. There are also indications that the hybrid fairy tale was to serve as an anti-fascist or anti-totalitarian text. The black mill is depicted more like a concentration camp than a workplace, and the evil miller has a clear resemblance to Hitler and other dictators.

Although Brĕzan endows Krabat with mythic features, he does not succumb to the hyperbolic pedantic style of Nowak-Neumann. In fact he makes
some major changes in the plot and themes in his novel that make it much
more compelling than Nowak-Neumann's adaptation of the Krabat material.
The young man Krabat, an orphan and a wanderer, appears out of the blue.
He seems to be a child of the folk. His quest is one for self-knowledge and
knowledge of the world, and the only reason he accepts the sinister miller's
offer to work at the mill for seven years is because he wants to acquire the
knowledge of the seven books that the miller keeps locked in a chest. Once
Krabat begins working at the mill, he realizes that it is a death camp, and he
joins forces with a co-worker named Markus. They escape with one of the
magic books. To earn some money so that they can free the other workers
and the peasant families surrounding the mill, Krabat changes himself first
into an ox and then into a horse to be sold at a market. The miller captures
Krabat, but with the help of Markus, Krabat changes himself into a lark,
then a fish, and finally a fox. However, the miller, who had transformed himself into a chicken, manages to escape and swears revenge. In fact the miller
becomes more powerful than ever in the region and knows that he must
separate Markus and Krabat to maintain absolute control of the peasants.
So he devises a strategy to spread rumors that Krabat is an evil sorcerer and
eventually he casts blame on Krabat for killing Markus during the war against
the Turks. However, with the help of Markus's mother, who tells the true
story of Krabat's struggle against the evil miller, the people become aware of
their need for knowledge and power. Eventually, Krabat leads them in a battle
against the miller, whom he kills. Then Krabat has the magic book destroyed,
and he disappears but remains within the spirit of the folk.

Clearly thanks to Brĕzan's efforts, the master-slave dialectic became
well-known throughout East Germany and parts of Central Europe in the
post–World War II period from the 1950s through the 1970s. Yet he was not
the only writer who contributed to the proliferation of Krabat tales. In my
opinion the most significant reworking of the legend for young adult readers
is the West German Otfried Preußler's *Krabat* (1971), translated into English
in 1972 with the title *The Satanic Mill* and adapted for the cinema in 1978
by the brilliant Czech animator Karel Zeman and later in 2008 by Marco
Kreuzpaintner.

Preußler (1923–2013), who grew up in Reichenberg, Bohemia, which is
part of the Czech Republic today, was steeped in Sorbian folklore. His family

could trace their ancestors back to the fifteenth century, and his parents were teachers who had a great interest in Sorbian, Czech, and German culture. After Preußler graduated from the gymnasium in 1942, he was drafted into the German Wehrmacht and captured by the Russians on the Eastern front in 1944. He spent the next five years in prisoner of war camps, and when he returned to Germany, he found that his family had been relocated to Rosenheim, a small city in Bavaria, where he spent the rest of his life. After attending the university, he began work first as a primary school teacher and then as a principal while writing books for children and became one of the most successful German children's book authors in the twentieth century. Among his noteworthy children's books translated into English are *The Robber Hotzenplotz* and *The Little Witch*. His novel *Krabat*, however, was the first book he ever wrote for young adults, and it was autobiographical and clearly political.

The novel is divided into three years. In the first Krabat is a fourteen-year-old Sorbian/Wendish orphan whose mother and father have died from a great plague, and he travels about begging in the countryside of Lusatia with other young men. He dreams about black ravens, which lure him to the Black Mill, where he becomes an apprentice to the tyrannical Master, who is a sorcerer of black arts and promises to teach Krabat magic to compensate him for his work at the mill. Once Krabat agrees, he makes the acquaintance of eleven other apprentices who are all afraid to tell him about the slave-like conditions at the mill. At the end of several months Krabat learns enough magic from the Master's *Koraltor*, the black book, to change himself into a raven and becomes friends with the head apprentice, Tonda. During Easter in a nearby village Krabat hears the voice of the congregation's lead singer, whose name is Kantorka, and is enchanted by her. Tonda warns him never to reveal her name because he had once loved a maiden from the village, and she had been mysteriously killed. Toward the end of the year on New Year's eve Tonda himself is also mysteriously murdered.

In the second year Krabat misses Tonda very much, and a new apprentice, Witko appears in his place so that there are always twelve apprentices. Krabat's best friend now is a youngster named Juro. Once again Krabat is drawn to the maiden Kantorka and leaves his body through magic to be in her presence in the village. He almost commits a grave error, but Juro saves him so that the sorcerer does not notice anything. In fact the Master is impressed by Krabat's knowledge of magic and takes him with him to Dresden, where Krabat learns how much influence the Master has on the German prince's militaristic politics. However, the suspicious Master has him tested when he commands him to go to the fair and sell Juro, who is changed into a horse. However, Krabat does not believe that Juro will be equal to the task and consequently transforms himself into the horse. To punish Krabat for his disobedience, the sorcerer appears as a merchant and buys Krabat at the fair. Then he beats him severely to humiliate him and teach him a lesson. Later a famous folk hero/apprentice by the name of Pumphutt visits the mill one day and defeats the Master in a magic competition. When New Year's eve arrives another apprentice is mysteriously killed, and it is clear that the Master is the murderer.

In the third year Krabat cannot get Kantorka out of his mind and constantly dreams about her. He uses magic to contact her, and since she, too, has dreams about him, they meet and declare their love for one another. However, Juro realizes that Krabat is still too unprepared in the art of magic and is endangering Kantorka's life and his own as well. So, Juro, who has secretly learned all of the sorcerer's magic knowledge, begins to teach Krabat everything as well. To protect Kantorka, Krabat does not leave the mill and breaks contact with her. However, he does arrange a quick meeting with her and informs her that, if she loves him, she can bring about his freedom by coming to the mill on New Year's Eve and asking for his freedom. At the same time she must be able to recognize him among the other apprentices, who will be ravens. She agrees, and when Krabat returns to the mill, the Master, who is impressed by Krabat's knowledge of magic, offers him the mill and tells him that he can be his successor and make a good deal of money. Krabat refuses, and it is clear that the sorcerer will now kill him on New Year's Eve. Consequently, Kantorka comes to the mill that evening and demands Krabat's freedom. The Master shows her the twelve ravens, and to his dismay, she recognizes Krabat, which means the sorcerer must die at midnight when the mill is to be destroyed by flames. Krabat leaves the mill with Kantorka and the apprentices, and he asks her how she had managed to recognize him. She replies that she sensed that he was the only bird who showed that he was worried about her.

This short plot summary does not do justice to the complexities in Preußler's fairy-tale novel, which reads like a chronicle or reportage that makes the shape-shifting and magic appear credible. There is no hype or fantasy. Magic was part of the quotidian life of most people in the sixteenth and seventeenth centuries. Magic was and is knowledge that equals power. Preußler tells the story as if it were matter-of-fact. It is true that Krabat does have a number of hallucinatory dreams, but Preußler does not exaggerate and depict the scenes as though they were beyond belief. He reports succinctly and bluntly because he seeks to grasp and depict the reality of poor, abused apprentices during a period of war when they are at the mercy not only of the sorcerer but also of the prince and an anonymous character who makes money off the work of the apprentices at the mill. More to the point Preußler metaphorically recalls his brief career in the German army and his five years in Russian prison camps. It is clear that he wants to recall the brutality of the Nazi and Stalinist periods and demonstrate how acts of human compassion and love can bring hope. There is no hint at the end of the narrative that magic will be used again. At least it will not be used to exploit other people. Krabat as apprentice has learned that the art and knowledge of black magic are too destructive to build humane relationships. Like the best of the apprentices in the tale type of "The Rebellious Apprentice," he is a rebel with a cause.

The historical evolution of Krabat tales in the region of Lusatia is a memetic cultural development that reveals how bits and pieces of legends were transformed into a hybrid fairy tale that relied heavily on the memeplex of the "Rebellious Apprentice" and "Humiliated Apprentice" tale types. In my opinion the memetic driving force is rooted in the cultural memory of worldwide master-slave conflicts that persist today, and the tales themselves appear to exploit all kinds of modalities to depict the conflicts and call upon us to engage in the conflicts as they pertain to our lives. The "Sorcerer's Apprentice" tale types emerge from human struggles for self-knowledge, magic (mana), and power. Magic and magical transformation are of essence. While the Krabat tales can be localized in Central Europe, they have spread and contribute to the much larger tradition of "Sorcerer's Apprentice" tales and consequently have greater ramifications. Magic and magical transformation are not only key components of all these tales, but they also form some of the modern modalities such as filmmaking and films. What is fascinating about the films that deal with the sorcerer's apprentice is that they continue the antagonistic memetic conflict between the rebellious and humiliated apprentices conveyed through the cinematic modality that provides greater dissemination of the tale types with diverse plots and characters.

THE CURIOUS CINEMATIC STRUGGLE OVER
THE "TRUE" SORCERER'S APPRENTICE

In Central Europe, the "Rebellious Apprentice" tales continue to flourish in print, in the theater, in local storytelling, on television, and on the Internet. In particular the tales that concern the hybrid fairy tale of Krabat have greatly appealed to German and Czech filmmakers, who have "grabbed" hold of these tales just as the tales have grabbed them. What stands out in their works is that the memetic dissemination of the "Rebellious Apprentice" tale type through the media of film tends to be stronger in Europe than it is in North America and the United Kingdom. Strangely—or, perhaps not so strangely—the three important Krabat films produced in East Germany, Czechoslovakia, and unified Germany have had very little distribution in the United Kingdom and the United States. Yet they have stuck in the cultural memories of people in Central Europe, I believe, because of Europe's experiences with fascism and war, and I want to discuss films by Celino Bleiweiß, *Die schwarze Mühle* (*The Black Mill*, 1975); Karel Zeman, *Krabat* or *The Sorcerer's Apprentice* (*Carodejuv ucen*, 1978); and Marco Kreuzpaintner, *Krabat* or *Krabat and the Legend of the Satanic Mill* (2008); before analyzing the curious and virtually unknown history of "Sorcerer's Apprentice" films in the United States. (In making this claim I do not want to discount the great significance of magic in Georges Méliès's films of the 1890s and how magic and magical transformation are key to understanding the general international fascination of the cinema and the popularity of the Harry Potter films.)

In her book *The Politics of Magic: DEFA Fairy-Tale Films*, Qinna Shen notes that Celino Bleiweiß's TV fairy-tale film, *The Black Mill*, was among ten or more East German fairy-tale films that didactically represented class struggles and ridiculed evil rulers during the existence of the German Democratic Republic.[72] She remarks that these "films all have a similar structure typical of fairy-tale narratives. They also reinforce Marxist ethics that sympathize with and empower the working class. They span four decades attesting to thematic consistency or, to use rather unflattering terms, monotony and anachronism. The preference to adapt class-conscious and leftist tales constitutes one of the hall marks of DEFA fairy tales in comparison to those of the West."[73]

While it may be true that there is a monotonous emphasis on anachronistic class struggle in many of the DEFA fairy-tale films, this viewpoint overlooks the contemporary relevant critique of East German conditions through metaphorical references in the films. In the case of Bleiweiß's adaptation of Jurij Brězan's *The Black Mill* (1968), it is clear and would have been clear to East German audiences that the film was not only about the exploitation of Krabat and the oppression of workers in the sixteenth and seventeenth centuries but also in the present-day of the German Democratic Republic and other Communist-bloc countries.

Bleiweiß follows the plot of Brězan's novella closely. However, the images of the workers in the film convey a critique of *contemporary* alienated work, "magical" deception, intimidation, and ruthless rule. Krabat, a free spirit, who appears to be eighteen or nineteen years old, is lured to work at the mill by the evil miller, who promises him powerful knowledge that will enable him to achieve and obtain whatever he wishes. Though the character of the miller is a stereotype of the wicked magician, and the characters of the workers and peasants are portrayed as flawless, noble but oppressed people, the film is not totally monotonous and kitsch, for it reveals the brutality of master-slave relations and false promises in a poignant manner. After all his desperate struggles to obtain power through magic, Krabat has the book of magic burned in the end and wanders freely into the forest, and the knowledge that he has gained about collective action in the conflict with his master appears to have given him hope for humanity that will guide him in future encounters.

Resistance and hope are the key themes in Karel Zeman's animated film, *Krabat,* which he made in Czechoslovakia and East Germany ten years after the Russians suppressed the cultural revolution in the Prague Spring of 1968. Based in part on the West German writer Otfried Preußler's 1971 novel, *Krabat,* the film has deep roots in European folk traditions. Zeman uses both folklore and Preußler's novel to form his own "contemporary" version of the tale type to comment on war, poverty, and tyranny. In his animated film Krabat, the protagonist, is a fourteen-year-old orphan wandering about Saxony in late medieval Europe. War is everywhere, and Krabat, a vagabond, begs and looks for food and shelter. During the warm weather, he is happy and manages to survive. However, the winter months are difficult. Starving, he is eventually lured to a mill by the sorcerer disguised as a raven. Once he arrives he believes that he will work as a miller's apprentice. However, he soon discovers that he will be compelled to study magic along with eleven other apprentices and to learn how to use it to help the evil sorcerer swindle people. At the end of each year one of the apprentices is to challenge the sorcerer in magic, and whoever wins the battle of transformations kills the other. The sorcerer always wins by cheating. In the course of time the sorcerer defeats a few apprentices, who are replaced by new recruits. Every now and then Krabat is allowed to test his magic in villages. On an Easter outing from the mill Krabat falls in love with a maiden, whose name he never learns. And as he visits her secretly over time he grows more and more torn between his dedication to magic and his love for the maiden. The sorcerer discovers Krabat's love, whips him in front of the other apprentices, and warns him that he will be killed if he betrays the sorcerer. This whipping and another incident in which the sorcerer almost forces Krabat to kill his best friend make him realize that he must somehow read the sorcerer's forbidden magic book to become as adept at magic as the sorcerer. However, Krabat is puzzled by the last magic formula in the book that states "love is stronger than any kind of magic power." He tries to solve this formula, but before he does, the sorcerer changes all the apprentices into crows and intends to punish Krabat and kill him in a duel. Krabat resists the challenge, and just as the sorcerer is about to murder him, the anonymous maiden appears. The sorcerer declares that if she can tell Krabat apart from the other eleven apprentices after he blindfolds her, he will let them go free. At first the maiden is troubled, but when she senses Krabat's anxiety and worry for her life, she succeeds in choosing him. As soon as she makes this choice, the sorcerer's head splits in two and a candle falls onto the magic book. The magic mill explodes into flames as if an atomic bomb had fallen on it. All the apprentices leave the mill as they were, young vagabonds without any knowledge of magic. Krabat joins the unknown maiden in a starlit evening in the snow. Together they hold hands and walk off into the distant field.

Zeman's *Krabat* was beautifully made with cell and cutout animation, and it is a profound analysis of the deadly consequences of forced labor in the service of a dreadful, powerful tyrant. The apprentices are all poor young men without hope; they succumb to the lure or call of the magician. These young men are also killed in a way that strengthens the sorcerer's rule of violence. Zeman's drawings are not realistic. The cutout figures have sharp angular contours; the perspectives of the frames are constantly altered with vividly colored backgrounds that constantly change and reveal different hues. Various motifs such as the transformation battles, wings of the bird, or Krabat's magic wings, are used in diverse ways. For Krabat the wings are a possible means to escape prison, while the sorcerer uses the wings to attack and kill. Landscapes and architecture indicate mood and spatial freedom. The film

is narrated in the first person by Krabat, and it commences with frames of
a peaceful summer meadow suddenly threatened by soldiers and war. The
music is solemn throughout most of the film. There is hardly any dialogue.
The sorcerer utters harsh commands. Otherwise the gazes of the characters indicate what they are thinking and feeling. Krabat never speaks to the
anonymous maiden. They understand each other through glances and facial
expressions. The end is a silent snowy winter evening of peace. The beauty
of Zeman's film of resistance and hope is that he weaves his tale with very
little dialogue or commentary. The startling images speak for themselves and
challenge viewers to think for themselves.

In contrast to Zeman's hopeful adaptation of Preußler's novel, Kreuzpaintner's stark realistic film of 2008 follows Preußler's novel more closely
than Zeman and covers the three years of Krabat's adolescence narrated at
times by a voiceover, an older Krabat, who reflects upon the trauma of his
youth. Darkness prevails throughout most of the film, indicating a more
sober consideration of Preußler's work. A good part of this story was filmed
in the rugged countryside of Rumania, and it develops into a chronicle of
the times, the Thirty Years War (1618–48) that makes the shape-shifting
and magic appear credible. As in the novel, the narrator of the film tells the
story matter-of-factly. He reports succinctly and bluntly because he seeks to
grasp and depict the reality of poor, abused apprentices during a period of
war, when they are at the mercy of the sorcerer as well as the Saxon prince
and an anonymous character who makes money off the apprentices' work at
the mill. The film's entire atmosphere and lighting are gloomy, the opposite
of spectacular American or light-hearted German fairy-tale films. The mill
in which Krabat and the apprentices work is depicted as a concentration
camp. The work is drudgery. The dominant color is black. The village nearby
is impoverished. The landscape is withered. Kreuzpaintner draws parallels
with the Nazi era—the Master is a ruthless dictator—and of course, parallels can be drawn to other historical figures and periods. Kreuzpaintner's
fairy-tale film significantly breaks with a tradition of happy endings. The
narrator remarks that he and the apprentices felt after all that happened that
they could determine their own futures without magic, for they had gained
freedom. Then they are pictured trudging into a forlorn wilderness. They
move on with bitter hope.

In all three Krabat films, the victorious rebellious apprentice is somewhat
battered at the end of the encounters with the sorcerer. Self-knowledge and

knowledge come with a price, but it is a price that is worth being paid. All three films were made by Germans and Czechs who suffered through World War II or have memories of World War II and were very familiar with conditions in the Communist-bloc countries in the postwar period. Overcoming the rampant evil of sorcerers was a struggle keenly felt and represented in these films. In contrast the films produced in America and England from 1930 to the present reveal a different attitude toward oppression and authoritarianism that is startling. For the most part the American films "celebrate" the omnipotence of sorcerers and the humiliation of apprentices. Of course this is not true in all of the films up to the present, especially in the Harry Potter films and in the cinematic adaptation of Ursula Le Guin's *Earthsea* and stories that stem from the Merlin legends.

Contrary to what most people may think, the cinematic history of adaptations of "The Sorcerer's Apprentice" did not begin with Walt Disney's *Fantasia* of 1940 but with Sidney Levee's *The Wizard's Apprentice* of 1930, an extraordinary 10-minute black and white film with animation. The similarities between the Levee and Disney films are so great that there cannot be any doubt but that the Disney version was influenced by Levee's film, even though it has never been given credit for being the first cinematic production of Goethe's version of "The Sorcerer's Apprentice."

At the beginning of Levee's film, which has only the music of Paul Dukas as sound, the wizard and his apprentice bring to life the statuette of a beautiful young woman. It is apparent that the apprentice is infatuated by the young woman as the wizard retransforms her into a small statuette. Then the wizard cautions him not to bring her to life again when he goes off to play chess. Left alone, however, the apprentice cannot resist the charm of the statuette and brings the lovely young woman to full life in a gothic castle. To impress her the apprentice casts a spell on a broom that sprouts arms and legs and begins to carry water from a well downstairs and to fill a fountain upstairs. The couple are delighted, but their delight is short-lived because the broom keeps bringing water from the downstairs well and begins to flood the upstairs and the entire castle. The couple must climb some stacks of books while the water mounts. The apprentice cannot stop the broom. He takes a knife and throws it at the broom, but the knife only manages to split the broom into many brooms. Now the water keeps rising, and the apprentice and the young woman may drown. Fortunately, while playing chess with a friend, the wizard sees water spilling out of the castle's windows, and he rushes to save the young couple from drowning through an incantation. The water disappears, the young woman is reduced to the size of the statuette, and the disappointed apprentice is briefly reprimanded while the wizard uses his magic power to unite the many brooms into one.

Dukas's music invigorates the romantic comedy. The action is set precisely to the movement of the music. Here the apprentice has some knowledge of magic but obviously not enough to keep the young woman alive and to stop the flooding of the palace. The wizard is not wicked and does not punish the apprentice. He just waves his finger at the apprentice, and that is that. Like Dukas's music, a scherzo, the story is a humorous sketch, more comic than serious.

This is not the case with the Disney adaptation of Goethe's "The Sorcerer's Apprentice," which is also comic but has more serious implications. Disney's film is not just an imitation of Levee's *The Wizard's Apprentice*; it also reflects more upon the master-slave dialectic in significant ways. In her analysis of Disney's ideological approach to the theme of apprenticeship, Erin Felicia Labbie explains the apprentice Mickey Mouse's desire to use magic to make his life less dolorous:

> Mickey's impatience is at once an endearing characteristic that encourages the audience to identify with him, as well as with a potentially dangerous impulse. Impatience is desire that is marked by temporality; it is a longing for the future enacted in the present. For children, impatience to acquire knowledge leads to a learning process that associates knowledge with power. In the context of an apprenticeship to a sorcerer, impatience is imbued with profound significance. The ambiguous length of time taken to master alchemy places the apprentice at the mercy of the sorcerer. The labor of the apprentice becomes a marker of time and knowledge, and it may produce impatience when juxtaposed with the desire for power. Such a medieval form of apprenticeship is illuminated in "The Sorcerer's Apprentice."[74]

While this interpretation has some merit, there is nothing in Mickey's expressions or behavior to indicate impatience. Instead, he can be best described as clever and curious, perhaps even daring. Mickey has been working hard, like a slave, and when left alone, he seeks a means to relieve his burden. He "rebels" against the sorcerer by taking his cone hat and replacing the sorcerer temporarily. He uses magic to lighten his burden by transforming the broom into a worker reminiscent of the broom in Levee's film. Here Mickey uses an axe to try to stop the broom from carrying too much water, and as in Levee's film, more brooms are created. In contrast to Levee's film, the sorcerer, named Yen-Sid (Disney spelled backwards), returns and angrily turns everything to "normal." He sneers at Mickey Mouse, swats him with a broom, and Mickey trudges off as a slave. In short the master-slave static relationship is reestablished.

There is something very alarming and distasteful about the in-joke, Yen-Sid, as autocratic magician. In fact it is a sour joke, for Disney really did imagine himself and became somewhat the master magician of fairy-tale films, superseding Georges Méliès, but his self-celebration was not just egotistical, it was also a proclamation in favor of authoritarianism and celebrity. We should remember that this was the period of the 1940s, one in which fascist leaders like Hitler, Mussolini, and Franco were dominating Europe. In Disney's film the scornful and abrupt dismissal of the curiosity of a young person by the sneering magician indicated and indicates a fear of young people who might learn the secrets of magic and indeed replace the master magician. Characteristic of almost all of the Disney films, even after Walt's death, is a celebration of elitism and dismissal of small people's needs and wants. In *Fantasia 2000* (1999), introduced well after Walt's death, the only episode retained from the original 1940 film was "The Sorcerer's Apprentice," and the only change made to this episode was the infantile and stupid introduction by the entertainers Penn and Teller, who made a mockery of magic. In fact the entire film was nothing but a commodification of the original *Fantasia*. As the *New York Times* film critic Stephen Holden wrote,

> From the movie's wraparound Imax images to its hosts (Steve Martin, Itzhak Perlman, Quincy Jones, Bette Milder, James Earl Jones, Penn and Teller, Angela Lansbury and James Levine) who introduce the segments, "Fantasia/2000" often has the feel of a giant corporate promotion whose stars are there simply to hawk the company's wares. As smooth as these introductions are, they give the film a choppy momentum and only underscore the grandiosity of the idea of "improving" mass culture by wedding classical music and animation. "Fantasia" was conceived as a glorified music-appreciation course designed to bring highbrow music to everyone. But while the synchronization of classical music with animated images certainly furthered the art of animation by encouraging abstract

design, it proved to be a hit-and-miss affair and not much more than high-flown kitsch, even at its best in the original production. Ideally the music and imagery should fuse into something larger than either. It has rarely worked out that way.[75]

There is something deprecating about the way music is used in both *Fantasia*s. In particular, Dukas's music is employed to emphasize the teaching of humiliation, or, put more simply as Holden does in his review: children are to listen to their parents and not endeavor to do anything without their supervision. In Levee's film Dukas's music is used to heighten the drama of the events, not to teach or preach. Nor is it used for synchronization with the animation. Though the apprentice is "humiliated" in Levee's *Wizard's Apprentice*, there is still a suggestion that he will continue to learn. The master-slave dialectic is kept open. In the two "Sorcerer's Apprentice" episodes of *Fantasia* and *Fantasia 2000*, the master-slave dialectic is abruptly stopped by Mickey's submission to Yen-Sid.

In the third Disney film, *The Sorcerer's Apprentice* (2010), there is no longer a trace of humiliation or submission. Instead, the film is a bombastic spectacle, very much influenced by the Harry Potter novels and movies. The film takes place in contemporary New York, when a ten-year-old boy named Dave, who evidently has magic in his blood and is related to Merlin, is discovered by a medieval magician named Balthazar, who has been roaming the world ever since Merlin's death and trying to protect it from the evil witch Morgan le Fay, who wants to destroy it. By the time Dave turns twenty, Balthazar takes him under his wing and teaches him all about "true" magic so that he can save the world from the witch and a bumbling cohort Horvath. There are a number of harrowing clashes with Horvath that quickly become boring because the audience knows that Dave and Balthazar will always escape and win. There is again another inside Disney joke when Dave wants to clean his messy apartment and take a shower at the same time. So he uses his magic to have a mop tidy his room for him. However, he loses control of this mop and other mops because he does not know enough magic. Balthazar, the master, must rescue him and convince him to continue to learn. Eventually, Dave proves that he is the authentic heir to Merlin's legacy and kills Morgan Le Fay and even saves Balthazar's life.

What is significant about this insignificant film is that the apprentice is not humiliated. Instead we learn from the action that in the hands of the right teacher, the apprentice learns to use the knowledge of magic to do good in the world, even if it means killing. In other words there is another strand in the texture of the "Sorcerer's Apprentice" memeplex: the apprentice is a chosen hero or genetically gifted young man, who must serve under an empathetic wise sorcerer of "white" magic, and/or discover his endowed gifts, so that he can defeat evil forces in the world. Hmm, this might make for a Harry Potter novel!

There are two other films that indulge in the spectacular achievements of a rebellious apprentice who is magically endowed with gifts that enable him to become a celebrated hero. In David Lister's *The Sorcerer's Apprentice* (2002), set in contemporary England, a young boy named Ben moves to a new town and discovers that his aging neighbor is Merlin, who teaches him all the magic he must know to defeat (yet again) the wicked Morgana before she can destroy the world. In *Merlin's Apprentice* (2006), a long and tedious TV mini-series, a handsome young thief named Jack arrives in Camelot, where he is chosen by Merlin to improve his magical skills. In the meantime the Holy Grail has been stolen, and the barbarians attack Camelot. Merlin learns somehow that Jack is his son who was born from the relationship that Merlin had with the Lady of the Lake. In combat with the barbarians, Merlin dies and passes on his legacy to Jack, who, of course, defeats the barbarians using magic and restores Camelot's fame.

Both of these "action" films are based on a feeble understanding of the late medieval Arthurian legends, and they basically foster hero worship and a narrow understanding of evil. It is what I call dichotomous thinking as opposed to dialectical thinking, and accordingly, the films paint the world black and white despite the colorful battles and the real complex developments that lead to evil actions. In two other films based on Ursula Le Guin's *Earthsea* stories, one of them, *Earthsea* (2004), followed the stereotypical pattern of transforming young Ged and an apprentice's quest for self-knowledge into a swash-buckling young hero and startling exploits to titillate TV audiences. Le Guin, whose novels served as the basis for this mini-series, was excluded from working on the filmic adaptation and wrote an angry critique in which she stated: "The books, *A Wizard of Earthsea* and *The Tombs of Atuan*, which were published more than 30 years ago, are about two young people finding out what their power, their freedom, and their responsibilities are. I don't know what the film is about. It's full of scenes from the story, arranged differently, in an entirely different plot, so that they make no sense."[76]

Though she was more receptive to the animated Japanese film, *Tales from Earthsea* (2006), directed by Gorō Miyazaki, she voiced strong objections to the way her tales have been adapted: "Much of it was, I thought, incoherent. This was because I was trying to find and follow the story of my books while watching an entirely different story, confusingly acted by people with the same names as in my story but with entirely different temperaments, histories, and destinies. . . . The moral sense of the books becomes confused in the film."[77] Indeed, Ged, the Archmage, who was the apprentice in Le Guin's first novel, now becomes the great magician who takes a murderer named Arren under his wing for no reason whatsoever. In the end, the conflict between good and evil is simplified in a battle unto death between his petite girl friend, Therru, and the evil Cob, who wants eternal life that would upset the balance in the world. However, the real imbalance is created by a meaningless stereotypical plot that once again divides the world's moral forces into black and white.

Perhaps the most interesting films since 1945 that have explored the underlying tensions and complexities of "The Sorcerer's Apprentice" tales are two short films, one a ballet directed by the multitalented Michael Powell, *The Sorcerer's Apprentice* (1955), and the other, an animated film, *The Sorcerer's Apprentice* (1980), directed by the gifted Canadian filmmaker Peter Sander. It is difficult to describe the tour-de-force dancing of Sonia Arova, the prima ballerina, cast as the apprentice, and the ballet company of the State Opera Hamburg, choreographed by Helga Swedlund. Suffice to say that the dancers who are mainly masked either as demons or cats blend with the haunted mansion. It is clear that this is the "home" of black magic, and the eerie music composed by Walter Braunfels reinforces the mood of dark magic. When the majestic magician departs, the apprentice is moved by temptation and mystery to transform a broom into a helper who is split into two helpers and almost swamps the haunted mansion. What is striking about the ending of the short ballet is the final shot of the apprentice groveling for pardon. More than the Disney version of Goethe's poem, this film represents the master-slave dialectic, which ends in total submission of the young pupil.

In contrast Sander's film is a stunning, simple depiction of the clever and rebellious apprentice, based allegedly on a tale by the Brothers Grimm and narrated by the well-known American actor Vincent Price. Actually this cinematic adaptation borrows greatly from other European tales and features a poor young boy named Hans wandering through a desolate landscape. Suddenly he encounters a black cat, which changes itself into the vicious sorcerer, named Spellbinder, who asks him to become his apprentice. In need of work and money Hans agrees to come with him, but when he tells Spellbinder that he can read and write, the sorcerer rejects him. Quickly Hans pretends that he cannot and convinces the sorcerer by saying that he had previously misunderstood him. So Spellbinder takes him to his majestic castle on the top of the mountain, where he meets Greta, the young modest maid, who keeps house for the sorcerer. Hans is put to work and made to do menial tasks that enable the sorcerer to develop his powers. Once Hans discovers that the sorcerer often leaves the castle to cause havoc in the world, he decides, with the help of Greta, to read the magic book of spells so that he can oppose Spellbinder. At one point the sorcerer discovers Hans's secret and challenges him to a duel that takes several days until Hans changes himself into a fly on the magic book, and Spellbinder replies by transforming himself into a spider. Just as Spellbinder is about to eat Hans as a fly, Hans changes himself back into a human and slams the magic book shut, thereby crushing Spellbinder. Then the castle begins to crumble and eventually explodes, as Hans and Greta escape with the magic book. Greta remarks that he can now change the world for the better with his magic. Hans agrees, and the first thing he wants to do, he tells Greta, is to teach her how to read. They hold hands as they march off to Hans's home.

Sander's open, hopeful ending is characteristic of various interpretations and adaptations of the "Sorcerer's Apprentice" tales that stand in opposition to the "Humiliated Apprentice" tales. In the post–World War II period, however, the most in-depth accounts of the struggles of young apprentices faced with malicious male wizards who want to exploit or kill them are generally to be found in novels for young and old readers, and I want to turn to a small selection of what I believe to be the more serious treatment of the master-slave dialectic.

OVERCOMING ABUSE IN THE NOVELS AND STORIES ABOUT APPRENTICES

The number of novels and tales written about the sorcerer's apprentice in English-speaking countries since 1940 is mind-boggling.[78] What is also fascinating is that there is a clear division in the memeplex between narratives written for children between the ages of four and ten and those written for young adults and adults. The books published for the very young tend to be picture books and ape Disney's *Sorcerer's Apprentice* film and book version of 1940. That is, they didactically promote the notion that "curiosity killed the cat." Young boys—and sometimes a girl or two—are depicted as foolish and whimsical and are to be taught that magic can be dangerous if they do not know fully how to control it, and therefore, they are not to dare, play, or experiment with this "secret" knowledge. They are to adhere to the commands or dictates of their masters. The humiliation of apprentices and pupils is always rationalized because children are considered irrational when they question authority. In the brightly colored picture books the punishment is not always severe because the master generally wants the apprentice simply to conform to his orders and work submissively and harmoniously for him. The magician must rescue the apprentice/pupil from himself because he does not know what he wants or who he is. For the most part American and British picture books are not even worth discussing because they rarely alter the Lucian/ Goethe/Disney plot, and the illustrations are bland and predictable, even when they are done by such subversive illustrators as Tomi Ungerer.[79] What is important to know is that, thanks to Disney, Golden Books, Ladybird Books, and other major publishers, the humiliated apprentice is "celebrated" for his foolhardiness throughout the world.

In contrast stories and novels for older readers stand in opposition to those created for the very young. Instead of humiliation and conformity these works complicate the dichotomy of humiliation and rebellion. Whereas some minimize the abuse that the apprentice suffers in his engagement with a master, most of the narratives tend to favor subversion and emancipation from arbitrary and authoritarian magicians who want to maintain power and control over apprentices and pupils. These works are very diverse and complex—even the popular ones written for the fantasy and fairy-tale trade market. Indeed, they are concerned with the physical, sexual, and psychological abuse of young people who are cultivated to serve masters and a master narrative. There can be no doubt that the memetic appeal of these works is due to the worldwide abandonment and maltreatment of young people and the conflicts that they have with their "superiors," and I want to discuss some of the more salient works that, I believe, shed light on different perspectives taken by writers who endeavor to provide alternatives to the humiliation of young people.

Unlike the optimistic fantasy novels or speculative fiction very much related to the Harry Potter novels, there are four somewhat disturbing "realistic" narratives that reveal the limitations of rebellion and yet keep the master-slave dialectic open to discussion. The works I want to consider here are François Augiéras's novella, *L'apprenti sorcier* (1964), translated into English in 2001; Charles Johnson's story, "The Sorcerer's Apprentice" (1986); Susanna Clarke's long novel, *Jonathan Strange & Mr. Norrell* (2004), adapted for television in 2015; and Elif Shafak's *The Architect's Apprentice* (2014).

Of the four works about sorcerers' apprentices, Augiéras's masochistic first-person narrative is the most disturbing because it is a coming of age novella that celebrates physical brutality as natural learning and love. The nameless sixteen-year-old narrator is sent one summer by his parents to live with a thirty-five-year-old "peasant" priest in the southwest French countryside of Sarladais, known for its mysterious woods and strange customs. No sooner does the boy arrive than the priest ties him up and rapes and beats him. The boy does not protest but finds his treatment somewhat pleasurable. Left alone in the presbytery because the priest travels about the region visiting different parishes, the boy explores the huge house and surrounding woods as places of enchantment. Whenever the priest returns, he does not speak much except to fondle and whip the boy. Eventually the narrator meets a twelve-year-old boy who delivers bread to different homes in the community. He immediately falls in love with the boy and seduces him. Under the "guidance" of the priest, who is more pagan than religious, the narrator has a love affair with the boy and thrills to the exposure of nature and the beatings of the priest. Finally, there is a possibility that the police will arrest the narrator because of his illicit relationship with the boy and place him on trial. But the boy protects him, and the narrator and the priest, who has known about this relationship, celebrate their victory after a strange adventure on a river with a glass of wine.

In the afterword to this novella, the translator, Sue Dyson, writes about the young narrator: "He will hide his soul, sheltering it from men, in a secret spring of the Vézière [nearby river]; he will triumph against the laws of society. And it becomes clear that this tense, shadowy tale, burning with love, is a eulogy in praise of difference, an apprenticeship to purity, and act of worship to beauty in the temple of *Périgordin* nature."[80] Despite these eulogistic comments, there is something disturbing in Dyson's simplistic praise for a novella that uses the pretext of an awakening in "pure" nature and distorted notions of spiritual pantheism to excuse the sadistic behavior of a priest and the submission of a helpless adolescent, who then practices what he has learned on a twelve-year-old. Augiéras's novella is a first-person account of deception and self-deception. He describes humiliation and degradation as pleasure and learning after he has undergone incarceration that he must explain to himself. If anything, the learning "process" has caused trauma that does not lead to self-knowledge but an avoidance. If anything, the novella twists the tale type of the "Sorcerer's Apprentice" into a celebration of "pure" pedophilia, a sickness that has plagued the Catholic Church and its legions of priests for quite some time, not to mention its tradition of authoritarianism.

At the end of Augiéras's novella there is a certain discomfort that the narrator expresses, despite his self-proclaimed "victory," and also an unease that a reader of this work might also experience for different reasons. This is also the case in Charles Johnson's short story, "The Sorcerer's Apprentice." However, there is very little self-deception or masochism. Ironically, the discomfort arises at the end of the narrative about the initiation of an African American into the secrets of sorcery because the young man, Allan Jackson, who goes to study with the old blacksmith sorcerer, Rubin Bailey, wants to succeed him too much. "Allan loved the Sorcerer, especially the effects of his craft, which comforted the sick, held back evil, and blighted the enemies of newly freed slaves with locusts and bad health."[81] Rubin, who lives in South Carolina at the end of the nineteenth century, teaches Allan all he knows with the warning that he should be careful about wanting to do good and to be too faithful or too eager; otherwise the good becomes evil. Yet Allan really does not understand what Rubin means and focuses mainly on learning the techniques of the craft, not its soul. Consequently, after five years, when Allan is twenty-five years old, he finishes his apprenticeship and is a superb technician but does not have confidence in himself and philosophical understanding of magic. In his first case he fails to save the life of a baby, and consequently, he is so discouraged that he conjures demon kings and wants to commit suicide. "For now he was sure that white magic did not reside in ratiocination, education, or will. Skill was of no service. His talent was for pa(o)stiche. He could imitate but never truly heal; impress but never conjure beauty; ape the good but never again give rise to a genuine spell. For that God or Creation, or the universe—it had several names—had to seize you, *use* you, as the Sorcerer said, because it needed a womb, shake you down, speak through you until the pain pearled into a beautiful spell that snapped the world back together. It had abandoned Allan, this possession."[82] Only his old father can save Allen from committing suicide at the end, when he breaks the demonic circle and grabs hold of his son. Allan is relieved, but it is unclear whether the young man will ever realize his goal of succeeding Rubin.

In a curious essay that seems to apologize for or rationalize the ending of Johnson's tale, Herman Beavers writes that "it would be wrong to read this [the ending] as Johnson's capitulation to an integrationist aesthetic that resituates blackness in the null space created for it by the Enlightenment. Rather, we find ourselves in a moment when Allan Jackson's life as a 'race man' is so uncertain, he can only imagine a life characterized by discomfort and disillusionment."[83] Beavers believes that Johnson's tale calls readers "to embrace our own forms of incompleteness, inviting us to recognize that who we are results from the ways that instruction and misguidedness constitute the Way."[84] Clearly, such a generalization has a certain truth to it. But this minimizes the pessimism of the tale. Written during the 1980s at a time when the civil rights movement was stalled and Ronald Reagan was president of the United States, there was little hope that the older generation, black or white, could pass on the knowledge and experience necessary to institute reforms and to carry out what the sorcerer, Rubin Bailey, could accomplish right after slavery. Allan is a figure of failure, and his fate indicates that dialectics do not lead to emancipation in a society in which perfect achievement and technique are worshipped above humanity. Allan is not humiliated. He is belittled by demons who think he is not worthy of their attention.

In contrast, the magicians Gilbert Norrell and Jonathan Strange are more than worthy of the attention by demonic fairy-tale creatures in a struggle for magic and power in England during the early part of the nineteenth century. For over 300 years practicing magicians seemed to have vanished from early modern England, but Susanna Clarke's unusual novel, *Jonathan Strange & Mr. Norrell*, an exemplary work of speculative fiction, restores magic not only to England and Europe plagued by the Napoleonic Wars but also to our contemporary world of fiction. Marek Oziewicz explains that

> speculative fiction is in fact a galactic span term for a great number of nonmimetic genres such as the gothic, dystopia, zombie, vampire, and postapocalyptic fiction, ghost stories, superheroes, alternative histories, steampunk, magic realism, retold or fractured fairy tales and so forth. Most of these genres are either derivatives of fantasy and science fiction or hybrids that elude easy classifications. . . . Characterized by extended thought experiments that involve the hypothetical, the supernatural, or

the impossible, speculative fiction is more cognitively stimulating than the mimetic genres. Unlike the mimetic genres, it offers no pretense of being of being factual or accurate, a denial that endows it with a deeper potential for ethical considerations.[85]

Clarke's garrulous 800-page novel, a pastiche of genres, can certainly be considered speculative fiction, for it employs a great number of nonmimetic genres to raise questions about the ethical use of magical knowledge to intervene in politics and in personal lives. At the heart of her mock historical novel is the master-slave dialectic related to the tradition of sorcerer's apprentice tales.

Mr. Norrell, a reclusive and eccentric practicing magician, is discovered by members of the Learned Society of York Magicians in 1806. Once he demonstrates his great powers by reviving the dead fiancée, Emma Wintertowne, engaged to the Cabinet Minister Sir Walter Pole, he becomes famous by reintroducing magic into England and begins to assist the English government in its battles against Napoleon. However, it should be noted that Mr. Norrell makes a bargain with a demonic fairy called "the gentleman with the thistle-down hair" that obliges Emma to spend half her time with this fairy in the Faerie Kingdom of Lost Hope along with her husband's black butler ironically named Stephen Black; the other half is to be spent in the so-called real world.

At a certain point a young man named Jonathan Strange, who is more or less a drifter from the upper class, takes an interest in magic once he marries a wealthy young woman named Arabella, who wants him to do something with his life. After studying by himself, Strange becomes a competent practicing magician. Then, to improve his skills and knowledge, he works as an apprentice under Norrell's tutelage for a few years, and once he becomes Norrell's equal, they have a dispute over the origins of magic in England, and Strange separates from his master. Their conflict leads to upheavals in England, for each one wants to prove that he is the best magician in the country. Taking advantage of this conflict, the wicked gentleman with the thistle-down hair causes havoc and goes on a destructive rampage that involves the kidnapping of Arabella, who is forced to live in the Kingdom of Lost Hope. To save his wife Strange makes peace with Norrell, and they unite to bring about the evil fairy gentleman's death, allowing Stephen Black to become the King of Lost Hope and Arabella to return to life. However, Norrell and Strange are trapped together in Eternal Night, a curse brought upon them by the gentleman with the thistle-down hair before his death. Though this ending may seem miserable to Arabella, who has been liberated from her enchantment, Strange explains to her:

> Do not be miserable, I beg you. Apart from anything else, I do not suffer. At little perhaps at first, but not now. And Norrell and I are hardly the first English magicians to labour under an enchantment.... Besides who is to say that Darkness may not be of advantage to us? We intend to go out of England and are likely to meet with all sorts of tricksy persons. An English magician is an impressive thing. Two English magicians are, I suppose, twice as impressive—but when those two English magicians are shrouded in an Impenetrable Darkness—ah, well! That I should think is enough to strike terror into the heart of any one short of a demi-god![86]

The optimistic resolution at the end of Clarke's novel is one that points to an ongoing negative dialectic or dialogue, for the two magicians do not want to destroy each other. Rather, they must bring light to themselves and other people to emerge from darkness. Their solipsistic and petty debate about the origins of magic and competition for laurels is transformed into a search for shared enlightenment. The work of master and apprentice is shared because both magicians have learned that they cannot defeat evil without cooperation.

There are no magicians in Elif Shafak's historical romance, *The Architect's Apprentice*, but there are plenty of master-slave conflicts and incidents of magic throughout the narrative that not only recall the ancient modes of apprenticeships and class and religious struggles in sixteenth- and seventeenth-century Turkey, India, and Europe but also speak to the present. Surprisingly, most of the reviews written soon after Shafak's book appeared in England and the United States during 2014 and 2015 did not deal with the major theme of apprenticeship and class and religious struggle, and yet Shafak's dedication makes it clear that she is most concerned with all types of relations between different masters and slaves: "For apprentices everywhere," she writes, "no one told us that love was the hardest craft to master."[87] Indeed, Shafak weaves a tapestry of master-slave incidents that focus on a twelve-year-old Indian boy named Jahan, who arrives in Istanbul as a stowaway, pretending to be the trainer of a white elephant called Chota, a gift for the Ottoman ruler Suleiman the Magnificent. A curious, outspoken, and creative boy, Jahan is soon taken under the wing of the great Ottoman architect Mimar Sinan as an apprentice to join three other young apprentices, and he begins to learn how to love and maintain his love for architecture, the sultan's daughter Mihrimah, and his noble elephant. This is not an easy task because most of the relations in the Ottoman Empire are based on strict laws, rules, and customs of obsequiousness, beginning with subservience to Allah and other gods. Sinan as master architect circumvents the authoritarian regulations of this time by sharing his knowledge with his apprentices and cultivating their creativity, especially because they had been broken and forsaken. At first Jahan, who cannot stop thinking of returning to India and taking revenge on his stepfather for murdering his mother, is bewildered and asks Sinan why he is helping him, and the architect replies:

> "You are talented, but you ought to be tutored. You must learn languages, If you promise to put your heart into this, I'll help you get lessons at the palace school. Men in the highest positions have been educated there. You have to strive as hard as they did. Year after year."
>
> "I am not afraid of work, *effendi*," said Jahan.
>
> "I know but you must let go of the past," said Sinan as he stood up. "Resentment is a cage, talent is a captured bird. Break the cage, let the bird take off and soar high. Architecture is a mirror that reflects the harmony and balance present in the universe. If you do not foster these qualities in your heart, you cannot build."
>
> His cheeks burning, Jahan said, "I don't understand. . . . Why do you help me?"
>
> "When I was about your age, I was fortunate enough to have a good master. He is long dead, may God have mercy on his soul. The only way I can pay him back is by helping others," Sinan said.[88]

Throughout the novel, Sinan serves as a model of humanity and tolerance, and time and again his humane comportment and dedication to the art of architecture over the eighty years that Jahan "serves" him enable the boy gradually to come into his own as a master architect later in India. This is not a minor accomplishment because Shafak weaves tales of treachery, arbitrary execution, violent wars, maltreatment of women, petty jealousies, torture, constant humiliation and exploitation of common people, laborers, and slaves, rivalries between religious groups, and revenge in her fantastical tapestry. It is clear that Shafak favors marginal figures such as the mischievous gypsy leader Balaban, who "magically" rescues Jahan several times. In the end, however, it is thanks to Sinan's wise teaching and love in contrast to the violence and violation of the times that Jahan learns how important the principles of tolerance, cooperation, and devotion to art can be in his struggle to define himself.

The themes of unity, cooperation, and social justice are common in many other stories and novels that recall the tradition of "Sorcerer's Apprentice" tales and are part of the cultural memory of post-1940 American and British fantasy. For instance, Ursula Le Guin's classic novel *A Wizard of Earthsea* (1968) and its sequels, *The Tombs of Atuan* (1971), *The Farthest Shore* (1972), *Tehanu* (1990), and *The Other Wind* (2001), are part of a major development in speculative fiction that is derived from the "Humiliated Apprentice" and "Rebellious Apprentice" tales. *A Wizard of Earthsea* is particularly important because it incorporates various elements and motifs of these tales that hark back to the Greco-Roman period and medieval Europe, and because it has had a major influence on numerous other stories and books that have followed its publication.

In Le Guin's fictional world of Earthsea the young protagonist Duny, who is nicknamed Sparrowhawk, is given his true name, Ged, on his thirteenth birthday and is "chosen" as a natural mage (magician) by the elderly sorcerer Orgion the Silent. However, Ged does not have a good sense of how magic can offset the natural balance of the world, Orgion must teach him to temper and control his gifts. In fact Ged misuses Orgion's magic books, compelling the wise mage to reprimand Ged and banish a shadowy creature. After this incident Ged begins to learn humility and modesty from Orgion, and he is sent to a magician's school on the island of Roke, where he competes with older boys to display his great powers. However, in a conflict with Jasper, his main rival, Ged upsets the balance of the natural order and releases a shadow creature from the dead that scars him for life. When he graduates from the school at Roke at age eighteen, he has various adventures in which he must use his powers to oppose dragons and other destructive forces. Finally, Ged learns from Orgion that he must confront the shadow creature if he is to come into himself—that is, to grasp who he is and what he wants to become. Instead of killing the shadow creature Ged embraces it as part of himself, and his friend Vetch, who watches this incident, believes at first that Ged might have been vanquished by the sinister creature. However, "now when he saw his friend and heard him speak, his doubt vanished. And he began to see the truth, that Ged had neither lost nor won but, naming the shadow of his death with his own name, had made himself whole: a man, who, knowing his whole true self, cannot be used or possessed by any power other than himself, and whose life therefore is lived for life's sake and never in the service of ruin, or pain, or hatred, or the dark."[89]

In Le Guin's dialectic, self-knowledge is obtained by absorbing the *Other*, which is actually part of oneself, not by effacing it. Ged and all the other young apprentices who follow him in speculative fiction can use their special magical gifts to combat injustice only if they recognize who they are and the potential they carry with them to unleash dark forces. The ethics of responsibility is fostered in all of Le Guin's works and in the best of popular fantasy up through J. K. Rowling's novels dealing with Harry Potter and Voldemort. In Raymond Feist's *Magician: Apprentice* (1982) and *Magician* (1986), the orphan boy, Pug, goes to study with the master magician Kulgan in the Kingdom of Isles and learns to use his unusual magic powers to protect it from menacing outsiders. In Margaret Mahy's *The Magician of Hoard* (2008), a twelve-year-old farmer boy, named Heriot Tarbas, who has all the signs of being a natural magician and can read minds, is taken by force to the king of Hoard's court, where he is more or less exploited to serve the king's ruling interests. Heriot gradually learns that a magician has other ethical responsibilities and breaks away from his masters to become more in touch with his own needs and to attain the independence and recognition that he has always desired. In Trudi Canavan's *The Magician's Apprentice* (2009), Tessia, a young woman living in a small village of ancient Kyralia, serves an apprenticeship in magic healing under Lord Dakon and becomes involved in a long and devastating war between Kyralia and another country called Sachaka. During the war she employs great powers of healing to serve friend and foe, and when the war is concluded, Tessia has become the greatest healing magician in the world. In James Morrow's *The Philosopher's Apprentice* (2009), a philosophy student named Mason Ambrose is hired by a wealthy woman to teach a young girl named Londa on a remote Caribbean island. She has lost her moral compass due to a car accident on an island. In her recovery, however, Londa causes more damage than good when she tries to apply her learning of social justice in extreme ways. Here ethical learning cannot be imposed even with good will because Londa does not have a good sense of herself and the world.

Nevertheless, in many of the novels, especially those for young readers, the protagonists are moral arbiters who expose the contradictions of society and use the magic that they learn to try to resolve those contradictions while coming into their selves. So, for instance, in Diana Wynne Jones's novel *House of Many Ways* (2008), a young "respectable" girl by the name of Charmain

Baker, whose main goal in life is to become a librarian, is called upon by her great-uncle William, the Royal Wizard of Nordland, to look after his magic house because he must depart to be cured of an illness. Charmain soon learns that not only is the house falling apart but also the kingdom. At one point she joins with a wizard's apprentice named Peter, who often bungles magic. Nurtured by the kindly William, the young girl and boy manage to restore order to the house and kingdom in comic adventures that demonstrate how wisdom can be a guiding principle in an ethical and cognitive learning process.

This is also the case in Sarah Prineas's *The Magic Thief* (2008). She uses an original narrative technique to tell her fairy tale about Conn by having the fourteen-year-old thief narrate a section of a chapter quickly followed by first-person comments written by the wizard Nevery in his diary. The chapters form a strange often comic dialogue with each character communicating his feelings. The setting of the novel is the realm of Wellmet during the late Middle Ages. Conn, who is wanted for thievery in Wellmet, tries to steal the great wizard Nevery Flingas's locus magicalicus, a stone used to work magic spells. Nevery catches the orphan, and despite Conn's rebellious and feisty ways, he takes a liking to him and decides to take him on as an apprentice. In the meantime, someone is stealing magic from the realm and thus causing living conditions to decline. Though Nevery does not always trust and agree with Conn, who must find his own magicalicus to be Nevery's official apprentice, it is Conn who eventually leads Nevery to discover who the real criminals are, and the great wizard is able to save Wellmet from destruction. But it is the cunning Conn, who perceives the menace of corruption better than even the wise wizard Nevery, who puts a tentative stop to the danger to Wellmet. It is the innocent eye of truth and youth that triumphs in the end, and it is an innocence that other novels seem to want to recuperate.

This can be seen in Anne Ursu's novel *The Real Boy* (2013), in which the eleven-year-old Oscar serves Master Caleb, the number-one magician on the island of Altheia, as a shop hand by running errands and by collecting herbs and flowers so that the magician can make them into potions, which he sells. Altheia is an island and the last bastion of magic in the world. Most people on this island think they are perfect, and there are many magicians. Oscar, however, is autistic and different, often treated in a demeaning manner especially by the magician's apprentice, Wolf. When Oscar leaves the island to sell his potions and Wolf seems to have been killed by a monster, Oscar joins with a young female magician named Callie to save the island from the monster and a strange sickness. Since Oscar can read—a fact that he kept from Callie and Wolf—he knows a good deal about magic and how it can be positive and destructive, while Callie is a healer. At one point, Oscar believes that his difficulties as an autistic boy might stem from the fact that he is an artificial puppet created by Caleb, but he comes to realize that he is simply different from other people, and that most people on the island had been deceiving themselves about how perfect they are. What becomes essential in Oscar's quest is a discovery that honesty means more than magic, and the entire island must come to terms with an honest self-revelation.

Almost all the stories and novels stemming from the tale type of the "Sorcerer's Apprentice" since the 1940s are both coming of age narratives or coming to terms with social and political contradictions in a particular society. Self-knowledge, exotic or supernatural knowledge, and technology as "mana" are fundamental in conflicts that involve consciousness and self-consciousness. Mistreatment of young people and misunderstandings can only be countered by the wise nurturing of young children and the empathetic comprehension of the problems the young face as they strive to gain an understanding of their situations.

One of the more interesting recent examples of how the master-apprentice conflict is played out to validate a negative dialectical approach to learning and maturation can be seen in the Japanese director Mamoru Hosada's *The Boy and the Beast* (2014), produced as an animated film and manga. In this story a forlorn nine-year-old boy named Ren runs away from home after his mother's death and lives alone on the streets of Tokyo. At a certain point a large hooded, bear-like beast named Kumatetsu offers him shelter and then leads him through some alleys to the other world of Jutengai, inhabited by beast people. Ren is renamed Kyuta. The young boy soon learns that Kumatetsu is vying to become the successor to the old master of Jutengai, who will soon retire and become a god, but Kumatetsu, who is somewhat lazy and carefree, must fight a popular, disciplined opponent named Iozen if he wants to become the new master. Consequently, Kumatetsu makes Kyuta his apprentice so that he can do serious training for the great combat. Interestingly, Kumatetsu does not know how to teach, and Kyuta is a stubborn learner. In their "master-slave" conflict they unexpectedly and gradually learn from one another and to respect one another. In the process Kyuta develops into an excellent fighter himself, while Kumatetsu deals with his laziness and gruffness. By the time Kyuta turns seventeen, he wanders back into the human world and meets a young girl named Kaede, who teaches him how to read and write and helps him reacquaint himself with his biological father. Since Kumatetsu does not like Kyuta to spend so much time in the human world, they have a falling out, and Kyuta leaves Jutengai right before Kumatetsu is to have his final combat with Iozen to determine who will be the new master of Jutengai. All three major protagonists, who were initially alone and lonely, learn in their conflicted relationships of mentor-pupil to gain meaning from one another and to prevent an evil spirit from creating a major disaster.

Although *The Boy and the Beast* does not include an evil sorcerer in the film and a battle for manga, it raises key themes of the master-slave conflict, self-knowledge, and the use of power. Indeed, it explores alternative ways to resolve conflict without a fight to death. Moreover, *The Boy and the Beast* reveals that we shall never lack for tales based on the master-slave dialectic so deeply embedded in most cultures. Tales about magical transformation will persist as long as voices of resistance to domination and exploitation continue to make themselves heard.

NOTES

1. *Folklore* 21.2 (June 1910): 147.

2. *The Philosophy of Enchantment: Studies in Folktale, Cultural Criticism, and Anthropology*, ed. David Boucher, Wendy James, and Philip Smallwood (Oxford: Clarendon Press, 2005), 129.

3. Jack Zipes, *Sticks and Stones: The Troublesome Success of Children's Literature from Slovenly Peter to Harry Potter* (New York: Routledge, 2002), 175.

4. William Alexander Clouston, *Popular Tales and Fiction*, vol. 1 (Edinburgh: William Black-wood and Sons, 1887): 413.

5. For an excellent study of the Harry Potter novels as fairy tale, see Elaine Ostry, "Accepting Mudbloods: The Ambivalent Social Vision of J. K. Rowling's Fairy Tales," in *Reading Harry Potter: Critical Essays*, ed. Giselle Liza Anatol (Westport, CT: Praeger, 2003): 89–101. Ostry writes: "Rowling intends to teach children that what matters is one's character, not color, pedigree, or wealth. However, her radical presentation of social issues is hindered by 'utter traditionalism.' This ideological doubleness mirrors the fairy tale, which is simultaneously radical and traditional. Because of Rowling's faithfulness to the fairy tale she often contradicts herself. Just as the fairy tale's radical qualities are matched by traditional inflexibility, so is Rowling's antimaterialism matched by an awe of wealth, her antiracism foiled by a reliance on 'color blindness' and stock types, and her hero simultaneously ordinary and princely" (89–90).

6. Hans-Jörg Uther, *The Types of International Folktales: A Classification and Bibliography*, 3 vols., FFCommunications 284 (Helsinki: Suomalainen Tiedeakatemia, 2004).

7. See Elisabeth Young-Bruehl, *Childism: Confronting Prejudice against Children* (New Haven, CT: Yale University Press, 2012).

8. See Ximena Gallardo-C. and C. Jason Smith, "Cinderfella: J. K. Rowling's Wily Web of Gender," in *Reading Harry Potter: Critical Essays*, ed. Giselle Liza Anatol (Westport, CT: Praeger, 2003): 191–205.

9. See Hans-Jörg Uther, "The Magician and His Pupil" (ATU 325), in *The Types of International Folktales: A Classification and Bibliography*, vol. 1 (Helsinki: Academia Scientiarum Fennica, 2004): 207–9.

10. For a full discussion of memeplex, see my *Grimm Legacies: The Magic Spell of the Grimms' Folk and Fairy Tales* (Princeton. NJ: Princeton University Press, 2015): 67–68.

11. Francis James Child, ed., *The English and Scottish Popular Ballads*, vol. 1 (New York: Houghton, Mifflin, 1882): 399–402.

12. Guido Görres, ed., *Altrheinländische Märlein und Liedlein* (Koblenz: 1843): 78–80.

13. Child, 401.

14. Graham Anderson, *Fairytale in the Ancient World* (London: Routledge, 2000): 104.

15. See Damian Kalitan, "In Search of the Sorcerer's Apprentice: Between Lucian and Walt Disney," *Journal of Education, Culture and Society* 1 (2012): 94–101.

16. Daniel Ogden, *In Search of the Sorcerer's Apprentice: The Traditional Tales of Lucian's Lover of Lies* (Swansea: Classical Press of Wales, 2007): 232–33.

17. Fritz Graf, *Magic in the Ancient World*, trans. Franklin Philip (Cambridge, MA: Harvard University Press, 1997): 1–2.

18. Ibid., 241–42.

19. Walter Burkert believes that tales and anecdotes about diviners and magicians began to be spread as early as the 8th century BCE and was part of an Orientalizing process in Greece and neighboring countries. See "Itinerant Diviners and Magicians: A Neglected Element in Cultural Contacts," in *The Greek Renaissance of the Eighth Century B.C.: Tradition and Innovation*, ed. Robin Hägg (Stockholm: Paul Åströms Förlag, 1983): 115–19.

20. See various versions in D. L. Ashliman's "The Sorcerer's Apprentice: Folktales of Aarne-Thompson-Uther Type 325* and Migratory Legends of Christiansen Type 3020" on his important website, http://www.pitt.edu/~dash/type 0325ast.html.

21. See *The Wizard's Apprentice* (1930)
USA, black and white, 10 minutes
Director: Sidney Levee
Music: Paul Dukas
Camera: Alfred Schmidt
Producer: William Cameron Menzies
Cast: Herbert Bunston, Fritz Feld, Greta Grandstedt

22. See also the section "Post-1945 Stories and Novels" in the bibliography.

23. Richard Rostron, *The Sorcerer's Apprentice*, illustr. Frank Lieberman (New York: William Morrow, 1941): unpaginated.

24. Donald Beecher, editor of Giovan Francesco Straparola, *The Pleasant Nights* (Toronto: University of Toronto Press, 2012): 221.

25. See Emmanuel Cosquin, "Les Mongols et leur pretendu rôle dans la transmission des contes indiens vers l'occident européen: étude de folk-lore comparé sur l'introduction du

'Siddhi-kur' et le conte du 'Magicien et son apprenti.'" *Revue des traditions Populaire* 27 (1912): 336–73, 393–430, 497–526, 545–66.

26. Eleaine Fantham, "Sunt quibus in plures ius est transire figuras: Ovid's Self-Transformers in the 'Metamorphoses,'" *Classical World* 87.2 (November–December 1993): 21.

27. It should be pointed out that there are various versions of the "Erysichthon and Mestra" tale in Greek antiquity, and my summary is based on a compilation of the Hesiod fragments.

28. Kirk Ormand, "Marriage, Identity, and the Tale of Mestra in the Hesiodic Catalogue of Women," *American Journal of Philology* 125.3 (Autumn 2004): 304–5.

29. See Noel Robertson, "The Ritual Background of the Erysichthon Story," *American Journal of Philology* 105.4 (Winter 1984): 369–408.

30. For an interesting discussion of magic and gender, see Frances Timbers, *Magic and Masculinity: Ritual Magic and Gender in the Early Modern Era* (London: I. B. Tauris, 2014).

31. For a history of different versions of *Siddhi Kür*, see Raffaella Riva, "The Tales of the Bewitched Corpse: A Literary Journey from India to China," in *India, Tibet, China: Genesis and Aspects of Traditional Narrative*, ed. Alfredo Cadonn (Florence: Leo Olschki, 1999): 229–56.

32. For different versions of this frame tale, see Bernhard Jülg, ed., *Kalmükische Märchen: Die Märchen des Siddhi-Kür oder Erzählungen eines verzauberten Todten* (Leipzig: F. A. Brockhaus, 1866); Rachel Harriette Busk, ed., *Sagas from the Far East; or, Kalmouk and Mongolian Traditionary Tales* (London: Griffith and Farran, 1873); Charles John Tibbitts, ed., *Folk-Lore and Legends: Oriental* (London: White and Allen, 1889).

33. Rachel Harriette Busk, ed. *Sagas from the Far East; or, Kalmouk and Mongolian Traditionary Tales* (London: Griffith and Farran, 1873): 342.

34. Riva, "The Tales of the Bewitched Corpse," 235.

35. See Emmanuel Cosquin, "Les Mongols et leur pretendu rôle dans la transmission des contes indiens vers l'occident européen: étude de folk-lore comparé sur l'introduction du 'Siddhi-kur' et le conte du 'Magicien et son apprenti.'"

36. See James Farr, *Artisans in Europe, 1300–1914* (Cambridge: Cambridge University Press, 2000).

37. Willem de Blécourt, "Der Zauberer und sein Schüler: Die Erzählung und sein historischer Ursprung," in *Faszination des Okkulten: Diskurse zum Übersinnlichen*, ed. Wolfgang Müller-Funk and Christa Agnes Tucza (Tübingen: Francke, 2008): 49.

38. See Rosa Salzberg, "In the Mouths of Charlatans: Street Performers and the Dissemination of Pamphlets in Renaissance Italy," *Renaissance Studies* 24.5 (2010): 638–53; *Ephemeral City: Cheap Print and Urban Culture in Renaissance Venice* (Manchester, UK: University of Manchester Press, 2014); and Rosa Salzberg and Massimo Rospocher, "Street Singers in Italian Renaissance Urban Culture and Communication," *Cultural and Social History* 9.1 (2012): 9–26.

39. See Georg Wilhelm Hegel, *Phenomenology of Spirit*, intro. J. N. Findlay, trans. A. V. Miller (Oxford: Oxford University Press, 1977). All future references to Hegel's book are noted in parentheses in the text.

40. See Maria Nikolajeva, "'Do We Feel Sorry for the Older Brothers?' Exploring Empathy and Ethics in Fairy Tales through Cognitive Poetics," in *Cambridge Companion to Fairy Tales*, ed. Maria Tatar (Cambridge: Cambridge University Press, 2015): 134–49.

41. Nicolas Laos, *The Metaphysics of World Order: A Synthesis of Philosophy, Theology, and Politics* (Eugene, OR: Pickwick Publications, 2015): 86–87.

42. For an important study of how Adorno's theory of dialectics and negative dialectics are related to Auschwitz, see Martin Shuster, *Autonomy after Auschwitz: Adorno, German Idealism, and Modernity* (Chicago: University of Chicago Press, 2014).

43. Georg Wilhelm Hegel, *Sämtliche Werke*, ed. Hermann Glockner, vol. 7: *Grundlinien der Philosophie des Rechts* (Stuttgart: Fromann, 1917): 231.

44. Theodor Adorno, *Negative Dialectics*, trans. E. B. Ashton (New York: Continuum, 1983): 329.

45. Ibid., 311.

46. Ibid., 320.

47. Ibid.

48. Alexandre Kojève, *Introduction to the Reading of Hegel: Lectures on* The Phenomenology of Spirit, ed. Allan Bloom, trans. James Nichols Jr. (New York: Basic Books, 1969): 29.

49. Elisabeth Young-Bruehl, *Childism: Confronting Prejudice against Children* (New Haven, CT: Yale University Press, 2012): 1.

50. Ibid., 25–26.

51. Ibid., 35.

52. Ibid., 36.

53. For a useful summary of the development of memetics, see "Memetics," from Wikipedia, the free encyclopedia: https://en.wikipedia.org/wiki/Memetics.

54. Some exceptions are Michael Drout, *How Tradition Works: A Meme-Based Cultural Poetics of the AngloSaxon Tenth Century* (Tempe, AZ: Arizona Center for Medieval and Renaissance Studies, 2006), and *Tradition & Influence in Anglo-Saxon Literature: An Evolutionary, Cognitivist Approach* (New York: Palgrave Macmillan, 2013). More recently, see Raffaele Cutolo, *Into the Woods of Wicked Wonderland: Musicals Revise Fairy Tales* (Heidelberg: Universitätsverlag Winter, 2014).

55. Francis Heylighen and Klaas Chielens, "Evolution of Culture, Memetics," *Encyclopedia of Complexity and Systems Science*, ed. Robert Meyers (New York: Springer, 2009): 3206.

56. Daniel Dennett, "The Cultural Evolution of Words," in *Evolution: The Molecular Landscape: Cold Spring Harbor Symposia on Quantitative Biology*, vol. 74 (Woodbury, NY: Cold Spring Laboratory Press, 2010): 435.

57. Ibid., 436.

58. Ibid., 437.

59. Ibid., 437.

60. Ibid.

61. Bernd-Christian Otto and Michael Stausberg, eds., *Defining Magic: A Reader* (Sheffield, UK: Equinox Publishing, 2013): 11.

62. See Jan Assmann, *Cultural Memory and Early Civilization: Writing, Remembrance, and Political Imagination* (Cambridge: Cambridge University Press, 2011); and Aleida Assmann, *Cultural Memory and Western Civilization: Functions, Media, Archives* (Cambridge: Cambridge University Press, 2011). See also Tristan Landry, *La mémoire du conte folklorique de l'oral à l'écrit: Les freres Grimm et Afanas'ev* (Laval, Canada: Les Presses de l'Université Laval, 2005), which is based on Jan Assmann's work.

63. Jan Assmann, *Cultural Memory and Early Civilization*, 2–3.

64. Susan Hose, "Krabat und die Erzählforschung. Eine Diskursbetrachtung," in *Krabat—Aspekte einer sorbischen Sage*, ed. Martin Neumann (Potsdam: Zentrum für Lehrerausbildung an der Universität Potsdam, 2008): 47.

65. See Susanne Hose, *Erzählen über Krabat: Märchen, Mythos und Magie* (Bautzen: Lusatia Verlag, 2013); Marie-Luise Ehrhardt, *Die Krabat-Sage: Quellenkundliche Untersuchung zur Überlieferung und Wirkung eines literarischen Stoffes aus der Lausitz* (Marburg: N. G. Elwert, 1982); Paul Nedo, "Krabat: Zur Entstehung einer sorbischen Volkserzählung," *Deutsches Jahrbuch für Volkskunde* 2 (1956): 33–50; Martin Neumann, ed., *Krabat—Aspekte einer sorbischen Sage* (Potsdam: Zentrum für Lehrerausbildung an der Universität Potsdam, 2008).

66. See Frank Schneider, "Chronik von Wittichenau und Umgebung," in Marie-Luise Ehrhardt, *Die Krabat-Sage: Quellenkundliche Untersuchung zur Überlieferung und Wirkung eines literarischen Stoffes aus der Lausitz* (Marburg: N. G. Elwert, 1982): 83.

67. See Joachim Leopold Haupt, "Von einem bösen Herrn in Groß-Särchen," *Neues Lausitzisches Magazin* 15.2 (1837): 203–4.

68. Hose, 213.

69. Martin Nowak-Neumann, *Meister Krabat der gute sorbische Zauberer*, trans. Jurij Brězan, illustr. Měrćin Nowak-Neumann, afterword Paul Nedo (Berlin: Kinderbuchverlag, 1954): 6.

70. See *Krabat, oder, Die Verwandlung der Welt* (Berlin: Verlag Neues Leben, 1976) and *Krabat oder die Bewahrung der Welt* (Bautzen: Dornowina-Verlag, 1995).

71. See *Die schwarze Mühle* (*The Black Mill*, 1975)
East Germany, color, 80 minutes
Director: Celino Bleiweiß
Screenplay: Celino Bleiweiß and Jurij Brězan's novel
Music: Andrzej Korzynski
Camera: Günter Marczinkowsky
Producer: Dieter Dormeier
Cast: Klaus Brasch, Leon Niemczyk, Monika Woytowicz
Company: DEFA-Studio

72. Qina Shen, *The Politics of Magic: DEFA Fairy-Tale Films* (Detroit: Wayne State University Press, 2015): 126. DEFA is the fomer East German film company, Deutsche Film Aktiengesellschaft.

73. Ibid., 126.

74. "The Sorcerer's Apprentice: Animation and Alchemy in Disney's Medievalism," in *The Disney Middle Ages: A Fairy-Tale and Fantasy Past*, ed. Tison Pugh and Susan Aronstein (New York: Palgrave Macmillan, 2012): 106.

75. Stephen Holden, "New Tricks," *New York Times* (December 31, 1999). http://www.nytimes.com/movie/review?res=9802E0D81538F932A05751C1A96F958260.

76. Ursula Le Guin, "A Whitewashed Earthsea," *Slate* (December 16, 2004). http://www.slate.com/articles/arts/culturebox/2004/12/a_whitewashed_earthsea.html.

77. Ursula Le Guin, "Gedo Senki. A First Response" (August 15, 2006). http://www.ursulakleguin.com/GedoSenkiResponse.html.

78. See the section of the present bibliography of this book regarding stories and novels about the sorcerer's apprentice since 1940.

79. See Barbara Hazen, *The Sorcerer's Apprentice*, illustr. Tomi Ungerer (New York: Lancelot Press, 1969).

80. François Augiéras, *The Sorcerer's Apprentice* (London: Pushkin Press, 2001): 106.

81. Charles Johnson, "The Sorcerer's Apprentice," in *The Sorcerer's Apprentice* (New York: Atheneum, 1986): 149.

82. Ibid., 164–65.

83. "The Pedagogy of Discomfort in *The Sorcerer's Apprentice*," in *Charles Johnson: The Novelist as Philosopher*, ed. Marc Conner and William Nash (Jackson: University of Mississippi, 2007): 53.

84. Ibid., 55.

85. Marek Oziewicz, *Justice in Young Adult Speculative Fiction: A Cognitive Reading* (New York: Routledge, 2015): 3–4.

86. Susanna Clarke, *Jonathan Strange & Mr. Norrell*, illustr. Portia Rosenberg (London: Bloomsbury, 2004): 761–62.

87. Elif Shafak, *The Architect's Apprentice* (New York: Viking, 2014): dedication page.

88. Ibid., 114–15.

89. Ursula Le Guin, *The Earthsea Trilogy* (New York: Penguin Books, 1982): 165–66.

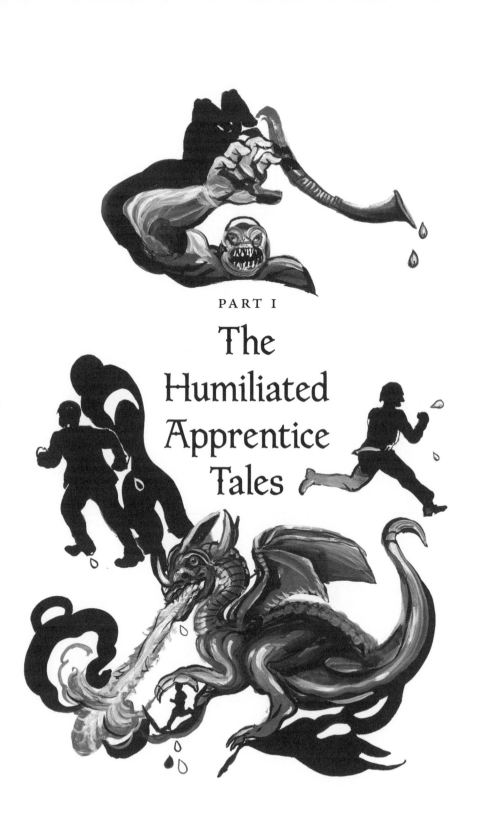

PART I

The
Humiliated
Apprentice
Tales

Early Tales

EUCRATES AND PANCRATES (CA. 170 CE)[*]

Lucian of Samosata

"I will tell you," [Eucrates said,] "another incident derived from my own experience, not from hearsay. Perhaps even you, Tychiades, when you have heard it, may be convinced of the truth of the story.

"When I was living in Egypt during my youth (my father had sent me traveling for the purpose of completing my education), I took it into my head to sail up to Koptos and go from there to the statue of Memnon in order to hear it sound that marvelous salutation to the rising sun. Well, what I heard from it was not a meaningless voice, as in the general experience of common people; Memnon himself actually opened his mouth and delivered an oracle to me in seven verses, and if it were not too much of a digression, I would have repeated the very verses for you. But on the voyage up the river, a man from Memphis chanced to be sailing with us. He was one of the scribes of the temple, wonderfully learned, familiar with all the culture of the Egyptians. He was said to have lived underground for twenty-three years in their sanctuaries, learning magic from Isis."

"You mean Pancrates," said Arignotus, "my own teacher, a holy man, clean shaven, in white linen, always deep in thought, speaking imperfect Greek, tall, flat-nosed, with protruding lips and thinnish legs."

"That self-same Pancrates, and at first I did not know who he was, but when I saw him working all sorts of wonders whenever we anchored the boat, particularly riding on crocodiles and swimming in company with the beasts, while they fawned and wagged their tails, I recognized that he was a holy man, and by degrees, through my friendly behavior, I became his companion and associate, so that he shared all his secret knowledge with me.

* *The Works of Lucian*, trans, A. M. Harmon, vol. 3 (London: William Heinemann; 1921).

"At last he persuaded me to leave all my servants behind in Memphis and to go with him quite alone, for we should not lack people to wait upon us; and thereafter we got on in that way. But whenever we came to a stopping place, the man would take either the bar of the door or the broom or even the pestle, put clothes upon it, say a certain spell over it, and make it walk, appearing to everyone else to be a man. It would go off and draw water and buy provisions and prepare meals and in every way deftly serve and wait upon us. Then, when he was through with its services, he would again make the broom a broom or the pestle a pestle by saying another spell over it.

"Though I was very keen to learn this from him, I could not do so, for he was jealous, although most ready to oblige in everything else. But one day I secretly overheard the spell—it was just three syllables—by taking my stand in a dark place. He went off to the square after telling the pestle what it had to do, and on the next day, while he was transacting some business in the square, I took the pestle, dressed it up in the same way, said the syllables over it, and told it to carry water. When it had filled and brought in the jar, I said, 'Stop! Don't carry any more water. Be a pestle again!'

"But it would not obey me now; it kept straight on carrying until it filled the house with water for us by pouring it in! At my wit's end over the thing, for I feared that Pancrates might come back and be angry, as was indeed the case, I took an axe and cut the pestle in two; but each part took a jar and began to carry water, with the result that instead of one servant I had now two.

"Meanwhile Pancrates appeared on the scene, and comprehending what had happened, turned them into wood again, just as they were before the spell, and then for his own part left me to my own devices without warning, taking himself off out of sight somewhere."

"Then you still know how to turn the pestle into a man?" said Deinomachus.

"Yes," said he. "Only halfway, however, for I cannot bring it back to its original form if it once becomes a water carrier, but we shall be obliged to let the house be flooded with the water that is poured in!"

"Will you never stop telling such buncombe, old men as you are?" said Tychiades. "If you will not, at least for the sake of these lads put your amazing and fearful tales off to some other time, so that they may not be filled up with terrors and strange figments before we realize it. You ought to be easy with them and not accustom them to hear things like this that will abide with them and annoy them their lives long and will make them afraid of every sound by filling them with all sorts of superstition."

THE STORY OF THE BRAHMIN PADMANABA
AND THE YOUNG HASSAN (1707)*

François Pétis de la Croix

Some time ago there was a shopkeeper by the name of Fyquaï in the city of Damas. He had a sixteen-year-old son whom he called Hassan, and who could pass for a prodigy. This young boy, who had the face of the moon, was as tall as a cypress tree, cheerful, and pleasant. Whenever he sang, his sweet voice charmed everyone, and he played the lute so well that he was capable of resuscitating a dead person. His talents were very useful for his father, who did good business by selling his *fiquàa*, a mixed drink of barley water and raisin, while his son provided his customers with so much pleasure. The drink, which did not cost more than a manghir, was sold for an aqta in the shop at his home. Fyquaï vainly sought to increase the sales of the drink, but when customers entered his shop, they came more to see his son than to drink, and there was quite a crowd. People even called the house *Tcheschémy Aby Hhayat*, that is, the fountain of youth, because the old people took so much pleasure in going there.

One day, when the young Hassan was singing and playing the lute to the great enjoyment of everyone in the shop, the famous Brahmin Padmanaba entered to refresh himself. He soon developed a certain admiration for Hassan, and after talking with the boy for a while, he was charmed by his conversation. Not only did Padmanaba return to the shop the next day, but he even dropped what he was doing to go there every day, and unlike the others in attendance who only gave an aqta, he gave a sequin to hear Hassan sing and play.

All this had been going on for a long time when Hassan told his father once: "There's a man who seems to be an important person, and he comes here every day. He takes so much pleasure in talking to me that he constantly calls out and asks me some questions. And when he leaves, he gives me a sequin."

"Oh, oh," the father responded, "there's something mysterious about all this! The intentions of this important person are perhaps not very good. Often these philosophers, despite their serious look, are very vicious. Tomorrow, when you see him, tell him that I wish to make his acquaintance. Ask him to mount the stairs to my room. I want to examine him. I have experience.

---

* "Histoire du Brachmane Padmanaba et du jeune Fyquaï," *Histoire de la Sultane de Perse et des Visirs. Contes Turcs* (Paris: 1707).

I'll get to the bottom of all this when I talk to him, and I'll know whether he is as wise as he appears to be."

The next day Hassan did what his father had instructed him to do, and he told Padmanaba to mount the stairs to his father's room, where a magnificent meal had been prepared for him. The shopkeeper paid all the honors imaginable to the Brahmin, who received this attention with great politeness and displayed such wisdom in his conversation that it was clear he was a very virtuous man. After the meal young Hassan's father asked him what country he was from and where he was lodging. As soon as Fyquaï learned that he was a stranger, he said to him: "If you would like to live with us, I can offer you lodging in my house."

"I accept the offer that you've made," Padmanaba responded, "because it is like a paradise in this world to be able to lodge with good friends."

So the Brahmin moved into the shopkeeper's house. His presence in the home was considerable, and he eventually developed a very strong friendship with Hassan. So, one day he said to him: "Oh, my son I must open my heart to you. I find you to contain the very spirit of the secret sciences. It is true that your character is a bit too cheerful, but I am persuaded that you will change, and you will eventually have all the seriousness, or rather all the melancholy necessary to become one of those sages whose mysteries I should like you to learn in an initiation. I intend to make your fortune, and if you want to accompany me outside of the city, I'll let you see from today onward the treasures that I claim you deserve to possess."

"My lord," Hassan responded, "you know that I depend on my father. I cannot go with you without his permission."

So the Brahmin went and spoke with his father, who was already convinced of the philosopher's wisdom and gave him permission to take his son to wherever he pleased.

Now Padmanaba left the city of Damas with Hassan. They walked toward a rundown cottage, and when they arrived, they found a well filled with water to the rim.

"Take good note of this well," the Brahmin said. "The treasures that I have intended for you are down there."

"Too bad," the young man replied with a smile. "How am I supposed to pull them out from this abyss?"

"Oh, my son!" Padmanaba exclaimed. "I'm not at all surprised that this seems difficult. Most people do not have the privilege that I have. Only those whom God wants to participate in the marvels of his omnipotence have the power to reverse the elements and to disturb the order of nature."

As he was saying this he wrote some letters on a piece of paper in Sanskrit, the language of the magi of India, Siam, and China. Next he only had to throw the paper down the well, and immediately all the water retreated and evaporated. The two of them climbed into the well, where some stairs appeared, and they descended to the bottom. There they found a door made of red copper locked by a large iron padlock. The Brahmin wrote a prayer and touched the padlock with the paper, and the lock opened instantly. They pushed the door and entered a cave, where they saw a very dark Ethiopian. He was standing and had a large rock made of white marble in his hand.

"If we approach him," young Hassan said, "he will throw the rock at our heads." Indeed, as soon as the Ethiopian saw the two of them advancing, he lifted this enormous rock as if to throw it. Padmanaba quickly recited a short prayer and whispered: "The Ethiopian cannot resist these words with force and will fall down because of the whisper."

Then they crossed the cave without encountering any obstacles and walked through a long and vast courtyard. There was a crystal in the middle of it, and the entrance was guarded by two dragons facing one another. Their mouths were open and spewed forth a whirl of fire. Hassan was terrified of them.

"Let's not go any farther!" he cried out. "Those horrible dragons will burn us."

"Don't be afraid of anything, my son," the Brahmin said. "Trust me, and have more courage. The supreme sagacity that I want you to attain demands fortitude. Those monsters that are terrifying you will disappear when they hear my voice. I have the power to command the demons and to dissipate all their spells."

Upon saying that he just needed to pronounce some cabalistic words, and the dragons retreated into two holes. Then the door to the dome opened by itself all at once. Padmanaba and the young Hassan entered, and they were pleasantly surprised to see a new dome made entirely of rubies in another courtyard. At the top there was a carbuncle six feet high that gave off a large light that shone all over and served as the sun in this subterranean place.

This dome was not like the first one guarded by frightening monsters. On the contrary there were six charming statues, each made from one solitary diamond, and they stood at the entrance and represented six beautiful women who played the Basque drums. The door was composed of one solitary emerald, and it was open and led to a magnificent salon. Hassan was daunted by what stood before his eyes.

After Padmanaba had carefully examined the statues and the dome, he entered with Hassan into the salon, which had a floor made of massive gold, and the ceiling was made of porphyry and scattered with pearls. There were a thousand different things, some more unique than others, that the young man's eyes avidly consumed. Then the philosopher took him into a large square room. In one corner there was a huge pile of gold; in another, a huge pile of extremely beautiful rubies; in a third, a pile of silver; and in the fourth, a pile of black dirt.

In the middle of the room a superb throne arose, and on it there was a silver coffin in which a prince was lying. On his head was a golden crown enriched by large pearls. One could see a large gold plaque on top of the coffin with words written in cabalistic hieroglyphs used by ancient the Egyptian priests: *People sleep until after they live. They only wake up at the hour of their death. What was important to me up to the present was to possess a great empire with tons of treasures that are here. There is nothing here that lasts so little as prosperity. And all the human power is nothing but a false blessing (fosblesse). Oh mortal who is in the shaky cradle do not glorify your fortune. Remember the time when the Pharaohs flourished. They no longer exist and make an offer to be just as good as they were.*

"What prince is in this coffin?" Hassan asked.

"One of the ancient kings of Egypt," responded the Brahmin. "It is he who created this subterranean realm and built this rich dome of rubies."

"I'm surprised by what you are teaching me," the young man answered. "What bizarre thing drove this king to construct this underground realm, a work that seems to have exhausted all the riches of the world? All the other monarchs who wanted to leave monuments of their grandeur to posterity displayed them instead of concealing them from the eyes of people."

"You are right," the Brahmin replied, "but this king was a great cabalist. He often slipped away from the court to come to this place to make discoveries in nature. He possessed many secrets, and among them was the philosopher's stone as one can see here in all the richness that is the product of this pile of black dirt that you can perceive in the corner."

"Is it possible," the young Hassan exclaimed, "that this black dirt was made for that?"

"Don't have any doubts," the Brahmin responded. "To prove this to you, I'm going to cite two Turkish verses that contain the secrets of the philosopher's stone. Here they are:

> *Wirghil Arons gharby Schahzadey Kibitays*
> *Bit Tift ola boulardam Sultan Khob'rouyan.*

This means literally: Give the son of the king of the Orient to the bride of the West; they will give birth to the sultan with a beautiful face. Now I'll tell you the mythic meaning of this. Mix the dry earth of Adam with the humidity that comes from the Orient. This mixture will engender the philosophical mercury that is omnipotent in nature and will engender the sun and the moon, that is, gold and silver. And when it is mounted on its throne, it will change the stones into diamonds and other precious gems. The pile of silver that is in the corner of this room contains water, that is, the humidity used for mixing with the dry earth and to convert it to the condition in which it is. If you were to take only a handful of this dirt, you could transmute it into silver or gold, or if you wanted, into all the metal in Egypt and all the stones of the houses into diamonds and rubies."

"I must admit," Hassan said, "that this is really marvelous dirt. I'm no longer surprised to see such riches here."

"They are even more admirable than I have already explained," the Brahmin replied. "They can cure all the enormous diseases. When an exhausted sick person who's about to surrender his soul swallows one solitary grain of the dirt, he'll suddenly feel his energy return, and he will get up straightaway full of vigor and good health. This dirt has another virtue that I prefer to all the others: Whoever rubs one's eyes with its sap will see the genies and will have the power to command them.

"After everything that I have just told you, my son," the Brahmin continued, "you are to value discreetly the treasures that are reserved for you."

"Without a doubt they are priceless," the young man said. "But while waiting for your permission to take possession of these treasures, may I take a part of them to show my father how fortunate we are to have a friend like you?"

"Yes, you may," responded Padmanaba. "Take as much as you would like."

So Hassan benefited from the opportunity to take some gold and rubies with him and followed the Brahmin who left the room of the king of Egypt. They crossed the beautiful salon, the two courtyards, and the cave, where they found the Ethiopian, who was still staggering. They opened the door made of red copper and departed, while the iron padlock shut by itself. Then they climbed the staircase, and after they were on top, the well filled itself with water and appeared just as it was before.

When the Brahmin noticed that Hassan was astonished to see the water return all at once, he said to him: "Where does that surprise come from that you've just shown? Haven't you ever heard of talismans?"

"No," the young man responded, "and I'd very much like it if you'd teach me what they are."

"I'm not ready to tell you," responded Padmanaba. "One day I'll teach you what they are made of. Right now, however, I'll explain to you what you wish to know. There are two kinds of talismans: the cabalist and the astrological. The first is the more sublime type and produces marvelous effects through the means of letters, words, and prayers. The second finds its effects through the relationship between the planets and the metals. The first type of strong talisman is the one I use. It was revealed to me in a dream by the great God Wistnou, the head of all the pagoda in the world.

"I want you to know, my son," he continued, "that the letters have a relationship with angels. There's not one letter that isn't governed by an angel. And if you ask me what an angel is, I would say to you that it is a ray or an emanation of the virtues of the omnipotence and the attributes of God. The angels who reside in the understandable world are in control of all the people who inhabit the celestial world, and the other angels control those in the suburban world. The letters form words, and the words compose prayers, and this only causes the angels represented by the letters and assembled in the written or spoken prayers to produce the marvels that astonish ordinary people."

While Padmanaba was talking to the young man, they gradually returned toward the city. After they arrived at the home of the shopkeeper, he was charmed when his son showed him the gold and the gems that he had carried with him. Then, they stopped selling the *fyquàa* in the shop and began to live a full and pleasurable life.

But Hassan had a stepmother who was greedy and ambitious. Even though the young boy brought her rubies that were worth immense sums, she complained that she didn't have enough money, and one day she said to him: "Oh, my son, if we continue to live as we have been doing, we shall soon be ruined."

"Don't you worry about all this, my mother," he responded. "The source of our wealth is not dried up. If you had seen the treasures that the generous

Padmanaba has intended for me, you would realize that your fear is senseless. The next time he takes me to the well, I'll bring you a handful of black dirt that will ease your mind for a long time."

"Instead of the dirt, bring me back gold and rubies," the stepmother replied. "I prefer those things than all the dirt of the world. But, Hassan," she added, "I have just had an idea. Since Padmanaba wants to give you all the treasures, why doesn't he teach you all the necessary prayers for descending to the place where they are? If he were to suddenly die, all our hopes would vanish. Moreover, we don't know whether he will get bored living with us. Perhaps he's at the point of leaving us and going somewhere else where he will share these treasures with other people. For me, my child, I'm of the opinion that you should press Padmanaba to teach you the prayers, and when you know them, we shall kill him so that nobody else will discover the mystery of the well."

The young Hassan was frightened by this conversation. "Oh, my mother!" he exclaimed. "How can you dare propose something like this? Could you really commit such a mean act? The Brahmin loves us. He has overwhelmed us with good deeds. He has promised me treasures capable of quenching the greed of the greatest monarchs on earth. And for the price of all his kindness you want to take away his life! No! Even if I had to return to my former condition and sell *fyquàa* for the rest of my life, I could never contribute to the death of a man to whom I owe so much."

"You have some very beautiful feelings, my son," the stepmother replied. "But it's necessary that we consider only our own interests. Fortune has presented us with just one opportunity that will allow us to enrich ourselves forever. We shouldn't let it escape us. Your father, who has more experience than you, applauds my plan, and you should also approve it."

Hassan continued to show a great repugnance about entering into this cruel conspiracy. Nevertheless, since he was young and easygoing, the stepmother presented so many arguments that he became too weak and yielded to her.

"All right," he said, "I'll go and find Padmanaba and get him to teach me the prayers."

Indeed, Hassan went out to look for the Brahmin, and he pressed him to teach him all that he knew for descending the well to the subterranean world. Well the Brahmin had such an extreme tenderness for the young boy that he could not refuse him. He wrote each prayer on paper and marked precisely the place where he was to pronounce the prayers along with all the other cabalist conditions. Then he gave the prayers to him.

As soon as he had the prayers, he alerted his father and stepmother, who set the day when all three of them could visit the treasures.

"When we return," the stepmother said, "we shall kill Padmanaba."

Once the day arrived, they left their home without telling the Brahmin where they were going, and they began walking to the rundown cottage. As soon as they arrived, Hassan took the paper from his pocket that had the first prayer written on it. He had barely thrown the paper down the well when the water disappeared. So they descended the stairs until they came to the door made of red copper. Hassan touched the padlock with another prayer, and the lock opened. Then they pushed the door open and saw the Ethiopian, who was standing and ready to throw the rock of white marble, frightening the shopkeeper and his wife. But Hassan quickly recited the third prayer and whispered, and the Ethiopian fell to the ground. Finally, they crossed the cave and entered the court where the crystal dome was standing.

Hassan compelled the dragons to withdraw into their holes so that he and his parents could advance into the second courtyard. They passed by the salon and entered the room where they found the rubies, the gold, the pile of silver, and the black dirt. The stepmother did not pay any attention to the king of Egypt's coffin and did not stop to read the moral inscription on the gold plaque. She did not deign to look at the heap of black dirt about which her stepson had told her so much. She threw herself greedily onto the rubies, and she took such a huge quantity of them that she could hardly move and carry them. Her husband gathered up gold, and Hassan was simply content to put two handfuls of black dirt into his pockets, determined to make use of them when he returned home.

After all this the three of them left the king of Egypt's room, and weighed down by all of the riches that they were carrying, they crossed the first court-yard cheerfully when suddenly three frightening monsters appeared and went straight at them. The shopkeeper and his wife were overcome by a dreadful fear and turned to Hassan, who did not have a prayer for chasing the monsters away and was just as afraid of them as his parents were.

"Oh, stepmother, you've been so unfair and wicked!" he exclaimed. "You are the reason why we are going to perish. Padmanaba knew for certain that we were going to come here. Perhaps he even discovered by his science that we had conspired to kill him, and to punish us for our ingratitude, he sent these monsters to devour us."

Barely had he spoken these works when he heard the voice of the Brahmin in the air who said: "All three of you are miserable and not worth my friendship. You would have done away with my life if the great God Wistnou had not alerted me to your evil plan. You are now going to feel my just resentment—you, woman, for having conceived the plan to assassinate me, and you others for having been willing to follow the advice of a woman whose wickedness you should have detested."

Upon saying these words, the voice could no longer be heard, and the three monsters began to tear the unfortunate Hassan, his father, and his guilty stepmother into pieces.

THE PUPIL IN MAGIC (1798)*

Johann Wolfgang von Goethe

I am now,—what joy to hear it!—
Of the old magician rid;
And henceforth shall ev'ry spirit
Do whate'er by me is bid;
    I have watch'd with rigour
      All he used to do,
    And will now with vigour
      Work my wonders too.

Wander, wander
    Onward lightly,
So that rightly
    Flow the torrent,
And with teeming waters yonder
    In the bath discharge its current!
And now come, thou well-worn broom,
And thy wretched form bestir;

* Edgar Alfred Bowring, trans., *The Poems of Goethe*, 2nd ed. (New York: Hurst, 1874); also known as "The Sorcerer's Apprentice." Published in German as "Der Zauberlehrling," in Friedrich Schiller, ed., *Musen-Almanach für das Jahr 1798* (Tübingen: J. G. Cotta, 1798).

Thou hast ever served as groom,
So fulfill my pleasure, sir!
  On two legs now stand,
    With a head on top;
  Water pail in hand,
    Haste, and do not stop!

Wander, wander
    Onward lightly,
  So that rightly
    Flow the torrent,
  And with teeming waters yonder
    In the bath discharge its current!
See! He's running to the shore,
And has now attain'd the pool,

And with lightning speed once more
Comes here, with his bucket full!
  Back he then repairs;
    See how swells the tide!
  How each pail he bears
    Straightway is supplied!

Stop, for, lo!
    All the measure
    Of thy treasure
    Now is right!—
  Ah, I see it! Woe, oh woe!
    I forget the word of might.
Ah, the word whose sound can straight
Make him what he was before!

Ah, he runs with nimble gait!
Would thou wert a broom once more!
  Streams renew'd for ever
    Quickly bringeth he;
  River after river
    Rusheth on poor me!

Now no longer
 Can I bear him;
 I will snare him,
  Knavish sprite!
  Ah, my terror waxes stronger!
   What a look! What fearful sight
Oh, thou villain child of hell!
Shall the house through thee be drown'd?

Floods I see that wildly swell,
O'er the threshold gaining ground.
  Wilt thou not obey,
   Oh, thou broom accurs'd?
  Be thou still I pray,
   As thou wert at first!

Will enough
  Never please thee?
  I will seize thee,
   Hold thee fast,
  And thy nimble wood so tough,
   With my sharp axe split at last.
See, once more he hastens back!
Now, oh Cobold, thou shalt catch it!

I will rush upon his track;
Crashing on him falls my hatchet.
  Bravely done, indeed!
   See, he's cleft in twain!
  Now from care I'm freed,
   And can breathe again.

Woe, oh woe!
  Both the parts,
  Quick as darts,
   Stand on end,
  Servants of my dreaded foe!
   Oh, ye gods protection send!

And they run! And wetter still
Grow the steps and grows the hail.
Lord and master hear me call!

Ever seems the flood to fill,

Ah, he's coming! See,
    Great is my dismay!
Spirits raised by me
    would I lay!
"To the side
    Of the room
    Hasten, broom,
    As of old!
Spirits I have ne'er untied
    Save to act as they are told."

Nineteenth-Century Tales

CORNELIUS AGRIPPA'S BLOODY BOOK (1801)*

Robert Southey

Cornelius Agrippa went out one day;
His study he lock'd ere he went away,
And he gave the key of the door to his wife,
And charged her to keep it lock'd on her life.

"And if any one ask my study to see,
I charge you to trust them not with the key;
Whoever may beg, and entreat, and implore,
On your life let nobody enter that door."

There lived a young man in the house, who in vain
Access to that study had sought to obtain;
And he begg'd and pray'd the books to see,
Till the foolish woman gave him the key.

On the study-table a book there lay,
Which Agrippa himself had been reading that day;
The letters were written with blood therein,
And the leaves were made of dead men's skin;—

And these horrible leaves of magic between
Were the ugliest pictures that ever were seen,
The likeness of things so foul to behold,
That what they were is not fit to be told.

* Matthew G. Lewis, *Tales of Wonder*, vol. 1 (London: Bulmer, 1801).

The young man he began to read
He knew not what; but he would proceed,
When there was heard a sound at the door
Which, as he read on, grew more and more.

And more and more the knocking grew;
The young man knew not what to do;
But, trembling, in fear he sat within,
Till the door was broke, and the Devil came in.

Two hideous horns on his head he had got,
Like iron heated nine times red-hot;
The breath of his nostrils was brimstone blue,
And his tail like a fiery serpent grew.

"What wouldst thou with me?" the Wicked One cried,
But not a word the young man replied;
Every hair on his head was standing upright,
And his limbs like a palsy shook with affright.

"What wouldst thou with me?" cried the Author of Ill;
But the wretched young man was silent still;
Not a word had his lips the power to say,
And his marrow seem'd to be melting away.

"What wouldst thou with me?" the third time he cried,
And a flash of lightning came from his eyes,
And he lifted his griffin claw in the air,
And the young man had not strength for a prayer.

His eyes red fire and fury dart
As out he tore the young man's heart;
He grinn'd a horrible grin at his prey;
And in a clap of thunder vanish'd away.

THE MORAL

Henceforth let all young men take heed
How in a Conjurer's books they read.

THE LAST EXORCISER (1838)*

Sir Walter Scott

A Mass John Scott, minister of Peebles, is reported to have been the last renowned exorciser, and to have lost his life in a contest with an obstinate spirit. This was owing to the conceited rashness of a young clergyman, who commenced the ceremony of laying the ghost before the arrival of Mass John. It is the nature, it seems, of spirits disembodied, as well as embodied, to increase in strength and presumption, in proportion to the advantages that they may gain over the opponent. The young clergyman losing courage, the horrors of the scene were increased to such a degree, that, as Mass John approached the house in which it passed, he beheld the slates and tiles flying from the roof, as if dispersed with a whirlwind. At his entry, be perceived all the wax tapers (the most essential instruments or conjuration) extinguished, except one, which already burned blue in the socket. The arrival of the experienced sage changed the scene: he brought the spirit to reason; but unfortunately, while addressing a word of advice or censure to his rash brother, he permitted the ghost to obtain the last word, a circumstance that, in all colloquies of this nature, is strictly to be guarded against. This fatal oversight occasioned his falling into a lingering disorder, of which be never recovered.

THE BOOK OF MAGIC (1874)†

John Naaké

A soldier was quartered in a certain town. He had taken to study the black art, and had got possession of books that dealt with it. One day, during his absence from his quarters, one of his comrades came to see him. Not finding him at home the visitor took up one of the soldier's books, and for want of other occupation began to read it. It was in the evening, and he read by the light of a lamp. The book was full of names and nothing else.

---

* *The Poetical Works of Sir Walter Scott; containing Minstrelsy of the Scottish Border, Sir Tristrem, and Dramatic Pieces* (Paris: Baudry's European Library, 1838).

† *Slavonic Fairy Tales: Collected and Translated from the Russian, Polish, Serbian, and Bohemian* (London: Henry S. King, 1874).

He had read about half of the names when he raised his head, and looking around him, saw that the room was full of diabolical-looking beings. The soldier was struck with terror, and not knowing what to do, began again to read the book. After reading for some little time, he again looked round him; the number of spirits had increased. Again he read, and having finished the book, looked again around him. By this time the number of demons had increased so much that there was barely space for them in the room. They sat upon each other's shoulders and pressed continually forward round the reader. The soldier saw that the situation was serious; he shut the book, closed his eyes, and anxiously awaited his comrade.

The spirits pressed closer and closer upon him, crying, "Give us work to do—quick!"

The soldier reflected awhile, and then said, "Fill up the cisterns of all the baths in the town with water brought there in a sieve."

The demons flew away. In two minutes they returned and said, "It is done! Give us some more work to do—quick!"

"Pull the Voivode's [governor's] house down, brick by brick—but take care you do not touch or disturb the inmates; then build it up again as it was before."

The goblins disappeared, but in two minutes returned. "It is done!" they cried. "Give us more work—quick!"

"Go," said the soldier, "and count the grains of sand that lie at the bottom of the Volga, the number of drops of water that are in the river, and of the fish that swim in it, from its source to its mouth."

The spirits flew away; but in another minute they returned, having executed their task. Thus before the soldier could think of some new labor to be done, the old one was completed, and the demons were again at his side demanding more work. When he began to think what orders he should give them, they pressed round him and threatened him with instant death if he did not give them something to do. The soldier was becoming exhausted, and there was no sign yet of his comrade's return. What course should he take? How was he to save himself from the evil spirits?

The soldier thought to himself, "While I was reading the book, not one of the demons came near me. Perhaps, if I try to read it again; that will keep them off."

Again he began to read the book of magic, but he soon observed that as he read, the number of phantoms increased, so that soon such a host of the spirit world surrounded him that the very lamp was scarcely visible. When the soldier hesitated at a word, or paused to rest himself, the goblins became more restless and violent, demanding, "Give us work to do! Give us work!"

The soldier was almost worn out and unfortunately did not know how to help himself. Suddenly a thought occurred to him, "The spirits appeared when I read the book from the beginning; let me now read it from the end, perhaps this will send them way."

He turned the book around and began to read it from the end. After reading for some time, he observed that the number of spirits decreased; the lamp began again to burn brightly, and there was an empty space around him.

The soldier was delighted, and continued his reading. He read and read until he had read them all away. And thus he saved himself from the demons. His comrade came in soon afterward. The soldier told him what had happened.

"It is fortunate for you," said his comrade, "that you began to read the book backward in time. Had you not thus read them away by midnight they would have devoured you."

THE MASTER AND HIS PUPIL; OR, THE MAGIC BOOK (1884)*

Alfred Cooper Fryer

There lived long ago in the north-country a man who was so learned that it was said of him he knew every language that was spoken, and all the mysteries of the universe. Now, this wise man had a book, bound in rough black leather, studded with brass nails, and fastened at each corner with iron clasps; and for further security it was chained to a heavy table that was made fast to the floor. Whenever the wise man desired to read in the book, he unlocked it with an iron key, which he always kept hanging at his girdle. He was the only person who ever glanced at its wondrous pages, for they contained secrets that other men might not know. Among other marvels it told how evil spirits might be held in bondage and become the slaves of men; and in the book were written

---

* *Book of English Fairy Tales from the North-Country* (London: W. Swan Sonnenschein, 1884).

the names of good spirits, what they did, and how they went about their work secretly, invisible to the human eye.

It was a queer old room in which the book was kept, and where the old magician—for that is what the wise man was—passed the greater part of his time. In one corner was a large stone furnace, fitted with a rusty iron grate and a deep copper. On the top of it, and on a row of shelves hanging above, was piled a confused heap of metal crucibles, pipes and tubes twisted into odd shapes, and squat bulging bottles of all the colors of the rainbow. This was the apparatus that the magician used in his experiments. Stuffed snakes, hedgehogs, and bats, and bunches of dried plants and grasses hung from the ceiling or were suspended from nails driven into the walls. In the dim light that struggled through the one barred window these objects could not be clearly seen; this added to the awe that was felt by the few visitors who came at times to consult the great magician.

A strange figure, too, was the old sorcerer himself, clad in a long robe, once black, but now of a rusty brown hue, which fell to his feet, and with a little velvet skull-cap drawn tightly over his head to his ears. A long white beard floated to his waist, but his eyebrows were as black as jet, and the deep-set eyes beneath them flashed with a keen and hawk-like glance, as if they could read the very secrets of the heart through its fleshly covering.

Now this learned magician had a pupil, and a very stupid boy he was. He usually acted as a servant to prepare his master's meals, or fetch him his cloak and staff when he went abroad. It was rarely that he entered the private chamber where the magic book was kept, and he was never by any chance permitted to peep into its contents.

One day, however, when the wise man went out as usual to visit the dwarfs in their mountain caves, or gather the plants of which he used to make his magic draughts, or some such errand, whatever it was, the boy ventured to enter the private chamber, as he had never before dared to do, except in obedience to his master's summons. With eager curiosity he gazed upon the marvelous objects that surrounded him. There was the apparatus for changing common metals into gold and silver. On the wall hung the magic mirror in which everything that was passing in the world was reflected, and beneath it was the magic shell, which, if held to the ear, repeated every word that was spoken anywhere. In the center of the room, upon a heavy table, fastened by strong iron bolts to the floor, lay the magic book.

The boy lighted a fire in the rusty grate, and having heated a crucible to redness, mixed together a lot of different ores; but he got neither gold nor silver. The copper remained copper still, and the lead remained lead. He only scalded his fingers and burned great holes in his clothes with the hot coals and fuming acids. Then he turned to the magic mirror and gazed long and steadily upon it. But he saw nothing clearly, only clouds and mist and smoke flitted over its shining surface. Then he took up the wonderful shell and held it to his ear; but he could hear only a confused medley of sounds, and a hoarse indistinct murmur like the breaking of waves on a distant shore.

"Oh, dear, how provoking!" cried the lad at last. "If I only knew the right word, I would soon hear and see everything the same as my master does."

He happened, as he spoke, to look in the direction of the magic book, which contained the spell that could render him as potent a wizard as his master, and he skipped with joy to perceive that the volume was unfastened. The magician had forgotten to lock it before he went out. Quickly he ran up to the massive table, opened the book, and turned over its mystic pages, inscribed in black and red ink with strange characters. The language was unknown to him, but putting his finger at random on a line, he began to spell the words aloud.

Immediately the room became as dark as if a thick cloud had suddenly overspread the sun's bright disk. The house trembled and rocked as if shaken by a mighty earthquake. A loud peal of thunder followed, and ere the echoes died away, a hideous and gigantic shape stood before the terrified youth. It breathed fire from its mouth and nostrils, and its deep-sunk eyes flashed and burned like lightning or the gleaming of a meteor. This was an evil spirit—the Slave of the Book—which the boy had unwittingly summoned from the dark shades in which it dwelt by pronouncing the magic spell.

"Set me a task, master!" cried the monster in a deep, hoarse voice, like the roaring and rumbling of a hidden furnace; but the rash pupil, who now thoroughly repented of his curiosity, trembled violently, unable to utter a word. His tongue clove to the roof of his mouth; his hair bristled, and cold drops of perspiration trickled down his face. He longed for the earth to open under his feet and swallow him up that he might escape from the dreadful sights.

Then the evil spirit, perceiving his terror, grew bolder and more threatening. "Set me a task at once," he repeated, in angry tones; "else will I strangle thee as a foolish impostor, who has dared to wield a power to which he can lay no claim!" The lad was still silent, and the hideous monster stretched forth his arm, till his fingers touched the boy's throat, and seemed to burn him. Then he shouted for the third time, in a voice that resembled the bellowing of a maddened bull, "Set me a task!"

But, as the burning fingers clasped his throat, the poor boy managed to stammer out, "Water that flower!" pointing to a plant with bright scarlet blossoms that stood in a corner of the room.

The spirit was pacified. His brow became smoother as he flew away to obey the order. He quickly returned, bearing upon his broad shoulders a barrel, the contents of which he poured upon the plant. Again he vanished and again reappeared, bringing with him a fresh barrel of water, which he poured upon the plant as before. When this operation had been repeated several times, the room was flooded ankle-deep.

"Enough! Enough! You may stop now!" cried the boy, in a new agony of fear. But, alas! He knew not the magic word with which to dismiss his terrible servant. So the spirit still went and came, pouring out fresh supplies of water, till the boy screamed with fear, for he saw that unless he could control the evil spirit, and make him cease his task, he would soon be drowned. Higher and higher in the room the water rose. The boy climbed upon the table, but inch by inch the water rose from his knees to his armpits, till at last it swirled and gurgled round his neck. Vain were his cries for help; vainly did he seek to dismiss the monster, who still plied his task, heedless of the youth's despairing shouts. To this very day probably the spirit would have gone on pouring water, and the water would have continued to rise, and all Yorkshire certainly would have been drowned as deep as the bottom of the sea, if the old magician had not luckily taken it into his head to return. In the middle of his journey he suddenly recollected that he had left the magic book unlocked. So he hurried back as fast as he could, and arrived just in time to utter the words of power that alone could dismiss the evil spirit, and thereby save the life of his inquisitive pupil.

What punishment was awarded to the latter the story does not tell. But one thing is certain, from that day forward the youth never entered the mystic chamber in the absence of his master, and the old magician, on his part, was very careful, before he took his walks abroad, to close and lock securely the clasps of his magic book.

THE LADY'S FIFTH STORY (1886)*

Sheykh-Zāda

There was of old time in a great city a sherbet-seller, and he had a son, a loveling of the age, who was so fair that he seemed a second Joseph,† and he used to sell sherbet in the shop. The folk would come to gaze upon this youth's beauty, and they would give a sequin for each cup of sherbet and drain it, and whenever they drank a cup, they would say it was the water of life.

Now one day a swarthy Moor came to that country, and as soon as he saw the youth, the hapless Moor's power of speech left him, and he could not stir one step from where he stood, but leaned against the opposite wall bewildered. After a time he recovered his understanding, and, rising and falling like one drunk, he came up as best he could to the youth, gave a sequin, drank a cup of sherbet, and went away. For a time he came every day and drank cups of sherbet at a sequin each and gazed at the beauty of the youth.

One day the youth told this thing to his father, and his father perceived that the Moor was ravished with the boy, and said, "Oh, my son, bring that Moor to the house tomorrow, and let us see what manner of man he is."

The next day when the Moor came to the youth, he invited him to his house, and took him and went to his father. After they had eaten, the father of the boy asked of the Moor's case and dwelling. The Moor saw what his intention was and answered, "I have no dwelling, I am a stranger."

The boy's father said, "Since you are a stranger, we will give you a dwelling. Stay with us."

The Moor was glad and counted it a boon to his soul. As they say, "the loved one's ward is Paradise."

So they showed the Moor a dwelling, where he lived for some days, and gradually his love for the boy increased. Then one day he showed him a precious stone and said, "If you let me give you one kiss, I will give you this stone."

With a thousand graces the boy consented, and the Moor gave him the stone, kissed him, and said, "My life, my master, I love you from heart and soul. Do not flee me. I know a talisman that will open before you. If you will

---

* Sheykh-Zāda, *The History of the Forty Vezirs, or The Story of the Forty Morns and Eves,* trans. Elias John Wilkinson Gibb (London: George Redway, 1886).

† Joseph is the type of youthful beauty.

come with me, I will open it and give you so much gold that you shall never again know poverty."

The youth told this thing to his father, and his father gave him leave. So the Moor took him, and they went outside the city, and he brought him to a ruin. Now there was a well there, full to the mouth with water, and the Moor wrote on a piece of paper and laid it on the well. Thereupon all the water vanished from the well. The Moor and the boy descended to the bottom of the well and saw a locked door. The Moor wrote a charm and fastened it on the lock, and it opened right away. They went in and saw a Negro holding in one hand a great stone to throw upon anyone who entered. The Moor repeated a charm and blew upon the Negro, and the Negro laid the stone that was in his hand upon the ground, and let them pass. They went on and saw a dome of crystal, and at the door of the domed building were two dragons, who stood facing one another with open mouths like caverns. When they came near, the dragons flew at them, but the Moor repeated a charm and blew on them, and they vanished. Then the door of the domed building opened, and they went inside and saw that in one corner was gold, in another corner silver, in another corner all manner of jewels, and in another corner a throne was raised upon black earth, and on that throne was a coffin, and in that coffin lay a renowned man dead. Upon his breast was a gold tablet, and on that tablet was written: "I was a king, and I ruled the whole earth, and wherever I went in this world I conquered. I had many many champions and great wealth and treasure. A little of the wealth I possessed I gathered here. Death did not spare me but made me just as though I had not come into the world. Now, oh, you, who sees me in this plight, heed my warning and remember my soul in prayer, and be not presumptuous through the wealth of this world for a few days' life."

And that was all. Then the Moor and the youth took as much as they desired of the gold and silver and precious stones and black earth, which was the philosopher's stone. Then they departed. The Moor repeated a charm and blew upon the well, and it was again all full of water, and he went back with the boy to their house, where they delighted in mirth and merriment. They spent day and night there and did not leave the house.

One day the boy asked the Moor to teach him the charms he had repeated in the talisman. The Moor consented, and instructed him for many days and taught him. One day, the boy suddenly went and said to his father, "Oh father, I have learned all the charms of the talisman, so we have no longer any need of the Moor. Let us poison him."

But his father did not consent and said, "Let us turn him away. Let him go somewhere else."

"This would not do if we just turned him away," said the youth. "He is a great master, and he might harm us. So let us poison him before he plays us some trick, and I will take as much gold and silver as is needed from that buried treasure."

The Moor heard him and knew that fairness purposed foulness, and he straightway disappeared from there.[*]

THE BLACKSMITH AND THE DEVIL (1890)[†]

Edith Hodgetts

Once upon a time there lived an old blacksmith who had an only son, a bright, intelligent boy of six. One day the blacksmith went to church, and began praying before a large holy picture. On looking at the picture more attentively, he saw painted on it a very big devil, such a dreadful-looking creature—all black, with long horns and fierce tail.

"That is something like a devil!" thought the blacksmith to himself. "I think I shall have one painted exactly like it in the smithy!"

So when he returned home he engaged a house-painter and told him to paint on the door of the smithy a devil exactly like the one he saw in the holy picture at church. The house-painter obeyed, and in a very short time he completed his order. From that day forth, whenever the blacksmith entered the smithy, he used to look at the devil on the door and say in a friendly way:

"Good-day to you, my countryman. I hope I see you well!"

He would then make a roaring fire and betake himself to his work. After living for over ten years in perfect harmony with the devil, the blacksmith

* In Pétis de la Croix's 1722 version, *L'Histoire de la Sultane de Perse et des Visirs*, the youth does not want to trick the Moor but is compelled by his mother-in-law to join a plot conceived by her and her husband to murder the magician. Before carrying out their design, all three descend the well and load themselves with treasures. However, as they are preparing to climb up the well, the youth realizes that he only knew the charm to gain entrance to the treasures in the well but did not know the charm that would enable them to exit. Consequently, the Negro and the dragons attack them and tear the would-be murderers into pieces.

† *Tales and Legends from the Land of the Tzar: Collection of Russian Stories* (London: Griffith Farran, 1890).

died and left his son to continue the business, who, being very fond of that sort of work, got on remarkably well. But one thing the young blacksmith would not do, and that was to regard the devil with the same respect with which his father had treated it before him. When he went into the smithy in the morning, he never by any chance greeted the devil, and instead of saying a kind word or two, he would take up a large iron hammer and give the unfortunate devil three blows on the forehead, and then go on with his work.

Three years went by, during which he continually treated the evil spirit to the hammer. The devil bore all this very patiently for some time, but at last he could stand it no longer.

"I have had enough of this!" thought the devil. "I can stand these insults no more. I will be artful and pay him out somehow or another!"

So the devil changed himself into a young man and entered the smithy.

"Good-day, uncle!" the devil said.

"Good-day, young fellow. What do you want?"

"I have come to ask you whether you would take me for an apprentice. I can, at any rate, carry the coals for you, and blow the bellows, to commence with!"

The blacksmith was delighted.

"Yes. Why not?" he cried. "It will be more amusing to have someone else with me!"

So the devil began to learn and help the blacksmith, and in about a month's time he knew everything much better than the master himself. What the blacksmith could not do, the devil did for him, and very soon he won the affections of the blacksmith, who became so fond of him and so pleased with everything he did, that it would be impossible to relate in this story. In fact, he very soon left off coming to the smithy, for he had such perfect confidence in the devil that he let him manage everything himself and left the shop in his charge.

One day the blacksmith was away from home, and the devil was quite alone in the smithy. After working a little, he went to the door to have a look at the passers-by. As he stood there, he saw an old lady driving along in her carriage and made a sign to the coachman to stop, and then he cried out to the old lady: "Walk in here, my lady. A new business has been started, whereby we can turn all old people into young ones again! Pray walk in!"

The old lady did not wait to think, but getting out of her carriage, entered the smithy.

"Is this really so," asked the old lady. "Can you change old people into young ones, or are you only boasting?"

"If I did not understand my business, my lady," said the evil spirit, "I should not have invited you in!"

"What do you charge?"

"Five hundred rubles."

"Very well, here is the money. Now make me young once more."

The evil spirit took the money and then sent the coachman into the village and said, "Go, and bring me two buckets full of milk."

This done, he seized the old lady and threw her into the furnace, where she was burnt up to her bones, which alone were left whole. When the coachman brought the two pails of milk, the devil poured them into a very large tub, and taking all the bones, threw them into the milk. And in about three minutes out came a young lady, alive and beautiful!

She thanked the devil, and seating herself in her carriage drove home to her husband, who stared at her in amazement when she entered the room in which he sat, and did not recognize his wife!

"Why do you stand staring there, like an idiot?" cried the lady. "Don't you see that I have become young and stately again? But now I do not wish to have a husband who is old and gray, so go to the blacksmith at once and be made young again, or I do not wish to know you, or have anything more to do with you. Go!"

The husband had to obey, or he knew he would suffer for it. So away he went.

Meanwhile the real blacksmith had returned, and after entering the smithy, he found his workman missing. He searched and searched, but all in vain. He asked his neighbors whether they had seen him, but no, no one knew anything, and no trace of him was to be found. The blacksmith then set to work by himself and began hammering away. Just as he was in the midst of his work, up drove a carriage, and the old lady's husband entered the shop.

"Make me into a young man!" he cried.

The blacksmith stared.

"I beg your pardon, sir," he said, "but are you in your right senses? How can I make you young again?"

"You ought to know that best yourself."

"But I assure you, sir, I don't know anything."

"You lie, you rascal! If you could make my wife young again, I suppose you can do the same with me. If you don't do this, I shall never be able to live with her any more."

"But I never set eyes on your wife."

"Never mind. Then your workman must have seen her and made her young again, and if he could do so, then you, who are the master, ought certainly to be able to do it also. Now, then, look alive, my friend! If you don't, woe betide you!"

The blacksmith was thus forced to change the old man into a young one, but how? He began asking the man what his workman had done, and how he did it and what it was he used, and any amount of other questions, which the old man answered as best he could, for his wife had told him something about the milk being ordered, and also about her sudden plunge into the fiery furnace.

"Well," thought the blacksmith to himself, "whatever happens, I must try and obey the extraordinary order. If I succeed, so much the better; if not, then I shall get into as bad a mess as if I had not obeyed the order at all."

So he caught the old man by the legs and threw him into the furnace, and then began blowing at him with the bellows. The unfortunate man was soon burnt to ashes, and nothing but the bones remained. These the blacksmith took and threw into the large tub, which he filled with milk, and waited, hoping to see a young man make his appearance. He waited an hour, and then another, yet nothing came. He looked into the tub, but only saw all the bones swimming about on the surface, and those were burnt almost black.

The wife was getting rather impatient, so she sent one of her servants round to the smithy to ask whether her husband would be ready soon.

The unfortunate blacksmith could only say in reply that her husband had wished her and all at home a long life, and asked them to remember his name.

When the wife heard this, she knew that the blacksmith had burnt her husband to ashes and had not made him young again. She flew into a great rage and ordered her servants to run to the smithy, seize the blacksmith, and take him to the gallows.

No sooner said than done. The servants ran into the smithy, caught hold of the unfortunate blacksmith, and dragged him to the gallows. Just as they were on their way, who should overtake them but the young fellow who had lived with the blacksmith as workman—in other words, the devil.

"Whither are they taking you, master?" he asked.

"They want to hang me," replied the blacksmith, and then he told the devil all that had happened.

"Well, uncle," the evil spirit whispered, "I am no other than the painting of the devil on the smithy door, but since you treated me so shamefully, I changed myself into a man, and vowed to pay you out. However, I will forgive you if you fall down on your knees and promise faithfully to treat me with the same respect that your father treated me with before you. If you promise this, the husband of the old lady who is sending you to the gallows shall become alive and well again."

The blacksmith did not wait to be told twice; anything would be better than being hanged. So he fell down before the devil and stammered out his promise, saying that he would never again think of knocking him about with the hammer, but would from henceforth treat him with all possible respect and courtesy.

The devil then ran to the smithy and very soon returned with the old gentleman, who had become youthful again.

"Stop!" cried the devil to the servants, who were about to hang the blacksmith. "Don't hang him! Here is your master for you!"

They at once untied the rope from around the blacksmith's neck and set him free again to do what he pleased.

From that day forth the blacksmith never attempted or even thought of giving the devil on the door of the smithy a blow with his hammer, or otherwise ill-treating him, but he always greeted the painting with the greatest possible politeness and lived on happily and prospered all his life, but his workman disappeared and was seen no more by anyone.

The husband and wife, whom the devil had turned into young people again, lived on double their time, and were as rich and happy as ever, and I believe they are still alive if not dead!

Twentieth-Century Tales

THE RASH MAGICIAN (1916)*

Henry Thomas Francis

Once on a time when Brahmadatta was reigning in Benares, the Bodhisatta was born into the family of a wealthy Brahmin. Arriving at years of discretion, he went to study at Takkasilā, where he received a complete education. In Benares as a teacher he enjoyed worldwide fame and had five hundred young Brahmins as pupils. Among those was one named Sanjīva, to whom the Bodhisatta taught the spell for raising the dead to life. But though the young man was taught this, he was not taught the countercharm. Proud of his new power, he went with his fellow pupils to the forest wood-gathering, and there came on a dead tiger.

"Now see me bring the tiger to life again," said he.

"You can't," said they.

"You look and you will see me do it."

"Well, if you can, do so," said they, and climbed up a tree forthwith.

Then Sanjīva repeated his charm and struck the dead tiger with a potsherd.† Up started the tiger and quick as lightning sprang at Sanjīva and bit him on the throat, killing him outright. Dead fell the tiger then and there, and dead fell Sanjīva too at the same spot. So there the two lay side by side.

The young Brahmins took their wood and went back to their master to whom they told the story.

"My dear pupils," said he, "mark herein how by reason of showing favor to the sinful and paying honor where it was not due, he has brought all the calamity upon himself."

And so saying he uttered this stanza:

* *Jātaka Tales* (Cambridge: Cambridge University Press, 1916).
† Potshard, a broken pottery fragment.

Befriend a villain, aid him in his need,
And, like that tiger which Sanjīva raised
To life, he straight devours your pains.

Such was the Bodhisatta's lesson to the young Brahmins, and after a life of almsgiving and other good deeds he passed away to fare according to his deserts.

THE SORCERER'S APPRENTICE (1941)*

Richard Rostron

Many years ago in far-off Switzerland, there lived a sorcerer. That is, this story took place many years ago. For all we know, the sorcerer may still be living yet. His name then was Willibald, which is a little odd, but no stranger than he was. He was tall and thin, and his nose was long and pointed to match. He wore long, loose, trailing gowns. What was left of his hair was white. A small black cap sat on the back of his head.

He was not a very ordinary sorcerer. For instance, his fellow sorcerers specialized in disappearing in puffs of smoke. Then they would bob up, at a moment's notice, in places far away from where they had been a second before. But Willibald felt such tricks were beneath his dignity. To him they were a trifle show-offy. *He* traveled from place to place on a donkey. Of course, this took a great deal more time. But no one knew better than he did that he was no ordinary sorcerer, and that his customers would wait.

However, he did have a weakness for service. It was his habit to command pieces of furniture—chairs, tables, footstools, even brooms—to do his bidding. Of course, once in a while a passerby would be frightened out of his wits to see a table capering along the street with a bucket of water on its top. But this didn't happen often. The sorcerer lived 'way on the edge of town on a street that wasn't all fashionable. And he was usually very careful not to let anyone see him work his spells. Not even Fritzl, his apprentice, knew how it was done.

Fritzl was a boy who was learning the sorcery business. He wasn't bright or industrious. He made mistakes, spilled things, and was a general nuisance. In fact, only Willibald's patience saved him from being sent home in disgrace.

---

* *The Sorcerer's Apprentice*, Richard Rostron, illustr. Frank Lieberman (New York: William Morrow, 1941).

Of course Fritzl was very pleased to have most of the unpleasant chores done for him. He didn't have to dust, or sweep, or scrub, or fetch water for the tank in the sorcerer's cellar workshop. Willibald used a good deal of water in his spells. And all this happened in the days before there were such things as faucets and sinks and city water supplies.

But in spite of all this, Fritzl wasn't satisfied. There were times when the sorcerer would go away and leave him to do all the work himself. Fritzl disliked those days terribly. So he decided to learn the spell his master used on the furniture. One day he crept to the top of the cellar stairs and peeped over. Willibald was busy stirring something in the kettle over the fire.

He stopped stirring to reach for a piece of firewood, and then exclaimed, "Out of wood again! That boy! Fritzl! Fritzl!!"

Fritzl trembled, but didn't answer. He was afraid his master would guess that he had been spying.

"Fritzl! Where is that boy? Never here when you want him."

The sorcerer grumbled a bit. Then he stopped stirring, and went over and stood a broom against the wall. He stepped back three paces, and forward two paces, and clapped his hands three times. Then he said, "Lif! Luf! Laf! Broom, fetch firewood!"

The broom immediately appeared to have arms—somewhat thin ones, and rather splintery, but still, arms. It came toward the stairs, hopping and thumping along on its straws. Willibald went back to his stirring, and Fritzl waited till the broom had thumped past his hiding place. Then he quietly crept away. Now he knew the spell, and he felt quite pleased with himself. He wouldn't have to work nearly so hard when old Willibald went off and left him to do everything alone.

There came a day when the sorcerer had to go off on business to the other side of town in a great hurry. In fact, he was almost tempted to travel in a puff of smoke instead of on his donkey. But he remembered in time who he was and soon he and his donkey were clip-clopping down the street. But before he went, he said to Fritzl: "This place is a mess. While I'm gone you set about clearing it out. And be sure to scrub the cellar floor clean. I dropped a spell I was mixing last night, and it's left quite a large stain. I'm expecting a visitor from the Sorcerer's Society of Silesia in a few days and I don't want him to think that I'm in the habit of spilling things. And then don't forget to refill the water tub in the workshop."

You see, Willibald was very vain of the reputation he had of being no ordinary sorcerer. When his master had gone, Fritzl went to work with a broom. He swept clouds of dust—both star and earth—in all directions. Then he started on the furniture, wiping and polishing till everything shone. After that he went downstairs to the workshop and scrubbed the floor there. The stain was very large and very dark, and he scrubbed a long time. By the time he had finished, the water tub was empty. It was a warm day and he had worked very hard. The idea of making many trips to the river with the water bucket didn't appear to him at all.

Then he had an idea: Why not let the broom fetch the water? Of course, if old Willibald found out, he would very likely be terribly angry. But surely the tub would be full by the time the sorcerer returned and no one would ever know. So Fritzl thought, and he wasted no time in thinking any further.

He seized the broom, stood it up against the wall, stepped back three paces, forward two paces, as he had seen Willibald do, then clapped his hands three times and said the magic words: "Lif! Luf! Laf! Broom, fetch water from the river!" He was delighted when the broom's arms appeared and it picked up the water bucket and started—thump-athump-athump!—up the stairs.

Soon it was back, and before Fritzl knew what was happening, it had tilted the bucket and flung the water across the room with a splash. Then it was off again—thump-athump-athump!—before Fritzl could stop it.

The water ran about and got in Fritzl's shoes, which wasn't very comfortable. He thought: "Well, perhaps I didn't think fast enough. When it comes back I'll make it put the water in the tub instead of spilling it out on the floor."

Almost before he knew it, the broom had returned. As soon as it appeared at the top of the stairs with another bucket of water, Fritzl called out: "Don't throw it. Pour it in the tub!"

But the broom paid no heed, flung the water as before, and went off—thump-athump-athump!—for more.

Poor Fritzl was frantic. "Something is wrong here," he thought. "Perhaps I'd better do the job myself and not try to get it done by magic."

And when the broom returned again, he clapped his hands three times and cried: "Lif! Luf! Laf! Broom, stop fetching water!"

But once more the broom paid no heed and flung the water across the room. And again it went off—thump-athump-athump!—for more.

Again and again the broom went back and forth, each time fetching and sloshing out a bucket of water and returning to the river for another. Fritzl became desperate. The water rose higher and higher until it reached his knees. Everything—even the big water tub—started floating around the room. And Fritzl's panic grew and grew. At last he seized an ax and next time the broom came with a bucket of water, he swung wildly and split it down the middle. But instead of stopping, the two pieces went merrily on. Each piece grew another arm, and another bucket appeared from nowhere. Off they went— thump-athump-athump!—to the river.

Higher and higher the flood mounted. The two brooms came and went faster and faster. Fritzl wept and pleaded. He repeated snatches of spells he had heard his master use. He tried to get out of the cellar, but the water had floated the wooden steps out of place. The brooms went on and on and the water rose and rose.

Just as it rose to his chin, Fritzl heard the clip-clop of his master's donkey coming along the street. Then he heard the donkey stop and Willibald coming in the front door.

"Help! Help!" he cried.

Willibald quickly appeared at the top of the stairs.

"What goes on here?" he howled.

Just then the brooms came in with more water and sloshed it down the stairs. Willibald was in the way and his gown was drenched. And there is nothing so angry as a wet sorcerer.

"Help, Master, quick!" poor Fritzl wailed. "I tried to make the broom fetch water, and then it wouldn't stop. Do something, before I drown!"

"Dumbhead!" roared Willibald. "I ought to let you drown. It's just what you deserve!"

As he said this, he jumped hastily aside, for the brooms could be heard thump-athump-athump!-ing into the house. When they appeared, the sorcerer clapped his hands *four* times. Then he gabbled a long string of words. But Fritzl didn't hear them, for just then the water tub bumped against his head. He lost his footing and went under the water with a gurgle.

Next thing he knew, he was lying on the floor coughing and gasping. He looked around him. The water was gone. In fact, there wasn't anything in the cellar that was even wet. The steps were back in their places in the stairs. One broom stood quietly and peacefully in the woodbox, with a bucket beside it. The other broom and bucket had disappeared.

Fritzl looked fearfully up at his master. The sorcerer stood at the top of the stairs, sputtering and fuming with rage.

"Get out of my sight, you blockhead! I've reached the end of my patience! Go on, get out! Go back where you came from!"

And he clapped his hands quite a bit and stamped his foot—the left one—and a puff of smoke appeared on the floor beside Fritzl.

The puff of smoke grew and grew. As it grew, it moved over and covered the apprentice. He shut his eyes in fright. He felt himself being lifted and heard a whistling in his ears like the wind. Then he was dropped with a hard bump. When he opened his eyes, he saw he was in his mother's front yard.

Fritzl lived to be a very old man, but he never saw the sorcerer again. And he didn't want to. In the fine summer evenings he would sit and tell stories to his grandchildren. They liked best the story of old Willibald and the broom. They remembered it and told it to their grandchildren. And *they* told it to *their* grandchildren. And so it has come down to us.

THE MOJO (1956)*

Richard Dorson

There was always the time when the white man been ahead of the colored man. In slavery times John had done got a place where the Marster whipped him all the time. Someone told him, "Get you a mojo, it'll get you out of that whipping, won't nobody whip you then."

John went down to the corner of the Boss-man's farm, where the mojo-man stayed, and asked him what he had. The mojo-man said, "I got a pretty good one and a very good one and a damn good one."

The colored fellow asked him, "What can the pretty good one do?"

"I'll tell you what it can do. It can turn you to a rabbit, and it can turn you to a quail, and after that it can turn you to a snake."

So John said he'd take it.

Next morning John sleeps late. About nine o'clock the white man comes after him, calls him: "John, come on, get up there and go to work. Plot

* *Negro Folktales in Michigan*, collected and edited by Richard M. Dorson (Cambridge, MA: Harvard University Press, 1956). Copyright © 1956 by the President and Fellows of Harvard College.

the taters and milk the cow and then you can go back home—it's Sunday morning."

John says to him, "Get on out from my door, don't say nothing to me. Ain't gonna do nothing."

Boss-man says, "Don't you know who this is? It's your Boss."

"Yes, I know—I'm not working for you any more."

"All right, John, Just wait until I go home; I'm coming back and whip you."

White man went back and got his pistol, and told his wife, "John is sassy, he won't do nothing I tell him. I'm gonna whip him."

He goes back to John, and calls, "John, get up there."

John yells out, "Go away from that door and quit worrying me. I told you once, I ain't going to work."

Well, then the white man he falls against the door and broke it open. And John said to his mojo, "Skip-skip-skip-skip."

He turned into a rabbit, and run slap out the door by Old Marster. And he's running son of a gun, that rabbit was. Boss-man says to his mojo, "I'll turn to a greyhound."

You know that greyhound got running so fast his paws were just reaching the grass under the rabbit's feet.

Then John thinks, "I got to get away from here."

He turns to a quail. And he begins sailing fast through the air—he really thought he was going. But the Boss-man says, "I will turn into a chicken hawk."

That chicken hawk sails through the sky like a bullet, and catches right up to that quail.

Then John says, "Well, I'm going to turn to a snake."

He hit the ground and began to crawl; that old snake was natchally getting on his way. Boss-man says, "I'll turn to a stick and I'll beat your ass."

Told by Abraham Taylor.

THE DO-ALL AX (1957)*

Harold Courlander

No, I don't know as I can tell you anything with magic in it. How you expect I can tell you about magic when they ain't no such thing? Of course, there's two-three exceptions, like those flyin' slaves in the old days. Folks say there was a couple of field hands down around Johnson's Landing who didn't like the way they was bein' treated as slaves, and they just flapped their arms and took off. When last seen they was over the water headed east like a ball of fire.

Then there was that do-all ax. It sure got magic in it, what I mean.

The way it was, in the old days there was a man who had this do-all ax. When it was time to clear the trees off the ground to do some plantin', this man'd take his ax and his rockin' chair and go out and sit down in the shade. Then he'd sing a kind of song:

> Bo kee meeny, dah ko dee,
> Field need plantin', get off my knee.

That ax would just jump off his knee and start choppin' wood without no one holdin' onto the handle or anything. All by itself it went around cuttin' down the timber till the field was cleared. Then it chopped up the trees into stovewood lengths and threw 'em in a pile in the barnyard.

And next thing you know, this ax turn itself into a plow and went to plowin' up the field to make ready for plantin'. And when that's done, the plow turn into a corn planter and plant the corn.

All the time this man who owned it was rockin' back and forth in the shade, fannin' himself with a leaf. Well, that corn was sure-enough magic corn, grew up almost as fast as it went in the ground; little sprouts start to pop out 'fore the sun went down.

'Bout this time the man sing another song:

> Kah bo denny, brukko bay
> Time for dinner, quit this play.

Then the corn planter turned itself back into an ax and stopped workin'.

Well, three-four days later that corn was tall and ready for hoein'. Man went out with his ax, and it turned into a hoe. It went up and down the rows by itself, hoein' corn till the whole field was done. Next week the man came back and the hoe turn itself into a corn knife to cut all them stalks down. You see, the whole job was done just by this here magic ax.

Other folks used to come around and watch all these goin's-on. Everybody figure if only they had an ax like that, life would be a powerful lot better for them.

There was one man named Kwako, who wanted that ax more'n anyone else. Said he reckoned he'd about die if he didn't get that ax. And when there wasn't nobody home one time, this Kwako went in and took it. Figured he'd get his own work done and then bring the ax back and wouldn't nobody know the difference.

He ran home and got his own rockin' chair and went out in the field. Laid the ax across his lap and sang like the other man did:

> Bo kee meeny, da ko dee
> Field need plantin', get off my knee.

Man that ax went to work. Chopped down all the trees, cut the wood up in stovewood lengths, and stacked it by the house. Then it turned itself into a plow and plowed the ground. Then it turned to a corn planter and planted corn. 'Bout the time it was done plantin', the corn sprouts was already pokin' through the ground.

Kwako he was mighty pleased when he see all that. He sat rockin' back and forth in the shade enjoyin' himself real good. So when the corn was all planted he hollered, "That's enough for now, come on home." But corn planter didn't pay no attention, just kept jumpin' all around. Kwako hollered, "Didn't you hear what I said? Quit all this foolishness and come on home." Trouble was, he didn't know the song to stop it. He should have said:

> Kah bo denny, brukko bay
> Time for dinner, quit this play.

But he didn't know the words, and he just kept hollerin', and the corn planter just kept jumpin' every which-way till the seed was all gone. Then it turned into a hoe and started hoein' up the field. Now, that corn wasn't tall enough to be hoed, and it got all chopped into little pieces. Man, that field was a mess. Kwako, he ran back and forth tryin' to catch the hoe, but he couldn't make it, hoe moved around too fast. Next thing you know, the hoe turned into a corn knife and started cuttin' in the air. But wasn't no corn to cut. So it went over in the cotton field and started cuttin' down everything in the way. When last seen it was followin' the settin' sun. After that it was gone for good.

Since that time there hasn't ever been a magic do-all ax in this part of the world, and folks has to do their farmin' the hard way.

But get it out of your head that there's magic things roundabout. What I told you is true, but it's an *exception*.

PART II

The
Rebellious
Apprentice
Tales

Early Tales

ERYSICHTHON AND MESTRA (8 CE)[*]

Ovid

Now Erysichthon's daughter, Mesta, had
that power of Proteus—she was called the wife
    of deft Autolycus.—Her father spurned
the majesty of all the Gods, and gave
no honor to their altars. It is said
he violated with an impious axe
the sacred grove of Ceres, and he cut
her trees with iron. Long-standing in her grove
there grew an ancient oak tree, spread so wide,
alone it seemed a standing forest; and
its trunk and branches held memorials,
as, fillets, tablets, garlands, witnessing
how many prayers the goddess Ceres granted.
And underneath it laughing Dryads loved
to whirl in festal dances, hand in hand,
encircling its enormous trunk, that thrice
five ells might measure; and to such a height
it towered over all the trees around,
as they were higher than the grass beneath.

But Erysichthon, heedless of all things,
ordered his slaves to fell the sacred oak,
and as they hesitated, in a rage
the wretch snatched from the hand of one an axe,

* Ovid, *Metamorphoses*, trans. Brookes Moore (Boston: Cornhill Publishing, 1922).

and said, "If this should be the only oak
loved by the goddess of this very grove,
or even were the goddess in this tree,
I'll level to the ground its leafy head."

So boasted he, and while he swung on high
his axe to strike a slanting blow, the oak
beloved of Ceres, uttered a deep groan
and shuddered. Instantly its dark green leaves
turned pale, and all its acorns lost their green,
and even its long branches drooped their arms.
But when his impious hand had struck the trunk,
and cut its bark, red blood poured from the wound,—
as when a weighty sacrificial bull
has fallen at the altar, streaming blood
spouts from his stricken neck. All were amazed.
And one of his attendants boldly tried
to stay his cruel axe, and hindered him;
but Erysichthon, fixing his stern eyes
upon him, said, "Let this, then, be the price
of all your pious worship!" So he turned
the poised axe from the tree, and clove his head
sheer from his body, and again began
to chop the hard oak. From the heart of it
these words were uttered; "Covered by the bark
of this oak tree I long have dwelt a Nymph,
beloved of Ceres, and before my death
it has been granted me to prophesy,
that I may die contented. Punishment
for this vile deed stands waiting at your side."

No warning could avert his wicked arm.
Much weakened by his countless blows, the tree,
pulled down by straining ropes, gave way at last
and leveled with its weight uncounted trees
that grew around it. Terrified and shocked,
the sister-dryads, grieving for the grove
and what they lost, put on their sable robes

and hastened unto Ceres, whom they prayed,
might rightly punish Erysichthon's crime;—
the lovely goddess granted their request,
and by the gracious movement of her head
she shook the fruitful, cultivated fields,
then heavy with the harvest; and she planned
an unexampled punishment deserved,
and not beyond his miserable crimes—
the grisly bane of famine; but because
it is not in the scope of Destiny,
that two such deities should ever meet
as Ceres and gaunt Famine,—calling forth
from mountain-wilds a rustic Oread,
the goddess Ceres, said to her, "There is
an ice-bound wilderness of barren soil
in utmost Scythia, desolate and bare
of trees and corn, where Torpid-Frost, White-Death
and Palsy and Gaunt-Famine, hold their haunts;
go there now, and command that Famine flit
from there; and let her gnawing-essence pierce
the entrails of this sacrilegious wretch,
and there be hidden—Let her vanquish me
and overcome the utmost power of food.
Heed not misgivings of the journey's length,
for you will guide my dragon-bridled car through lofty ether."

And she gave to her
the reins; and so the swiftly carried Nymph
arrived in Scythia. There, upon the told
of steepy Caucasus, when she had slipped
their tight yoke from the dragons' harnessed necks,
she searched for Famine in that granite land,
and there she found her clutching at scant herbs,
with nails and teeth. Beneath her shaggy hair
her hollow eyes glared in her ghastly face,
her lips were filthy and her throat was rough
and blotched, and all her entrails could be seen,

enclosed in nothing but her shriveled skin;
her crooked loins were dry uncovered bones,
and where her belly should be was a void;
her flabby breast was flat against her spine;
her lean, emaciated body made
her joints appear so large, her knobbled knees
seemed large knots, and her swollen ankle-bones protruded.

When the Nymph, with keen sight, saw the Famine-monster, fearing to
    draw near
she cried aloud the mandate she had brought
from fruitful Ceres, and although the time
had been but brief, and Famine far away,
such hunger seized the Nymph, she had to turn
her dragon-steeds, and flee through yielding air
and the high clouds;—at Thessaly she stopped.

Grim Famine hastened to obey the will
of Ceres, though their deeds are opposite,
and rapidly through ether heights was borne
to Erysichthon's home. When she arrived
at midnight, slumber was upon the wretch,
and as she folded him in her two wings,
she breathed her pestilential poison through
his mouth and throat and breast, and spread the curse
of utmost hunger in his aching veins.

When all was done as Ceres had decreed,
she left the fertile world for bleak abodes,
and her accustomed caves. While this was done
sweet Sleep with charming pinion soothed the mind
of Erysichthon. In a dreamful feast
he worked his jaws in vain, and ground his teeth,
and swallowed air as his imagined food;
till wearied with the effort he awoke
to hunger scorching as a fire, which burned
his entrails and compelled his raging jaws,
so he, demanding all the foods of sea

and earth and air, raged of his hunger, while
the tables groaned with heaps before him spread;
he, banqueting, sought banquets for more food,
and as he gorged he always wanted more.
The food of cities and a nation failed
to satisfy the cravings of one man.
The more his stomach gets, the more it needs—
even as the ocean takes the streams of earth,
although it swallows up great rivers drawn
from lands remote, it never can be filled
nor satisfied. And as devouring fire
its fuel refuses never, but consumes
unnumbered beams of wood, and burns for more the more
'tis fed, and from abundance gains
increasing famine, so the raving jaws
of wretched Erysichthon, ever craved
all food in him, was only cause of food,
and what he ate made only room for more.

And after Famine through his gluttony
at last had wasted his ancestral wealth
his raging hunger suffered no decline,
and his insatiate gluttony increased.
When all his wealth at last was eaten up,
his daughter, worthy of a fate more kind,
alone was left to him and her he sold.
Descendant of a noble race, the girl
refusing to be purchased as a slave,
then hastened to the near shore of the sea,
and as she stretched her arms above the waves,
implored kind Neptune with her tears, "Oh, you
who have deprived me of virginity,
deliver me from such a master's power!"

Although the master, seeking her, had seen
her only at that moment, Neptune changed
her quickly from a woman to a man,
by giving her the features of a man

and garments proper to a fisher-man:
and there she stood. He even looked at her
and cried out, "Hey, there! Expert of the rod!
While you are casting forth the bit of brass,
concealed so deftly in its tiny bait,
gods-willing! let the sea be smooth for you,
and let the foolish fishes swimming up,
never know danger till they snap the hook!
Now tell me where is she, who only now,
in tattered garment and wind-twisted hair,
was standing on this shore—for I am sure
I saw her standing on this shore, although
no footstep shows her flight."

By this assured
the favor of the god protected her;
delighted to be questioned of herself,
she said, "No matter who you are, excuse me.
So busy have I been at catching fish,
I have not had the time to move my eyes
from this pool; and that you may be assured
I only tell the truth, may Neptune, God
of ocean witness it, I have not seen a man
where I am standing on this shore—myself
excepted—not a woman has stood here."
Her master could not doubt it, and deceived
retraced his footsteps from the sandy shore.
As soon as he had disappeared, her form
unchanged, was given back to her. But when
her father knew his daughter could transform her
body and escape, he often sold
her first to one and then another—all
of whom she cheated—as a mare, bird,
a cow, or as a stag she got away; and so
brought food, dishonestly, to ease his greed.

And he lived until the growing strength
of famine, gnawing at his vitals, had

consumed all he could get by selling her:
his anguish burned him with increasing heat.
He gnawed his own flesh, and he tore his limbs
and fed his body all he took from it.

Ah, why should I dwell on the wondrous deeds
of others—Even I, O gathered youths,
have such a power I can often change
my body till my limit has been reached.
A while appearing in my real form,
another moment coiled up as a snake,
then as a monarch of the herd my strength
increases in my horns—any strength increased
in my two horns when I had two—but now
my forehead, as you see, has lost one horn.
And having ended with such words,—he groaned.

THE SAGA OF THE WELL-AND-WISE-WALKING KHAN (CA. 3ᴿᴰ CENTURY TO 11ᵀᴴ CENTURY)*

Rachel Harriette Busk

In the kingdom of Magadha[†] there once lived seven brothers who were magicians. At the distance of a mile from their abode lived two brothers, sons of a khan. The elder of these went to the seven magicians and said, "Teach me to understand your art," and he lived with them for seven years. Though they continually trained him to learn difficult tasks, they were never able to teach him the true key to their mystic knowledge. However, his brother, who came to visit him one day, merely looked through a crack in the door of the apartment where the seven brothers were at work and acquired perfectly the whole *krijâvidja*.[‡]

---

  * *Sagas from the Far East; or, Kalmouk and Mongolian Traditionary Tales* (London: Griffith and Farran, 1873).

  † Magadha was one of the sixteen kingdoms in ancient India. The center was the area of Bihar south of the Ganges. Magadha grew to include most of Bihar and Bengal. The ancient kingdom of Magadha is mentioned in numerous Jain and Buddhist texts and also in some Vedic texts much earlier in time than 600 BCE.

  ‡ Writings concerned with the study of magic.

After this they both went home together, the elder because he perceived he would never learn any thing from the magicians, and the younger because he had learned everything they had to impart.

As they went along, the younger brother said, "Now that we know all their art, the seven magicians will probably seek to do us some mischief. Therefore, go to our stable, which we left empty, and you will find there a splendid steed. Put a rein on him and lead him forth to sell him. Just take care that you don't go in the direction of the dwelling of the seven magicians. After you have sold the horse, bring back the money you will have received."

When he had finished speaking, he went and transformed himself into a horse and placed himself in the stable until his brother arrived. But the elder brother, knowing the magicians had taught him nothing, was not afraid of them. Therefore, he didn't do what his brother had instructed him to do, but said to himself: "Since my brother is so clever that he can conjure this fine horse in the stable, let him conjure another one, if he wants it sold. This one I will ride myself."

Accordingly he saddled and mounted the horse. However, all his efforts to guide the horse were in vain, and in spite of his best endeavors, the horse, impelled by the power of the magic that the younger brother had learned, carried the older brother straight to the door of the magicians' dwelling. Once there he was also unable to induce the horse to go away. Instead the horse persistently stood still before the magicians' door. When the older brother found he could not in any way command the horse, he determined to sell it to these same magicians, and he offered it to them at a great price.

The magicians immediately recognized that it was a magic horse, and they said, among themselves, "If our art is to become this common, and everybody can produce a magic horse, no one will come to our market for wonders. We had best buy the horse up and destroy it."

Accordingly, they paid the high price that was demanded and took possession of the horse and shut it up in a dark stall. When the time came to slaughter it, one of the magicians held it down by the tail, another by the head, and the other four by the four legs, so that there was no way the horse could break away, while the seventh bared his arm ready to beat the horse to death. When the khan's son, who had transformed himself into the horse, realized what the magicians intended to do, he said, "May I quickly transform myself into any kind of living thing that I can!"

Hardly had he uttered the wish when a little fish was seen swimming down the stream. This was actually the khan's son, who had transformed himself. The seven magicians knew what had occurred and immediately transformed themselves into seven larger fish and pursued the little one. When they were very close to the little fish, with their gullets wide open, the khan's son said to himself, "May I transform myself into any other kind of living being."

Immediately a dove was seen flying in the heavens, for the khan's son had transformed himself into the dove. Once they saw what he had done, the seven magicians transformed themselves into seven hawks, pursuing the dove over hill and dale. Once again they were near overtaking him when the dove took refuge in the Land Bede.* Southward in Bede was a shining mountain and a cave within it called Giver of Rest. It was there that the dove took refuge, right in the very bosom of the Great Master and Teacher, Nâgârg'una.†

The seven hawks flew very fast in pursuit of the dove and also arrived at the entrance of Nâgârg'una's cave, where they showed themselves once more as men, clothed in cotton garments. Then spoke the Great Master and Teacher, Nâgârg'una, "Why, oh Dove, are you fluttering so full of fright, and what do these seven hawks have to do with you?"

So the khan's son told the Master all that had happened between himself, his brother, and the seven magicians, and he added these words, "Even now seven men clothed in cotton garments are standing before the entrance of this cave. These seven men will come in and ask the Master for the boon of the *ârâmela*, which he holds in his hand. Meantime, I shall transform myself into the large bead of the *ârâmela*, and when the Master hands the chaplet to the seven men, I beg him to put one end of it in his mouth and bite the string in two so that all the beads shall be set free."

The Master benevolently did just as the khan's son had pleaded. Moreover, when all the beads fell showering on the ground, they were all turned into little worms, and the seven men clothed in cotton garments transformed themselves into seven fowls, who pecked up the worms. But when the Master dropped the large bead out of his mouth on to the ground, it was transformed into the form of a man with a staff in his hand. With this staff the khan's son

---

* Bede is Botha, or Bothanga, the Indian name of Tibet.

† According to Busk, Nâgârg'una was the 15th Patriarch in the Buddhist succession, born in South India, and educated a Brahman; he wrote a treatise on the wisdom of the Buddhist theology and died 212 BCE.

killed the seven fowls, but the moment they were dead they bore the forms of men's corpses.

Then the Master spoke: "You have done something evil. Behold, while I gave you protection for your one life, you have taken the lives of these men, seven of them. By doing this you have done evil."

But the khan's son answered, "To protect my life there was no other means except to take the lives of these seven, who had vowed to kill me. Nevertheless, to testify my gratitude to the Master for his protection, and to take this sin from off my head, I am ready to devote myself to whatever painful and difficult task the Master will be pleased to lay upon me."

"Then," said the Master, "if this is so, I want you to go to the cool grove at the cîtavana,* where you will find the Siddhi-kür.† From his waist upward he is made of gold; from his waist downward, of emerald. His head is of mother-of-pearl, decked with a shining crown. This is how he is made. If you bring him to me from his mango tree, you will have testified your gratitude for my protection and shall have taken off this sin that you have committed from your head. Once you have done this and I have the Siddhi-kür in subjection under me I shall be able to bring forth abundant gold to give lives of a thousand years' duration to the men of Gambudvîpa‡ and to perform all kinds of wonderful works."

"Behold, I am ready to do everything just as you say," answered the khan's son. "Just tell me the way I have to take and how to proceed and what devices I must take."

Then the Great Master and Teacher, Nâgârg'una, spoke again: "When you will have wandered for approximately one hundred miles, you will come to a dark and fearsome ravine where the bodies of the giant-dead are lying. As you approach they will all rise up and surround thee. But you call out to them, 'You giant-dead, *hulu hulu svâhâ!*§ At the same time you will scatter around you these barley-corns, consecrated by the power of magic art, and continue on your way without fear. After you go about another hundred miles farther, you will come to a smooth meadow by the side of a river where

---

   * A burial place.

   † A dead body endowed with supernatural or magic powers (*Siddhi*, Sanskrit, perfection of power).

   ‡ Native name for India.

   § Magic words that have no meaning.

the bodies of the pigmy-dead are lying. As you approach they will all rise up and surround you. But you will cry out to them, 'You pigmy-dead, *hulu, hulu svâhâ!*' and after you spread your offering of barley-corns, you will again continue on your way without fear. After you walk another hundred miles you will come to a garden of flowers with a grove of trees and a fountain in the middle. Here lie the bodies of the child-dead. As you approach they will rise up and run and surround you. But you must cry out to them, 'You child-dead, *rira phad!*' and spread your offering of barley-corns. Then you will continue on your way without fear. Out of the midst of these the Siddhi-kür will rise and will run away from you until he reaches his mango tree, where he will climb up to the top. Then you will swing the axe that I will give you, namely the axe White Moon,* and pretend as though you would really chop down the tree. Rather than let you chop down the mango tree, he will come down. Then seize him and bind him in this sack of many colors, which has enough space for a hundred people. Tie the mouth of the sack tightly with this cord, twisted of a hundred threads of different colors. You will take your meals from this cake that never diminishes. Then place the sack on your shoulder, and bring him to me here. ONLY BEWARE THAT YOU ARE NOT TO OPEN YOUR LIPS TO SPEAK ALONG THE WAY!

"In the past and until the present, you have been called the khan's son, but now, since you have found your way right to the cave 'Giver of Rest,' you will no longer be called the khan's son, but the Well-and-Wise-Walking Khan. Now, be off with you."

After the Master, Nâgârg'una, had given him this new name, he further provided the young man with all the provisions for the undertaking that he had promised him, and, pointing out the way, dismissed him in peace.

BHAVAŠARMAN AND THE TWO WITCHES (CA. 1070)†

Somadeva

"This is my story, but tell me now, my friend, how you came to this inaccessible wood, and why."

---

* The "white moon" was the designated name of the moon in the waxing quarter. In other words, the axe had the form of a sickle.

† Charles Henry Tawney, trans., *The Ocean of Story* (Somadeva's *Kathā Sarti Sāgara*), 1924.

When Nischayadatta was thus requested by the Brahmin Somasvāmin, he told him his story, how he came from Ujjayinī on account of a Vidyādharī, and how he was conveyed at night by a Yakshinī, whom he had subdued by his presence of mind. Then the wise Somasvāmin, who wore the form of a monkey, having heard that wonderful story, went on to say: "You, like myself, have suffered great woe for the sake of a female. But females, like prosperous circumstances, are never faithful to anyone in this world. Like the evening, they display a short-lived passion, their hearts are crooked like the channels of rivers, like snakes they are not to be relied on, like lightning they are fickle. So that Anurāgaparā, though she may be enamored of you for a time, when she finds a paramour of her own race, will be disgusted with you, who are only a mortal. So desist now from this effort for the sake of a female, which you will find like the fruit of the colocynth, bitter in its aftertaste. Do not go, my friend, to Pushkāravatī, the city of the Vidyādharas, but ascend the back of the Yakshinī and return to your own Ujjayinī. Do what I tell you, my friend. Formerly in my passion I did not heed the voice of a friend, and I am suffering for it at this very moment. For when I was in love with Bandhudattā, a Brahmin friend named Bhavašarman said this to me in order to dissuade me: 'Do not put yourself in the power of a female, for the heart of a female is a tangled maze.' In proof of it I will tell you what happened to me. Listen!"

BHAVAŠARMAN AND THE TWO WITCHES

"In this very country, in the city of Vāranasī, there lived a young and beautiful Brahmin woman named Somadā, who was unchaste and secretly a witch. And as Destiny would have it, I had secret interviews with her, and in the course of our intimacy my love for her increased. One day I willfully struck her in the fury of jealousy, and the cruel woman bore it patiently, concealing her anger for the time. The next day she fastened a string round my neck, as if in loving sport, and I was immediately turned into a domesticated ox. Then I, thus transformed into an ox, was sold by her, on receiving the required price, to a man who lived by keeping domesticated camels. When he placed a load upon me, a witch there, named Bandhamochinī, beholding me sore burdened, was filled with pity. She knew by her supernatural knowledge that I had been made an animal by Somadā, and when my proprietor was not looking, she loosed the string from my neck. So I returned to the form of a man, and that master of mine immediately looked round, and thinking that

I had escaped, wandered all about the country in search of me. And as I was going away from that place with Bandhamochinī, it happened that Somadā came that way and beheld me at a distance. She, burning with rage, said to Bandhamochinī, who possessed supernatural knowledge: 'Why did you deliver this villain from his bestial transformation? Curses on you! Wicked woman, you shall reap the fruit of this evil deed. Tomorrow morning I will slay you, together with this villain.'

"When she had gone, after saying this, that skillful sorceress Bandhamochinī, in order to repel her assault, gave me the following instructions: 'She will come tomorrow morning in the form of a black mare to slay me, and I shall then assume the form of a bay mare. And when we have begun to fight, you must come behind this Somadā, sword in hand, and resolutely strike her. In this way we will slay her, so come tomorrow morning to my house.'

"After saying this, she pointed out to me her house. When she had entered it, I went home, having endured more than one birth in this very life. And in the morning I went to the house of Bandhamochinī, sword in hand. Then Somadā came there in the form of a black mare. And Bandhamochinī, for her part, assumed the form of a bay mare, and then they fought with their teeth and heels, biting and kicking. Then I struck that vile witch Somadā a blow with my sword, and she was slain by Bandhamochinī. Then I was freed from fear, and having escaped the calamity of bestial transformation, I never again allowed my mind to entertain the idea of associating with wicked women. Women generally have these three faults, terrible to the three worlds, flightiness, recklessness, and a love for the congregation of witches. So why do you run after Bandhudattā, who is a friend of witches? Since she does not love her husband, how is it possible that she can love you?"

THE MAGICIAN'S APPRENTICE (CA. 1220)*

Farīd al-Dīn 'Attār

When the first prince asks his father to tell him what the princess of the fairies whom he desires so much actually is, the father answers him with a story.

* Hellmut Ritter, *The Ocean of the Soul: Man, the World and God in the Stories of Farīd al-Dīn 'Attār*, trans. John O'Kane with Bernd Ratke (Leiden: Brill, 2003), pp. 640–41.

A man in India has a clever son who early on has learned all the sciences but is especially interested in astrology. In the astrological books he's read about the king of China's daughter and fallen in love with her. In a far-off city lives a famous astrologer and doctor who's stingy with his knowledge, however, and doesn't accept any students. But through a ruse the clever youth figures out a way to smuggle himself into his presence as a student. He makes believe he's deaf and dumb, and the father must convince the master to take on the deaf mute as a domestic servant for the sake of God's reward. To confirm that the youth is really a deaf mute, the master gives him a sleeping potion. But the youth knows how to undo its effect, and once the master has gone out, he runs about the house and makes movements so as not to succumb to sleep. When the master returns, the youth pretends to be sleeping. The master sticks him in the leg with an awl, but the young man controls himself and only makes sounds as one would expect from a deaf mute. And he prudently leaves unanswered the questions of the master. After that he is accepted as a domestic, and he now secretly reads through the master's books and pays close attention when the latter talks about his knowledge. Only there's one chest which he can't examine because the master is careful to keep it locked. The youth is convinced that what he seeks is contained in this particular chest.

One day the master is called to attend on the king's sick daughter. The student, dressed in women's clothes, sneaks into the women's quarters of the palace. The king's daughter has an abscess in her scalp. Sitting inside it is a crab-like animal that's dug its claws into her skin. When the doctor cuts open the swelling and approaches the animal with an instrument, the animal digs deeper into the skin so that the princess cries out in pain. When the student sees this, he can no longer hold back and cries to the master: "You're driving the animal deeper into the skin with the metal instrument. You must burn it with a glowing iron. Then it will let go of her skin!"

When the master realizes he's been deceived, he dies from anger. The student brings the treatment to a happy conclusion, and he's awarded the title of Sarpāysk.

After returning to the dead master's house, he opens the aforementioned chest and performs an incantation following the instructions of a book he finds in the chest. Then after forty days the "fairy-daughter" he's in love with actually appears to him. When he looks at her carefully, he notices that she's

sitting in his own breast. In response to his surprised question, the peri*
informs him: "I've been with you from the first day. I'm your soul (yourself).
You're only seeking yourself. If you look properly, all the world is you."

There follow teachings about the various souls mentioned in the Koran.
In the epilogue of the story the poet says:

"Now, oh son, you're the thing you sought. Everything is in you, but you're
weak at doing work. If you remain manly in God's work, then you're everything and you're a co-habitant of the house. Suddenly, without yourself, you
became lost because you seek yourself on this path. You're your own beloved.
Arrive unto yourself! Don't go out into the field, return to the homeland (to
yourself)!"

MAESTRO LATTANTIO AND HIS APPRENTICE DIONIGI (1553)[†]

Giovan Francesco Straparola

In Sicily, an island that surpasses all others in antiquity, there is a noble city
commonly called Messina, renowned for its safe and deep harbor. It was in
this city that Maestro Lattantio was born, a man who exercised two kinds
of trades and was highly skilled in both. One of these he practiced in public,
namely his trade of a tailor, while the other, the art of necromancy, he did
in secret.

Now, one day Lattantio took the son of a poor man as his apprentice in
order to make a tailor out of him. This young man was called Dionigi, an
industrious and smart fellow, who learned everything as soon as it was taught
him. One day, when Maestro Lattantio was alone, he locked himself in his
chamber and began conducting experiments in magic. When Dionigi became
aware of this, he crept silently up to a crack in the door and saw clearly what

---

* In Persian and Armenian mythology, a peri (pari) is a fairy spirit who has wings and
sometimes appears to mortals. The peri are female and male and have magical powers somewhat comparable to angels and evil spirits.

† "Maestro Lattanzio sarto ammaestra Dionigi suo scolare; ed egli poco impara l'arte
che gl'insegna, ma ben quella' sarto teneva ascosa. Nasce odio tra loro, e finalmente Dionigi
lo divora, e Violante figliuola del re per moglie prende," in *Le Piacevoli Notti*, 2 vols. (Venice:
Comin da Trino, 1550/53).

Lattantio was doing. As a result, he became so entranced and obsessed by this art that he could think only of necromancy and cast aside all thought of becoming a tailor. Of course he did not dare tell his master what he had discovered.

When Lattantio noticed the change that had come over Dionigi and how he had become ignorant and lazy and was no longer the skilled and industrious fellow he had been before and no longer paid any attention to tailoring, he dismissed the apprentice and sent him home to his father. Now, since Dionigi's father was a very poor man, he lamented greatly when his son came home again. After he scolded and punished the boy he sent him back to Lattantio, imploring the tailor to keep him on as an apprentice, and he would pay for his board and chastise him if Dionigi did not learn what Lattantio had to teach. Lattantio knew quite well how poor the apprentice's father was and consented to take back the boy. Every day he did his best to teach him how to sew, but Dionigi appeared always to be more asleep than anything else and learned nothing. Therefore, Lattantio kicked and beat him every day, and more than once he smashed his face so that blood streamed all over it. In short, there were more beatings than there were handfuls of food to eat. But Dionigi endured all this with patience and went secretly to the crack in the door every night and watched everything that Lattantio did in his chamber.

When Maestro Lattantio saw what a simpleton the boy was and could learn nothing that he taught him, he no longer concealed the magic that he practiced, for he thought that if Dionigi could not grasp the simple art of tailoring, he would certainly never understand the difficult art of necromancy. This is why Lattantio no longer shunned Dionigi but did everything in front of him. Of course this pleased Dionigi very much. Even though it seemed to his master that he was awkward and simple-minded, Dionigi was easily able to learn the art of necromancy and soon became so skilled and sufficient that he could perform wonders greater than his master.

One day Dionigi's father went to the tailor's shop and noticed that his son was not sewing. Instead he was performing menial household chores such as carrying the wood and water for the kitchen and sweeping the floors. When he saw this, he was very disturbed and removed him from Lattantio's service and led him straight home. The good father had already spent a fair amount of money so his son would be dressed properly and learn the art of tailoring, but when he saw that he could not prevail upon him to learn this trade, he was very sad and said, "My son, you know how much money I've spent to make a man out of you. But you've never availed yourself of this opportunity to help me. So now I find myself in the greatest of difficulties and don't know how I can provide for you. Therefore, I would appreciate it very much if you could find some honest way to support yourself."

"Father," Dionigi replied, "before anything else I want to thank you for all the money and trouble you've spent in my behalf, and at the same time I beg you not to get upset even though I've not learned the trade of tailoring as you wished. However, I've learned another that is much more useful and satisfying. Therefore, my dear father, calm yourself and don't be disturbed because I'll soon show you how we can profit from this and how you'll be able to sustain the house and family with the fruits of my art. Right now I shall use magic to transform myself into a beautiful horse. Then you're to get a saddle and bridle and lead me to the fair, where you're to sell me. On the following day I'll resume my present form and return home. But you must make sure not to give the bridle to the buyer of the horse. Otherwise, I won't be able to return to you, and you'll perhaps never see me again."

Thereupon Dionigi transformed himself into a beautiful horse, which his father led to the fair and then showed to many people attending the event. All of them were greatly astonished by the beauty of the horse and the feats that it performed. Now just at that time it happened that Lattantio was also attending the fair, and when he saw the horse, he knew that there was something supernatural about it. So he quickly returned to his house, where he assumed the guise of a merchant, took a great deal of money, and went back to the fair. When he approached the horse, he realized at once that it was really Dionigi. So he asked the owner whether the horse was for sale, and the old man replied that it was. Then, after much bartering, the merchant offered two hundred gold florins, and the owner was content, but he stipulated that the horse's bridle was not to be included in the sale. However, the merchant used many words and money to induce the old man to let him have the bridle as well. Then the merchant led the horse to his own house and put him into the stable. After tying him tightly, he began to beat him severely. Indeed he continued to do this every morning and evening until at last the horse became such a wreck that it was pitiful to behold.

Now Lattantio had two daughters, and when they saw how ruthlessly their cruel father treated the horse, they were greatly moved and sympathized with the horse. So every day they would go to the stable and fondle and caress it. One day they took the horse by the bridle and led it to the river so that it might drink. As soon as the horse came to the bank of the river, it dashed into the water at once and transformed itself into a small fish and dove deep down. When the daughters saw this strange and unexpected thing, they were stunned. After they returned home, they began to weep tears, beat their breasts, and tear their blonde hair. Shortly after this Lattantio came home and went straight to the stable to beat the horse as he usually did, but he couldn't find it. Immediately he burst into a fit of anger and went to his daughters who were shedding a flood of tears. Without asking why they were crying (because he already had suspected their mistake), he said to them, "My daughters, tell me everything right away, and don't be afraid."

As soon as the father heard their story, he took off his clothes and went to the bank of the river, where he threw himself into the water and transformed himself into a tunfish. Immediately he began pursuing the little fish wherever it went and tried to devour it. When the little fish saw the vicious tunfish, it was afraid of being swallowed. So it swam to the edge of the river, changed itself into a precious ruby ring, and leapt out of the water right into a basket carried by one of the handmaidens of the king's daughter, who had been amusing herself by gathering pebbles along the river's bank. It was there that the ring remained concealed.

When the maiden returned to the palace and took the pebbles out of the basket, Violante, the only daughter of the king, happened to see the ruby ring. After picking it up, she put the ring on her finger, and it became very dear to her. When night came, Violante went to bed, wearing the ring on her finger, but suddenly it transformed itself into a handsome young man, who caressed her white bosom and felt her two firm little round breasts. The damsel, who had not yet fallen asleep, was very scared and was about to shriek. But the young man put his hand over her lips and prevented her from screaming. Kneeling down before her, he asked her pardon and implored her to help him because he had not come there to sully her name, but was driven there out of necessity. Then he told her who he was and the reason why he had come, how he was being persecuted, and by whom. Violante was somewhat reassured by the words of the young man, and when she saw how charming and handsome he was as he stood in the light of the lamp, she was moved to pity and said, "Young man, in truth you have shown great arrogance by coming here and even greater impudence by touching restricted areas that are off limits to you. However, now that I have heard the full tale of your misfortunes, and since I'm made of marble with a heart as hard as a rock, I am ready and prepared to provide you with any aid that I can honestly give you, provided that you will promise faithfully to respect my honor."

The young man thanked Violante at once, and since dawn had arrived, he changed himself once more into a ring, and Violante put it away in a place where she kept her most precious jewels. But she would often take it out so that it could assume human form and hold sweet conversations with her.

One day, the king, Violante's father, was stricken with a serious disease which could not be cured by any of his doctors, who reported that the malady was indeed incurable. From day to day the king's condition grew worse and worse. By chance the news of the king's malady reached the ears of Lattantio, who disguised himself as a doctor, went to the royal palace, and gained admission to the king's bedroom. Then, after asking the king something about his malady and carefully observing his face, he felt his pulse.

"Sacred king," Lattantio said, "your sickness is indeed grave and serious, but cheer up. You'll soon recover your health, for I know a remedy that will cure the deadliest disease in a short time. So keep up your good spirits, and don't worry."

Thereupon the king said, "Good doctor, if you cure my disease, I shall reward you in such a fashion that you may live according to your heart's content for the rest of your life."

But Lattantio replied that he did not want land or money, but only one single favor. Then the king promised to grant him anything that might be within his power, and the doctor replied, "Sacred king, I ask for no other reward than a single ruby stone, set in gold, which is at present in the possession of the princess, your daughter."

When he heard this modest request, the king said, "If this is all you desire, rest assured that I shall readily grant your wish."

After this the doctor applied himself diligently to develop a cure for the king, who in the course of ten days found that the malady had disappeared. When the king had completely recovered and was in pristine health, he summoned his daughter, and in the presence of the doctor, he ordered her to fetch all the jewels that she had. The daughter did as he commanded, but she did not bring back the one jewel that she cherished above all others. When the doctor saw the jewels, he said that the ruby, which he desired so much, was not among them and that, if the princess were to search more carefully, she would find it. The daughter, who was already deeply enamored of the ruby, denied having it. When the king heard these words, he said to the doctor, "Go away for now and come back tomorrow. In the meantime, I shall speak to my daughter in such a way that you can count on having the ruby tomorrow."

When the doctor departed, the king called Violante to him, and after the two were alone in a room with the door closed, he asked her in a kindly manner to tell him about the ruby that the doctor was so intent on having, but Violante firmly denied that she had it. After she left her father, Violante went straight to her own chamber, locked her door, and began to weep. She took the ruby, embraced and kissed it, and pressed it to her heart, cursing the hour in which the doctor had come across her path. As soon as the ruby saw the hot tears that streamed down from the eyes of the princess and heard her sighs that came from her tender heart, it was moved to pity and changed itself into the form of Dionigi, who with loving words said, "My fair lady, to whom I owe my life, do not weep or sigh on my account, for I am beholden to you. Rather, let us find a way to overcome our anguish. Indeed, this doctor, who is so keen to possess me, is my enemy and wants to do away with me. But since you are so wise and prudent, you will not deliver me into his hands. Instead, when he asks, you are to hurl me violently against the wall, and I shall provide for what may come after."

On the following morning the doctor returned to the king, and when he heard the unfavorable report, he became somewhat disturbed and affirmed that the ruby was in the damsel's hands. In the presence of the doctor, the king summoned his daughter once more and said to her, "Violante, you know full well that, if it had not been for this doctor's skill, I would not have recovered my health. Moreover, he did not request land or treasure as a reward but only a ruby which is said to be in your hands. I should have thought that on account of the love you have for me, you would have given me not merely the ruby but your own blood. Therefore, because of the love I have for you, and because of the suffering your mother has undergone for your sake, I implore you not to deny this favor that the doctor requests."

When his daughter heard and grasped her father's wish, she withdrew to her room. Then she took the ruby along with many other jewels and went back to her father and showed the stones one by one to the doctor. As soon as the magician saw the one that he so greatly desired, he cried out, "There it is!" And he extended his hand to pick it up.

However, when Violante realized what he was about to do, she said, "Stand back, doctor, and you'll get the stone!"

Then she angrily took the ruby in her hand and said, "Now that I realize this is the precious and lovely jewel you've been seeking, I want you to know that I would regret losing it for the rest of my life. So I won't give it to you of my own free will. I am only doing so because my father has compelled me to do it."

As she spoke these words, she threw the beautiful ruby against the wall, and when it fell to the ground, it opened immediately and became a fine large pomegranate, which scattered its seeds on all sides when it burst. As soon as the doctor saw the pomegranate seeds spread all over the floor, he immediately transformed himself into a cock, thinking he could kill off Dionigi by pecking the seeds with his beak. But he was deceived because one of the seeds hid itself and waited for the right opportunity to change itself into a cunning and agile fox, which swiftly pounced on the cock, seized it by the throat, killed it, and devoured it in the presence of the king and princess.

When the king saw all this, he was astonished. But once Dionigi reassumed his proper human form, he told the king everything, and then with full royal consent, he was united with Violante, who became his lawful wedded wife. They lived together many years in tranquility and glorious peace. Dionigi's father rose from poverty to become a rich man, while Lattantio had been killed by his own envy and hate.

THE DECEIVER SHALL BE DECEIVED (CA. 1770)*

Sangendhi Mahalingam Natesa Sastri

Listen, oh you best of womankind! There was a town called Dharmâpurî, ruled by a king named Dharmananda. He regarded the lives of his subjects as his own life, and he reigned with the help of his fellow officers—the ministers, councilors, commanders, captains, and lieutenants—in a fair and just manner. During the fifty years of his prosperous rule there was not even a single day on which he swerved from the Codes of Manu. But for all his charitable

---

* Pandit S. M. Natesa Sastri, *The Dravidian Nights Entertainments: Being a Translation of Madanakamarajankadai* (Madras, India: Excelsior Press, 1886). Based on a Tamil text first published in 1848. The twelve tales in this collection stem from the 17th century and were set in a frame narrative in which Prince Madanakāmarāja falls in love with two young women in a painting. Since he believes they exist, he sends his friend, a minister's son, to find them. Once the friend brings them back, the prince will wed one and allow his friend to marry the other. So the friend begins his journey, discovers the young women, and begins the return trip, Since he does not know which of the young women he will wed, he tells them twelve stories to postpone the decision until he reaches home. The tales were probably disseminated in the 17th century.

disposition, he had not the happiness of a son to his allotment. Of course, this defect was constantly on his mind. He consecrated several shrines to Brahmâ, Rudra, Vishnu, and other Gods; had their festivals regularly conducted; distributed food to the poor; made the sixteen kinds of donations to deserving men; and sent up prayers to God on the three occasions of morning, noon, and evening with the intention of securing a son. Eventually all his devotions seemed to have had an effect, and God gave him a son. Due to his happy news, the king distributed sugar to his subjects, and he brought up his son with tender care. In the third year after this event the king had another son, who was also to be raised with tender care. However, a few days after his birth, an enemy suddenly invaded the town of Dharmâpurî and totally defeated the king, driving him from the town with his wife and children. The king was very vexed at the calamity that came over him, and cursing his own evil star, he went to another town and earned his livelihood there by begging in the streets until his elder son was seven years of age and his younger five. Thinking that it was a sin to ruin the boys without giving them an education, he took them to a distant village, where an old learned Brahmin was keeping a school. He gave the sons over to the charge of that village schoolmaster and addressed him as follows: "These two are my sons. I am extremely poor and so quite unable to pay anything for their education. But if you would kindly educate them, I intend to reward your pains by presenting you with one of these boys."

The schoolmaster agreed to the conditions, and so the king and his queen, after leaving their children there, went away to some other town to pass their days like the lowest of men in begging.

The Brahmin teacher selected the eldest son to do the domestic tasks of grazing the cows and buffalos and educated with all possible means the second son, who duly learnt the four *Védas*,[*] six *Sâstras*, sixty-four varieties of philosophy, the Codes of Manu, and even the objectionable science of jugglery, the magic art of infusing one's own soul into different bodies, and other tricks in which his master the old Brahmin was a great expert. He also acquired from him the faculty of *Jñānadrishti*.[†] Thus he passed several years in study and acquired perfection in one and all the departments of knowledge.

---

[*] The four *Védas*—(1) *Ríg Véda*, (2) *Yajur Véda*, (3) *Sâma Véda*, (4) *Atharva Véda*—are the celebrated holy writings on the religion of the Hindus.

[†] The knowing eye, a faculty of diving into others' inward feelings and motives.

One day, just when he had attained mastery of the science of *Jñānad-rishti*, he experimented with it to see where his parents were dwelling at that time. When he discovered their whereabouts by his newly acquired power, he wanted to go and see them in secret. "They have been separated from us so long that they have forgotten us and are now mere beggars in the streets," he said to himself. "I shall now go and see them and make arrangements to relieve them from their calamity. They may then ask me about my brother. Why doesn't my master educate him but chooses him only to do lowly works? Let me now try to divine his motives by my *Jñānadrishti*."

Thus pondering over in his mind, he thought for a time and exclaimed, "Vile wretch! For henceforth I must only regard you so, as you want to deceive my parents when they come to demand one of us. You also intend to make me sit in the sun as a student who is very careless and never pays any attention whatsoever to his books. Of course, they will choose my elder brother since they will be deceived by his position of a monitor in the class, though he knows nothing. Thus you mean to deceive my poor parents. Oh! I know how to deceive you."

These were the thoughts of the prince—the second son—and they were quite natural. He saw through the evil intentions of his teacher. He wanted to inform his parents about them and waited until nightfall to go to them. And soon night came, and after his duties of the evening as a student were over, he retired to rest or rather pretended to retire for rest. For no sleep could now close down his eyelids since the evil intentions of his master had become clear to him. He, therefore, left his bed and walked out to the public road. To his joy he found the dead body of a kite. So he transferred himself into its corpse, flew at once to his parents, and reached them in the dead of night. Then, resuming his own shape, he awakened them from their slumber. They were surprised at first, and when they were certain that it was one of their sons who stood before them, they kissed their boy and inquired into the welfare of his brother and the way by which he managed to come such a long distance. Their second son hastily related everything to them: how he had acquired all the rare arts, how his elder brother had been ruined, what the master was intending, and how they must act themselves. He also requested them to come soon and reclaim him and not to take the elder brother, who would be quite useless for them. He assured them that he would afterward himself manage to arrange for the rescue of his brother. Having advised his parents in this way, the second son assumed the shape of a kite and flew back that same night to his master's house, where he once again assumed his former shape and fell asleep in a sound slumber.

As soon as the morning dawned, the father-king and the mother-queen set out to the Brahmin teacher's village, which they reached after several days' journey. When they entered his house, the teacher welcomed them with a cheerful countenance and made arrangements to offer them a grand dinner. Secretly, however, he called a student to his side and sent him to fetch the eldest son, who was looking after the grazing cattle. As soon as the boy arrived, the student dressed him up with all pomp and sent him to the school as the monitor of the highest class. And he made the second son sit in the scorching sun as a fit punishment, he said, for not having studied his lessons well.

When the parents saw what was before them, they concluded by themselves that the younger son had told the truth. After the festivities were over, the master was overly hospitable to his poor but royal guests. He extolled the eldest son's high proficiencies and how he had raised himself through his own efforts to a monitor's position in the highest class of the school. The master also spoke very poorly of the attainments of the second son, who had to spend the greater portion of the day sitting in the sun because of his carelessness and stupidity.

The king saw all too well through the tricks of the master. Consequently, he spoke to the Brahmin in this way: "Sir, many thanks for your having devoted so much attention to my first son. I am going to give him to you. Indeed, I think he may not obey me because he has learned too much and may be too proud. I prefer the second son because he is so stupid, and I can make him obey me."

Upon saying this the king took the second son and returned with him to his place. The master was sorely very disappointed so see his own plans ruined and sent the eldest son as usual to look after his cattle.

The old king and queen returned to a certain town with their second son, who now asked for some food. They said that he must fast that night with them, and as soon as morning dawned, they would beg in the streets and give him his breakfast. The son was extremely vexed by the imprudence of his parents, who had never saved anything during all their past period of begging. So he said to them, "My dear father, I am very sorry to see that you have been begging so long without having saved even a single pie for the future. Let what is past be past, and let us no longer think about it. For the present kindly do as I request. The king of this town owns a big cock, and he has been searching for a hen to go with this cock his entire life. But he has not succeeded in procuring one for it. So, I shall transform myself into a hen by the power of the magic art that I have recently learned. When I begin to crow in the morning, people will be attracted to me by my voice and report to the king that there is a hen suitable for his cock. He shall then demand to purchase me. If you ask for one hundred pagodas, he shall match your offer and take me from you disguised as a hen. Then I shall rejoin you later on."

After thus advising his father, the son assumed the shape of a hen and began to crow. Early morning crowds began to collect before the abode of the beggar king. The news reached the ears of the king of that town, who at once came in person to the spot to see the hen reported to be a fair match for his cock. Indeed, his obsession for these fowls had always been very great. The father, who was now the owner of the hen, demanded one hundred pagodas for it, which the king of the town offered without grudging and walked home rejoicing that he had obtained such a good fowl. He handed her over to the fowlers, who put her in an iron basket, which they set over her and placed a weight over the basket. But no sooner had these people left the hen to herself than she—rather the prince in disguise—assumed the shape of a bandicoot. After boring a hole in the ground, he escaped his confinement, crossed all the palace mansions until he reached the outside of the town, and went to the place where his father was staying. The parents had kept meals ready and were waiting for their son. So they were highly pleased to see him return safely. After they first served him his meals, they sat down themselves for their dinner.

Now the king of that country, who had been constantly thinking of that highly expensive hen, ordered his fowlers, as soon as he had some leisure time, to bring the hen to him. When they went for her, they found only a hole in that place. You can imagine their confusion! So they rushed back in anguish and reported the strange phenomenon of a hole in the place of a hen that they had safely secured in an iron basket over which they had put a heavy weight.

The king was extremely vexed by the mystery of his hen's disappearance and cried out: "Is it possible for a bandicoot ever to kill a hen and eat her up? It may kill the hen perhaps, but let us now examine the hole and its tunnels, and where the bandicoot dragged it out to kill."

So thinking, he ordered his men to bring him, at the very least, the murderer of his hen—the bandicoot. Pickaxes, spades, hoes, and crowbars were freely used to dig up all the winding tunnels of the bandicoot's hole until more than half the palace was plowed down. However, all the searching, of course, proved in vain, and the king was doubly mortified and had to deal with new estimates for the repair of his mansion.

Let us turn now to the prince, who was living in peace outside the town with his parents. They took great care of him until every pie of the hundred pagodas was spent. When that sum was exhausted, they informed their son, who was now devising another scheme and said to his father: "There is a rich merchant named Dhanapâla Setti living in this town. He has an only son who prefers walking only instead of riding, which his father compels him to do every day. I shall assume the shape of a Panchakaylyani* horse, and you shall walk with me to the tank side where the merchant's son comes in the morning for his bath. He will take a liking to the horse and ask you what it costs. I want you to demand one thousand pagodas. Then he will conduct you to his father, who will count out the money and then take me to the stables. I shall somehow manage to come away from my confinement."

After giving his father these instructions, the son assumed the shape of a horse and stood before his father neighing most melodiously. The father was extremely delighted by the beauty of the horse, which was no other than his own son, and as instructed he took him to the tank side. The merchant's son came, and just as the prince had already predicted, promised to offer one thousand pagodas for it. So he took the seller with his horse to Dhanapâla Setti, his father. Now, unfortunately, the Brahmin master, who had instructed the transformed prince, happened to be sitting by the merchant's side. As soon as he saw the horse, he immediately grasped that it was no other than the tricky disciple of his who had outsmarted him by using his own art. So he now conceived plans to kill him by using some tricks, and with this evil design in mind, he said to the merchant: "My dear merchant, you only have one son, and since this horse is a very rough and mischievous animal, it's not fit to be used by such untrained riders like your boy. In short, it's not fit for him. And if you or he persist in buying the horse, you'll never see your son's face getting down from it. Therefore, since I know riding better, I wish to have this horse. Please lend me one thousand pagodas, and I shall return the money to you as soon as I return home. You'll soon see yourself the tricks this animal plays."

---

* A horse whose four feet and forehead are white.

Upon saying this, the Brahmin master procured one thousand pagodas from the merchant, and counting them out to the seller, he purchased the horse—that is, his student whom he had hated ever since his father had walked away with him. The master got on top of the horse and began to whip it to the right and left. The horse carried him to all the places that he was driven until it was entirely exhausted. Then the rider took it to a dirty pool to water it and to kill it. The transformed prince saw the evil intentions of his master-enemy, and so he entered the body of a dead fish inside the water, leaving that of the horse. The horse no longer had any life, and hence it fell down. The Brahmin now saw through his *Jñānadrishti* that his student had transformed himself into a fish, and so he called all his pupils and ordered them to pour out all the water in the tank and to kill all the fish in it. As they were executing their master's order, the prince in the shape of the fish became confused. He saw the dead body of a buffalo on the side of the tank that the cobblers had left there while they had gone to fetch their weapons to dissect it. So the prince entered its body and began to run away. The master was watching all the prince's movements, and as he followed the buffalo, he ordered the cobblers to torture it. In his confusion, the prince assumed the shape of a parrot whose carcass he discovered in a tree. So the master took the shape of a kite (*garuda*) and followed him furiously through mountains, forests, thickets, and jungles, until at last both of them reached a town. Since the prince found it impossible to escape the beak of a kite, he flew in the direction of the palace. To his joy the windows of the princess's room were open, and she herself was sitting on her cushion undoing the braids of her hair over her head. When the parrot-prince flew through the windows and fell on her lap, she was extremely delighted. As she lifted the parrot with her hands, she hugged it close to her breast. Then she immediately sent for a goldsmith, and after counting rubies from her treasury, she asked him to make a suitable cage for her parrot. And the goldsmith complied with her wishes. Meanwhile, the kite waited for some time outside the window and indicated by signs that he would take the parrot's life within a week. Afterward, he flew away.

The prince-parrot showed by signs that he *poo-pooed* the idea, for he felt entirely secure in the cage. The princess fondled her pet the entire day, and at night fed it with milk, fruits, and condiments and retired for her usual sleep. At about midnight the parrot left its cage, and after assuming its own form of a prince, he sat beside the sleeping princess, smeared sandal over her body, ate all the sweetmeats that she had left on her table, converted himself again into a parrot, and then quietly dozed away the night in its cage. At about the tenth *ghatikâ** in the night, the princess arose from her deep slumber. It was then that she realized something that had been placed on her without her knowledge while she was asleep. The sandal cup was empty; the contents of the scent boxes had been depleted; her entire body had been rubbed over with sweet scent.

"Who could have done all this in this strictly guarded place? The *Zanâna* is tightly guarded by soldiers and eunuchs. Who could have managed to throw dust into the eyes of all of the guards? Why should that expert man who had managed to cross all the many barriers not draw attention? I shall keep close watch the following night."

So thought the princess, and with that thought the morning dawned. During the day she nursed the parrot as usual, and when it became dark, she retired and kept herself awake until midnight, when she fell unconscious into a deep slumber. The prince-parrot watched how careful the princess was and never left its cage until she was snoring. Then it came out, and resuming its original shape, he rubbed sandal on the sleeping princess's body and went back into the cage. When the princess got out of her bed the next morning, she saw the signs of the shameful act to her body repeated and was very astonished by her own carelessness and the dexterity of the secret frequenter of her room. Consequently, she became fully determined to catch the thief the next night. After she took her little breakfast, she slept the whole day so she could be alert during the night. Despite all her preparations, the parrot kept careful watch.

Before going to bed the princess fed him well, and on rising from her sleep in the evening, she nourished him with milk and fruit. After she had a light supper to keep herself awake, she retired to her bed and covered her body with a blanket from head to toe and pretended to sleep. The parrot-prince watched all her movements. He knew quite well that she was wide awake. So he thought it best to come out of the cage and disclose his secret to her. He was also eager to instruct her about what course to take in the future. Consequently, he came out of the cage and assumed his original form. As he chewed betel and sat next to the princess on her couch, she took hold of his arm, sat up in her bed, and said: "I have watched you separate from your

* *Ghatikâ* is equal to 24 minutes. Since the story is *Hindû*, the *Hindû* mode of reckoning time is maintained in these tales.

parrot's body and assume this princely shape. Now tell me who you are, why you have assumed this shape, and what made you come to me."

The prince then told her about his family, education, and adventures, how his older brother had been ruined, how he had first transformed himself into a hen, then a horse, then a fish, then a buffalo, and at last into a parrot, and how his bitter enemy the teacher pursued him throughout his transformations and teased him. He then addressed the princess as follows: "I intuited that you were to become my wife, and this is why I made secret visits to your bed. Even now, when I knew that you were wide awake, I came to you because I need to instruct you in advance about the course of action you should follow. My master hates me from the very bottom of his heart and has vowed to kill me within a week. Three days have already passed. In four days he will go to your father, the king of this country, with a band of rope-dancers. He will perform before him in such an excellent manner that your father will make up his mind to give him whatever he demands. The master will demand the parrot because his sole intention is to kill me. Your father will send some female servants to you, and they will request that you give them the bird. It's best that you refuse their request. Then they will come again for it. Then you are to break the parrot's neck and place it into their hands. Don't be afraid of having killed me, for I shall then run over to your pearl necklace. The servants will come to you once again and tell you that your father wants the necklace. Then it would be best if you break the necklace into pieces and throw them into the courtyard. Then a miracle will take place, and you'll be able to see it from the top of this mansion."

This was how the prince ended his talk, and the princess was delighted by what her lover had said. Indeed, this is what he must be called from now on, for the princess was enslaved by all his qualities, personal as well as mental, and she sent up prayers to God for his having given her such a noble and clever husband. Everything that the prince had related to her seemed more a fairy tale to her. She was tremendously amazed by all his wonderful accomplishments and was glad after all that the intruder was no one else but him. With an elated mind she slept soundly by the side of the prince that night, and as soon as it was morning, she asked him to assume the shape of a parrot. Five days passed in this way. During the day the prince continued to be a parrot, and during the night he assumed his own shape again.

Soon a band of rope-dancers arrived at the palace portals on the morning of the sixth day, just as the prince had predicted. The king himself was enthusiastic about such entertainment. Therefore, he invited them into the palace and ordered them to perform there. The master and his band of dancers did their tricks so very well that the king was delighted by their performance. After rewarding them with clothes and money, he told them to demand whatever presents they wanted. The chief dancer, who was the Brahmin master in disguise, demanded the princess's parrot. He said that he would not descend from the rope-swing unless the parrot was given to him. So the king sent some maid-servants to fetch the parrot, but they returned with a negative reply from the princess. Nevertheless, the rope-dancer persisted with his request, and the king ordered his daughter to give up the parrot. When the servants went to her with the king's order, she strangled the parrot's neck and threw the pieces into their hands. Upon returning to the king, they placed the bits before him, and though vexed by his daughter's disobedience, he didn't pursue the matter any further,

However, the rope-dancer would not come down from the rope-swing. He now asked the king to give him his daughter's necklace. So the king sent for it, and the princess became so enraged by the pliancy of her father to the words of a rope-dancer that she tore off her necklace and threw the pearls into the courtyard. Then she was unusually astonished by the events that were literally following the prince's words, and she watched what more would take place.

As soon as the pearls fell down into the courtyard, they were all converted to worms. The master used his *Jñānadrishti* and was able to see that the prince was in one of the worms. So he remained on the rope as a man and then assumed another shape as a cock and began to peck at every worm. But the prince, who knew how to use tricks better than the master who had taught them to him, now assumed the shape of a cat and pounced on the cock and caught it by its neck.

The spectators were startled by what they saw, especially when the cock cried for help in a human voice. The cat responded in a younger human voice and cried out that he had to kill his enemy. The king and the other spectators interfered and wanted to know who they were, why they fought in such a beastly shape, and why they had become enemies. So the prince told them everything that concerned his master and himself, while the master acknowledged his evil intentions in front of all the people who had gathered there. He also swore before them that he would give up all such intentions from that day onward because his student had become a better expert than he himself. Consequently, they both returned to their original shapes.

The king was greatly pleased by the beauty of the prince, and he also respected the teacher. When he called the prince to his side, he said: "Even though it was in the shape of a parrot, you stayed with my daughter for one week. So you must now stay with her forever—that is, marry her."

In keeping with the sayings that happy events must be instantly celebrated, the king celebrated the marriage that very day. The master, too, who was overwhelmed by the superiority of the prince, became reconciled with him. Indeed, he gave a grand feast to the royal pair and also gave back the brother, who was still looking after the cows, to the prince. Once the prince reclaimed his elder brother and also received all sorts of presents from his father-in-law, he returned to the country of his birth and prepared for a battle to reconquer it, while his parents also followed him.

The usurper of Dharmâpurî was so unprepared that he thought it best to surrender the kingdom without a fight and did so accordingly. Thus the second son recaptured his lost country Dharmâpurî without a blow. He then educated his elder brother and also had him married to a princess. He ruled over that country for several years, bringing peace and prosperity to the inhabitants.

Thus Buddhichâturya finished his story. Before concluding, he added one sentence. "Shouldn't such a prince be the one to become your husband? Oh my love!" By that time the day dawned and the minister's son and the princess left their bed chamber.

[The moral of the story is that whoever deceives will himself be deceived. We find here that the Brahmin teacher, who troubled and harassed his student—the second prince—was in the end overpowered by his own intended victim.]

Nineteenth-Century Tales

THE NIMBLE THIEF AND HIS MASTER (1819)*

Jacob and Wilhelm Grimm

Jan wanted his son to learn a trade. So he went into a church and prayed to our Lord to ask him what would be suitable for his son. The sexton was standing behind the altar and cried out, "Thieving, thieving."

Afterward Jan went to his son and said that God had told him that he should become a thief. He then set out with his son to look for a man who knew something about thieving. After they had traveled a long time, they reached a large forest, where they found a small cottage with an old woman sitting inside.

"Do you happen to know a man good at thieving?" Jan asked.

"You can learn what you want here," said the woman. "My son's a master thief."

Then Jan talked with her son and asked him whether he was really good at thieving.

"I'll teach your son well," said the master thief. "Come back in a year, and if you can still recognize him, I won't take any money for my services. But, if you can't recognize him, you must give me two hundred talers."

The father went home again, and the son learned all about thieving. When the year was over, the father set out by himself and began to fret because he didn't know how he'd be able to recognize his son. As he was walking along and fretting, he encountered a little man, who said, "What are you worrying about, my man? You look quite gloomy."

"Oh," Jan said, "I hired my son out as an apprentice to a master thief a year ago. He told me to return about now, and if I can't recognize my son, I

* "De Gaudeif an sien Meester," *Kinder- und Haus-Märchen. Gesammelt durch die Brüder Grimm*, 2 vols. (Berlin: G. Reimer, 1819).

must pay him two hundred talers. But if I can recognize my son, I won't have to give him anything. Now I'm afraid I won't be able to recognize him, and I don't know where I'll get the money to pay him."

Then the little man told him to take a crust of bread with him and stand beneath the chimney once he was there. "You'll see a basket up on the crossbeam, and a little bird will peep out of it. That will be your son."

So Jan went there and threw a crust of black bread in front of the basket, and a little bird came out and looked at it.

"Hello there, my son, is that you?" said the father.

The son rejoiced to see his father, but the master thief said, "The devil must have told you how to recognize your son!"

"Let's go, father," said the boy.

Then the father and his son set out for home. On the way a coach came driving by, and the son said to his father, "I'm going to turn myself into a big greyhound. Then you can earn a lot of money by selling me."

Just then a nobleman called from the coach, "Hey, my good man, do you want to sell your dog?"

"Yes," said the father.

"How much money do you want for it?"

"Forty talers."

"Well, my man, that's certainly a lot, but since it's such a good-looking dog, I'll pay."

The nobleman took the dog into his coach, but after they had driven along for a while, the dog jumped out of the coach window. All of a sudden he was no longer a greyhound and ran back to his father.

They made their way home together, and on the following day, there was a fair in the neighboring village. So the boy said to his father, "Now I'm going to turn myself into a handsome horse, and you'll sell me at the fair. But when you sell me, make sure that you take off the bridle so I can become human again."

The father took the horse to the fair, and the master thief came and bought the horse for a hundred talers. However, the father forgot to take off the bridle. So the master thief went home with the horse and put him in the stable. Later, when the thief's maid happened to enter the stable, the horse cried out, "Take off my bridle! Take off my bridle!"

The maid stopped and listened.

"You can talk!" she remarked and went and took off the bridle. Immediately, the horse became a sparrow and flew out the door. Then the master thief also became a sparrow and flew out after him. Soon they met and clashed in a battle in midair. The master lost and fell into the water, where he turned himself into a fish. The boy also turned himself into a fish, and they fought another battle. Once again the master lost, and he turned himself into a rooster, while the boy turned himself into a fox and bit the master's head off. So the master died, and he has remained dead up until this very day.

THE SORCERER AND HIS APPRENTICE (1839)*

Kazimierz Wladyslaw Woycicki

Once there was a poor woman who walked through a dark forest leading her little son by her hand. As she went, she wept because she had many children and little to feed them properly and to raise them in a good way. Suddenly a man who had been sitting beneath an oak tree stood up, and when he saw the hot tears of the poor woman, he asked her why she was crying. When she told him the reason for her sorrows, the stranger comforted her and told her that he was a tailor. However, that was a lie because he was in fact a powerful sorcerer.

Then he took the young boy by his hand and led him into a cave, while he promised his mother to return him to her in three years. So the woman went home with a happy heart, and little Hans began to learn the black art. Indeed the boy soon surpassed the master. When the end of the three years was almost over, the boy escaped from the sorcerer's cave and encountered his mother on a green meadow.

The good mother wept tears of joy when she saw how big and strong her son had become. Then the boy said to her: "Dear mother, in a week the three years that I have served my master will end. Then you must go to the sorcerer and demand my release. In response he'll show you a lot of pigeons and insist that you recognize your son among them. These birds are not really pigeons; rather, they are nothing but young boys that he's taken in as apprentices. When he spreads some peas on the ground for the pigeons, you must pay attention and look for the pigeon that does not eat any of the peas but cheerfully flaps its wings. This one will be your son."

---

* "Der Hexenmeister und sein Lehrling," *Polnische Volkssagen und Märchen*, trans. Friedrich Heinrich Lewestam (Berlin: Schlefinger'sche Buch-und Musikhandlung, 1839).

One week later the mother went to the sorcerer and demanded that he release her son. The old man took a copper trumpet and blew it in all four corners of the world. Suddenly, many pigeons arrived, and the sorcerer spread peas on the ground. While they were all eating, he ordered the woman to pick out her son. The mother looked for the one that was not eating but was hopping joyfully and flapping its wings. Then she pointed to this pigeon with her finger, and the sorcerer correctly returned her son to her.

Well, the boy's father was an honest shoemaker, who lived in great poverty with his large family. One time, Hans, who knew all the arts of magic, said to his father: "I'm going to make you rich, but it won't happen quickly. I'm going to change myself into a cow, then into an ox, and finally into a sheep. Then you are to lead me to the market place and sell me for a tidy sum of money. But you must beware not to enchant me into a horse or to sell the halter with which you will lead me to the market. Otherwise, you'll lose all the earnings you make, and you'll do me harm."

So the shoemaker first enchanted his son into an ox, then into a cow, and finally into a sheep, and each time he did this, he struck a good bargain at the market. He used the money he earned to build a new hut, and from then on he never suffered from hunger. However, in spite of his son's warning, his greed drove him to enchant his son into a horse, and then he led the poor boy to the marketplace, where the sorcerer was already waiting for this moment. He bought the horse and paid so much for it that the wicked father let him have the halter as well.

So this is how the sorcerer was able to catch clever Hans in his net once more. He led him to a stable, tied him with a chain, starved him, and beat him brutally with a whip. The poor little horse groaned in a painful voice until the sorcerer's maid took pity on him. She went into the stable, and the emaciated horse wept and told her his unfortunate story. All this touched her heart, and she removed the chain. Then Hans transformed himself into his natural form and thanked the maiden sincerely. Immediately thereafter he became a sparrow and flew in fear of his master onto the stable roof, where he began to chirp out of joy.

The sorcerer noticed that Hans had fled and recognized the boy in the shape of a sparrow. So he changed himself into a black raven and pursued the poor little bird. The sparrow flew as fast as it could, but the furious raven did not let him rest. Finally, the sparrow fell down into the royal garden. But the enraged raven fluttered over him with its beak wide open. Then Hans transformed himself into a wren, and the sorcerer changed himself into a sparrow as the hunt continued with the same bitterness.

Just about the same time, the princess went into the garden to take a walk, and as soon as she noticed this battle, she thought to herself: "Dear God! What is going on between these two small birds? Why are they such enemies? That will lead to war throughout the world!"

Since Hans had now exhausted all his living energy and could no longer escape the furious sparrow, he changed himself into a beautiful ring and jumped onto the princess's finger. The sparrow searched for him in vain until he finally discovered the wren's trick and was determined to use any possible means to get him in his power.

No sooner had the princess returned to her chamber than she was amazed to perceive the beautiful ring, and lo and behold! the ring changed itself at the same time into the handsome Hans. Then the young man told her about his sufferings and warned her about the sorcerer, who would appear at the court the next day richly dressed as a prince and with a large retinue and would ask the princess to show him the ring.

"If the master gets hold of the ring," he continued his story, "then I shall be done for. It would be best, if he insists on seeing the ring, that you throw it on to the ground with all your might."

Everything happened just as he said it would. The next day the sorcerer came to the court dressed as a prince and with numerous servants. He was led into the hall, and as soon as he was introduced to the princess, he asked her immediately to show him the ring. However, the princess, who had taken a great liking to Hans, did not even want to extend her hand with the ring on it to the sorcerer so that he could kiss it. Since he began to insist, she vehemently threw the ring on to the ground. Then the ring burst into a large amount of peas. The sorcerer blew on his copper trumpet to all four corners of the world, and a large swarm of pigeons came and began eating the peas. But one pea shoved itself into the white hand of the princess. Then she threw it on the ground, and a large amount of black poppy seeds sprang from this pea.

So the sorcerer blew on this copper trumpet toward all four corners of the world once more, and a large amount of sparrows came flying. And since the sorcerer wanted the seeds to be eaten as quickly as possible, he changed himself into a sparrow as well.

This is what Hans had been waiting for, and he immediately changed himself into a raven and bit the sorcerer to death. Then he carried parts of his body to the four corners of the world so that they could never grow back together again.

Now the princess chose the handsome Hans for her husband. After the wedding there was a splendid meal. People ate and drank well into the late evening. I, too, was there and ate and drank so much that everything dripped from my chin.—But take a look! Now my mouth is completely empty.

THE DEVIL AND HIS PUPIL (1845)*

Arthur and Albert Schott

A farmer, to be sure one of the few whose plow had earned him enough money that he could put away in his chest, used all that he had earned to send his only son far away to study in a famous city. After his son had completed his studies, he returned home. But as it frequently happens, he soon showed that he now did not understand how to live without a good deal of money. Since all the farmer's savings had been depleted, the father didn't know what else to do but now to have his son practice his own profession and work the land with his plow. Yet, the young man didn't agree to this at all, and therefore, he proposed to this father to allow him some time until he had learned the black art. After that he'd easily manage to generate some money in some way. At first the father didn't want to give his consent, but after a while he yielded and went with his son to look for the devil. After they had traveled a good distance, they encountered the devil himself along the way, and he asked them where they were going,

"To see the devil."

"And what do you want when you get there?" came the second question.

The father answered, "My son wants to learn the black art."

The stranger laughed and said, "Well then, give him to me. I am the devil himself!"

"And what must I pay you to have my son spend one year in your school?" the farmer responded.

"If you can recognize your son after one year has passed," the devil answered, "you can take him back with you without paying for his apprenticeship. However, if you don't recognize him, he will remain mine."

---

* "Der Teufel und sein Schüler," *Walachische Märchen* (Stuttgart: J. G. Cotta, 1845).

The farmer felt some concern about all this. So he waved his son to come to his side and whispered: "Look, my son, one long year, and the devil's school will distort you so that I won't be able to recognize you, and then you will belong to the devil forever."

"Oh, don't be afraid, father," the son replied. "I'll give you a signal that will easily help you recognize me among many others. I'll simply bend my index finger on my left hand, and then you'll be able to see that I am the one that you've been looking for."

And this is also what happened when the father went to the devil's school one year later to fetch his son. However, the devil asked the father to let him keep his pupil one more year and promised to teach him even more than he had learned. Well, the father and son agreed, and since the same condition was to count as before, they arranged a secret signal once more so that the father would be able to recognize his son, who intended to scrape the ground with his foot when his father came back to the devil's school after one year.

So another year passed, and the farmer appeared at the devil's school to select his son from the many young men who were studying there. The secret signal worked once more, but when the father wanted to take his son away, the devil asked him whether he'd let his son stay one more year so that he could learn three more spells in addition to those that he now already knew. So the father and son discussed this proposal by themselves, and the son said: "Father, when you come to fetch me after a year, the devil will not let you enter the school out of precaution. Instead, he will send each one of the pupils outside separately. Well, I'll brush you with my clothes as I walk by you so that you'll easily be able to recognize me."

When the farmer agreed to this signal, he gave his son to the devil for a third time and departed.

After a year had passed the farmer appeared at the door of the devil's school and demanded his son. In response the devil shoved each one of the pupils, one after the other, through the door. When the farmer's son came, he brushed his father with his clothes so that the farmer immediately recognized him. Then he demanded that the devil release his son to him, and he did this, too, even though he was highly annoyed.

When the two of them had returned home, the son said: "Father, now I know how to make some money!"

Since the father wanted to know how, the son said: "I'm going to transform myself into an ox greater and more beautiful than any other ox in the world.

Then you will bring it to the market to sell it. Many buyers will come, but you are not to sell it for less than two large buckets of ducats. In addition you must remember not to give the rope away when you sell the ox!"

Upon saying all this, the son transformed himself into a huge beautiful ox, and when it became known that this animal was for sale, a large crowd of buyers gathered together around the ox at the market. But when they learned that they would have to spend so much money to buy it, they quickly left. Finally, a group of traveling actors came and bought the wondrous animal that they wanted to exhibit for money, and the farmer rushed home with two large buckets of ducats.

Meanwhile, the actors set up a tent and crowned the ox with garlands. They intended to show the ox at an evening performance when there would be many people eager to see the animal. However, in the meantime, the wondrous ox had returned to its human form behind the curtain and had scampered away as fast as it could. When the curtain was raised after this, there was great confusion and consternation. Everyone began yelling, "Fraud! Fraud!" They all wanted their money returned to them, spectators and actors, and the ridicule of the crowd was mixed into this so that the authorities had to intervene and sort things out.

In the meantime the father and his son lived comfortably from the two buckets of ducats and didn't think about earning anything more until their entire treasure was depleted. Then the son spoke to his father again: "Dear father, I'm now going to transform myself into a horse more beautiful than any other horse in the entire land. The devil will be among the many buyers who come to the market, but don't sell the horse for anything lower than six buckets of ducats. In addition, don't forget to remove the bridle when you sell me. Otherwise, I won't be able to return any more!"

After he had spoken these words, there was indeed an extraordinarily beautiful horse standing in front of the old farmer, who took it to sell at the fair in the neighboring city. There were many interested buyers who appeared, but few who could pay the enormous price of six buckets of ducats. Finally, the devil appeared just as the son had predicted. He bought the horse, paid the six buckets of ducats, but he absolutely wanted the bridle and, after the sale, he refused to leave until he obtained it. The farmer, who had already grown fond of so much gold, listened to the remarks of people in the crowd who felt that the bridle was meaningless in such an enormous sale, and so he finally gave into the devil.

Now the devil rode home and was highly pleased. Along the way he spurred and whipped the horse and mistreated it instead of feeding it properly and giving it water to drink. Soon after he arrived home there was a devil's wedding, and the devil, who owned the horse, sent his son on it with the instructions neither to feed nor give water to the horse. All the young devils who went to the wedding on horseback did all the things that young people usually do. And especially at such an event as this they didn't ride to the wedding slowly. They rode their horses at breakneck speed until they sweated, and this is why they rode them through a brook and let them drink the water except for the horse of devil's son who had been forbidden to do this. However, his companions convinced him to do it. "Otherwise," they said, "you will trail far behind us with your thirsty, emaciated nag, and you will be dishonored at the wedding."

All these remarks led the young devil to allow his horse to drink some water. However, the horse had hardly swallowed the water between the bit than he changed himself into a small gudgeon fish. And to the astonishment of his companions, the young devil sat on the water instead of on the saddle, while the gudgeon swam away.

The old devil, who saw all this right away thanks to his command of the black art, came as quickly as he could and swam after the gudgeon. Since the little fish had such an early start, he encountered another fish and said: "Dear fish, when you continue swimming in this direction and you come upon a devil, then tell him, when he asks about me, you had swum from the depths and hadn't seen me."

The fish promised him he would do this, and when the devil really came swimming toward it and asked about the gudgeon, the small fish kept its word by saying: "I haven't seen a gudgeon and have just come from the depths of the water."

Upon hearing this, the devil turned around and swam upstream until he came to the source of the water, and when he didn't find the gudgeon there, he turned around and swam downstream again as fast as lightning so that he was close to catching the gudgeon. When the gudgeon saw, however, that the devil was about to catch him and that he had no more time to lose, he changed himself into a beautiful gold ring and jumped onto the finger of the emperor's daughter, who was standing on the banks of the brook and bathing herself at that moment.

"I implore you, most beautiful princess," he said to her, "do not surrender me to the devil!"

No sooner did he say these words than the devil approached the astonished emperor's daughter. He declared to her that the ring that had just
jumped onto her finger belonged to him, and he demanded it from her. But
the princess boldly replied that she didn't have one like that. The ring that
she had on her finger had been hers for some time. Thereupon, she turned
her back on him and returned to her father's palace.

The devil, who insisted on having the ring on her finger, followed her
and revealed his great desire to have to the ring to the emperor, whom he
promised to give all possible kinds of wealth and treasures. Meanwhile, the
ring spoke to the princess along the way and said: "Dearest, most beautiful
princess, do not surrender me to the devil until he builds a golden bridge on
which beautiful green trees flourish with a golden fountain in the middle.
Once there, tell him you'd like to hand me over. However, don't place me in
his hand. Instead, throw me on the ground."

The princess noted all that he had said, and when her father, the emperor,
pressed her to give the ring to the devil, she did what the ring had told her
to do.

No sooner did she express her wishes to the devil and her father than a
beautiful golden bridge with a fountain in the middle arose in the courtyard
below them, and on both sides there were glorious green trees. The emperor
and the empress along with the princess went downstairs in order to observe
this miracle more closely. Also the devil followed them, expecting the ring.

When the princess, as promised, was to give over the ring to the devil
at the fountain and he greedily approached her, she let the ring fall to the
ground. During the fall, however, the ring transformed itself into numerous
seeds of fruit spread all about. When the devil saw this, he transformed
himself into a chicken and began pecking and eating the seeds as fast as it
could. One seed, however, that fell into the princess's shoe transformed itself
into a lapwing, which constantly flew around the chicken and hacked out its
eyes and brains so that he soon was able to fly better than the chicken. Then
the lapwing bit the chicken to death, and he took on his human shape again
and appeared as a handsome young man before the astonished royal couple
and their daughter, the princess, who was more than happy that she had
courageously stood by the handsome stranger. The emperor and the empress
and all the other people present at this incident were very curious to hear
the story about this unusual stranger's life and therefore invited him to come
into the castle and tell it. Of course, he did this willingly, and he told about
the devil's school that he had attended and how he had constantly managed

to evade the devil and about all the other adventures that we already know. Immediately thereafter the emperor did not hesitate to give his daughter to the farmer's son, who was smarter than the devil, as his wife. The princess had no objections to this, nor did the young man, and the story tells that the emperor was always satisfied with his son-in-law as long as he lived because he gave him the best advice in all his affairs. After the emperor's death, the young man took over the throne and scepter and ruled with his dear wife for many years in pleasure and happiness.

THE MAGIC COMBAT (1857)*

Ludwig Bechstein

Once there was a young journeyman, a bookbinder by trade, who went off to see foreign places. He wandered for a long time and took in the large beautiful world. He wandered until there wasn't a single penny jingling in his pocket. So his slack wallet finally strained and compelled him to begin looking seriously for some work. Soon thereafter he was hired by a master bookbinder, and the conditions for work were very agreeable.

"You'll have it good in my place, boy!" the master said to him. "The daily work here is slight. You're to wipe all the books clean every day and then put them back in the same order. But you're not to touch this small little book standing here off to a side, much less to look inside it. Otherwise, things will go bad for you, my fellow. Remember this! As far as the other books are concerned, you can read them as much as you like."

The journeyman took his master's words very much to heart, and for two years he spent the best time cleaning the books every day. He also read many of them and in the process had the finest fare and didn't touch the forbidden little book at all. Consequently, he won the complete confidence of his master so that the bookbinder often stayed away from the house for the entire day and sometimes took longer trips. Now, when the master went off for several days, the journeyman felt a great longing, as is always the case with the human heart that desires to explore the forbidden in life, to know finally what was in the little book, which constantly stood in its designated and sacred place, for he had already read through the other books. To be sure his conscience

* "Der Zauber-Wettkampf," *Deutsches Märchenbuch* (Leipzig: Hartleben, 1857).

resisted this desire to do the forbidden, but his curiosity was stronger. He took the little book, opened it, and began reading in it. Soon he saw that the little book contained the greatest and most valuable secrets, and the most powerful magic formulas were also included. Gradually the astonished young man, who at first was extremely dazzled, was able to sort things out so that they were as clear as daylight, and he began right away to make attempts to perform magic. Indeed, he succeeded in everything. Whenever the young man uttered a powerful magic spell from the little book, his wish was immediately fulfilled. In addition, the little book taught him how to transform himself from one shape into another. So he kept trying things out until he finally changed himself into a swallow, took the little book, and flew to his home in the twinkling of an eye. His father was completely astonished when a swallow flew through his window and suddenly transformed itself into his son, whom he had not seen for two years. Then the young man embraced the old man warmly and said: "Father, now we are fortunate and secure. I've brought a little book of magic with me, and by using it we can become the richest of people."

The old man was pleased by this, for he lived very meagerly. Right after this the young magician transformed himself into an extraordinarily large and fat ox, and he said to his father: "Now take me to the market and sell me, but I want you to demand a good deal, and I mean a good deal of money. People will pay tons for me, and don't forget to untie the little piece of rope that's tied on my rear foot and take it home with you. Otherwise, I'll be doomed."

The father did as he was told, and when he appeared at the marketplace with only the ox, a large group of people gathered around him, and he sold the animal for a good deal of money. Everyone admired the rare ox, and Christians and Jews fought with one another to buy the beast. The man who purchased the ox, however, and who had made the highest bid, paid the price, and led the ox away in triumph. Then the next morning he found a bundle of straw lying in his stall instead of the marvelous ox. And the young journeyman was once again at home with his father in good spirits, and he lived with him wonderfully and joyously profiting from the round gold coins they had earned.

Soon thereafter the young man cast a spell and changed himself into a splendid mare and had his father take him to the horse market to sell. People gathered again to see the marvelous glistening steed. In the meantime the master bookbinder had returned home from his trip and realized right away what had happened, and since he wasn't actually a bookbinder but a powerful magician, who only pretended to practice this trade, he also knew immediately just what the score was and set out after the young journeyman. So now the master arrived at the horse market and was among the buyers, and since he knew each and every sentence of the little book, he perceived right away the reason why the horse was there and thought: "Stop, now I'll catch you."

So he sought to buy the horse no matter what the price was, and he succeeded without much effort because he was ready to pay the first high price. The father didn't know the buyer, but the horse began to tremble intensely and to sweat and behaved extremely shyly and anxiously. Nevertheless the father could not sense his son's desperate situation that had now become dangerous. When the horse was led into the new owner's stall and was put into the place reserved for it, the father wanted to take off the little piece of rope. But the buyer didn't allow him to do this because he knew that if he did, he would lose what he had just caught. Consequently the father had to depart without the little piece of rope and thought to himself: "My son will know how to get himself out of this jam. If he knows how to change himself into a horse, then he can certainly use his magic art once again and find a way to break loose and return home."

Now there was a huge crowd of people, big and little, old and young who filled the horse's stall. They all wanted to gaze at the excellent beautiful steed. A plucky little boy dared to stroke and fondle the horse, and the horse let itself, so it seemed, be caressed. And when the little boy came closer to the horse in a friendly way and stroked the horse on its head and neck, the horse whispered very quietly to the boy: "My dearest boy, do you happen to have a little pocket knife with you?"

And the astonished boy, who was very happy about this, answered: "Oh, yes, I have a very sharp one."

So the mare said once again very quietly: "Cut off the little rope on my left rear hoof."

And quickly the boy cut the rope in two.

Immediately thereafter the beautiful horse vanished before the eyes of everyone present and a bundle of straw stood in its place. Then a swallow flew out of the stall and up high into the blue sky. The master had let the horse out of his sight for just a brief moment, and now there was no time to lose. He used his art to change himself rapidly into a vulture and zoomed into the sky to chase the fleeting swallow. Within only a short time the vulture had the swallow in its claws, but the little swallow was aware of his enemy, and it looked down upon the earth and saw that there was a beautiful castle right beneath them. There was also a princess sitting in front of the castle, and without delay the little swallow transformed itself into a golden ring, fell down, and landed right on the lap of the princess. She had no idea how that happened and stuck the little ring on her finger. However, the vulture's sharp eyes had seen everything, and the master magician speedily changed himself into an elegant squire, approached the princess in a refined way, and requested politely and humbly to have the little ring with which he had just performed a trick. He told her he'd be pleased to have her hand it back to him. The beautiful princess blushed and smiled. She took the little ring from her finger and wanted to hand it to the artist. But, lo and behold, it slipped from her tender finger and rolled into the crack of a stone as a tiny millet seed. In a split second the squire transformed himself into a proud rooster that began busily pecking in the stone's crack with its beak. But just at this point, the millet seed became a fox, which bit off the rooster's head. And this was how the master magician was defeated. Now the young journeyman changed back into his human form, sank to his knees before the princess, and praised her gratefully for putting him as a ring on her finger. He also added that, by doing this, she had become engaged to him. The princess was greatly shocked by all that had just happened, for she was still very young and inexperienced. So she granted him her heart and hand but under the condition that he would not do any more changing and would remain true to her without any transformations. The young man swore an oath to her and sacrificed the little book of magic by throwing it into a fire. But by doing this, dear reader, he did something bad, for in the end he could have bequeathed it to you or to me as a gift.

THE TEACHER AND HIS PUPIL (1864)*

Johann Georg von Hahn

Once upon a time there lived a king and a queen who could not produce any children. Well one time a demon in disguise came to them and promised the king that they could have children if the king would give him the oldest among them. The king was satisfied with this offer, and the demon pulled

---

* "Der Lehrer und sein Schüler," *Griechische und albanische Märchen*, vol. 2 (Leipzig: W. Engelmann, 1864).

out an apple, cut it into two slices, and gave him one and the queen the other to eat. Soon thereafter the queen gave birth to three sons one after the other.

The king, however, regretted that he had made a promise to the demon. Therefore, he had a tower made out of pure glass and put his children inside it. Then the demon said to him: "If you don't keep your word and don't give me your son, then I'll bend over and shine so that their hearts will burn."

When the three boys had grown up, the eldest asked his father to let him leave the tower and go out into the world and see his father's glorious kingdom. However, the king denied him this request because he was afraid of the demon. Yet his sons grew more curious from day to day and wanted to see the world. So one time they secretly left the tower to explore the surroundings a bit.

As they ran about cheerfully and were in a good mood, a huge storm erupted with thunder and lightning and covered everything in pitch-black darkness. The storm scooped up the oldest son and carried him away. So the other two brothers ran to their father and told him what had happened. Then the king in his grief had his castle painted black and announced that no one would be allowed to sing and dance any more in the city. From then on, all the people were to mourn.

Meanwhile, the demon led the oldest son to a wasteland, where he pounded the ground with his fist so that the earth immediately opened, and the two of them began to descend until they came to the demon's home, which consisted of forty rooms. The demon treated the boy as if he were his very own son. He fed him all kinds of wild game and gave him the keys to thirty-nine rooms and allowed him to enjoy all the different kinds of treasures that were piled up in them. He also gave him a book to read, and when the boy, now a young man, had learned his lessons very well, the demon hugged and caressed him.

One day, the demon said, "Come here and delouse me a bit."

As he was doing this, the young man discovered a small golden key tied to the demon's forehead. He guessed right away that it was the key to the locked door, and during the night he took the key from the demon's head and opened the door. Once inside he found a beautiful maiden who shone like the sun, but she was hanging in the room by her hair. So the young man untied the hair and set her loose, and she kissed and hugged him. Then she cried out: "Oh, you poor young man! How did you get here? My time is now up, and so the demon will replace me with you and hang you. In the end he will eat us both. Did he give you a book that you were to memorize? And didn't he already ask you whether you knew it by heart? Well, if he continues to ask you, you must tell him that you couldn't learn it. As for me, you must let me hang at the place where I was."

The young man did what the maiden instructed him to do. He locked the door of her room and tied the key to the demon's head again. The next morning the demon gave the book of lessons to the young man, and when the young man retuned in the evening, the demon asked him: "Have you learned your lessons well?"

And when the young man replied that he hadn't learned them, the demon became angry, and instead of giving him dinner, he gave him a good beating. In the evening the young man fetched the key again from the demon's forehead, and he went to the maiden, untied her, and gave her some water.

"You must make an effort," she said, "to memorize the entire book as much as possible. But you must pretend, when you are with the demon, that you can't accomplish this. Then, when you have learned the entire book by heart, you're to come and fetch me because, if we were to stay here, we'd be lost."

Now the young man made every effort to memorize the entire book as fast as possible without letting the demon notice anything. Because he was accused of laziness, he tolerated the demon's beatings patiently, and after he had learned the entire book by heart, he prepared a shell with salt, a piece of soap, and a comb just as the book instructed him to do, and he took a large bag of gold coins with him. That night he fetched the key from the demon's forehead and went to the maiden. After he untied her, he gave her a slap and changed her into a mare. Then he mounted her and rode away as fast as he could.

The next morning the demon looked for the young man in vain, and as he was doing this, he discovered that the maiden had also disappeared. Therefore he transformed himself into a wolf and pursued her and the young man. When he approached them, the mare said to the young man: "What are you gaping at?! Throw the shell with salt at him!"

After the young man did this, a huge fire arose with thick smoke that prevented the wolf from following them. Now the young man had a head start. After half an hour had passed, the mare asked the young man: "Do you see whether anything is coming after us?"

As the young man looked backward, he answered: "Yes, I see a sinister wolf following us up the mountain."

"Quick! Throw the soap at him!" yelled the mare.

Then a large stream of water arose and prevented the demon from following them.

Once again, after an hour had passed, the mare asked once more: "Do you see anything coming toward us or following us?"

"Yes," he said. "I see a wild boar grunting and running after us."

Then the mare ordered him to throw the comb at the boar, and a swamp arose from the comb. Then the boar charged into the swamp and tossed and turned in it. And this is how the young man escaped the demon along with the maiden.

Now the young man rode to the city in which his father was living, and when he dismounted, he gave the mare a slap, and she was immediately transformed into a maiden. Thereupon, the young man said to her, "You are single, and I'm single. So let's join together in marriage."

She told him that she was content with his proposal, but she thought that each one of them should first visit their parents. Then she took a ring from her finger and gave it to the young man. Immediately thereafter each took half a sack of the gold coins and went off to visit their parents.

However, the young man didn't return to his father's castle. Instead, he went to an old woman and said to her: "Good evening, little mother! Would it be possible to spend the night here?"

She agreed but told him that she didn't have any bed sheets. So, he gave her a handful of gold coins so that she could obtain whatever was necessary. And after the old woman had taken care of everything for eating, drinking, and sleeping, he said to her before he went to bed: "Early tomorrow morning I'll be transformed into a mule, and you are to take me and bring me to the market and sell me. But you are not to sell the halter, which you must bring back to your home with you. And when they ask you how much you want for the mule, you must say: 'I want what it's worth,' and you are not to take anything less than six thousand drachmas for it."

The next morning the old woman brought the mule to the market and sold it for six thousand drachmas and kept the halter. As she went home the young man came running after her, for he was the halter. So she continued to do this day after day, and the old woman earned a good deal of money with him.

However, one evening the young man said: "Early tomorrow morning I am going to transform myself into a bathhouse that will stand opposite the king's castle, and when you sell this bathhouse, you are not to include the key in the sale. You are to pretend that the bath and your house have only one key, and that you are an old woman and don't have any other key to your house except this one. If you were to sell or give away the key, then I would be lost."

When the old woman stood in front of the bathhouse the next day, the demon approached her in the form of a man and bought the bathhouse from her for fifty thousand drachmas. However, she sold it only under the condition that she could keep the key because it was the key to her house, and the buyer was content with this. Then, when the old woman had left and taken the key with her, the demon went into the bathhouse and said to him: "Now I shall ruin you."

"Tomorrow morning," answered the bath, "you will be rolling like a pig in its own excrement."

And the next morning the demon was stuck on the spot where the bath had been, and he was covered with excrement from head to toe.

Now when the young man returned to the home of the old woman, he revealed to her that he was the king's son, and as soon as she heard this, she bowed in front of him and kissed his hand. Then she promised him that she wouldn't tell anyone else all that she had seen him perform. Meanwhile, he went into the royal garden and transformed himself into a pomegranate which was so large and heavy that the tree on which it was hanging could hardly support it. When the king took notice of this pomegranate, he picked it and placed it on a little bench in his room.

Now the demon transformed himself into a human being, went to the king, and said: "I have come to bring you greetings from your eldest son, and if you should have a pomegranate, he requests that you send it to him because he is sick and has a great longing for this fruit."

When the king heard this, he ordered his maid to fetch the large pomegranate and give it to the man. But just as she was reaching out to hand the pomegranate to the demon, it fell to the ground and splintered into many small pieces so that all the seeds were spread out on the ground. Immediately the demon transformed himself into a hen with its chicks, and they began to peck and eat up all the seeds. Now, however, the final seed was the eldest son, and he transformed himself into a fox and devoured the hen with all her chicks. Yet, after he had done all this, he noticed that he had become blind in both eyes. Immediately thereafter he changed himself back into his own shape and said to the king: "I am your son whom the demon had stolen from you," and he told him his entire story.

On the one hand, the king was extremely pleased that he had found his son again. On the other, he was distressed that his son had become blind. Nevertheless, the king held a great celebration to honor the return of his son, and it lasted for five days.

After the celebration the blind young prince wanted to search for his bride, and his father said to him: "Oh, my son, you have been away from me for such a long time, and now, after five days, you want to leave me again?"

Then his son told his father about the maiden to whom he was engaged and that he wanted to set off and bring her back home. After saying this, he set out on his journey. Once again, however, the king began to mourn and had his entire castle painted black once more.

Now we want to see what happened to the maiden after she had returned to look for her father. Along the way she was followed by a darling little dog, and she liked it so much that she took the pup with her. After five days, however, it became blind, and when the maiden jumped over a brook, the little dog wanted to follow her. But since it was blind, it fell into the water, which brought back the dog's sight.

Shortly thereafter the maiden came to her father, and out of gratitude for her return, the king built a large hospital where any kind of sick person was accepted and healed. Each morning the maiden went to the sick people and asked them whether they were satisfied and whether they needed anything. So, now, when the blind young man entered the maiden's city, he went to her hospital as a blind man. The next morning the maiden came and saw him as he was searching for his ring, which he had lost from his finger. She asked him what he was looking for, and he answered that he was looking for a ring that had fallen off his finger. The maiden helped him look for it and found the ring which was her own. So she asked him: "Where did you find this ring? It belongs to me."

And he answered that he had found it on his way to this city. However, she didn't believe him and kept asking him questions until he told her that he had received the ring from a certain princess with whom he had surmounted many dangers. As soon as the maiden heard this, she embraced and kissed him.

"How did you become blind?" she asked.

Then he told her what had happened to him, and she led him to her father and said: "He is the one who saved my life in the demon's cave."

Now the two of them went to the brook where the dog had recovered its sight, and they both jumped in. Immediately thereafter the young man recovered his sight, and they returned to the castle and celebrated their wedding. And if I had attended the ceremony, I would have probably also received a spoonful of pea pudding.

THE TUFT OF WILD BEET (1875)*

Giuseppe Pitrè

Here's a tale people like to tell.

Once upon a time there was a father and mother who had an only child named Vicenzu. One day, when they couldn't find anything to eat, the father said, "What do you say, my boy? Let's go looking for something to make for tonight's soup."

And that's what they did. But as they walked far and wide, they found the whole countryside as smooth as the top of a hat, not a cabbage, fennel, or beetroot in sight. After walking some two miles without finding anything, they grew tired and discouraged. Then, all at once, Vicenzu saw a large, handsome tuft of wild beet, enough for two days' food.

When he went to pull it up, he couldn't get it out of the ground because it was so firmly rooted. So he called his father, and they pulled together and took turns until finally they yanked it out, leaving a big hole in the ground. Dark smoke began pouring out of this hole, and into the midst of the smoke leaped what looked like a sack of black cloth. Who could it be? None other than Papa-Dragu the ogre.

The father and son were struck speechless with fear. But Papa-Dragu said,

"Have no fear! I'm not going to hurt you. Just give me Vicenzu for a year, a month, and a day. If at the end of this time"—he said to the father—"you can recognize your son, you'll have him back. If you can't recognize him, he stays with me."

The poor father felt trapped and could do nothing but bow his head in consent. The ogre dismissed him with these words:

"Here, take these two hundred ducats. They will make your wife feel better, and you both can eat for a year."

---

* "La troffa di la razza," *Fiabe, novelle e racconti populari siciliani*, 4 vols. (Palermo: Lauriel, 1875).

After the father had gone, the ogre tapped Vicenzu and turned him into a little chick. Then he picked him up and put him in a cage full of chicks, all of them little boys whom he had similarly bewitched.

Now let's leave him and go back to the father. When the year, month, and day had passed, he had a dream in which his son appeared to him and said, "Father, the ogre has turned me into a little chick. If you want to break the spell, you must be able to recognize me amongst a group of chicks. I can help by giving you a signal: when you put your hand into the cage of chicks, I'll be the one that jumps onto your hand."

The father woke up, went out, and walked until he came to the ogre's house. When he yanked up the wild beet, smoke poured out, and the black sack appeared. It was Papa-Dragu.

"Come here and tell me if you recognize your son. He is one of the chicks in this cage."

The father felt completely at a loss because all the chicks were white, and all came right up to him. But when one of them jumped onto his hand, he was filled with joy.

"This is my son! This is my son!" he declared.

The ogre, angry and frustrated, had no choice but to give him his son.

"Go! Leave this place! But don't think that I won't get even with you!"

Father and son departed. Then Vicenzu immediately returned to his human form and said, "We should have something to bring back to mother. Look here, I have magical powers. I'll turn myself into a dog, and we'll go hunting. We'll meet some hunters, and when they want to buy me, you'll sell me for two hundred ducats that you can bring to mother. However, you must be very careful to say you're selling me *without the collar*. If you forget, there's no way for me to come back to you."

And that's what they did. He became a dog and began catching hares and rabbits in large numbers, then roosters, wild doves, and partridges, and he brought them all to his father. The father, loaded down with all this game, met a royal hunting party, all princes and barons and king's sons, who were leading a big pack of dogs. They were greatly discouraged because they hadn't been able to catch a single thing. When they saw Vicenzu's father with such rich game, they asked, "My good fellow, how did you manage to catch so much?"

"Oh, it was because of this dog I have."

"What an exceptional animal! Is he for sale?"

"My lords, I really couldn't do without him. But to show my great respect for your lordships, let me say two hundred ducats, *but without his collar.*"

"We certainly don't need this cheap collar. Here, take it, along with the two hundred ducats, and the dog is ours."

The father left with the two hundred ducats, and the hunters left with the dog.

When they began hunting, the dog went after a rabbit and vanished from sight. The instant he was alone, he said, "Dog I am, and man I shall become," and he turned back into Vicenzu.* Soon after, he met the hunters, all tired and out of breath.

"You there, my lad, did you see a handsome dog, about this size?"

"No, sir."

And so they went off this way and that, running around looking for the dog. Vicenzu rejoined his father, and the two of them went home.

A few days passed, and there happened to be a fair in a nearby town. Vicenzu said to his father, "Do you know what I'm thinking? I can turn myself into a horse, and you can take me to the fair and sell me for two hundred ducats, *without the halter.* But be very careful to say *without the halter.* If you forget, I have to remain a horse."

So Vicenzu became a horse, and his father took him to the fair. But Papa-Dragu also happened to be there. He was looking for the little boys whom he had turned into chicks but who had escaped and then learned to make money by turning themselves into animals. When the ogre came upon Vicenzu in the shape of a handsome horse, he recognized him at once.

"My good man, how much do you want for this horse?"

"Two hundred ducats . . ." began the father. But before he had time to add *without the halter,* the ogre tossed him a sack of two hundred ducats and seized the horse.

"Wait, sir, I'm selling him *without the halter,*" said the father.

"Oh no, he's all mine now. You had to say those words before making the sale!"

"But sir, please listen . . ."

"No way." And Papa-Dragu took away the horse, or, to be precise, Vicenzu.

* Vicenzu's words are "Cani sugnu e cristianu mi fazzu." *Cristianu,* "christian," is a standard Sicilian expression to denote "man" or "human."

He took him to an inn and tied him to a feeding trough, but gave him neither food nor drink. Then he took a very big stick, and—*whack! whack!*—he
began beating him all over.

"Do you remember, Vicenzu, when you got away from me? Well, I'm the
ogre, and you're not getting away from me again! Your life is now entirely in
my hands. Didn't I say I'd get even with you?"

He beat him night and day and kept him starving so that the poor horse's
condition would move even stones to pity.

One day the ogre happened to go out, and the stable boy found the horse
and felt sorry for him.

"Poor beast!" he said. "What a terrible master you have! Let me at least
give you something to drink, and wash these wounds on your back."

So he brought the animal to the fountain, and in order to clean him better,
he took off the halter. At this very moment the ogre returned.

"You there! What are you doing? Why are you taking that off? Put it
back on at once!"

But Vicenzu heard the voice of the ogre approaching, and having no wish
to wait for him, he uttered the words, "Horse I am, and eel I shall become,"
and threw himself into the fountain.

The ogre said, "Man I am, and shark I shall become!" and jumped into the
fountain to pursue the eel. The eel eventually grew tired and said, "Eel I am,
and vulture I shall become!" and he flew off in a great burst of speed. Then
the ogre said, "Shark I am, and eagle I shall become!" and began chasing the
vulture with even greater speed.

The vulture was about to be caught, when he spied the king's daughter
on her balcony. "Vulture I am, and ring I shall become!" he cried, and turned
into a ring and landed on the brim of the princess's hat. "What a beautiful
ring!" she exclaimed when she saw it fall and then put it on her finger. The
ogre in his eagle form was just about to swoop down to catch the ring, but
when he saw the princess put it on, there was nothing he could do. He had
to turn back and fold his wings.

Now let's leave him and follow Vicenzu, who had taken the form of a ring.
Night came, and the princess was asleep. "Ring I am, and man I shall become!"
he said, and turned back into the handsome lad he was. The princess awoke
and saw him and was afraid. But Vicenzu calmed her, telling her his whole
story, and the two of them spent the night together. In the morning he became
a ring again, and she kept him on her finger.

THE TUFT OF WILD BEET

Now the princess began to worry that her father would find out the truth one of these evenings, and since she was constantly anxious and worried, she fell ill. This became an illness that nobody could cure because nobody knew its cause.

When Papa-Dragu the ogre heard of this, he decided to disguise himself as a doctor and go to the palace.

"Your majesty, I can make your daughter well again," he said to the king, "but you must promise to give me the ring from her finger."

The king agreed, but the princess would not hear of it. That evening she told all this to Vicenzu.

"All right," he said, "you can give me to him, but on one condition, if you love me. When the ogre holds out his hand, instead of giving the ring to him, you must let it fall to the ground."

The next day the ogre arrived promptly to fetch the ring. As the princess took it off her finger, she let it fall to the ground. "Ring I am, and pomegranate I shall become!" Vicenzu said, and turned into a pomegranate, split open with all its seeds scattered on the ground. "Man I am, and rooster I shall become!" said the ogre, and he began pecking up all the pomegranate seeds until there was only one seed left, and just as he was about to gobble it up, Vicenzu said, "Pomegranate I am, and weasel I shall become!"

The weasel sprang at the rooster's head and swallowed it whole in a single bite. Then he turned back into a man and asked the king's permission to marry his daughter. The king wasn't ready to say yes, but the princess grew so insistent that, in the end, they were married that very day.

The next day Vicenzu went to where the tuft of wild beet was, entered the dead ogre's palace, and released all the little chicks from the spell that kept them bewitched. Then he gathered up all the ogre's treasures and brought them to his own palace.

Now we can leave Vicenzu, happy with his new bride, and turn to the prince of a neighboring kingdom, whose wealth and power had no limits. This prince had been planning to marry the princess who was now wed to Vicenzu, and so now he was furious about losing her. Consequently, he assembled an army so vast that it blotted out the sun, and he declared war against the king, who was Vicenzu's father-in-law. One morning the king woke up, looked out his window, and saw that his castle was surrounded by soldiers, who were preparing to demolish the walls.

"Vicenzu, what can we do? Surely we're lost!"

"Leave it to me," said Vicenzu, "I'll take care of it."

He went to his room, made a circle, and spoke three words of black magic.

"At your command!" said a voice.

"I command all the devils in hell to come here and defend this castle!"

In the wink of an eye it was raining devils. Indeed, a hundred thousand devils poured down, each with a red beret, red moustache, and red eyes that flashed sparks of flame. They made the earth itself shake with fear.

The soldiers were about to attack, but when they saw these devils facing them all along the castle walls, they cried out, "Who in the world would want to attack *them?*" and they turned and ran away as fast as they could. The prince himself became so frightened that he immediately asked to make peace with Vicenzu's father-in-law.

Eventually it came to pass that Vicenzu himself became king of the land. He remained happy living there with his royal wife, while we here lead a beggar's life.

Told by Francesca Leto to Salvatore Salomone-Marino in Borsetto.

OH, RELIEF! (1875)*

Domenico Comparetti

There was once a husband and wife, and they had only one son. At one point the father wanted to take their son to the city to learn magic. His wife was happy about this, but only under the condition that their son would not stay away from her in the city for longer than a year because she loved him so very much. Her husband promised to do as she wished and departed with their son.

When they arrived in the city, they saw a water fountain, and they stopped there to have a drink. After he had drunk some water, the father felt glad to be relieved of his thirst that had tormented him, and he cried out: "Oh, relief!"

And all at once a man with a beard appeared at his knees and said: "What is your wish, oh good man, who has called me?"

"Me? I didn't call anyone?"

"What do you mean? Didn't you cry out 'oh, relief'?"

---

* "Bene mio" in *Novelline popolari italiene* (Bologna: Forni, 1875).

The father of the young man began to laugh. But the circumstance was such: the man called himself exactly that, "oh, relief," and he was a magician and whenever he heard anyone who called his name "oh, relief," even from afar, he would immediately appear at any place whatsoever.

Now that the father knew this, he offered him one hundred ducats if he agreed to teach magic to his son in one year. The magician accepted, and the father left his son with him and returned home. Then, after one year had passed, the wife asked her husband to travel to the magician and retrieve their son. So the husband departed, and when he arrived at the fountain where the magician had appeared for the first time, he heard a wind coming from inside the fountain and then a voice that said: "Wind I am, and man I shall become."

And, behold, his son stood in front of him.

"I've learned magic so well," he said to his father, "that the master wants to keep me. He won't release me unless you pass a test. I shall become a crow, and you are supposed to recognize me among many other crows. Now here's how you are to do this: keep an eye out for the crow that flutters its wings a bit because that will be me."

Well, his father did just what his son told him to do, and he regained his son who was now much better in magic that his own master.

"Well," the son said to his father, "we must think about making money. First I shall become a hunting dog, the best the world has ever seen, and you will take me and sell me for a thousand ducats. After you sell me, I'll become a human again and return to our home. Then I'll become a magnificent huge ox, which you'll sell for two thousand ducats. And finally, I'll become a horse in the same way, a thoroughbred stallion, which no king has ever ridden. Then the greatest noblemen and the magician, my master, will come to buy me, and you're to sell me for ten thousand ducats. But pay attention that when you sell me as a dog that you keep the collar; when you sell me as ox, you're to keep the bell around its neck; and when you sell me as a horse, you're to keep the bridle. If you don't do these three things, I'll be very unfortunate for a long time."

The father did what his son instructed him to do the first two times, and everything went well. But when he sold his son as a horse to the magician, he forgot to take off the bridle. The horse stamped its feet and neighed to remind the father what he should do, but he didn't understand and let the bridle stay on the horse's neck. Because of this the horse could not return to its human form. The son became so enraged that it began to kick up tons of sand from the ground that flew into his father's face and eyes, causing him to become blind.

Meanwhile the master magician was extremely happy to have bought his disciple who had left him, and he avenged himself by having his servants frustrate the horse for many hours each day, for they were to give him very little hay to eat or water to drink. Fortunately for the horse, he forgot to tell his servants that they were never to take off the bridle. After three years of torturing the poor animal, a servant led the horse one day to a fountain to drink some water. Seeing how lean and crippled the horse was due to the master's cruelty, the servant pitied the horse, and he removed the bridle so that it would be able to drink better. Immediately, the horse reacquired its magic qualities that it had lost and said: "Horse I am, and eel I shall become." And it jumped into the water in front of the fountain. Even though the master magician was far from there, he became aware of what had happened and said: "Man I am, and large eel I shall become." And all at once he found himself in the water right behind the small eel, and he began pursing his disciple, who had transformed himself into the small eel.

Then his disciple said, "Eel I am, and a dove I shall become," and he flew away.

In reply the magician said, "Large eel I am, and a falcon I shall become." And he flew off in pursuit of the dove. For three days they flew that way, the dove ahead, and the falcon right behind it, until they came to the king's palace. The falcon was about to grab hold of the dove when the king's daughter, who was the most beautiful young woman in the realm, appeared at a balcony. So the dove said: "Dove I am, and ruby I shall become," and the ruby inserted itself into the ring on the princess's finger.

The magician was furious, and he caused the king himself to become so crippled that he couldn't move. As a result, a proclamation was issued: "Whoever Cures the King Will Wed the Princess." So the magician presented himself to the king and promised to cure him under the condition that he did not have to wed the princess but that he would be given the ring that she wore on the finger of her right hand. The king was most happy about this, but not the princess because the ruby in her ring had turned one time into the most handsome young man in the world, and they had fallen in love with each other. And he had told her: "If you love me, don't give the ring to the magician. If your father compels you to give the ring to him, do not deliver it with your hands, but throw it on to the ground."

And that is what she did. No sooner than the ring was thrown onto the ground, a voice could be heard: "Ruby I was, and garnet I shall become," and this is what happened. Then the master said: "Man I am, and rooster I shall become." And the rooster began to peck at the garnet. But a grain escaped the rooster's beak and jumped onto the handkerchief that the princess had in her hand. As soon as the magic spell was broken, there was another voice: "Garnet I am, and fox I shall become."

And so the magician's very best disciple ate the rooster who was indeed the master. Then the king was cured, and he married off his daughter. In the end, the young man sent for his old mother and blind father from his home country, and he restored his father's sight. Then his father-in-law gave him his crown, and the young man became a powerful king thanks to his riches, soldiers, and magic and lived happily with his wife.

Collected in Basilicata.

THE MAGICIAN AND HIS SERVANT (1885)*

François-Marie Luzel

All this happened some time ago
When the chickens had teeth.

Once upon a time there was a farmer from Breton, named Mélar Dourduff, who went to a fair on the mountain of Bré. He was accompanied by his fifteen-year-old son, who was called Efflam. This good man wasn't rich, and since he no longer had much money at home, he went to the fair to sell a cow. He chided his son along the way and called him lazy and a good-for-nothing. The young boy answered and made his father so irritated that he finished by crying out: "May the devil come and take you away!"

No sooner did he pronounce these words than he saw a stranger mounted on a beautiful black stallion behind him.

"Why are you scolding your son in this way?" he asked the father.

"It's because, monsieur," the man replied, "this rogue here can't do anything well. He's slothful, stubborn like a mule, and only argues so that I often feel enraged."

* "Le magicien et son valet," *Bulletin de la Societé Archéologique du Finistère* (1885).

"Give him to me as my servant for a year, and I'll give you a hundred crowns."

"I couldn't ask for anything better. You can take him right away."

And the stranger counted out a hundred crowns for Mélar Dourduff. Afterward he had Efflam mount on the back of the horse behind him and said to the farmer:

"We'll meet here at the end of a year and a day, and I'll return your son to you. But if you are not exactly on time for the rendez-vous, you'll never see him again."

And the stranger galloped away with Efflam.

The good man returned to his home with the cow, happy that he didn't have to sell it. But let us leave him for the present to follow the other two.

They arrived toward sunset at the walls of an old chateau in the middle of a forest and stopped before a large iron gate. The stranger blew on a horn, and immediately the gate opened, and they entered. It was the gate of hell. There were an infinite number of steaming cauldrons in a large hall under which a fire of hell was maintained. And there were stifled cries and heartbreaking moans that emanated from them. The devil—for the stranger was a devil—said to Efflam: "You are to maintain the fire beneath the cauldrons, and no matter what you may hear, you are not to let yourself be moved by your emotions. Most of all you are not to lift the cover of any of the cauldrons. Otherwise, I'll arrive instantly and shall throw you inside one of them. You will not lack for anything here, and you will always find a well-set table in the dining room. As for me, I am going to depart again in search of some people, and you won't see me again until a year and a day have passed. If I am satisfied with you upon my return, you'll be rewarded. But if I'm not . . . woe is you!"

After saying this, he departed.

Efflam tended to the fire beneath the cauldrons every day, deaf to the wailing and the anguished cries for help that came from them, and one time, after his work was done, he took a walk around the chateau and saw all sorts of things that astonished him very much. He also discovered books of magic and sorcery in a cabinet, and since he knew how to read quite well, he learned many secrets.

The day before his year of service to the magician was to be completed, he set out for his father's home and arrived at the door toward midnight. He knocked three times at the small window that led to his bed. "Knock-knock! Knock-knock! Knock-knock!"

"Who's there?" his father asked getting out of bed.

"It's me, your son Efflam, who's returned to remind you that tomorrow will be one year and a day since I left you and it's necessary for you to return exactly to the place of the rendez-vous that you agreed upon with my master, or else you'll never see me again."

Farmer Dourduff had never given a thought to his son and would have certainly missed the rendez-vous without this warning.

"My master," Efflam continued, "will take you with him to his chateau to get me. He will show you three iron gates and will tell you to enter through the one that he designates. But you're not to listen to him. Rather you're to enter through one of the other two. Once you are in the courtyard of the chateau, you'll see all kinds of birds—chickens, cocks, ducks, geese, swans, and turkeys, and he'll say to you, pointing with his hand: 'Your son is among all of them. Try to recognize him if you want to have him.' The moment when you enter the courtyard, a red cock will flap its wings three times. Take good note of this cock because it will be me. My master, who is a great magician, will have changed me into this cock. And now, good night, for I must return before daylight. Don't forget what I've told you!"

"Why don't you stay here since you're already here?" the old man asked.

"Because my master knows how to find me no matter where I hide. Above all, be on time for the rendez-vous tomorrow, otherwise all will be lost."

"I'll be on time," the good man responded.

And Efflam departed.

His father found everything that he had just heard to be extraordinary. However, the next day he was exactly on time for the rendez-vous. Soon he saw the magician coming toward him on his horse.

"Mount my horse behind me," the magician said, "and I'll take you to your son."

When they reached the walls of the chateau, they dismounted.

"Enter through that gate," the magician said to Mélar Dourduff, pointing to one of the three iron gates.

But the good man went through another one of the gates that was on the side. The magician grumbled and looked at him with a menacing glare. However, he didn't say anything.

"Let us first go and dine together," the magician continued. And he led the father to the dining room, where a good steaming meal was served. However, when they sat down at the table, Mélar Dourduff only ate and drank a little, following his son's advice.

"Go ahead and eat and drink more!" the magician said. "Don't you think that the wine is good?"

"I think it's excellent, but I usually don't drink much. Please excuse me, and now show me my son."

"First come with me and let me show you my courtyard."

And the magician led him into a vast courtyard filled with chickens, cocks, ducks, geese, turkey, and other birds of different kinds. At the very moment they entered the courtyard, a beautiful red cock flapped its wings and cried out three times, and the good man noticed it. Then the magician and the father visited the stables filled with handsome horses and also ponies.

"Choose one of my animals, anyone that you want, one of the beautiful horses, for example," the magician said.

"I'd prefer," the father responded, "something from your courtyard."

"Indeed, you have a peculiar taste! However, I'll let you choose as you wish."

And when the old man reentered the courtyard, he spied the red cock that had crowed, and said, "That's what I want!" And he grabbed the cock, which let this happen willingly.

"A thousand curses on you!" the furious magician exclaimed. "You must have been given advice. Get out of here! Quick! Get out of my eyesight, you and your cock. But I'll catch you again!"

And Mélar Dourduff departed, carrying the cock under his arm. As soon as he left through the gate the cock became a man, and Mélar Dourduff recognized his son Efflam, who had now become a big and strong handsome lad. Then they set out on their way to return home.

As they passed by another chateau not far from the other in the same forest, Efflam said to his father, "Here's a place where you can sell me for a high price. I often amused myself by watching the dances and games of all kinds that continually took place here from the windows of the chateau that we've just left. This is another chateau of hell, and the people entertain themselves a great deal. I've read the magician's books, and as I've already told you, he himself is a devil, and I've learned, among other secrets, how to change myself into any kind of animal that pleases me. I'll become a handsome hunting dog. I'll catch a great deal of game that you'll give to the master of the chateau, and he'll offer to buy your dog. You'll ask for a basket of money for me, and you'll get it. Don't worry about a thing, by the way. I know how to get out of any kind of trouble that concerns either you or me. All this depends on the condition that you keep the collar when you deliver the dog. Do you understand me? You're to keep the collar when you deliver the dog; otherwise everything will be lost."

"I understand," the good man responded. "I'm to sell the dog and keep the collar. Nothing could be simpler."

"That's it. I'll stay for some time in this chateau, and you'll stay with me. You will be well fed and treated well, and you'll have nothing to do other than to take care of me. Let me repeat: if you keep the collar, everything will go well, and we'll get out of there, when we want. But if you leave the collar with the dog, we'll pay for it, first me and then you. So don't forget. Keep the collar no matter what happens."

"I certainly won't forget," the old man replied.

In the woods that surrounded the chateau there was abundant game of all kinds. Efflam changed himself into a handsome hunting dog and caught rabbits and hare as well as partridges. During the hunt the master of the chateau was attracted by the barking of the dog, and he went to see what was happening. He was astonished by the beauty, the skill, and the intelligence of the animal and said to the old Dourduff: "What a good dog you have there! Would you like to sell it to me?"

"If you give me enough money for it," the good man replied.

"What do you want?"

"A basket full of money filled to the brim."

"That's a great deal, but I'll give it to you."

"I also want to keep its collar."

"Not at all. The collar is always given with the dog, just as the bridle's given with the horse."

"That depends on the conditions. For me, I prefer to keep my dog's collar; otherwise I won't give him to you for anything in the world."

"I'm paying a pretty high price, and it seems to me that I should have the collar along with the dog."

"I tell you, either I keep the collar, or there's no deal."

"Oh, all right, you stubborn old man! Keep your collar and give me the dog and take your money."

"There's one more thing."

"What now?"

"I want to stay for some time in your chateau to take care of the dog until he's adapted to the customs of your household, and I want to be treated as one of the masters."

"All right. Follow me with your dog."

At the end of a week, the good man became tired of the lifestyle at the chateau and returned to his home. Efflam also left the chateau in the form of the dog and took the road toward his father's house. But the master of the chateau quickly realized that he had disappeared and began to pursue him with a pack of dogs. When Efflam heard their barking behind him, he noticed a farmer cutting wheat on a field. So, he ran to him and said, "Quick! Give me your clothes for a moment, and I'll reward you well."

The man was surprised to hear a talking dog. Since he was afraid, he threw his sickle to the ground and took off his clothes. Now the dog became a man dressed in the peasant's clothes and began calmly to cut the wheat after saying to the peasant: "Go to the side of the road and pretend to be a merchant dying of hunger. Within minutes you'll see a man on horseback with a pack of dogs in front of him, and he'll ask you whether you've seen a lone dog run by here. You're to respond that the dog passed by about half an hour ago and he was following the road straight ahead."

Indeed, soon thereafter the man on horseback arrived at a triple gallop, and he was accompanied by numerous dogs in a pack that made an infernal racket.

"Have you seen a lone dog pass by here?" the man asked the beggar.

"Yes, monsieur," the beggar responded. "It passed by here about half an hour ago and kept running straight down the road."

So the man on horseback and his pack of dogs continued their pursuit. Meanwhile Efflam returned the sickle and clothes to the peasant along with a gold coin. Then he became a dog again and ran across the fields to return to his father's home. He arrived happily, having thrown the devil and his pack of infernal dogs off his scent. Then he reassumed his natural form.

Some time later, when he had become bored of things at home, Efflam said to his father once again, "Father, tomorrow there's a big fair on the mountain of Bré. I'm going to change myself into a handsome horse, and you're to take me to the fair. A man will arrive to bargain for me. He'll say that he's a dealer from Normandy, but in reality he'll be nothing but my master from the first chateau. He'll be trying to catch me just as he told us. If you follow my instructions point by point, we'll trick him again. You're to ask for a barrel of money filled to the top, that's to be delivered to your home. He'll agree to the deal because the money costs him nothing. But when you give him the horse, you're once again to keep the bridle just as you kept the dog's collar. Otherwise, you'll never see me again."

"I'll do exactly as you say," the good man responded.

Early the next morning Mélar Dourduff took the road for Bré, mounted on his superb horse. Everyone admired it along the way, and when he arrived at the fair, a group of people gathered around him. There were many dealers among them from Léon, Cornouaille, Vantnes, Tréguier, and Goëlo. But the price was so high that nobody could meet it. Finally, toward dusk, a strange dealer arrived, who said he was from Normandy. Nobody knew him except for the good man Dourduff, who was aware exactly with whom he was dealing. They easily reached an agreement about the price—a barrel of money. But when it came time to deliver the animal, Dourduff got ready to take off the bridle.

"What are you doing there?" asked the stranger.

"I've just sold you the horse," the good man responded, "but not the bridle. I'm keeping the bridle."

"But the bridle is always taken with the horse, you old imbecile."

"Either I keep the bridle, I tell you, or there's no deal."

"Well then, there's no deal," the dealer said, and he turned his back in a bad mood and got ready to leave the fair. But the people, excited by the stranger who paid a great deal for their drinks, began to hoot at the good man and call him an imbecile and an old idiot until he lost his nerve and let the dealer have the horse with the bridle.

As soon as the magician mounted the horse, he flew off into the air to the great astonishment of everyone present. When Mélar Dourduff saw this, he realized his great fault and began to weep.

"Why are you crying, you old imbecile?" some one asked. "You've got a barrel full of money for your horse. Why are you so concerned now what happens to the horse?"

"I sold my son!" he exclaimed. "The horse was my son! The devil took him away!"

And he lamented all that he had done and tore out his hair. But nobody understood anything he said, and they believed that he was drunk and saying crazy things.

So now Efflam returned to hell in the form of a horse. A servant was placed in charge to keep watch over him in the stable and to bring him water with the express order never to allow him to drink at the river. The horse was to be fed a bunch of spinach and greens on the rack of the stall. The poor beast began to lose weight in plain sight because of this diet. It drank a great deal so that the man in charge of furnishing the water with caution became tired of going to the fountain to fetch it because the fountain was a long way off. He found that it was more convenient to lead the horse to the nearby river.

When he did this, the horse jumped into the water, got rid of the bridle as well as the rider, and changed himself into an eel. The servant got back on his feet and returned to his master.

"The horse is gone!" he wept as he spoke.

"Where to, you idiot?"

"He jumped into the river and changed himself into an eel!"

"Curses!" the magician exclaimed. "I ordered you not to let him approach the river!"

And he ran to a spot next to the river where the horse had entered. Then he jumped into the water and quickly became a pike and began to search for the eel. Sensing that the pike was near, the eel sprang out of the water and became a hare and began to run. In his turn, the pike became a hunting dog and chased the hare. As they crossed through a village at this very moment, there was a wedding at the church, and the curious people, who were at the wedding, cried out: "Look at that! A hare chased by a dog!"

The hare fled from the cemetery into the church. The dog stopped at the entrance to the cemetery because the devil cannot set foot on sacred ground. The wedding couple were on their knees at the rail of the choir, and the priest was getting ready to take the wedding rings and place them on their fingers, those poor silver wedding rings that a child from the choir held on a tin plate. All of a sudden one of the rings changed itself into a beautiful golden ring with a precious gem. The priest put it on the finger of the newlywed bride. It was the hare—that is, Efflam Dourduff—who had changed himself into a ring.

The wedding couple left the church. The bride went to her home, took off the ring from her finger, and locked it in her closet. Everyone was sitting at the table and chatting noisily. They were joking and laughing when an unknown fiddler entered the room and began to play a violin. He played so well and with such spirit and cheerfulness that everyone got up from the table and began to dance. At the end of the day they asked the fiddler what he would like for his troubles.

"I ask for nothing," he said, "but something that I've lost that is in this house."

"What is it?" asked the newlywed bridegroom, who was intrigued.

"A beautiful golden ring with a precious gem."

"It may be my wife's ring, which came out of nowhere."

And the newlywed bride went to look for the ring in her room, and the fiddler accompanied her. But just as she picked up the ring, it slipped from her fingers and fell to the floor and was lost in a pile of nearby wheat.

"Ah!" she cried out. "The ring's fallen to the ground and has rolled into the wheat."

And she began to search, and since she couldn't find it again, the fiddler changed himself into a red cock and began to swallow the wheat. He swallowed and swallowed until there were only three or four grains left when one of them changed itself into a fox that threw itself upon the cock and devoured it whole!

That's how the battle was finished, and Efflam triumphed again. He went back to his father's home in his natural form, and since he was now quite rich, he spent his time peacefully at home and married the richest heiress of the country.

Told by Fiacre Briand, mason, in the commune of Cavan (Côtes-du-Nord).

FARMER WEATHERSKY (1888)*

George Webbe Dasent

Once upon a time there was a man and his wife, who had an only son, and his name was Jack. The old dame thought it high time for her son to go out into the world to learn a trade, and bade her husband be off with him.

"But all you do," she said, "mind you bind him to someone who can teach him to be master above all masters."

And with that she put some food and a roll of tobacco into a bag, and packed them off.

Well, they went to many masters, but one and all said they could make the lad as good as themselves, but better they couldn't make him. So when the man came home again to his wife with that answer, she said: "I don't care what you make of him, but this I say and stick to: you must bind him to someone where he can learn to be master above all masters."

And with that she packed up more food and another roll of tobacco, and father and son had to be off again.

Now when they had walked a while they got upon the ice, and there they met a man who came whisking along in a sledge and drove a black horse.

"Whither away?" said the man.

---

* *Popular Tales from the Norse* (Edinburgh: David Douglas, 1888).

"Well," said the father, "I'm going to bind my son to someone who is good to teach him a trade, but my old dame comes of such fine folk, she will have him taught to be master above all masters."

"Well met then," said the driver. "I'm just the man for your money, for I'm looking out for such an apprentice. Up with you behind!" he added to the lad, and whisk! Off they went, both of them, and sledge and horse, right up into the air.

"Nay, nay!" cried the lad's father, "You haven't told me your name, nor where you live."

"Oh!" said the master. "I'm at home alike north and south, and east and west, and my name's Farmer Weathersky. In a year and a day you may come here again, and then I'll tell you if I like him."

So away they went through the air and were soon out of sight.

When the man got home, his old dame asked what had become of her son.

"Well," said the man, "heaven knows, I'm sure I don't. They went up aloft."

And so he told her what had happened. But when the old dame heard that her husband couldn't tell at all when her son's apprenticeship would be out, nor whither he had gone, she packed him off again and gave him another bag of food and another roll of tobacco.

When he had walked a bit, he came to a great wood, which stretched on and on all day as he walked through it. Soon it got dark, and he saw a great light and went toward it. After a long, long time he came to a little hut under a rock, and outside stood an old hag drawing water out of a well with her nose, so long was it.

"Good evening, mother!" said the man.

"The same to you," said the old hag. "It's hundreds of years since any one called me mother."

"Can I have lodging here tonight?" asked the man.

"No! That you can't," said she.

But then the man pulled out his roll of tobacco, lighted his pipe, and gave the old dame a whiff, and a pinch of snuff. All at once she was so happy she began to dance for joy, and the end was, she gave the man leave to stop the night.

So next morning he began to ask after Farmer Weathersky.

"No!" she never heard tell of him, but she ruled over all the four-footed beasts. "Perhaps some of them might know him."

So she played them all home with a pipe she had and asked them all, but there wasn't one of them who knew anything about Farmer Weathersky.

"Well," said the old hag, "there are three sisters of us; maybe one of the other two knows where he lives. I'll lend you my horse and sledge, and then you'll be at her house by night; but it's at least three hundred miles off, the nearest way."

Then the man started off, and at night reached the house, and when he came there, there stood another old hag before the door, drawing water out of the well with her nose.

"Good evening, mother!" said the man.

"The same to you," said she. "It's hundreds of years since any one called me mother."

"Can I lodge here tonight?" asked the man.

"No!" said the old hag.

But he took out his roll of tobacco, lighted his pipe, and gave the old dame a whiff, and a good pinch of snuff besides, on the back of her hand. Then she was so happy that she began to jump and dance for joy, and so the man got leave to stay the night. When that was over, he began to ask after Farmer Weathersky.

"No!" she had never heard tell of him, but she ruled all the fish in the sea. "Perhaps some of them might know something about him."

So she played them all home with a pipe she had, and asked them, but there wasn't one of them who knew anything about Farmer Weathersky.

"Well, well!" said the old hag. "There's one sister of us left; maybe she knows something about him. She lives six hundred miles off, but I'll lend you my horse and sledge, and then you'll get there by nightfall."

Then the man started off, and reached the house by nightfall, and there he found another old hag who stood before the grate, and stirred the fire with her nose, so long and tough it was.

"Good evening, mother!" said the man.

"The same to you," said the old hag. "It's hundreds of years since any one called me mother."

"Can I lodge here tonight?" asked the man.

"No," said the old hag.

Then the man pulled out his roll of tobacco again, and lighted his pipe, and gave the old hag such a pinch of snuff it covered the whole back of her hand. All at once she got so happy she began to dance for joy, and so the man got leave to stay. But when the night was over, he began to ask after Farmer

Weathersky. She never heard tell of him she said; but she ruled over all the birds of the air, and so she played them all home with a pipe she had, and when she had mustered them all, the eagle was missing. But a little while after he came flying home, and when she asked him, he said he had just come straight from Farmer Weathersky. Then the old hag said he must guide the man thither; but the eagle said he must have something to eat first, and besides he must rest till the next day. He was so tired with flying that long way, he could scarce rise from the earth.

So when he had eaten his fill and taken a good rest, the old hag pulled a feather out of the eagle's tail and put the man there in its stead. So the eagle flew off with the man, and flew, and flew, but they didn't reach Farmer Weathersky's house before midnight. So when they got there, the eagle said: "There are heaps of dead bodies lying about outside, but you mustn't mind them. Inside the house every man Jack of them are so sound asleep, 't will be hard work to wake them; but you must go straight to the table drawer, and take out of it three crumbs of bread, and when you hear someone snoring loud, pull three feathers out of his head; he won't wake for all that."

So the man did as he was told, and after he had taken the crumbs of bread, he pulled out the first feather.

"OOF!" growled Farmer Weathersky, for it was he who snored.

So the man pulled out another feather.

"OOF!" he growled again.

But when he pulled out the third, Farmer Weathersky roared so, the man thought roof and wall would have flown asunder, but for all that the snorer slept on. After that the eagle told him what he was to do. He went to the yard, and there at the stable-door he stumbled against a big gray stone, and that he lifted up. Underneath it lay three chips of wood, and those he picked up too. Then he knocked at the stable-door, and it opened of itself. Once it was open, he threw down the three crumbs of bread, and a hare came and ate them up; that hare he caught and kept. After that the eagle bade him pull three feathers out of his tail, and put the hare, the stone, the chips, and himself there instead, and then he would fly away home with them all.

So when the eagle had flown a long way, he lighted on a rock to rest.

"Do you see anything?" it asked.

"Yes," said the man. "I see a flock of crows flying after us."

"We'd better be off again, then," said the eagle, who flew away.

After a while it asked again, "Do you see anything now?"

"Yes," said the man, "now the crows are close behind us."

"Drop now the three feathers you pulled out of his head," said the eagle.

Well, the man dropped the feathers, and just as soon as he dropped them, they became a flock of ravens, which drove the crows home again. Then the eagle flew on far away with the man, and at last it lighted on another stone to rest. "Do you see anything?" it said.

"I'm not sure," said the man. "I fancy I see something coming far far away."

"We'd better get on then," said the eagle; and after a while it said again: "Do you see anything?"

"Yes," said the man. "Now he's close at our heels."

"Now you must let fall the chips of wood that you took from under the gray stone at the stable door," said the eagle.

So the man let them fall, and they grew at once up into tall, thick wood so that Farmer Weathersky had to go back home to fetch an axe to hew his way through. While he did this, the eagle flew ever so far, but when it got tired, it lighted on a fir to rest.

"Do you see anything?" it said.

"Well, I'm not sure," said the man, "but I fancy I catch a glimpse of something far away."

"We'd best be off then," said the eagle; and off it flew as fast as it could. After a while it said: "Do you see anything now?"

"Yes! Now he's close behind us," said the man.

"Now, you must drop the big stone you lifted up at the stable door," said the eagle.

The man did so, and as it fell it became a great high mountain, which Farmer Weathersky had to break his way through. When he had got halfway through the mountain, he tripped and broke one of his legs, and so he had to limp home again and patch it up.

But while he was doing this, the eagle flew away to the man's house with him and the hare, and as soon as they got home, the man went into the churchyard and sprinkled Christian mold over the hare, and lo! it turned into Jack, his son. Well, you may fancy the old dame was glad to get her son again, but still she wasn't easy in her mind about his trade, and she wouldn't rest till he gave her a proof that he was "master above all masters."

So when the fair came round, the lad changed himself into a bay horse and told his father to lead him to the fair.

"Now, when any one comes," he said, "to buy me, you may ask a hundred dollars for me; but mind you don't forget to take the headstall off me. If you forget, Farmer Weathersky will keep me forever, for he it is who will come to deal with you."

And this is the way it turned out. Up came a horse dealer, who had a great wish to deal for the horse, and he gave a hundred dollars down for him; but when the bargain was struck, and Jack's father had pocketed the money, the horse dealer wanted to have the headstall.

"Nay, nay!" said the man, "There's nothing about that in the bargain; and besides, you can't have the headstall, for I've other horses at home to bring to town to-morrow."

So each went his way, but they hadn't gone far before Jack took his own shape and ran away, and when his father got home, there sat Jack near the fireplace.

Next day he turned himself into a brown horse, and told his father to drive him to the fair.

"And when any one comes to buy me, you may ask two hundred dollars for me—he'll give that and treat you besides. But whatever you do, and however much you drink, don't forget to take the headstall off me, else you'll never set eyes on me again."

So all happened as he had said. The man got two hundred dollars for the horse and a glass of drink besides, and when the buyer and seller parted, it was as much as he could do to remember to take off the headstall. But the buyer and the horse hadn't got far on the road before Jack took his own shape, and when the man got home, there sat Jack near the fireplace.

The third day it was the same story over again: the lad turned himself into a black horse, and told his father someone would come and bid three hundred dollars for him, and fill his skin with meat and drink besides; but however much he ate or drank, he was to mind and not forget to take the headstall off, else he'd have to stay with Farmer Weathersky all his life long.

"No, no, I'll not forget, never fear," said the man.

So when he came to the fair, he got three hundred dollars for the horse, and as it wasn't to be a dry bargain, Farmer Weathersky made him drink so much that he quite forgot to fake the headstall off, and away went Farmer Weathersky with the horse. Now when he had gone a little way Farmer Weathersky thought he would just stop and have another glass of brandy, so he put a barrel of red-hot nails under his horse's nose, and a sieve of oats under his tail, hung the halter upon a hook, and went into the inn. Well, the horse stood there and stamped and pawed, and snorted and reared. Just then out came a lassie, who thought it a shame to treat a horse so.

"Oh, poor beastie," she said, "what a cruel master you must have to treat you so," and as she said this, she pulled the halter off the hook, so that the horse might turn round and taste the oats.

"I'M AFTER YOU!" roared Farmer Weathersky, who came rushing out of the door.

But the horse had already shaken off the headstall and jumped into a duck-pond, where he turned himself into a tiny fish. In went Farmer Weathersky after him, and turned himself into a great pike. Then Jack turned himself into a dove, and Farmer Weathersky made himself into a hawk, and chased and struck at the dove. But just then a princess stood at the window of the palace and saw this struggle.

"Ah! Poor dove," she cried, "if you only knew what I know, you'd fly to me through this window."

So the dove came flying in through the window, and turned itself into Jack again, who told his own tale.

"Turn yourself into a gold ring, and put yourself on my finger," said the princess.

"Nay, nay!" said Jack. "That'll never do, for then Farmer Weathersky will make the king sick, and then there'll be no one who can make him well again till Farmer Weathersky comes and cures him, and then, for his fee, he'll ask for that gold ring."

"Then I'll say I had it from my mother, and can't part with it," said the princess.

Well, Jack turned himself into a gold ring and put himself on the princess's finger, and so Farmer Weathersky couldn't get at him. But then followed what the lad had foretold. The king fell sick, and there wasn't a doctor in the kingdom who could cure him till Farmer Weathersky came, and he asked for the ring off the princess's finger for his fee. So the king sent a messenger to the princess for the ring, but the princess said she wouldn't part with it, her mother had left it to her. When the king heard that, he flew into a rage and said that he would have the ring, no matter who left it to her.

"Well," said the princess, "it's no good being cross about it. I can't get it off, and if you must have the ring, you must take my finger too."

"If you let me try, I'll soon get the ring off," said Farmer Weathersky.

"No, thanks. I'll try myself," said the princess and flew off the grate and put ashes on her finger. Then the ring slipped off and was lost among the ashes. So Farmer Weathersky turned himself into a cock, who scratched and pecked after the ring in the grate till he was up to ears in the ashes. But while he was doing this, Jack turned himself into a fox and bit off the cock's head. And so if the Evil One was in Farmer Weathersky, it is all over with him now.

THE FISHERMAN'S SON AND THE GRUAGACH OF TRICKS (1890)*

Jerome Curtin

There was an old fisherman once in Erin who had a wife and one son.

The old fisherman used to go about with a fishing rod and tackle to the rivers and lochs and every place where fish resort, and he was killing salmon and other fish to keep the life in himself and his wife and son.

The son was not so keen nor so wise as another, and the father was instructing him every day in fishing, so that if himself should be taken from the world, the son would be able to support the old mother and get his own living.

One day when the father and son were fishing in a river near the sea, they looked out over the water and saw a small dark speck on the waves. It grew larger and larger, till they saw a boat, and when the boat drew near, they saw a man sitting in the stern of it.

There was a nice beach near the place they were fishing. The man brought the boat straight to the beach, and stepping out, drew it up on the sand.

They saw then that the stranger was a man of high degree (*duine uasall*).

After he had put the boat high on the sand, he came to where the two were at work, and said: "Old fisherman, you'd better let this son of yours with me for a year and a day, and I will make a very wise man of him. I am the Gruagach na g-cleasan† (Gruagach of tricks), and I'll bind myself to be here with your son this day year."

"I can't let him go," said the old fisherman, "till he gets his mother's advice."

"Whatever goes as far as women I'll have nothing to do with," said the Gruagach. "You had better give him to me now, and let the mother alone."

---

* *Myths and Folk-Lore of Ireland* (Boston: Little Brown, 1890).

† Pronounced "ná glássan."

They talked till at last the fisherman promised to let his son go for the year and a day. Then the Gruagach gave his word to have the boy there at the seashore that day year.

The Gruagach and the boy went into the boat and sailed away.

When the year and a day were over, the old fisherman went to the same place where he had parted with his son and the Gruagach and stood looking over the sea, thinking would he see his son that day.

At last he saw a black spot on the water, then a boat. When it was near he saw two men sitting in the stern of the boat. When it touched land the two, who were *duine uasal* in appearance, jumped out, and one of them pulled the boat to the top of the strand. Then that one, followed by the other, came to where the old fisherman was waiting, and asked: "What trouble is on you now, my good man?"

"I had a son that wasn't so keen nor so wise as another, and myself and this son were here fishing, and a stranger came, like yourself today, and asked would I let my son with him for a year and a day. I let the son go, and the man promised to be here with him today, and that's why I am waiting at this place now."

"Well," said the Gruagach, "am I your son?"

"You are not," said the fisherman.

"Is this man here your son?"

"I don't know him," said the fisherman.

"Well, then, he is all you will have in place of your son," said the Gruagach.

The old man looked again and knew his son. He caught hold of him and welcomed him home.

"Now," said the Gruagach, "isn't he a better man than he was a year ago?"

"Oh, he's nearly a smart man now!" said the old fisherman.

"Well," said the Gruagach, "will you let him with me for another year and a day?"

"I will not," said the old man. "I want him myself."

The Gruagach then begged and craved till the fisherman promised to let the son with him for a year and a day again. But the old man forgot to take his word of the Gruagach to bring back the son at the end of the time, and when the Gruagach and the boy were in the boat and had pushed out to sea, the Gruagach shouted to the old man: "I kept my promise to bring back your son today. I haven't given you my word at all now. I'll not bring him back, and you'll never see him again."

The fisherman went home with a heavy and sorrowful heart, and the old woman scolded him all that night till next morning for letting her son go with the Gruagach a second time.

Then himself and the old woman were lamenting a quarter of a year, and when another quarter had passed, he said to her: "I'll leave you here now, and I'll be walking on myself till I wear my legs off up to my knees, and from my knees to my waist, till I find where my son is."

So away went the old man walking, and he used to spend but one night in a house, and not two nights in any house, till his feet were all in blisters. One evening late he came to a hut where there was an old woman sitting at a fire.

"Poor man!" said she, when she laid eyes on him, "it's a great distress you are in, to be so disfigured with wounds and sores. What is the trouble that's on you?"

"I had a son," said the old man, "and the Gruagach na g-cleasan came on a day and took him from me."

"Oh, poor man!" said she. "I have a son with that same Gruagach these twelve years, and I have never been able to get him back or get sight of him, and I'm in dread you'll not be able to get your son either. But tomorrow, in the morning, I'll tell you all I know, and show you the road you must go to find the house of the Gruagach na g-cleasan."

Next morning she showed the old fisherman the road. He was to come to the place by evening.

When he came and entered the house, the Gruagach shook hands with him, and said: "You are welcome, old fisherman. It was I that put this journey on you and made you come here looking for your son."

"It was no one else but you," said the fisherman.

"Well," said the Gruagach, "you won't see your son today. At noon tomorrow I'll put a whistle in my mouth and call together all the birds in my place, and they'll come. Among others will be twelve doves. I'll put my hand in my pocket, this way, and take out wheat and throw it before them on the ground. The doves will eat the wheat, and you must pick your son out of the twelve. If you find him, you'll have him. If you don't, you'll never get him again."

After the Gruagach had said these words the old man ate his supper and went to bed.

In the dead of night the old fisherman's son came.

"Oh, father!" said he, "it would be hard for you to pick me out among the twelve doves, if you had to do it alone, but I'll tell you. When the Gruagach calls us in, and we go to pick up the wheat, I'll make a ring around the others, walking for myself, and as I go, I'll give some of them a tip of my bill, and I'll lift my wings when I'm striking them. There was a spot under one of my arms when I left home, and you'll see that spot under my wing when I raise it tomorrow. Don't miss the bird that I'll be, and don't let your eyes off it. If you do, you'll lose me forever."

Next morning the old man rose, had his breakfast, and kept thinking of what his son had told him.

At midday the Gruagach took his whistle and blew. Birds came to him from every part, and among others the twelve doves. Then he took wheat from his pocket, threw it to the doves, and said to the father: "Now pick out your son from the twelve."

The old man was watching, and soon he saw one of the doves walking around the other eleven and hitting some of them a clip of its bill, and then it raised its wings, and the old man saw the spot. The bird let its wings down again and went to eating with the rest. The father never let his eyes off the bird. After a while he said to the Gruagach: "I'll have that bird there for my son."

"Well," said the Gruagach, "that is your son. I can't blame you for having him, but I blame your instructor for the information he gave you, and I give him my curse."

So the old fisherman got his son back in his proper shape, and away they went, father and son, from the house of the Gruagach. The old man felt stronger now, and they never stopped traveling a day till they came home.

The old mother was very glad to see her son, and see him such a wise, smart man. After coming home, however, they had no means but the fishing; they were as poor as ever before.

At this time it was given out at every crossroad in Erin, and in all public places in the kingdom, that there were to be great horse-races. Now, when the day came, the old fisherman's son said: "Come away with me, father, to the races."

The old man went with him, and when they were near the race-course, the son said: "Stop here till I tell you this: I'll make myself into the best horse that's here today, and you take me to the place where the races are to be, and when you take me in, I'll open my mouth, trying to kill and eat every man that'll be near me, I'll have such life and swiftness, and you are to find a rider for me that'll ride me, and don't let me go till the other horses are far ahead on the course. Then let me go. I'll come up to them, and I'll run ahead of them and win the race. After that every rich man there will want to buy me of you, but don't you sell me to any man for less than five hundred pounds, and be sure you get that price for me. And when you have the gold, and you are giving me up, take the bit out of my mouth, and don't sell the bridle for any money. Then come to this spot, shake the bridle, and I'll be here in my own form before you."

The son made himself a horse, and the old fisherman took him to the race. He reared and snorted, trying to take the head off every man that came near him.

The old man shouted for a rider. A rider came; he mounted the horse and held him in. The old man didn't let him start till the other horses were well ahead on the course. Then he let him go, and the new horse caught up with the others and shot past them. So they had not gone halfway when he was in at the winning-post. When the race was ended, there was a great noise over the strange horse. Men crowded around the old fisherman from every corner of the field, asking what would he take for the horse.

"Five hundred pounds," said he.

"Here 'tis for you," said the next man to him.

In a moment the horse was sold, and the money in the old man's pocket. Then he pulled the bridle off the horse's head and made his way out of the place as fast as ever he could.

It was not long till he was at the spot where the son had told him what to do. The minute he came, he shook the bridle, and the son was there before him in his own shape and features.

Oh, but the old fisherman was glad when he had his son with him again, and the money in his pocket!

The two went home together. They had money enough now to live and quit the fishing. They had plenty to eat and drink, and they spent their lives in ease and comfort till the next year, when it was given out at all the cross-roads in Erin, and every public place in the kingdom, that there was to be a great hunting with hounds in the same place where the races had been the year before.

When the day came the fisherman's son said: "Come, father, let us go away to this hunting."

"Ah!" said the old man. "What do we want to go for? Haven't we plenty to eat at home, with money enough and to spare? What do we care for hunting with hounds?"

"Oh! They'll give us more money," said the son, "if we go."

The fisherman listened to his son, and away they went. When the two came to the spot where the son had made a horse of himself the year before, he stopped, and said to the father: "I'll make a hound of myself today, and when you bring me in sight of the game, you'll see me wild with jumping and trying to get away, but you are to hold me fast till the right time comes, then let go. I'll sweep ahead of every hound in the field, catch the game, and win the prize for you. When the hunt is over, so many men will come to buy me that they'll put you in a maze. But be sure you get three hundred pounds for me, and when you have the money, and are giving me up, don't forget to keep my rope. Come to this place, shake the rope, and I'll be here before you, as I am now. If you don't keep the rope, you'll go home without me."

The son made a hound of himself, and the father took him to the hunting-ground. When the hunt began, the hound was springing and jumping like mad, but the father held him till the others were far out in the field. Then he let him loose, and away went the son. Soon he was up with the pack, then in front of the pack, and never stopped till he caught the game and won the prize.

When the hunt was over, and the dogs and game brought in, all the people crowded around the old fisherman, saying: "What do you want of that hound? Better sell him. He's no good to you."

They put the old man in a maze, there were so many of them, and they pressed him so hard. At last he said: "I'll sell the hound, and three hundred pounds is the price I want for him."

"Here 'tis for you," said a stranger, putting the money into his hand.

The old man took the money and gave up the dog without taking off the rope. He forgot his son's warning.

That minute the Gruagach na g-cleasan called out: "I'll take the worth of my money out of your son now." And away he went with the hound.

The old man walked home alone that night, and it is a heavy heart he had in him when he came to the old woman without the son. And the two lamented their lot till morning. Still and all, they were better off than the first time they lost their son, as they had plenty of everything, and could live at their ease.

The Gruagach went away home and put the fisherman's son in a cave of concealment that he had, bound him hand and foot, and tied hard knots on his neck up to the chin. From above there fell on him drops of poison, and every drop that fell went from the skin to the flesh, from the flesh to the bone, from the bone to the marrow, and he sat there under the poison drops, without meat, drink, or rest.

In the Gruagach's house was a servant-maid, and the fisherman's son had been kind to her the time he was in the place before. So on a day when the Gruagach and his eleven sons were out hunting, the maid was carrying a tub of dirty water to throw it into the river that ran by the side of the house. She went through the cave of concealment where the fisherman's son was bound, and he asked of her the wetting of his mouth from the tub.

"Oh! The Gruagach would take the life of me," said she, "when he comes home, if I gave you as much as one drop."

"Well," said he, "when I was in this house before, and when I had power in my hands, it's good and kind I was to you, and when I get out of this confinement, I'll do you a turn, if you give me the wetting of my mouth now."

The maid put the tub near his lips.

"Oh! I can't stoop to drink unless you untie one knot from my throat," said he.

Then she put the tub down, stooped to him, and loosed one knot from his throat. When she loosed the one knot, he made an eel of himself and dropped into the tub. There he began shaking the water, till he put some of it on the ground, and when he had the place about him wet, he sprang from the tub, and slipped along out under the door. The maid caught him but could not hold him, he was so slippery. He made his way from the door to the river, which ran near the side of the house.

When the Gruagach na g-cleasan came home in the evening with his eleven sons, they went to take a look at the fisherman's son, but he was not to be seen. Then the Gruagach called the maid, and taking his sword, said: "I'll take the head off you if you don't tell me this minute what happened while I was gone."

"Oh!" said the maid. "He begged so hard for a drop of dirty water to wet his mouth that I hadn't the heart to refuse, for 'tis good he was to me and kind each time he saw me when he was here in the house before. When the water touched his mouth, he made an eel of himself, spilled water out of the tub, and slipped along over the wet place to the river outside. I caught him to bring him back, but I couldn't hold him. In spite of all I could do, he made away."

The Gruagach dropped his sword and went to the waterside with his sons.

The sons made eleven eels of themselves, and the Gruagach their father was the twelfth. They went around in the water, searching in every place, and there was not a stone in the river that they passed without looking under and around it for the old fisherman's son.

And when he knew that they were after him, he made himself into a salmon, and when they knew he was a salmon, the sons made eleven otters of themselves, and the Gruagach made himself the twelfth.

When the fisherman's son found that twelve otters were after him, he was weak with hunger, and when they had come near, he made himself a whale. But the eleven brothers and their father made twelve cannon whales of themselves, for they had all gone out of the river, and were in the sea now.

When they were coming near him, the fisherman's son was weak from pursuit and hunger, so he jumped up out of the water and made a swallow of himself. But the Gruagach and his sons became twelve hawks and chased the swallow through the air, and as they whirled round and darted, they pressed him hard till all of them came near the castle of the king of Erin.

Now the king had made a summer-house for his daughter; and where should she be at this time but sitting on the top of the summer-house.

The old fisherman's son dropped down till he was near her. Then he fell into her lap in the form of a ring. The daughter of the king of Erin took up the ring, looked at it, and put it on her finger. The ring took her fancy, and she was glad.

When the Gruagach and his sons saw this, they let themselves down at the king's castle, assuming the form of the finest men that could be seen in the kingdom.

When the king's daughter had the ring on her finger, she looked at it and liked it. Then the ring spoke and said: "My life is in your hands now. Don't part from the ring, and don't let it go to any man, and you'll give me a long life."

The Gruagach na g-cleasan and his eleven sons went into the king's castle and played on every instrument known to man, and they showed every sport that could be shown before a king. This they did for three days and three nights. When that time was over, and they were going away, the king spoke up and asked: "What is the reward that you would like, and what would be pleasing to you from me?"

"We want neither gold nor silver," said the Gruagach; "all the reward we ask of you is the ring that I lost on a time, and which is now on your daughter's finger."

"If my daughter has the ring that you lost, it shall be given to you," said the king.

Now the ring spoke to the king's daughter and said: "Don't part with me for anything till you send your trusted man for three gallons of strong spirits and a gallon of wheat. Put the spirits and the wheat together in an open barrel before the fire. When your father says you must give up the ring, you are to answer back that you have never left the summer-house, that you have nothing on your hand but what is your own and paid for. Your father will say then that you must part with me, and give me up to the stranger. When he forces you in this way, and you can no longer keep me, then throw me into the fire, and you'll see, great sport and strange things."

The king's daughter sent for the spirits and the wheat and had them mixed together and put in an open barrel before the fire. Then the king called the daughter in and asked: "Have you the ring that this stranger lost?"

"I have a ring," said she, "but it's my own, and I'll not part with it. I'll not give it to him nor to any man."

"You must," said the king, "for my word is pledged, and you must part with the ring!"

When she heard this, she slipped the ring from her finger and threw it into the fire. That moment the eleven brothers made eleven pairs of tongs of themselves, while their father, the old Gruagach, was the twelfth pair. The twelve jumped into the fire to know in what spark of it would they find the old fisherman's son, and they were a long time working and searching through the fire, when out flew a spark and into the barrel.

The twelve made themselves men, turned over the barrel, and spilled the wheat on the floor. Then in a twinkling they were twelve cocks strutting around. They fell to and picked away at the wheat to know which one would find the fisherman's son. Soon one dropped on one side, and a second on the opposite side, until all twelve were lying drunk from the wheat.

Then the old fisherman's son made a fox of himself, and the first cock he came to was the old Gruagach na g-cleasan himself. He took the head off the Gruagach with one bite, and the heads off the eleven brothers with eleven other bites. When the twelve were dead, the old fisherman's son made himself the finest-looking man in Erin and began to give music and sport to the king, and he entertained him five times better than had the Gruagach and his eleven sons.

Then the king's daughter fell in love with him, and she set her mind on him to that degree that there was no life for her without him. When the king saw the straits that his daughter was in, he ordered the marriage without delay.

The wedding lasted for nine days and nine nights, and the ninth night was the best of all. When the wedding was over, the king felt he was losing his strength, so he took the crown off his own head and put it on the head of the old fisherman's son and made him king of Erin in place of himself.

The young couple were the luck, and we the stepping-stones. The presents we got at the marriage were stockings of buttermilk and shoes of paper, and these were worn to the soles of our feet when we got home from the wedding.

THE WONDERFUL TRADE (1890)*

Edith Hodgetts

In a certain kingdom there lived an old woman who was almost penniless. She had an only son, whom she wished to apprentice where he would not be required to work, but only eat, sleep, and wear fine clothes. But, unfortunately, such places were scarce, and whenever she told her wishes to others they only laughed at her, saying, "You will have to go right 'round the world first, and then you won't get what you want! No one would be such a fool!"

The old woman was highly indignant and said she was not going to be *done*. So after selling all she had, which, needless to say, was very little, she turned to her son and told him to get ready, and they would start off to seek their fortunes.

They traveled from one town to another, but nobody seemed inclined to take the son into such apprenticeship as she wanted, especially without money. They went through the whole kingdom without any success. At last the old woman, finding that her search was fruitless, decided to turn homeward once more, not in the highest spirits, when suddenly they came upon a man, who, seeing that the old woman looked very sad, asked her the reason.

"How can I be otherwise?" replied she. "I have walked and walked through the whole kingdom with my son, to bind him apprentice to a trade where he need do no work, only eat, drink, sleep, and dress well, but nobody will have him without money."

"Give him to me," said the stranger, "and on this day three years hence you may come and fetch him away. For teaching him I will take nothing, but mind

* *Tales and Legends from the Land of the Tzar: Collection of Russian Stories* (London: Griffith Farran, 1890).

you recognize him again. If you don't, you can come twice more after three years, but if you do not know him then, he must be mine for ever."

The old woman thought this very extraordinary. Was it possible not to know her own child again? However, she was glad that she had at any rate found someone who would take him. Now she could return to her own country and laugh at the people who had once laughed at her. It was not a very Christian way of looking at things, but, nevertheless, so thought the old woman. In her joy she forgot to ask this stranger who he was and where he lived, but gave him her son and left, to return after three long years to that very spot to claim her boy.

Now this stranger was a sorcerer. All his companions having died, he alone was left with his daughter to perform his magic arts. He kept a school, in which he taught the most wonderful things possible to some dozen young men who boarded with him.

The three years passed away very rapidly, and at last the important day arrived when the old woman was once more to behold her beloved son, and take him home with her. She got up very early and went to the place where she had first met the stranger. The time approached, and with it the sorcerer.

"Ah, little mother! I see you have not forgotten to fetch your boy."

He gave two loud whistles, and in another moment twelve bees came buzzing round the old woman, who was terribly frightened and began waving her hands about to keep them off.

"Don't be afraid, little mother," said the sorcerer, laughing, "for your son is among them. I have taught him all kinds of clever things, and if you really want him back, you must try and find him."

"Find him, indeed! Why, I gave you a boy, and these are only a lot of horrid bees! Why, good man, do you want to make such a fool of me? Don't you think I know the difference between a boy and a bee?"

"These are not bees really, but twelve young men, who, like your son, wished to have the same easy kind of apprenticeship. They fell into my hands and have been taught all kinds of cunning and wonderful things. One of the things being that they can change themselves into whatever they wish, whenever they please. Eleven of these are staying with me forever because their parents did not succeed in recognizing them, and—"

"I should think not," exclaimed the old woman. "This is the greatest fraud I ever came across, and you ought to be punished for cheating a poor old woman like me."

"Hush! Don't speak like that, little mother. I was just going to tell you that your son is the twelfth, and if you don't recognize him, he must stay with me like the others."

"But, great heavens, how can I possibly recognize him when they are each and all alike?"

Suddenly one of the bees flew to the old woman's face and began to sting her.

"Get away, you nasty thing, do!" she cried, beating it away from her.

"Well, don't you recognize your son?"

"No, I don't!"

"Very well, then you must come again on this day three years hence. The bee that stung you was your son. However, it is too late now. You must come again."

The old woman burst into tears and left the place, promising to come again in three years.

When the time came round, the old woman once more went to meet the sorcerer.

When he whistled this time, twelve white doves flew round the old woman.

"Try and recognize your son. He is among them," said the sorcerer.

She looked, and looked, but grew no wiser: All the twelve doves sat in a row; all had exactly the same feathers, and how was she to find him? She looked again and saw one of the doves put its head under its wing. Yet, although she noticed this, nothing crossed her mind.

"No," she said at last, "I do not recognize my son."

"The little dove that had its head under its wing was your son. Now you must come again at the end of another three years, but that will be the last time. If you do not know him then, he will be lost to you forever."

"Old swindler!" muttered the old woman as the sorcerer and the doves disappeared.

The years passed away, and the old woman found herself for the last time at the place where she and the sorcerer first met. This time she determined to keep her eyes open. The sorcerer whistled again, and twelve little ponies came galloping up and stood in two rows before the old woman.

"Now, then, little mother, which is your son?" asked the sorcerer.

The old woman passed up one row, then down the other, but no sign of any kind did she see. She passed by again, and this time one of the ponies began stamping on the ground.

"This is my son!" she said, stopping in front of the little pony.

"Right for once, little mother. You have recognized him this time!" cried the sorcerer. "But you are not so very clever, you know. If it had not been for your son's stamping in the way he did, you would have passed him. However, you may take him home now, and may the Lord bless you both!"

The horse then changed itself into the old woman's son, who had grown wonderfully handsome in those few years.

"How did you get on without me, mother mine?" asked the young fellow as they walked homeward.

"Very badly, my boy. I have hardly had anything to eat all the time."

"Well, mother, I shall see that you have plenty of everything now. Will a hundred rubles be enough to start with?"

"A hundred rubles!" cried the old woman. "I never had so much in all my born days. In fact, I never saw so much. Where have you got them?"

"I haven't got them yet, but I shall get them for you in a minute. Listen. Do you see those hunters galloping about yonder after a fox? Well, I shall change myself into a hound and catch the fox for them. They will then want to buy me, and ask you how much you want for me. 'A hundred rubles, gentlemen,' you must say. They will, of course, bargain with you, but you must not on any account give me for less. And another thing you must not forget—that is, to be sure and take my collar off before you part with me. The hunters are sure to make a fuss, but no matter, do as I tell you, and all will be right."

As soon as he had finished speaking he changed himself into a beautiful dog and ran after the fox, which he very soon caught. The old woman went up to the hunters, who had ridden up to the dog and were now stroking it, wondering whose it was.

"Why do you interrupt our hunting, old woman?" they asked, when they saw her coming up to them.

"Because, gentlemen, it is my dog, and I have come to fetch it away."

"No, old woman, don't take him away. We want to keep him ourselves."

"Very well, gentlemen, if you would like to buy him you are welcome."

"How much do you want?"

"A hundred rubles, gentlemen."

"That is rather high, my good woman."

"No, gentlemen, not at all. Look at the dog yourselves, and see what a splendid animal it is."

The hunters, after a little bargaining, counted out the money, while the old woman began taking the collar off. However, when the hunters saw what she was doing, they would not hear of it.

"But I don't intend selling the collar," said the old woman. "I only sell the dog."

"Nonsense!" cried the hunters. "We must have the collar, too. Who ever thought of buying a dog without a collar? Why, the animal would be sure to get lost."

The old woman, after a great deal of arguing, at last consented, and giving them the dog as well as the collar, took the money, and went away.

Off rode the hunters, when suddenly a fox ran past. They loosened their dogs and away they went, but the creature was not to be caught so easily.

"Let us try the new hound. He may be able to catch it," said one of the hunters.

So they loosened him, too, but the cunning dog had hardly been set free when away he went in exactly the opposite direction of the fox, and when at a safe distance from the hunters, he changed himself quickly into his proper shape and overtook the old woman.

"Oh, mother! Why on earth did you sell the collar? I warned you not to, and if we had not met a fox, I should have been lost to you forever."

Then they began building a new hut for themselves, where they lived for some time without starving, but at last only a hundred kopeks remained out of the hundred rubles.

"My dear son," said the old woman one day, "I wish we could get a little more money to buy a few things with."

"Very well. How much do you want? Will two hundred rubles be enough for you?"

"Two hundred rubles? Why, we could build quite a large house, as well as buy all the things I want."

"Well then, look here. I will change myself into a beautiful bird, and you must take me to market and sell me for two hundred rubles. But mind, mother, and on no account sell me in a cage, or else I can never come home again."

So saying he changed himself into a bird with such lovely feathers that the like had never been seen. The old woman was greatly astonished and carried it to market in a pretty little cage, and in a very short time she had quite a crowd round her, who came to admire the beautiful creature and wanted to buy it.

Unfortunately, however, the price was too high for them, so they shook their heads, whistled, and went away. The old woman was beginning to think that she would never get rid of it at all, when suddenly who should turn up but the sorcerer. He knew her at once and went up to her and began admiring the bird. The old woman did not recognize him since he was disguised to look like somebody else. He asked how much she wanted for the bird, and she told him. He did not hesitate a moment, but gave her the money, and was just about to take the cage, when she stopped him.

"I did not sell the cage as well," said she.

After a long argument, the sorcerer and the old woman kept quarreling. But the assembled crowd took the old woman's part and would not let the sorcerer have the cage. So he had to give it back to her. The sorcerer, on seeing that he could not do anything, took the bird and tied it up in his handkerchief and went home.

"Well, daughter," said he, "I have brought back our young man after all, and a nice lot of trouble he gave me."

"Oh! Where is he?" she exclaimed.

He untied the handkerchief very carefully; but just as he opened it, out flew the bird through the open window and away high up into the air, quite out of sight, leaving the sorcerer stamping about in at awful rage, and his pretty little daughter to lament her loss.

When the old woman returned home from market, she was greatly surprised, as well as overjoyed, at seeing her son seated very comfortably in a chair, waiting for her.

"Thank Heaven," said he, embracing her, "that you did what I told you this time. It would have been awfully unpleasant for me as well as for you had you done otherwise, for the man who bought me was no other than the sorcerer. He is trying to get me back to marry his daughter, who seems to have taken a great fancy to me, but as I don't particularly care for the young lady myself, I am by no means anxious to return to him."

Things went on very well for some time. The old woman got all she wanted, and everything was very comfortable in the little hut, till one day she looked out of the window into the little yard at the back, and sighed.

"What is the matter now, mother mine?" asked the son." Is there anything more that you are in need of?"

"Oh, it's not worth talking about, dear! I was only thinking what a pity it is that such a nice piece of ground as we have at the back here should be so empty. Now, if I had the means, I should buy some horses, cows, pigs, poultry, or something to make it look cheerful, but it's no use my wishing for things when we can't afford to have them."

"I don't know, mother. I think we shall soon be able to get all you want. I told you that I would try and please you in every possible way, and get you everything you like. So take me to the market again, and I shall change myself into a lovely little pony, and you must try and sell me for three hundred rubles; but be careful not to sell me with the bridle."

So off went the old woman once more to market, leading a sweetly pretty, plump little pony. The crowd again surrounded her, admiring the wicked-looking little horse, and began bargaining, but the old woman firmly kept to her price. "Three hundred rubles, and not a kopek less," she had said, and stuck to it.

"How much did you say, little mother?" asked a voice.

It was the sorcerer again.

"Three hundred rubles, and not a kopek less."

"There you are, three hundred rubles, well counted," he cried, throwing the money down before her, while the old woman began taking off the bridle,

"No, no, old woman!" the sorcerer exclaimed, taking the bridle roughly out of her hands. "What next? Where in the wide world did you see a horse sold without a bridle? How do you expect me to take him home?"

And before anyone could stop him, he jumped on to the little pony and galloped off as hard as he could, leaving the old woman wringing her hands, bemoaning her hard fate.

"Oh, my son, my son, my darling son! I have lost you now forever!"

The people tried to comfort her as best they could, though they themselves were sorely puzzled by her cries of "my son!" and wondered how a pony could be so nearly related to her. But they at last came to the conclusion that the "poor old woman was not quite right in her upper story," and told her that she had best go home and console herself with a glass or two of vodka, which she could well afford out of the three hundred rubles. But the old woman had recognized the sorcerer as he mounted the pony, and regarded the money he had given her with disgust. What was it to her, if she were never to see her beloved son again?

Meanwhile the sorcerer, thinking that he would pay the "youngster" back for flying out the window when last he bought him as a bird, rode him about for three whole days and three whole nights without giving the tired horse a moment's rest. He rode over stock and stone, up hill and down dale, until the perspiration poured down his face in streams. He was at length obliged to go home. When he arrived in his garden, he tied the unfortunate animal's head to a tree in such an uncomfortable position that the poor creature could hardly breathe.

"Well," said the sorcerer aloud to himself as he walked into the hut, "I think I have pretty well done for him this time."

"Done for whom, father?" asked his daughter.

"Why, for that young fellow I used to have, whom you took such a fancy to. There he is. Just look at him. Not likely to get away this time, is he?"

The damsel at once ran off into the garden, and on seeing the poor little pony tied up with his head high up in the air, she could not help being sorry for him and angry with her father for his cruelty.

"Poor thing," she cried. "How my father has tormented you! How cruel of him to have tied you up like this, and without any food, too!"

She untied the horse's head very gently from the tree and patted him fondly. But the horse loosened himself from her grasp, and, after thanking her, he bounded off into the fields and far away.

The girl was so alarmed that she ran trembling to her father, exclaiming, "Forgive me, father, but I loosened the little pony, as I felt so sorry for him, and he has run away."

Hardly had the sorcerer heard these words when he changed himself into a gray wolf and gave chase. The pony, on hearing someone chasing him, turned himself into a white dove. The sorcerer then changed himself into a kite, and flew after the dove. They were very close to each other now, but the dove suddenly perceiving a river below him, flew down, changing himself into a stickleback, and stood on the defensive. The sorcerer, not wishing to be beaten, changed himself into a pike, and dashed into the water. The stickleback shot rapidly through a hole in the shell of a crawfish and waited.

"Turn your head round, friend stickleback," said the pike, "and I will eat you."

"You had better not, friend pike, for it would not agree with you. You would very soon suffocate. And besides, pikes never eat sticklebacks; it is not at all fashionable."

And then they stood looking at each other for nearly three hours, till at last the pike fell fast asleep. Meanwhile the stickleback slipped out of the shell and swam through the water. He swam and swam till he came to a raft. After he climbed on to it, he floated on it until he came near to the shore where, to his surprise, he saw a most beautiful princess sitting and watching the tide. The stickleback changed himself at once into a golden ring and rolled before the princess's feet. She took it up, put it on her beautiful little white finger, and gazed at it in admiration as she said softly in a low, musical voice, "Ah, how I should like to find a good and handsome young man to marry me! I don't care for any of the men I have seen. They are none of them to my taste. But I suppose I am difficult to please and shall have to die an old maid!"

At this moment the pike, who had been left sleeping, appeared on the scene, and, on hearing these words, changed himself at once into a handsome young man, and came up to the princess, saying, "I beg your pardon, princess. I lost my ring just now, and I think you picked it up. Will you please give it back to me, or keep it, and take me for your husband, if you think I am good-looking enough for you."

The princess was very angry at the cool way in which the stranger spoke.

"Marry *you*, you impudent creature!" she cried. "There, take your ring, and be gone!"

So saying, she took the ring from her finger, and threw it down on the ground before the sorcerer, but the moment the ring fell it turned into a number of very small seeds, one of which rolled under the princess's shoe. On seeing this, the sorcerer changed himself quickly into a cock and began picking the seeds. When he had finished eating them all up, he cried out in a loud voice: "Cock-a-doodle-doo! I have done the very thing I wanted!"

But at that moment the last seed rolled out from under the shoe, and, changing itself into a handsome hawk, threw itself on to the cock, and sent its sharp claws into his breast.

"Cock-a-doodle-doo, brother," cried the cock. "Let me go! Let me go!"

"Not I," replied the hawk. "Did you ever know a hawk to be such a fool as all that?"

And the unfortunate cock was torn in two. After that the hawk changed himself into a young man, so handsome that it would be simply impossible to describe him, or even to imagine his equal!

The princess fell so much in love with him that in a very few days they were married. Of course the old woman came to the wedding, and everybody was happy all round, especially the old woman.

"I never thought—I never dreamt—that he would ever marry a princess!" she cried in her joy. "Now I shall be able to spend the rest of my days in peace and happiness. This is what has come out of the apprenticeship that every one laughed at."

Her son did not keep up the arts which the sorcerer had taught him, but very soon forgot them all since he had not much chance to practice now.

Many years after some other people went in search of the same kind of apprenticeship for their sons, but all in vain, for the last sorcerer had been killed and with him died the wonderful trade.

THE STORY OF ALI THE MERCHANT
AND THE BRAHMIN (1892)*

Charles Swynnerton

There was once a Brahmin who had two sons. But the Brahmin was very old, and his sons were unlettered and ignorant. So the old man began to think: "My sons are so ignorant that they cannot even recite the creeds and the prayers on which we beggars depend for our daily food. How will they live? Who will give them a morsel of food when I am taken away?"

The thought of this preyed on his mind and gradually rendered him silent and desponding.

One day he was sitting at a shop in the bazaar, brooding over his troubles, when a fakeer† came up, and seeing him so sad and woebegone, he began to ask him the reason.

"Why are you so deep in thought?" said he.

"For no reason," said the Brahmin. "There is nothing the matter."

"Nay, but there is," replied the fakeer.

"But even if I were to tell you," said the Brahmin, "you could not divide my sorrows with me."

"You are mistaken," returned the fakeer. "I am a fakeer. Therefore, tell me your trouble."

"Well," said the Brahmin, "my only trouble is this: I am old and not likely to live. My sons are untaught and ignorant. They cannot say even a creed, and when I die they must both starve."

---

* *Indian Nights' Entertainment, or, Folk-Tales from the Upper Indus* (London: Elliot Stock, 1892).

† A Muslim or Hindu religious ascetic, who lives solely on alms. Also spelled *fakir*.

"Nay," said the fakeer, "not so bad as that, not so bad as that. Listen to me, and I will make you an offer. You say you have two sons who want training. Hand them over to me for a year, and I will be their tutor, if only at the end of the year you will agree to give me one of the boys, keeping the other for yourself."

This proposal seemed so reasonable to the Brahmin that he joyfully accepted it, and, rising up, he led the way to his home. There he introduced the boys to their future master, and the fakeer took them away to his own village. But both the Brahmin and the fakeer had quite omitted to specify which of the sons was to be the property of the fakeer at the end of the year. It was the habit of the fakeer to sit at the door of his miserable hut, where he had two hookahs for all passers who chose to stop and smoke hubble-bubble. Very few thought of passing without giving him alms, and by this means he was able to provide food for himself and the two boys, and he had ample time as well for teaching them their letters. Very soon it became apparent to him that, of his two pupils, the younger developed far greater intelligence than his elder brother, so to him the fakeer determined to communicate all the secrets and the arts of fakeers, such as witchcraft, magic, and soothsaying, while he taught the elder only such ordinary knowledge as was suitable to poor Brahmins.

When the year was up the fakeer said to the boys: "Now come along with me. Let us go and visit your father."

So they set out together, and came and put up in the town where the children's father and mother were living. The next morning the younger boy asked the fakeer's permission to go and see his parents, to which the fakeer agreed, and both brothers took their way to their old home. When the younger son had greeted his father, who was overjoyed to see them both, he whispered to him: "Remember, father, when you choose between us, you are to choose me."

In a few minutes the fakeer himself arrived, and said: "Brahmin, you see I have fulfilled my side of the bargain. Now let me choose which of the two I shall have."

"Nay," said the Brahmin, "I will choose for you. Take the elder; the younger is mine."

But the fakeer would not have this on any account. "Nay, master," said he, "the younger boy I love. Let me have him."

So there arose a dispute between the two men, the father and the teacher, until at last, after much argument, they agreed to call in arbitrators to settle their differences. When the arbitrators entered the room, the Brahmin addressed them, explained to them all the circumstances of the case, and concluded by saying: "I have decided to retain my younger son for myself, but do you judge between us."

Upon this the neighbors turned to the fakeer and said, "It is evident that both the boys are the sons of the Brahmin. Therefore, do you take the elder and be satisfied."

But the fakeer flew into a rage, and cried: "The younger is mine; I will have him or none! I will have him or none!"

Upon saying this, he instantly left the Brahmin's house, muttering a dreadful revenge. After a day or two the father said to his younger son, "You advised me to choose you, and you I have chosen. But know we are poor and destitute, and you must help us to live."

"Father," answered the lad, "I know something of magic. If you will trust me, we shall have no lack of money. This very night I will enter the empty house on the opposite side of the street. You shall see me enter, but you must not follow me till the morning, and then you will find there a bullock that is tied. Him you must lead out, and sell him for not less than a hundred rupees. But remember, you are not to part with the headstall, and, above all, beware of the fakeer."

In the evening the boy entered the empty hut, as he had said, and the next morning it was found that a fine bullock had been brought into the world by his magic. When the Brahmin had examined him, he untied him and led him by the rope into the marketplace for sale.

"What is the price of your bullock?" cried half a dozen voices at once.

"One hundred rupees without the headstall," answered the Brahmin.

After some discussion, a farmer counted out one hundred rupees and bought the bullock. "But you must give up the headstall as well," said the people.

The Brahmin, however, refused to part with it, and the purchaser then agreed to buy another. Then the Brahmin took the headstall, laid it on his shoulder, and turned himself homeward. After a time, he noticed that the headstall was missing from his shoulder. He supposed it to have fallen, but as it was useless to search for it. Then, he continued his way. Arriving at his house, he said: "Son, I have sold the bullock, and, see, here are the hundred rupees. But, alas, by some misadventure, I have lost the headstall."

"Don't be distressed, father," answered the son. "I was myself the headstall, and you see I have found my way back all right."

The Brahmin, who had been wretchedly poor, was now rich enough to pay off his debts, and to live in less discomfort. But as the money was not inexhaustible, it was soon spent, and then he had to turn to his son once more.

"Always depend on my power," said the boy, "and you will never need anything."

In a few days he took his father aside and revealed to him another scheme. "Tonight I shall again go into the empty hut and shut the door. In the morning you will find there a handsome horse. Take him and sell him for not less than one hundred rupees, but remember you are not to part with the bridle, and, above all, beware of the fakeer, who is still lurking somewhere in the village. He is the master of magic, and I am only the pupil."

Early before sunrise the Brahmin opened the door of the house and saw before him a beautiful riding-horse fully bridled. Leading him forth, he mounted the horse's back and rode to the marketplace to sell him.

"How much?" cried the people.

"One hundred rupees without the bridle," said he.

Now the fakeer himself happened to be one of the crowd assembled around the horse. Laying aside his bag, and retaining his staff, he began to walk round the animal as if to observe its points, and as soon as he saw that the Brahmin was absorbed in making terms with the dealers, he suddenly lifted his staff and struck the horse a violent blow on the back. The horse sprang several feet into the air, tossed off the Brahmin, and instantly galloped away, while the fakeer ran after him at the top of his speed.

As he ran in pursuit, he kept crying out, "My young fellow, I was the making of you. You know it. It seldom happens that the moustaches grow longer than the beard. How far do you intend to make me run—two miles, three miles? In the end you simply cannot escape me. I am the master."

Hearing these words, the lad in the shape of the bridle began to consider that escape was impossible under these conditions, and he compelled the horse to stop short. Then, by the power of his magic art, the horse suddenly vanished, and the boy himself became a dove.

"Ho! Ho!" said the fakeer. "You turned yourself into a bridle, and you are now a pigeon. But do you not know that I can become a hawk?"

And the fakeer, in the form of a hawk, gave instant chase. The poor dove wheeled, and turned now here, now there—sometimes in the open, sometimes in the tangled wood, until at last he found that it was all of no avail. He would have been struck down by his pursuer if he had not happened to arrive at a lake, when, changing the form of a dove, he became a fish and plunged into the water.

"Ha, ha!" laughed the fakeer. "A horse, a pigeon, and now a fish! But what is the use? I shall now become an alligator, and you cannot possibly escape, for I will devour every fish in the lake."

So the fakeer then changed himself from a hawk into an alligator, and in that shape he raged through the waters of the placid lake, eating voraciously every fish he could find. At last he came to the dark creek where his pupil was biding, and peering in he made a hideous dart at him. Caught in extremity of despair, his intended victim made one final effort and succeeded in leaping onto the bank, whence, perceiving that the corpse of a man was hanging from the branch of a tree, he transformed himself into a mosquito and hid himself in the dead man's nostrils. Out now came the alligator, having observed the whole proceeding, and resuming his original form of a man, he took up a small piece of soft clay, and with it he stopped up the nostrils of the corpse, determined that this time there should be no escape. He then slid down from the tree and squatted on the ground beneath to consider how he should next proceed. Just then there passed by a respectable countryman riding on a horse, to whom the fakeer cried out, "O beloved of God, give me, I pray you, a little cloth."

"I can give you but little," answered the traveler. "Why do you not go into the town, where Ali the merchant lives? He is rich, and freely gives away everything."

"So I shall," said the fakeer, "but, meanwhile, I am begging you to give me a little cloth."

So, the traveler handed a piece of linen to the fakeer and continued his journey. Meanwhile the fakeer tore the linen into three slips, and after climbing the tree once more, he tied up the corpse's head, binding it round over the nostrils with the linen slips, so that the mosquito could not possibly force his way out. After doing this, he came down.

"Now I shall visit Ali," said he.

And without any more delay, he went to Ali's house and took up a position with other beggars outside the door. By and by Ali the merchant came out and sat down to his prayers. As soon as he appeared the fakeer approached him and put up his joined hands, as beggars always do.

"O Ali," said he, "your name and your liberality are spoken of everywhere. I have traveled to see you from a distant land, but just now I want your help, for God's sake, in a matter of importance."

When Ali looked at him and perceived that he was a fakeer, he answered: "My goods are your goods. If you want a horse, speak, and I will give it you, or money or clothes."

"I want neither horse, nor money, nor any clothes," replied the fakeer. "I only want you to do me a small favor. For God's sake promise me that you will do it."

"Of course," said Ali. "I will oblige you, and it is not necessary for you to invoke the name of God so much. Why do you do it when you see I do not refuse?"

"Never mind," said the fakeer. "Come aside and hear my story."

So the fakeer took simple Ali the merchant to the side and said, "For God's sake, my friend, perform this favor for me. You are a Hindoo, I am a Mussulman. In a certain spot there is a body hanging from a tree. Go yourself, cut it down, and bring it here to me."

"Oh, what a difficult task you have set me!" cried the merchant. "I certainly cannot do this thing in the daytime. What would the people say? Still, for your sake, and as I have given my word, and because you are a fakeer, I will go at night and bring the body to you."

When darkness had set in, Ali mounted his horse and rode out of the town, and when he had arrived at the spot indicated, he dismounted and began, in spite of his unwieldy bulk, to climb up the tree. When he got within reach, he cut the rope with a knife, which he had been holding between his teeth, and down fell the corpse with a thud. He then descended, thinking to take up the body in order to set it on his horse, and so to carry it back to the town. But, lo! when he got to the ground, he was astounded to perceive that the corpse was once more hanging from the same branch. Believing that he had made some mistake, he again climbed the tree and again cut down the body. But precisely the same thing was repeated, for as soon as he had reached the ground the corpse was seen to be still dangling from the bough. A third time he essayed his difficult task, and the third time this extraordinary corpse resumed his position in the tree. Ali now began to feel seriously alarmed.

"There is something wrong here!" cried he, and getting on his horse, he rode swiftly back to the town.

When the fakeer, who had been looking out for him, saw that he had not brought in the body, he began to reproach him. "What!" said he. "You could not do such a trifling service for a poor fakeer as that?"

"The blame is not mine," said the merchant. "The corpse is bewitched. Every time I cut it down, it jumped up again into the tree, and there it is hanging now!"

"Ali!" replied the fakeer. "If this had been so easy a thing, I would have brought in the corpse myself. But, as you say, there is magic in it. O Ali! To me you are a king, though only a merchant, and a king you shall really be if you will only bring me that body! And now remember my directions. First, do not dismount from your horse; and next, for God's sake, try to manage it so that the corpse will fall on the horse and not on the ground."

With these instructions, Ali set out again, and coming to the tree, he called upon God and cut the string. He had so stationed himself that the corpse fell in front of him on the horse's withers. So he settled it evenly, with his stirrup-leathers, and then, uttering a sigh of relief, he started once more for the town.

As he went along, Ali cast his eye over this singular corpse and began to address it with playful humor: "Now, here you are," said he, "a dead body, though how long dead I don't know. Pretty tricks, indeed! I wonder how you managed to get up into that tree again and again!"

Hardly had he spoken the words, when the dead body began to quiver and shake and wriggle as if it had ague. Seeing this, Ali seized it and held onto it with all his strength. But he held on in vain, for the body easily shook itself off the horse, and in another second it was suspended once more from the branch of the tree.

"The devil!" muttered Ali. But he was in no mood to turn back that night, for the sky was dark and murky, and his mind was confused. So he made the best of his way back to his home.

When the fakeer saw that he had returned a second time without the body, he began to reproach him once more.

"O Ali!" said he. "What, no body yet? How is this? For God's sake, tell me!"

"Why are you perpetually calling on the name of God?" said Ali peevishly. "Listen, and judge if I am to blame."

Then Ali related to the fakeer the whole of his adventure.

"I see how it is," said the fakeer. "The body is certainly bewitched. I knew that before, but, Ali, the next time, you are not to open your mouth to speak a single word to it on any account whatsoever."

The night following Ali again saddled his horse and rode out to the fatal tree. He acted precisely as on the last occasion, and, with the body balanced in front of him, he began his journey to the town. As he rode along, the body began to mutter and to appeal to soft-hearted Ali's feelings.

"Ali!" moaned he, "we all know you to be a great man, wise and prudent, and of excellent judgment. For God's sake, then, stop a moment until I ask you a question!"

So Ali pulled up his horse in the moonlight, for the night was fair, and then the corpse resumed his speech: "Listen," said the corpse. "I'll tell you a story of a frightful tyranny, a piece of consummate cruelty, which has been witnessed in this very country. There is a certain Brahmin. The Brahmin's family consists of four persons—himself, his wife, his son, and his daughter. What the mother orders, the daughter does not obey, and what the father orders, the son does not obey. In the midst of all this domestic disunion, the daughter grows up and becomes marriageable. Without consulting with his wife, the father goes out to the house of a neighbor, betroths his daughter to a certain youth, and receives for her a hundred rupees. The marriage is fixed for the fifteenth day after the betrothal. Having done this, he returns home, but he keeps the business secret from every member of his family. About the same time the mother also goes out, and betroths her daughter to someone else, and she also receives one hundred rupees for her. Then she comes home, but she also keeps her deed a secret from the rest of her family. After a day or two the son thinks to himself, 'It is time now for my sister to be married. I had better go and get her betrothed somewhere.' So he goes to the house of one of his friends, and betroths her to an acquaintance, receiving a hundred rupees for her, and fixing the same day for the wedding as his father and mother had chosen. Then he, too, comes home; but he takes care not to breathe a word of the matter to anyone. On the morning of the wedding day the father gets up, and, going to the bazaar, he buys five rupees' worth of rice and curry-stuffs, which he brings back with him to the house. When his wife sees him entering with such a quantity of food, she asks: 'What is all this rice for?'

"'This is our daughter's wedding-day,' answers the Brahmin. 'The guests will all assemble here this evening, and this rice is for their entertainment.'

"'Alas!' exclaims the wife. 'Something dreadful has happened. I also have betrothed our daughter, and this is the day fixed for the wedding. My friends will also be here this evening.'

"She has no sooner spoken these words when the son enters the door, and says: 'Why, father, what's the meaning of all these preparations?'

"'It is your sister's wedding day,' answers his father. 'I have betrothed her, and the guests will be here to-night.'

"'Sir,' replies the son, 'I also fixed this day as the day of my sister's wedding, and the guests whom I have invited will also be here immediately.'

"After hearing these heavy tidings they all sit down in silence and await the issue of events. By and by the three grooms and the whole of the three parties of invited guests arrive at the house and begin to ask for explanations.

"Now the poor young girl herself knows nothing of these arrangements. She is playing innocently with some of her companions in the court, when one of them who has overheard the angry expostulations of the guests runs to her and says: 'Your father and your mother and your brother have engaged you to three different persons. Today is your wedding day, and all those people are the guests.'

"The daughter now thinks to herself: 'Can this be so? But if I go with the man of my father's choice, my mother and brother will be angry. Neither can I consent to marry any of the others. Let me go and see whether this can be true.'

"So she goes to her mother and learns what fatal mistakes have been made. Beginning to weep, the poor girl says to herself: 'What's to be done now? Better die than survive this disgrace. If I leap from the house-top, it will be all over, and my troubles will end.' And she mounts the outer steps and throws herself down, but life is extinct before her body reaches the ground. Her playmates, seeing this catastrophe, cry out: 'Alas, alas! Help! Your daughter has killed herself!'

"And the whole assembly comes rushing to the spot. But it is too late. The child lies upon the ground with her eyes open, and her spirit has gone forever. Such is the mournful end of an innocent girl!

"This," continued the corpse, "is the tyranny to which I referred as going on in this country. And now, O merchant, answer, what have you to say to it?"

Since Ali had been adjured in the name of God he felt bound to answer. Besides, in his indignation, he had utterly forgotten all about the fakeer.

"My opinion is this," said he. "The unhappy girl saved her whole family from well-merited disgrace. That is my reply."

As soon as the merchant had finished speaking, the corpse began to shake as before, and in another minute, it fell, glided rapidly over the earth, and once more it hung itself up in the tree.

By this time it was close upon dawn, and the astonished Ali, not willing to be seen near so unlucky a spot in the light of day, hastened away home. As soon as he appeared, the fakeer again began to upbraid him. "Such a trifle it is, Ali," said he, "which I ask of you, and all in the name of God! Have you not accomplished it yet?"

"O fakeer, do not be hard on me," answered Ali. "Have I not given you my word? If it costs me my head, that wretched corpse, I am determined to bring it to you."

At the close of day, Ali the merchant once more rode forth to try his luck on the bewitched corpse. He arrived at the tree, cut down the body, settled it on the horse, and set off for the town once more. He had not gone half a mile when the corpse began to wheedle and coax him again. "O merchant," said the body, "you are a great man—who can deny it? Listen to me, for I have something more to tell you of what is going on in this country.

"In the morning her friends bathe the poor girl's dead body and, laying it on a stretcher, carry it away to the place of burning. The three wedding parties now separate and betake themselves to their homes. Not so the three young men. 'Let us all perish with her,' cries one, and sadly they join in the funeral procession. When the mourners arrive at the pile, the same youth, he to whom the brother had betrothed her, exclaims: 'For me life is over. I will ascend too.'

"'Nay,' answer the people, 'do not be foolish. A woman might indeed make this sacrifice for a man, but a man should know better.'

"Yet, when the body is laid on the top of the pile, he springs up, and sits himself down beside it, wringing his hands. Then the faggots are lighted, and in an hour this devoted couple are burnt to ashes. When this is all over, the youth, to whom the girl had been betrothed by the mother, collects all the charred bones together and buries them on the spot. Then he becomes a fakeer, and, taking up his station there, watches by the bones day after day, and never leaves them, except on those rare occasions when he goes into the village to beg for his food. When the third youth, he to whom the father betrothed the child, witnesses all these things, he goes up to the one who is sitting over the bones, and he says to him: 'Friend, we all loved the girl. We all had a share in her, for each gave his hundred rupees. The bones of one of us are mingling with her own. You are now the guardian of her dear remains. As for me, I shall also turn fakeer, and for the sake of that bright one I will travel over the whole world.'

"So he dons the garb of a fakeer, and with a wallet on his back and a staff in his hand, he starts on his travels. After traveling many a weary mile, at last, one day toward evening, he arrives at a village, and sees a woman spinning at the door of a house. To her he goes forward and says: 'O mother, I have here a little flour, bake me some bread!'

"The woman merely answers, 'Oh yes,' and goes on with her spinning.

"The fakeer, being tired, sits down and waits patiently. At last he speaks again. 'Mother,' says he, 'the sun is now setting. By this time I could have walked on some three or four miles. Bake me, I pray you, a little bread.'

"The woman, who was a witch, answered, 'Don't be in a hurry. Your bread shall be baked, and you shall have it immediately.'

"Upon saying this she rises from her spindle, takes a handful of dry grass, puts it in the stove, and on it she drops a little fire. Then she catches up her little girl, who was sleeping on a couch hard by, and puts the child's feet into the fire, and they begin to burn and burn like dry wood, nor does the child once awake, though the whole of her feet, almost to the knees, consume slowly away. The fakeer looks on with speechless horror, watching the woman baking his bread over that horrible fire.

"When the bread is quite ready, the woman enters the house and brings out a little vase. Pouring some colored liquid from it into a large vessel, she fills it up with water, and lifting her child, she puts both her legs into the mixture. Then, snatching her up once more, she lays her as before on the bed, and covers her over with a sheet.

"'O fakeer,' she cries, 'come and eat. Your bread is ready.'

"'Nay, woman,' answered he. 'I eat not, I am a fakeer. As for you, you are worse than a cannibal. Such tyranny as this is outrageous!'

"'Your eyes beguile you,' says she. 'This is true bread, fit for fakeers. Come and eat it.'

"As they are arguing and disputing, the husband with his two sons approaches the spot and cries in angry tones: 'Woman, will you never be quiet? Whenever I come home, I find you quarreling with fakeers. You must be worse than human. You are a devil, and no woman at all!'

"He then turns to the fakeer and says: 'Eat the bread! Eat the bread!'

"'No, no!' replies the fakeer. 'Never shall I eat bread that has been baked with the feet of a poor child.'

"'What nonsense, man!' exclaims the husband. 'Was it ever heard of that a child's feet could be burnt like that? It is quite impossible.'

"'But, what if I saw it with my own eyes?' says the fakeer. 'What would you say if I prove it to you?'

"With this the fakeer steps forward to the couch and lifts up the sheet that covers the sleeping child. But he jumps back astonished still more than before, for the child's feet are whole and well, and there is not a sign of fire upon them. Meanwhile the mother comes and rouses the child, who wakes up crying.

"'Come and eat bread, child,' says the mother, 'come and eat bread.'

"'Don't give me any bread, mother,' says she. "Oh, no, I don't want bread, mother. Give me some dal.'*

"But the fakeer, sitting apart upon the ground, loses himself in reflection, thinking of the wonderful power of the witch. 'If I only knew her secret,' says he to himself, 'I might throw some enchanted water on the bones of my betrothed, and we might marry and be happy still.'

"So the fakeer feigns a complaisance that he does not feel and eats a little bread. He then, says: 'Oh, mother, have you any old bedstead you can lend me? If so, let me have it, as I am tired and would like to sleep.'

"Early in the morning the fakeer rises, takes up his wallet and goes out to beg. On his return in the evening he hands over all his alms to the woman. In short he takes up his abode with her, and each day he walks as many as ten or fifteen miles to all the villages round, but he never fails on his return to give the woman everything he collects. At last she says to him: 'O fakeer, once you scorned to touch my very bread. But now there is nothing which you do not give to me. What is it you really want of me?'

"'All I want,' answers he, 'is some of your skill in the art of magic. Teach me a little of your knowledge.'

"So the woman imparts to him all the knowledge she possesses herself, and he soon acquires it, after which he leaves that country and hastens back to visit his own. Four days is the length of the journey from the one country to the other, but his eagerness to visit the grave of his betrothed is such that he accomplishes it in a single day. It happens that when he arrives at the spot the other fakeer is in the village begging. So he digs up the whole of the bones and lays them reverently on the ground, after which he throws over them a sheet, and, sitting down, he keeps reading his magic words, and sprinkling the remains with his enchanted water. Presently he removes the sheet, and sees lying under it the living forms of his betrothed and of the other youth who was burnt with her on the funeral pile. At this moment the other fakeer also

* Dâl is a vetch used for food in India.

returns. And so it happens that they all find themselves sitting side by side at the tomb, the three suitors and the young girl, all four living and breathing face to face, as they lived on the earth before.

"And now, O merchant," concludes the corpse, "this is the question which in God's name I implore you to answer. Of all these three, whom is the girl to marry?"

In spite of his promise the forgetful merchant hastened to give his opinion. "My judgment is this," said he. "The two who were burnt together, the youth and the maiden, having been the same dust, must be regarded as brother and sister now that they are restored to life. Therefore they cannot marry. The suitor who raised the pair from the dead must be viewed as their father, since he was the author of their second birth. Therefore the maiden cannot be married to him. But the third suitor, who merely watched by the bones, must be considered differently. He bears no relationship whatever to these children of resurrection, and to him therefore the girl belongs, and him she must marry."

Having so delivered himself, Ali the merchant looked for the corpse, but it had slipped down from the horse, and was moving with surprising swiftness over the fields toward the tree, from which in a few minutes it was once more swinging in the wind.

Again the merchant rode on to encounter the disappointed greeting of the fakeer, who met him at the city gates, and cried: "O Ali, Ali, lacs and crores* of rupees in charity you squander abroad, yet for poor me you will not do this trifling favor."

"I was beguiled again into speaking," pleaded Ali. "Let me try my hand once more."

"For the love of God," urged the fakeer, "speak not a word to the body on any account."

That night Ali rode away again and acted precisely as on former occasions, cutting down the corpse and bringing it away on the neck of his horse. And as on former occasions so now, the corpse endeavored to take advantage of Ali's simplicity.

"For God's sake," he implores, "hear me but this once. Listen to the rest of my story, and I promise to go wherever you please. All the former part of the adventure I have reported exactly, and you cannot accuse me of perverting

---

* Hundreds of thousands.

the truth. Yet once more will I speak. Only, as the night is warm, undo these bandages, and take from my nostrils the clay that closes them up."

Ali felt glad when he heard the corpse's promise, and he had no hesitation in complying with his request. He first untied the bands of linen and then removed the clay. In a moment the mosquito escaped with a buzz, and, flying to the earth, turned at once into the son of the Brahmin, who walked rapidly away in the direction of the town, to the intense amazement of the bewildered Ali.

"Hullo!" cried he. "Who are you? Hi! Stop and say who you are and whence you have come."

But the boy did not say a word to him.

Meanwhile, the corpse had fallen heavily to the ground where it lay perfectly still. Then the merchant dismounted, and having replaced it once more, he continued his journey, and arrived with it safely at the town.

The fakeer was overjoyed. He advanced to meet the merchant, and helped him lift down the corpse. But when he did not see the bandages and the clay with which he had secured the mosquito, he turned away and set up a howl. "Ah, miserable Ali!" cried he. "What have you done? You have let my enemy escape me!"

He was not a man, however, to lose time in useless recriminations, so he made his way at once to the house of the Brahmin, and, peeping in through a hole in the door, he saw, as he expected, his runaway pupil. He therefore decided to remain in that town a little while longer. When a day or two elapsed, he sent a request to the boy to come and see him. The boy knew well that all this time he had been withstanding his master, and, as the old influence was still upon him, he said to his father: "I have been called by my master. Will you also come along with me?"

He went, therefore, to the house at which the fakeer was lodging and made his salaams to him.

"Bravo!" cried the fakeer. "You have done your old master credit. The world used to say that moustaches never grew longer than the beard, but you have proved the old saying to be false. Come, sit down."

The boy with a smile of triumph sat down by his master, who then said: "All this time you have outwitted me by mere tricks. If you trick me this time, I promise you something which will be the death of you outright."

"O, master," answered the boy, "let me give you a friendly challenge, and so let us decide who is the better man, you or I. I propose that you turn yourself into a tiger, while I shall turn myself into a goat. Should the goat eat the tiger, then the world will see that the pupil has surpassed his master. But should the tiger devour the goat, it will acknowledge the master to be still paramount."

The fakeer at once agreed to this proposal, but in the boy's mind there existed treachery unsuspected by his master. It was arranged between them that the boy in the form of a goat should be tied outside the town, and that at a certain hour in the evening the tiger should approach the spot and endeavor to carry him off.

Leaving the house of the fakeer, the boy and his father, the Brahmin, went round to a certain number of the inhabitants and revealed to them that the next evening a large tiger would be prowling about outside a certain part of the town, and that, in order to capture it effectually, it would be necessary for marksmen to be stationed in ambush behind the neighboring walls. So everyone was on the alert, armed, some with guns, and some with bows and arrows. Then the boy turned himself, as agreed upon, into a goat and was tied by the Brahmin to a stake near one of the entrances of the town. Presently a large, full-grown tiger was seen issuing from the jungle and creeping cautiously up the slope in the direction of his prey. Just then one of the concealed marksmen fired, but missed his aim, and the next moment the tiger had leaped upon the goat and had seized it by the neck. An indiscriminate volley was now poured in from all sides, and tiger and goat, both pierced in a score of places, rolled over and over dead upon the ground. And so ends the story of Ali the Merchant and the Brahmin, or, as it might be named with greater exactness, the Story of the Fakeer and the Brahmin's Son.

Twentieth-Century Tales

THE TALE OF THE SORCERER (1902)[*]

Leo Wiener

There once was a rich man who had no children. So he went to a wonder rebbe[†] in hopes that the rebbe would ask for a child for him.

"You were born with two fates," the rebbe told him. "Either you can be rich or you can have a child. Now which do you want? If you want a child, you must become poor."

The man replied that he would rather have a child than be rich. So the rebbe said, "Go home. In nine months your wife will give birth to a son."

Within a few months after the man returned home all his possessions were destroyed in a fire and his entire fortune was lost. When nine months passed his wife bore him a son. Then, for thirteen years, he struggled along but realized that he could do nothing to help the family. Consequently he took his son and went out into the world to beg. They wandered from city to city, from village to village, until they arrived in Odessa, where the father went into the poorhouse and saw how all the poor people there seemed happy and excited.

"What are you all so excited and happy about?" the father asked.

"Don't you know?" they replied. "Here in Odessa there's a rich man who holds a banquet for the poor every week, and if you want, you can come with us."

So he went to his son and asked him if he wanted to attend, and he said yes.

Soon after they went to the banquet, and when they got there, they were provided with all kinds of good things to eat and drink. At one point a carriage

* "Di Majnse vin dem Pojps," *Mitteilungen der Gesellschaft für jüdische Volkskunde* 9.2 (1902): 104–7.

† A wonder rabbi, who has special magical powers.

arrived, pulled by four beautiful horses, and a very handsome man stepped out of the carriage. The host of the banquet went up to him, brought him inside, and told everyone that this man would entertain them. Then he introduced him, saying he was a sorcerer, and this sorcerer began amazing the people by turning himself into a horse, an elephant, a loaf of bread, a cat, and anything in the world. And so they entertained themselves until two o'clock in the morning.

Afterward the father went to his son and said, "Come, my child, let's go."

But his son answered, "I won't leave until I can perform magic like the sorcerer."

The man began to weep bitterly and said to his son, "How do you think you're going to do that?"

His son answered, "Nothing can help. I must learn how to perform magic!"

So the father went to their host and told him the whole story—that his son wouldn't leave until he could perform magic as well as the sorcerer. The host replied that he couldn't help him, but he advised him to take the path that the sorcerer would take and lay himself down in front of the sorcerer's horses. The sorcerer would bring his carriage to a stop, and the man could then ask him to take his son on as an apprentice.

Well that's what he did, and the sorcerer ordered his driver to stop the horses. Then the man asked him to teach his son, and the sorcerer responded by asking the man to give him a contract that stipulated his son would stay with him for three years. Consequently, the man signed the contract with the sorcerer, and the sorcerer took the boy and told the man to return in three years to fetch his son.

At the end of three years the man went to retrieve his son at the sorcerer's house, which was difficult to reach because there were all kinds of beasts surrounding it. At first he was afraid to approach, but he took his life into his hands and made his way to the house, and the animals did not harm him. When he entered the house, he found the sorcerer sitting with his son and with the sorcerer's daughter.

The sorcerer recognized him at once and said to him, "I see you've come to retrieve your son."

The man said yes, and the sorcerer replied, "You can take your son back on one condition. My daughter and your son will become doves, and you must choose between them. If you choose your son, you can have him back, but if you choose my daughter, your son will be lost forever."

So the father became angry and left. He went into a forest and began to weep bitterly, and soon he fell asleep. While he was asleep, someone came and gave him a kick, and he leapt up. He saw a gray old man standing there.

"Why are you weeping, my friend?" the old man asked him.

"I gave up everything in the world to have a child," the man replied, "and now my son is with the sorcerer. When I went to fetch him, he said that my son would become a dove, and his daughter, a dove, and if I wanted to retrieve my son, I'd have to choose which one is my son. If I pick his daughter, my son is lost."

"Leave the forest," the old man said to him, "and you'll find a wheat field. Pluck several stalks of the wheat, and take out the grain. Then you are to go to the sorcerer and tell him that you're ready to pick one of the doves. When he shows you two doves, you are to throw the grain on the ground. The dove that gobbles up the grain quickly is the sorcerer's daughter. The dove that eats slowly is your son because he will be worried and concerned because you're his father. That's the one you're to choose."

And that's what the father did. He picked his son right away, and the sorcerer declared: "Well, you've found your son, but you can't take him home until you sign a contract stipulating that, as long as I live, your son won't perform any magic. After I die, he can do whatever he wants."

So the man agreed to sign that contract too, and off he went with his son.

Along the way the son said to his father, "Dear father, since you're so very poor, I'm going to change myself into a good horse, and you're to take me to the market and sell me. The merchants will offer a lot of money for me, but listen: when you sell me, you must remove the bridle. If you don't remove my bridle, then I'll remain a horse forever. If you take it off, then I can become a dove and will fly into the sky, and I'll see where you're walking. Then I'll fly down to you and turn back into a human."

The father agreed to the plan, and the son turned himself into a horse. Then the father brought the horse to the market in order to sell him. There were a great many merchants there, and they wanted to buy him. But the sorcerer was also there and understood everything: he knew that this was not a real horse, but one produced from magic. So he went to the father and asked him, "How much do you want for this horse?"

"A thousand rubles," said the father.

"Let me test him," replied the sorcerer, "to see if he is indeed worth that much."

"Go ahead," the father said.

So the sorcerer mounted the horse and said to the father, "You've got as much hope of seeing your son again as you can see your own ears. We agreed to a contract stipulating that he wouldn't perform magic during my lifetime, and you broke the contract."

Upon saying this, the sorcerer whipped the horse and rode away. He rode the horse all the way home, took him into the stable, and gave him ten lashes, some water to drink, and nothing to eat. Several days went by just like this. Soon a letter arrived from Odessa, requesting that the sorcerer come and perform his magic. Before he left, he told his daughter to go into the stable every day and to give the horse ten lashes and some water to drink.

In the morning she went into the stable and was about to whip the horse when she saw that it was quite a beautiful horse, and she felt sorry for him and caressed his head. Then, as she took off his bridle, the horse immediately turned into a human, and she recognized him.

"Get me a bit of water," he said, and when she left to fetch water, he turned himself into a dove and flew away.

On his way to Odessa the sorcerer saw that there was a dove flying overhead, and he realized that it was not a normal dove. So he turned himself into a hawk and went in pursuit of the dove. When the dove glanced back and saw that the hawk was about to catch him, he turned into a ring and fell into the sea. Immediately, the hawk turned into a duck with a copper bill and began searching for the ring in the sea. But the ring had gradually made its way up onto the shore, and when the tsar's daughter went to bathe in the sea, she found the ring.

Once the duck saw that the tsar's daughter had picked up the ring, he flapped his wings and said, "I can no longer get him now, but if I put all my powers to the test, I will get him in the end."

When the tsar's daughter arrived home, the ring began to squeeze her finger. So she tugged and removed it from her finger. Then it fell on the floor and turned into a man!

She was terrified, but he told her, "Don't be afraid; I'm a sorcerer, a man— but there's a sorcerer more powerful than I am, and he wants to harm me. Soon he'll come here and will want to take me away from you. I beg you not to abandon me, even when he offers you mountains of gold. Don't trust him! It'll all be a lie. Before he comes, I'll turn myself back into a ring, and you're to put me on your finger. When he tries to grab the ring, you're to throw me onto the floor. Then I'll turn into some peas, and he'll turn into a hen to eat the peas. When that happens, you must step on one of the peas, and I'll turn into a polecat and wring the hen's neck."

And that's what happened. The sorcerer came and wanted to buy the ring, but she refused to sell it. He persisted so much that she threw the ring on the ground. All at once it was transformed into peas, and the sorcerer became a hen. Then the princess stepped on one of peas, which became a polecat, and the polecat wrung the hen's neck. Afterward the servants took the hen's carcass and threw it outside on the street.

Later the young man went back to the sorcerer's daughter and married her, and they are alive and well. Now he is the one who goes to Odessa, as the sorcerer once did, to perform magic for the poor. Moreover his father lives with him and has no need to go begging anymore. He is just happy enough to take great joy in his children.

Translated from the Yiddish by Adelia Solemsli-Chrysler.

THE TWELFTH CAPTAIN'S TALE (CA. 1904)*

Joseph Charles Mardrus

Now, when the nine-hundred-and-fifty-second night came, Shahrazade said:

It is related—but is there knowledge save with Allah?—that there was once a king who had a barren queen. One day a Moor sought audience with him, saying: "If I give you a remedy by which your queen shall conceive and bear, will you give me your first son?"

"Certainly," answered the king.

So the Moor handed him two sweetmeats, one green and the other red, with these words: "Eat the green yourself, make your wife eat the red, and Allah will do the rest." Then he departed.

---

* J. C. Mardrus and E. Powys Mathers, eds., *The Book of the Thousand and One Nights,* vol. 4 (London: Casonova Society, 1923). First printed in French in Joseph Charles Mardrus, *Le livre des mille nuits et une nuit,* 16 vols. (Paris: Éditions de la Revue Blanche, 1889–1904). Mardrus took this tale from Guillaume Spitta-Bey's "Histoire de Mohammed l'Avisé" ("The Story of Clever Mohammed") in *Contes arabes modernes* (Leiden: E. J. Brill, 1883): 1–11. The original tale was told to Spitta-Bey, printed in Arabic, and translated into French.

After the king had eaten the green sweetmeat and given his wife the red one, the woman conceived and bore a son, whom his father called Muharaad (a blessing be upon that name!). And the child grew up rich in all learning and with a most sweet voice.

Then the queen bore a second son, whom his father called Ali; and the child grew up unhandy in everything. Finally she bore a third son, Mahmud, who grew up as an idiot.

At the end of ten years the Moor sought audience of the king again, saying: "Give me your first son."

So the king went to the queen and told her of the Moor's demand.

"Never, never," she cried, "Let us rather give him Ali, the unhandy."

The Moor left the palace with Ali, and walked with him along the roads in the great heat till noon. Then he asked: "Are you not hungry or thirsty?"

"By Allah, what a question!" exclaimed the boy, "How can you expect me not to be both, after half a day without food and drink?"

Then the Moor exclaimed: "Hum!" and led Ali back to his father, saying: "This is not my son. Let me see the three of them together, and I will know my own."

So the king made the three boys stand in line, and the Moor picked out Muhamad, the eldest, rich in all learning and with a most sweet voice. The Moor walked for half a day, and then asked: "Are you hungry? Are you thirsty?"

"If you are hungry or thirsty," answered Muhamad, "then I am hungry and thirsty also."

The magician embraced him, saying: "That is well, that is very well, O Learned! You are indeed my son."

He led Muhamad into his own land in the heart of Morocco, and, taking him to a garden, gave him food and drink. Then he put a grimoire* into his hand, and said: "Read this book!"

The boy turned the pages but could not read a word; so the Moor flew into a rage, and cried: "You are my son, and yet you cannot read this grimoire? By Gog and Magog, and by the fire of the turning stars, if you have not learnt it by heart in thirty days, I shall cut off your right arm!" Then he left Muhamad, and walked out of the garden.

The boy pored over the grimoire for twenty-nine days, but at the end of that time, he did not even know which way up to hold it. Suddenly he cast it

---

* A book of magic with symbols.

from him, crying: "If there be only one day left before my loss, I would rather spend it in the garden than wearying my eyes with this old thing!"

He began to walk under the heavy trees, deep in the garden, and saw a young girl hanging by her hair from one of them. He hastened to free her, and she embraced him, saying: "I am a princess, who fell into the power of the Moor. He hung me up here because I learnt his grimoire by heart."

"And I am a king's son," answered Muhamad, "The sorcerer gave me thirty days in which to learn the grimoire, but I cannot read it, and my loss is certain tomorrow."

"I will teach you," said the girl with a smile, "but when the Moor comes back, you must say that you have not been able to read one word."

She sat down by his side and taught him the grimoire, kissing him much the while. Then she said: "Hang me up as I was before," and Muhamad did so.

At this point Shahrazade saw the approaching of the morning and discreetly fell silent. But when the nine-hundred-and-fifty-third night had come, she said:

When the moon returned at the end of the thirtieth day, he bade the boy recite the grimoire.

"How can I recite it," asked Muhamad, "when I cannot read a word of it?"

Then the Moor cut off his right arm and cried: "I give you another thirty days! If, at the end of that time, you have not learnt the grimoire, you may say farewell to your head."

As soon as the sorcerer had departed for a second time, Muhamad went out to the girl, carrying his right arm in his left hand. When he had taken her down, she said: "Here are three leaves of a plant that I have found by chance. The Moor has been seeking it for forty years, to complete his knowledge of the chapters of magic. Apply them to the two parts of your arm, my dear."

The boy did as he was told, and his arm was restored to its former state.

Then the girl read out of the grimoire and rubbed another of the magic leaves the while. Hardly had she spoken when two racing camels came up out of the earth and knelt down near them. At once the princess mounted one of these, and said: "Let us each return to our parents. Afterward, you can come and ask for my hand in marriage. My father's palace is in such a place, in such a land."

She kissed him tenderly, and they departed, one riding to the right and the other to the left. Muhamad came to his father's palace, shaking the earth with the formidable gallop of his camel. But there, instead of telling his story, he handed over his mount to the chief eunuch, saying: "Sell it in the camel market, but be sure to keep the halter from its nose."

When the eunuch offered the camel for sale, a hashish seller came along and wished to buy it. After a great deal of chatting and chaffering, the animal changed hands at a very moderate price, for the eunuch, like all his kind, was no great hand at a bargain. He even sold the halter as a makeweight.

The hashish seller led the camel to the space in front of his shop and showed it off to the hashish eaters, his habitual customers. He set a bowl of water before it, while the takers of the drug laughed as if their hearts would break. But the camel placed its forefeet in the bowl, and when its new owner beat it and cried: "Back, back, you pimp!" the camel threw up its hind legs and, diving head first into the water, disappeared.

The hashish seller beat his hands together, showing the halter that still remained to him, and crying: "Help, help, good Mussulmans! My camel is drowning in the bowl."

Folk ran up from all sides and said to him: "Be quiet, O man, for you are mad! How could a camel drown in a bowl?"

"Be gone!" he answered, "What are you doing here? I tell you that he dived in head first and disappeared. If you want further proof than this halter, ask the honorables who were with me."

But the sensible merchants departed, calling over their shoulders: "You and your honorables are all mad together!"

While this scene was in the happening, the Moor bit his finger for rage at the disappearance of the prince and the princess.

"By Gog and Magog," he exclaimed, "and by the fire of the turning stars, I will catch them, even if they are on the seventh planet!"

He hastened to Muhamad's city and entered the market just as the hashish eater was bewailing his loss. Hearing talk of a halter and of a bowl which was both sea and tomb, he approached a man, saying: "My poor fellow, if you have lost your camel, I am ready for Allah's sake to reimburse you. Give me the halter which remains to you, and I will refund the price you paid for the animal with a hundred dinars in addition."

The bargain was quickly concluded, and the Moor danced off with the halter so light for joy that his toes scarcely touched the ground.

Now beside other powers, this halter had the power of capture. The Moor had only to hold it out toward the palace, and Muhamad came at once to pass his nose into the loop of it; also at contact with the cord the boy was changed into a camel, which knelt before the sorcerer.

The Moor mounted his new steed and urged it toward the dwelling of the princess. When the two came below the walls of the garden that surrounded the palace, the magician worked the cord to make the camel kneel, but this movement brought the halter within reach of Muhamad's teeth, and he at once snapped it through, so that its power of capture was destroyed. Then, to escape his persecutor, the prince used the virtue of the cord to change into a large pomegranate and hang himself among the pomegranate flowers in the garden.

The Moor at once sought audience with the princess's father and, after humble greeting, said to him: "O king of time, I come to beg you for a pomegranate. My wife is pregnant and ardently desires to eat one. You know how great a sin it is to thwart the yearning of a woman in her state!"

"But, my good man," answered the astonished king, "the season of pomegranates is not yet! All the trees of my garden are in flower only."

Then said the Moor: "O king of time, if there is no pomegranate in your garden, I give you leave to cut off my head."

The king called his chief gardener and asked: "Are there any pomegranates in my garden'?" and when the man answered: "But master, this is no time for pomegranates!" he turned to the Moor, saying: "Your head is forfeit!"

At this point, Shahrazade saw the approach of morning and discreetly fell silent. But when the nine-hundred-and-fifty-fourth night had come, she said:

The Moor cried: "O king, before you cut off my head, will you not tell the gardener to look among pomegranate trees?"

The king consented to do this, and the gardener, going down to his trees, found a large pomegranate, the like of which he had never seen before.

When the king received the fruit, he was so astonished that he did not know whether to keep it for himself or to cede it to the childing woman. He sought the advice of his wazir, and the man asked this question in return: "If the pomegranate had not been found, would you have cut off this Moor's head?"

"Certainly," said the king, and the wazir replied: "Then justice demands that he be given the pomegranate."

The king held forth the fruit in his hand, but, as soon as the Moor touched it, it burst asunder, and all the grains were scattered on the floor. The sorcerer picked them up, one by one, until he came to the last grain, which had sought refuge in a little hole near the throne's foot, and which contained the vital essence of Muhamad. As the vile magician stretched out his neck toward this final grain, a dagger came up out of it and stabbed him to the heart so that he spat out his unbelieving soul in a stream of blood.

Then Prince Muhamad appeared in his own delightful form and kissed the earth between the king's hands. At that moment, the princess entered and said to her father: "This was the youth who loosed me when I was hung by my hair from a tree."

"Since that is so, you cannot do less than marry him," answered the king.

The wedding was celebrated with all due pomp, and that night for the young lovers was blessed among all other nights.

They dwelt together in sweet content, and had many sons and daughters. This is the end.

But praise and glory to the Only, to the One, who knows neither end nor beginning!

THE BATTLE OF THE ENCHANTERS (1907)*

Fletcher Gardner

There was once a poor boy who was very ambitious to learn, and with the consent of his parents, he bound himself to an enchanter who was a very wise man. The boy remained with him for a very long time, until at last his master sent him home, saying that he could teach him nothing more. The boy went home, but there he found nothing in the way of adventure, so he proposed to his father that he should become a horse, which his father could sell for twenty pesos to his late teacher. He cautioned his father that, as soon as he received the money for the horse, he should drop the halter as if by accident.

The young man then became a horse, and his father took him to the en-chanter, who gave him twenty pesos. As soon as the money was in the father's hand, he dropped the halter, and the horse at once became a bird, which flew away. The enchanter metamorphosed himself into a hawk and followed. The bird was so hard pressed by the hawk that it dived into the sea and became a

* "Tagalog Folk-Tales. II," *Journal of American Folklore* 20.79 (October–December 1907): 309–10.

fish. The hawk followed and became a shark. The fish, being in danger from the shark, leaped out onto the dry ground and took the shape of a crab, which hid in a spring where a princess was bathing. The shark followed in the shape of a cat, which began to search under the stones for the crab, but the crab escaped by changing itself into a ring on the finger of the princess.

Now it chanced that the father of the princess was very sick, and the enchanter went to the palace and offered to cure him for the ring on the finger of the princess. To this the king agreed, but the ring begged the princess not to give him directly to the enchanter, but to let him fall on the floor. The princess did this, and as the ring touched the floor it broke into a shower of rice. The enchanter immediately took the form of a cock and industriously pecked at the grains on the floor. But as he pecked, one of the grains changed to a cat, which jumped on him and killed him.

The young man then resumed his own form, having proven himself a greater man than his master.

THE BLACK KING OF MOROCCO (1908)*

Peter Buchan

One of those farmers in the North of Scotland who delight in educating their sons had a favorite son who had got all the education that part of the country could bestow, and his father thought of improving it still a little further by travel. Accordingly the father and son set off together to procure more knowledge when they met with a stranger, who, in a familiar manner, asked where they were going.

The old father told him that he was going in quest of knowledge for his son, who had been tutored at the best schools in Scotland, but was still deficient in the principal requisites of human education.

The stranger then said that if he would entrust him to his care, he would complete his education and make him perfect in all that was necessary for any of the learned professions in the course of seven years.

To this the old man consented, having himself a thirst for knowledge, but asked, at the expiry of the term, where he would find his son.

---

* *Ancient Scottish Tales*, intro. John Fairley (Peterhead, UK: 1908).

The stranger then replied that if he did not get him ere the seven years were expired, he would not get him at all, and where he was to find him, he did not let him know.

Then they went their several ways, the farmer back to his farm, and his son and teacher to a place beyond the ken of man.

Before the end of seven years the farmer began to weary for the return of his son, so went in pursuit of him. When traveling in a solitary part of the road in an uninhabited part of the country, he met with an old man dressed in pilgrim's weeds who said he knew his errand, and desired him to go to Dr. Brazen-nose of Cambridge, who could inform him of his son, as it was he who gave him to the black king of Morocco, where he feared he would have to go before he received his son.

On arriving at Cambridge he was told by the doctor that he would get his son if he could find him. This was all the information he received from the learned Brazen-nose, so he set off for the court of the black king, where he arrived after having seen many sights in safety. Here he asked for his son, when seven doves were set before him, and he was desired to make his choice; he did so, and made choice of one with a broken wing, which chanced to be his son in the likeness of a dove. Happy to meet again, they now took leave of the black king's court, and they pursued their journey homeward with all the speed they may.

On their way home hunger began to prey upon their vitals, but having no money wherewithal to pay for meat, the son said he would turn himself into a horse, which the father could sell at the first market, but to be sure he was to be on his guard not to let the bridle slip out of his hand, for if he did, the consequences might be fatal to him.

The old man promised, but thoughtlessly forgot the serious injunction and let the bridle fall from his hand, which put the young man into much danger, being pursued by the king and his companions.

The young man then changed himself into an eel, which the king observing, who with six of his nobles, turned themselves into seven sharks and pursued the eel. Being hard beset, he next turned himself into a bird, when they did the same into eagles, and gave him chase, till he took shelter in a lady's window, and became a ring on her finger.

When night came, he became a man, which put the lady in great fear. He told her the danger he was in, and begged her assistance in making his escape from the king and his nobles, who were his pursuers, and were at that time at her gate as musicians, who would ask nothing of her but the ring. Instead of complying with their request, he asked her to throw him into the fire, and he would save himself.

Accordingly, as he had said, they asked her for the ring, but she threw it into the fire. In turn, they became goldsmiths in order to beat the ring. However, he turned himself into a sack of barley, and as soon as they became geese to eat the barley, he immediately turned himself into a fox, and before they knew what was happening, he devoured them all, which put an end to his troubles.

He then married the lady and went in search of his father, who had caused him so much pain. On his travels he happened to see a man who had two old wives, and he asked what he was going to do with them. Receiving no answer, he said he could grind them together, and out of the two, produce a beautiful young one. This he did to the astonishment of every beholder. He next made a fine young horse out of two useless old ones. Two men who had observed this tried to do the same thing, but out of two horses, they produced nothing. One man also endeavored to make a young woman out of two old ones that he had, but was still more unfortunate than the two men with useless horses, for they only lost their horses, but he lost his wives and was condemned to death for murder.

At length he put all things to right again, found his father, went back to his wife, and for many years lived happy and peacefully, much and justly esteemed by all who knew him for his great learning.

THE BOY WHO LEARNT MAGIC (1909)*

Cecil Henry Bompas

Once upon a time there was a raja who had seven wives, and they were all childless, and he was very unhappy at having no heir. One day a jogi came to the palace begging, and the raja and his ranis asked him whether he could say what should be done in order that they might have children. The jogi asked what they would give him if he told them, and they said that they would give him anything that he asked for and gave him a written bond to this effect. Then the jogi said, "I will not take elephants or horses or money, but you shall give me the child that is born first and any born afterward shall be yours, do you agree?"

* *Folklore of the Santal Parganas* (London: David Nutt, 1909).

And the ranis consulted together and agreed. "Then," said the jogi, "this is what you must do: you must all go and bathe, and after bathing you must go to a mango orchard, and the raja must choose a bunch of seven mangoes and knock it down with his left hand and catch it in a cloth without letting it touch the ground. Then you must go home, and the ranis must sit in a row according to their seniority, and the raja must give them each one of the mangoes to eat, and he must himself eat the rinds that the ranis throw away. Then you will have children."

And so saying the jogi went away, promising to return the next year. A few days later the raja decided to give a trial to the jogi's prescription, and he and the ranis did as they had been told. But the raja did not eat the rind of the youngest rani's mango, for he did not love her very much. However, five or six months after it was seen that the youngest rani was with child, she became the raja's favorite; but the other ranis were jealous of her and reminded the raja that he would not be able to keep her child. Soon her time was full, and she gave birth to twin sons. So the raja was delighted to think that he would be able to keep the younger of the two, and he loved it much.

When the year was up, the jogi came and saw the boys, and he said that he would return when they could walk. So when they could run about he came again and asked whether the raja would fulfill his promise. The raja said that he would not break his bond. Then the jogi said that he would take the two boys, and when the raja objected that he was only entitled to one, the jogi said that he claimed both as they were born at the same time; but he promised that if he took both, he would teach them magic and then let one come back. Also he promised that all the ranis would have children. So the raja agreed and sent the boys away with the jogi, and with them he sent goats and sheep and donkeys and horses and camels and elephants and furniture of all sorts.

The jogi was called Sitari Jogi, and he was a raja in his own country. But before they reached his country, all the animals died, first the goats, then the sheep and the donkeys and the horses and the camels and the elephants. And when the goats died, the boys lamented:

> "The goats have died, father.
> How far, father,
> Is it to the country of the Sitari Jogi?"

and so they sang when the other animals died.

At last they reached the jogi's palace, and every day he taught them in-cantations and spells. He bought them each a water pot and sent them every morning to fill it with dew, but before they collected enough, the sun came out and dried up the dew. One day they got a cupful, another day half a cupful, but they never were able to fill the pots. In the course of time they learnt all the spells the jogi knew, and one day when they went out to gather dew, the younger boy secretly took with him a rag, and he soaked this in the dew and then squeezed it into the pot and so he soon filled it. Meanwhile, the elder boy seeing his brother's pot full, filled his pot at a pool of water, and they took them to the jogi, but the jogi was not deceived by the elder boy and told him that he would never learn magic thoroughly. However, the younger boy, having learned all that the jogi knew, learnt more still from his friends, for all the people of that country knew magic.

Then one day the jogi took the two boys back to their home, and he told the raja that he would leave the elder boy at home. The raja wanted to keep the younger one, but the jogi insisted, and the younger boy whispered to his mother not to mind as he would soon come back by himself. So they let him go.

The jogi and the boy used to practice magic: the jogi would take the form of a young man, and the boy would turn into a bullock, and the jogi would go to a village and sell the bullock for a good price. But he would not give up the tethering rope, and then he would go away and do something with the tethering rope, and the boy would resume his shape again and run off to the jogi. Then, when the purchasers looked for their bullock, they found nothing, and when they went to look for the seller, the jogi would change his shape again so that he could not be recognized, and in this way they deceived many people and amassed wealth.

Then the jogi taught the boy the spell he used with the rope, and when he had learnt this, he asked to be taught the spell by which he could change his own shape without having a second person to work the spell with the rope. The jogi said that he would teach him that later, but he must wait. Then the boy reproached the jogi and said that he did not love him, and he went away to his friends in the town and learnt the spell he wanted from them so that he was able to change his shape at will.

Two or three days after the boy again went to the jogi and said, "Teach me the spell about which I spoke to you the other day," and the jogi refused. "Then," said the boy, "I shall go back to my father, for I see that you do not love me."

At this the jogi grew wrathful and said that if he went away, he would kill him. So the boy at this ran away in terror, and the jogi became a leopard and pursued him. Then the boy turned himself into a pigeon, and the jogi became a hawk and pursued him, so the boy turned himself into a fly, and the jogi became a paddy bird and pursued him. The fly alighted on the plate of a rani who was eating rice, and the jogi took on his natural shape and told the rani to scatter the rice that she was eating on the ground, and she did so. But the boy turned himself into a bead of coral on the necklace that the rani was wearing, and the jogi did not notice this but became a pigeon and ate up the rice that the rani had thrown down. When the jogi did not find the boy among the rice, he turned himself into a jogi again and saw the boy in the necklace. Then he told the rani to break her necklace and scatter the beads on the ground, and she did so. Then the jogi again became a pigeon and began to pick up the beads, but the boy turned himself into a cat and hid under the verandah, and when the pigeon came near, he pounced on it and killed it and ran outside with it. Then he became a boy again and twisted off the bird's head and wrapped it in his cloth and went off home. Looking behind, he saw the jogi's head come rolling after him. So when he came to a blacksmith's fire by the side of the road, he threw the pigeon's head into it. Then the jogi's head also ran into the fire and was consumed.

And the boy went home to his parents.

THE MAGICIAN'S HEART (1912)*

Edith Nesbit

We all have our weaknesses. Mine is mulberries. Yours, perhaps, motor cars. Professor Taykin's was christenings—royal christenings. He always expected to be asked to the christening parties of all the little royal babies, and of course he never was, because he was not a lord, or a duke, or a seller of bacon and tea, or anything really high-class, but merely a wicked magician, who by economy and strict attention to customers had worked up a very good business of his own. He had not always been wicked. He was born quite good, I believe, and his old nurse, who had long since married a farmer and retired into the calm of country life, always used to say that he was the duckiest little boy in

* Edith Nesbit, *The Magic World* (London: Macmillan, 1912).

a plaid frock with the dearest little fat legs. But he had changed since he was a boy, as a good many other people do—perhaps it was his trade. I dare say you've noticed that cobblers are usually thin, and brewers are generally fat, and magicians are almost always wicked.

Well his weakness (for christenings) grew stronger and stronger because it was never indulged, and at last he "took the bull into his own hands," as the Irish footman at the palace said, and went to a christening without being asked. It was a very grand party given by the king of the Fortunate Islands, and the little prince was christened Fortunatus. No one took any notice of Professor Taykin. They were too polite to turn him out, but they made him wish he'd never come. He felt quite an outsider, as indeed he was, and this made him furious. So that when all the bright, light, laughing, fairy godmothers were crowding round the blue satin cradle, and giving gifts of beauty and strength and goodness to the baby, the magician suddenly did a very difficult charm (in his head, like you do mental arithmetic), and said: "Young Forty may be all that, but *I* say he shall be the stupidest prince in the world," and on that he vanished in a puff of red smoke with a smell like the Fifth of November in a back garden on Streatham Hill, and as he left no address the king of the Fortunate Islands couldn't prosecute him for high treason.

Taykin was very glad to think that he had made such a lot of people unhappy—the whole Court was in tears when he left, including the baby— and he looked in the papers for another royal christening, so that he could go to that and make a lot more people miserable. And there was one fixed for the very next Wednesday. The magician went to that, too, disguised as a wealthy.

This time the baby was a girl. Taykin kept close to the pink velvet cradle, and when all the nice qualities in the world had been given to the princess he suddenly said, "Little Aura may be all that, but *I* say she shall be the ugliest princess in all the world."

And instantly she was. It was terrible. And she had been such a beautiful baby too. Everyone had been saying that she was the most beautiful baby they had ever seen. This sort of thing is often said at christenings.

Having uglified the unfortunate little princess, the magician did the spell (in his mind, just as you do your spelling) to make himself vanish, but to his horror there was no red smoke and no smell of fireworks, and there he was, still, where he now very much wished not to be. Because one of the fairies there had seen, just one second too late to save the princess, what he was up to, and had made a strong little charm in a great hurry to prevent his vanishing. This fairy was a white witch, and of course you know that white magic is much stronger than black magic, as well as more suited for drawing-room performances. So there the magician stood, "looking like a thunder-struck pig," as someone unkindly said, and the dear white witch bent down and kissed the baby princess.

"There!" she said, "you can keep that kiss till you want it. When the time comes you'll know what to do with it. The magician can't vanish, Sire. You'd better arrest him."

"Arrest that person," said the king, pointing to Taykin. "I suppose your charms are of a permanent nature, madam."

"Quite," said the fairy, "at least they never go till there's no longer any use for them."

So the magician was shut up in an enormously high tower, and allowed to play with magic, but none of his spells could act outside the tower, so he was never able to pass the extra double guard that watched outside night and day. The king would have liked to have the magician executed, but the white witch warned him that this would never do.

"Don't you see," she said, "he's the only person who can make the princess beautiful again. And he'll do it someday. But don't you go *asking* him to do it. He'll never do anything to oblige you. He's that sort of man."

So the years rolled on. The magician stayed in the tower and did magic and was very bored,—for it is dull to take white rabbits out of your hat, and your hat out of nothing when there's no one to see you.

Prince Fortunatus was such a stupid little boy that he got lost quite early in the story, and went about the country saying his name was James, which it wasn't. A baker's wife found him and adopted him, and sold the diamond buttons of his little overcoat, for three hundred pounds, and as she was a very honest woman she put two hundred away for James to have when he grew up.

The years rolled on. Aura continued to be hideous, and she was very unhappy, till on her twentieth birthday her married cousin Belinda came to see her. Now Belinda had been made ugly in her cradle too, so she could sympathize as no one else could.

"But *I* got out of it all right, and so will you," said Belinda. "I'm sure the first thing to do is to find a magician."

"Father banished them all twenty years ago," said Aura behind her veil, "all but the one who uglified me."

"Then I should go to *him*," said beautiful Belinda. "Dress up as a beggar maid, and give him fifty pounds to do it. Not more, or he may suspect that you're not a beggar maid. It will be great fun. I'd go with you only I promised Bellamant faithfully that I'd be home to lunch." And off she went in her mother-of-pearl coach, leaving Aura to look through the bound volumes of *The Perfect Lady* in the palace library, to find out the proper costume for a beggar maid.

Now that very morning the magician's old nurse had packed up a ham, and some eggs, and some honey, and some apples, and a sweet bunch of old-fashioned flowers, and borrowed the baker's boy to hold the horse for her, and started off to see the magician. It was forty years since she'd seen him, but she loved him still, and now she thought she could do him a good turn. She asked in the town for his address, and learned that he lived in the Black Tower.

"But you'd best be careful," the townsfolk said, "he's a spiteful chap."

"Bless you," said the old nurse, "he won't hurt me, as I nursed him when he was a babe, in a plaid frock with the dearest little fat legs ever you see."

So she got to the tower, and the guards let her through. Taykin was almost pleased to see her—remember he had had no visitors for twenty years—and he was quite pleased to see the ham and the honey.

"But where did I put them eggs?" said the nurse, "and the apples—I must have left them at home after all."

She had. But the magician just waved his hand in the air, and there was a basket of apples that hadn't been there before. The eggs he took out of her bonnet, the folds of her shawl, and even from his own mouth, just like a conjurer does. Only of course he was a real magician.

"Lor!" said she, "it's like magic."

"It *is* magic," said he. "That's my trade. It's quite a pleasure to have an audience again. I've lived here alone for twenty years. It's very lonely, especially of an evening."

"Can't you get out?" said the nurse.

"No. King's orders must be respected, but it's a dog's life." He sniffed, made himself a magic handkerchief out of empty air, and wiped his eyes.

"Take an apprentice, my dear," said the nurse.

"And teach him my magic? Not me."

"Suppose you got one so stupid he *couldn't* learn?"

"That would be all right—but it's no use advertising for a stupid person—you'd get no answers."

"You needn't advertise," said the nurse; and she went out and brought in James, who was really the prince of the Fortunate Islands, and also the baker's boy she had brought with her to hold the horse's head.

"Now, James," she said, "you'd like to be apprenticed, wouldn't you?"

"Yes," said the poor stupid boy.

"Then give the gentleman your money, James."

James did.

"My last doubts vanish," said the magician, "he *is* stupid. Nurse, let us celebrate the occasion with a little drop of something. Not before the boy because of setting an example. James, wash up. Not here, silly; in the back kitchen."

So James washed up, and as he was very clumsy he happened to break a little bottle of essence of dreams that was on the shelf, and instantly there floated up from the washing-up water the vision of a princess more beautiful than the day—so beautiful that even James could not help seeing how beautiful she was, and holding out his arms to her as she came floating through the air above the kitchen sink. But when he held out his arms she vanished. He sighed and washed up harder than ever.

"I wish I wasn't so stupid," he said, and then there was a knock at the door. James wiped his hands and opened. Someone stood there in very picturesque rags and tatters.

"Please," said someone, who was of course the princess, "is Professor Taykin at home?"

"Walk in, please," said James.

"My snakes alive!" said Taykin, "what a day we're having. Three visitors in one morning. How kind of you to call. Won't you take a chair?"

"I hoped," said the veiled princess, "that you'd give me something else to take."

"A glass of wine," said Taykin. "You'll take a glass of wine?"

"No, thank you," said the beggar maid who was the princess.

"Then taketake your veil off," said the nurse, "or you won't feel the benefit of it when you go out."

"I can't," said Aura, "it wouldn't be safe."

"Too beautiful, eh?" said the Magician. "Still—you're quite safe here."

"Can you do magic?" she abruptly asked.

"A little," said he ironically.

"Well," said she, "it's like this. I'm so ugly no one can bear to look at me. And I want to go as kitchenmaid to the palace. They want a cook and a scullion and a kitchenmaid. I thought perhaps you'd give me something to make me pretty. I'm only a poor beggar maid. . . . It would be a great thing to me if . . ."

"Go along with you," said Taykin, very cross indeed. "I never give to beggars."

"Here's two pence," whispered poor James, pressing it into her hand, "it's all I've got left."

"Thank you," she whispered back. You *are* good."

And to the magician she said: "I happen to have fifty pounds. I'll give it you for a new face."

"Done," cried Taykin. "Here's another stupid one!" He grabbed the money, waved his wand, and then and there before the astonished eyes of the nurse and the apprentice the ugly beggar maid became the loveliest princess in the world.

"Lor!" said the nurse.

"My dream!" cried the apprentice.

"Please," said the princess, "can I have a looking-glass?" The apprentice ran to unhook the one that hung over the kitchen sink, and handed it to her. "Oh," she said, "how *very* pretty I am. How can I thank you?"

"Quite easily," said the magician, "beggar maid as you are, I hereby offer you my hand and heart."

He put his hand into his waistcoat and pulled out his heart. It was fat and pink, and the princess did not like the look of it.

"Thank you very much," said she, "but I'd rather not."

"But I insist," said Taykin.

"But really, your offer . . ."

"Most handsome, I'm sure," said the nurse.

"My affections are engaged," said the princess, looking down. "I can't marry you."

"Am I to take this as a refusal?" asked Taykin; and the princess said she feared that he was.

"Very well, then," he said, "I shall see you home, and ask your father about it. He'll not let you refuse an offer like this. Nurse, come and tie my necktie."

So he went out, and the nurse with him.

Then the princess told the apprentice in a very great hurry who she was. "It would never do," she said, "for him to see me home. He'd find out that I was the princess, and he'd uglify me again in no time."

"He shan't see you home," said James. "I may be stupid but I'm strong too."

"How brave you are," said Aura admiringly, "but I'd rather slip away quietly, without any fuss. Can't you undo the patent lock of that door?"

The apprentice tried but he was too stupid, and the princess was not strong enough.

"I'm sorry," said the apprentice who was a prince. "I can't undo the door, but when *he* does I'll hold him and you can get away. I dreamed of you this morning," he added.

"I dreamed of you too," said she, "but you were different."

"Perhaps," said poor James sadly, "the person you dreamed about wasn't stupid, and I am."

"Are you *really*?" cried the Princess. "I *am* so glad!"

"That's rather unkind, isn't it?" said he.

"No, because if *that's* all that makes you different from the man I dreamed about I can soon make *that* all right."

And with that she put her hands on his shoulders and kissed him. And at her kiss his stupidity passed away like a cloud, and he became as clever as anyone need be, and besides knowing all the ordinary lessons he would have learned if he had stayed at home in his palace, he knew who he was, and where he was, and why, and he knew all the geography of his father's kingdom, and the exports and imports and the condition of politics. And he knew also that the princess loved him.

So he caught her in his arms and kissed her, and they were very happy, and told each other over and over again what a beautiful world it was, and how wonderful it was that they should have found each other, seeing that the world is not only beautiful but rather large.

"That first one was a magic kiss, you know," said she. "My fairy godmother gave it to me, and I've been keeping it all these years for you. You must get away from here, and come to the palace. Oh, you'll manage it—you're clever now."

"Yes," he said, "I *am* clever now. I can undo the lock for you. Go, my dear, go before he comes back."

So the princess went. And only just in time, for as she went out one door Taykin came in at the other.

He was furious to find her gone, and I should not like to write down the things he said to his apprentice when he found that James had been so stupid as to open the door for her. They were not polite things at all.

He tried to follow her. But the princess had warned the guards, and he could not get out.

"Oh," he cried, "if only my old magic would work outside this tower. I'd soon be even with her."

And then in a strange, confused, yet quite sure way, he felt that the spell that held him, the white witch's spell, was dissolved.

"To the palace!" he cried, and rushing to the cauldron that hung over the fire he leaped into it, leaped out in the form of a red lion, and disappeared.

Without a moment's hesitation the prince, who was his apprentice, followed him, calling out the same words and leaping into the same cauldron, while the poor nurse screamed and wrung her hands. As he touched the liquor in the cauldron he felt that he was not quite himself. He was, in fact, a green dragon. He felt himself vanish—a most uncomfortable sensation—and reappeared, with a suddenness that took his breath away, in his own form and at the back door of the palace.

The time had been short, but already the magician had succeeded in obtaining an engagement as palace cook. How he did it without references I don't know. Perhaps he made the references by magic as he had made the eggs, and the apples, and the handkerchief.

Taykin's astonishment and annoyance at being followed by his faithful apprentice were soon soothed, for he saw that a stupid scullion would be of great use. Of course he had no idea that James had been made clever by a kiss.

"But how are you going to cook?" asked the apprentice. "You don't know how!"

"I shall cook," said Taykin, "as I do everything else—by magic." And he did. I wish I had time to tell you how he turned out a hot dinner of seventeen courses from totally empty saucepans, how James looked in a cupboard for spices and found it empty, and how next moment the nurse walked out of it. The magician had been so long alone that he seemed to revel in the luxury of showing off to someone, and he leaped about from one cupboard to another, produced cats and cockatoos out of empty jars, and made mice and rabbits disappear and reappear till James's head was in a whirl, for all his cleverness, and the nurse, as she washed up, wept tears of pure joy at her boy's wonderful skill.

"All this excitement's bad for my heart, though," Taykin said at last, and pulling his heart out of his chest, he put it on a shelf, and as he did so his magic notebook fell from his breast and the apprentice picked it up. Taykin did not see him do it; he was busy making the kitchen lamp fly about the room like a pigeon.

It was just then that the princess came in, looking more lovely than ever in a simple little morning frock of white chiffon and diamonds.

"The beggar maid," said Taykin, "looking like a princess! I'll marry her just the same."

"I've come to give the orders for dinner," she said, and then she saw who it was, and gave one little cry and stood still, trembling.

"To order the dinner," said the nurse. "Then you're—"

"Yes," said Aura, "I'm the princess."

"You're the princess," said the magician. "Then I'll marry you all the more. And if you say no, I'll uglify you as the word leaves your lips. Oh, yes—you think I've just been amusing myself over my cooking—but I've really been brewing the strongest spell in the world. Marry me—or drink—"

The princess shuddered at these dreadful words.

"Drink, or marry me," said the magician. "If you marry me you shall be beautiful forever."

"Ah," said the nurse, "he's a match even for a princess."

"I'll tell papa," said the princess, sobbing.

"No, you won't," said Taykin. "Your father will never know. If you won't marry me you shall drink this and become my scullery maid—my hideous scullery maid—and wash up forever in the lonely tower."

He caught her by the wrist.

"Stop," cried the apprentice, who was a prince.

"Stop? *Me?* Nonsense! Pooh!" said the magician.

"Stop, I say!" said James, who was Fortunatus. "*I've got your heart!*"

He had—and he held it up in one hand, and in the other a cooking knife.

"One step nearer that lady," said he, "and in goes the knife."

The magician positively skipped in his agony and terror.

"I say, look out!" he cried. "Be careful what you're doing. Accidents happen so easily! Suppose your foot slipped! Then no apologies would meet the case. That's my heart you've got there. My life's bound up in it."

"I know. That's often the case with people's hearts," said Fortunatus. "We've got you, my dear sir, on toast. My princess, might I trouble you to call the guards."

The magician did not dare to resist, so the guards arrested him. The nurse, though in floods of tears, managed to serve up a very good plain dinner, and after dinner the magician was brought before the king.

Now the king, as soon as he had seen that his daughter had been made so beautiful, had caused a large number of princes to be fetched by telephone. He was anxious to get her married at once in case she turned ugly again. So before he could do justice to the magician, he had to settle which of the princes was to marry the princess. He had chosen the prince of the Diamond Mountains, a very nice steady young man with a good income. But when he suggested the match to the princess she declined it, and the magician, who was standing at the foot of the throne steps loaded with chains, clattered forward and said: "Your Majesty, will you spare my life if I tell you something you don't know?"

The king, who was a very inquisitive man, said "Yes."

"Then know," said Taykin, "that the princess won't marry *your* choice because she's made one of her own—my apprentice."

The princess meant to have told her father this when she had got him alone and in a good temper. But now he was in a bad temper, and in full audience.

The apprentice was dragged in, and all the princess's agonized pleadings only got this out of the king—"All right. I won't hang him. He shall be best man at your wedding."

Then the king took his daughter's hand and set her in the middle of the hall, and set the prince of the Diamond Mountains on her right and the apprentice on her left. Then he said: "I will spare the life of this aspiring youth on your left if you'll promise never to speak to him again, and if you'll promise to marry the gentleman on your right before tea this afternoon."

The wretched princess looked at her lover, and his lips formed the word "Promise."

So she said: "I promise never to speak to the gentleman on my left and to marry the gentleman on my right before tea today," and held out her hand to the prince of the Diamond Mountains.

Then suddenly, in the twinkling of an eye, the prince of the Diamond Mountains was on her left, and her hand was held by her own prince, who stood at her right hand. And yet nobody seemed to have moved. It was the purest and most high-class magic.

"Dished," cried the king, "absolutely dished!"

"A mere trifle," said the apprentice modestly. "I've got Taykin's magic recipe book, as well as his heart."

"Well, we must make the best of it, I suppose," said the king crossly. "Bless you, my children."

He was less cross when it was explained to him that the apprentice was really the prince of the Fortunate Islands, and a much better match than the prince of the Diamond Mountains, and he was quite in a good temper by the time the nurse threw herself in front of the throne and begged the king to let the magician off altogether—chiefly on the ground that when he was a baby he was the dearest little duck that ever was, in the prettiest plaid frock, with the loveliest fat legs.

The king, moved by these arguments, said: "I'll spare him if he'll promise to be good."

"You will, ducky, won't you?" said the nurse, crying.

"No," said the magician, "I won't, and what's more, I can't."

The princess, who was now so happy that she wanted every one else to be happy too, begged her lover to make Taykin good "by magic."

"Alas, my dearest Lady," said the Prince, "no one can be made good by magic. I could take the badness out of him—there's an excellent recipe in this notebook—but if I did that there'd be so very little left."

"Every little helps," said the nurse wildly.

Prince Fortunatus, who was James, who was the apprentice, studied the book for a few moments, and then said a few words in a language no one present had ever heard before. And as he spoke the wicked magician began to tremble and shrink.

"Oh, my boy—be good! Promise you'll be good," cried the nurse, still in tears.

The magician seemed to be shrinking inside his clothes. He grew smaller and smaller. The nurse caught him in her arms, and still he grew less and less, till she seemed to be holding nothing but a bundle of clothes. Then with a cry of love and triumph she tore the magician's clothes away and held up a chubby baby boy, with the very plaid frock and fat legs she had so often and so lovingly described.

"I said there wouldn't be much of him when the badness was out," said the prince Fortunatus.

"I will be good; oh, I will," said the baby boy that had been the magician.

"I'll see to that," said the nurse. And so the story ends with love and a wedding, and showers of white roses.

THE TWO MAGICIANS (1916)*

Claude-Marius Barbeau

It's good to tell you that there was once a king who had only one son, and one day he said to him: "My little boy, I'm going to have you educated about good and evil."

"Good, Papa," the child responded, "I'd like to be instructed about good and evil. There is an old magician in the city, and he could teach me quite well."

So the child went to the magician.

"Good day, old magician."

"Good day, my little boy."

"I've come to have you teach me about good and evil."

Well, the magician taught him all that he knew.

After a long time had passed, the young man returned to his father and said: "Now I've learned all about good and evil."

"Well, yes, my son, what do you know?"

"Tomorrow I'm going to change myself into a handsome brown horse, and you'll take me to the city, where you're to sell me for a thousand francs, and you're to keep the bridle and saddle."

So the father went to the city and sold the brown horse as agreed. As soon as he sold the horse he took the bridle and saddle with him. Then later the brown horse escaped, ran off, and disappeared. The buyer ran after the horse, but soon thereafter he encountered only a handsome prince. His brown horse had turned into a prince.

"My sire, prince, have you seen a handsome brown horse pass by here?"

"Yes, and it was running with lightning speed."

The next morning the prince said to his father, "Today I am going to be a handsome black horse. You're to go to the city again and sell me for a thousand francs. And you are to keep the bridle and the saddle."

Well soon the old magician learned about all this, and he said to himself: "I'm going to go and buy the horse."

---

* "Les deux Magiciens," *Journal of American Folklore* 29.61 (January–March 1916): 87–99.

So he went to the city with his own bridle and saddle, and when he met the king with the black horse, he asked: "Is your horse for sale?"

"Yes, for a thousand francs."

"Very well then. Take the money! The horse is mine."

"But I want to keep the bridle and the saddle."

When the king went to take the bridle and the saddle, the old magician replaced them with his own. Then, turning to the horse, he said: "Now, my friend, I'm going to put you in my stable and make you suffer."

Then he turned to his servants and said: "I'm going away today, and I don't want you to give my horse anything to eat or drink."

After the magician had departed, the servants went to the stable, and they saw the horse rubbing against the bar indicating that he was hungry and thirsty. "The poor horse," they said, "it's thirsty and starving. Let's take it from the stable and give it something to drink."

So they led the horse to the river, but since it was wearing the bridle and the saddle, the horse didn't want to drink and rubbed and tried to take them off. The servants said: "The poor horse. Let's remove the bridle and the saddle so that it can drink."

As soon as the horse was no longer saddled and bridled, it escaped them and plunged into the river. That night the old magician returned and asked: "Did you give the horse something to drink?"

"Something extraordinary happened!" they responded. "We went to the river to give the horse some water to drink, but it didn't want to drink anything as long as the bridle and saddle were on it. When we removed them, it escaped and plunged into the river."

The magician hired five hundred fishermen and five hundred boats to go fishing for carp in the river. In order to avoid being caught, the prince transformed himself into a beautiful yellow diamond on the bank of the river. Just then a princess passed by, and when she discovered the diamond, she put it in her corsage and went away. After she had gone some distance, the diamond jumped out of the corsage and changed itself into the prince.

"Yes," he said, "I changed myself into a yellow diamond because they were searching for me in the river. I'm now going to change myself into a pomegranate, and when the old magician comes to your home, you're to take the pomegranate and throw it against the wall. All the seeds will scatter on the ground. You're to put your foot on top of the seed that comes close to you."

The next day the magician arrived at the princess's home and said: "Princess, did you find a beautiful yellow diamond along the shore of the river yesterday? I would like to have it."

"Yes," she replied. "I'll give it to you."

Then she took the pomegranate and threw it against the wall. As the seeds scattered all over the place, the magician transformed himself into a rooster and began to eat the seeds. Just then the princess raised her toe, and lo and behold, the seed changed into a fox. All of a sudden there was a crack! The fox devoured the rooster, and the magician was destroyed. Then the fox became the prince once again and said: "Now, princess, you and I are going to get married."

Once they were wed, the prince returned to his father's chateau, and his father said: "My son, you got married on your journey?"

"Yes," he responded. "I married the woman who protected me from the old magician and who saved my life."

As for myself, they sent me here to tell this story.

This tale was told at Sainte-Anne, Kamouraska (Canada) in July 1915, by Achille Fournier, who had learned it twenty-five years ago from an old woman, Louis Dionne, eighty years old, also from Sainte-Anne.

THE FOREST DWELLER (1917)*

Hermann Hesse

At the dawn of civilization, quite some time before human creatures began wandering over the face of the earth, there were forest dwellers. They lived close together fearfully in the dark tropical forests, constantly fighting with their relatives, the apes, and the only divine law that governed their actions was—the forest. The forest was their home, refuge, cradle, nest, and grave, and they could not imagine life outside it. They avoided coming too close to its edges, and whoever, through unusual circumstances while hunting or fleeing something, made his way to the edges would tremble with dread later when reporting about the white emptiness outside, where the terrifying nothingness glistened in the deadly fire of the sun.

* "Der Waldmensch," first published as "Kubu" in *Simplicissimus* (1917).

There was an old forest dweller who decades before had been pursued by wild animals and had fled across the farthest edge of the forest. He had immediately become blind and was now considered a kind of priest and saint with the name Mata Dalam, or "he who has an interior eye." He had composed the holy forest song chanted during the great storms, and the forest dwellers always listened to what he had to say. His fame and mystery rested on the fact that he had seen the sun with his eyes and lived to tell about it.

The forest dwellers were small, brown, and very hairy. They walked with a stoop, and they had furtive, wild eyes. They could move both like human beings and like apes and felt just as safe in the branches of the forest as they did on the ground. They had not yet learned about houses and huts. Nevertheless, they knew how to fabricate many kinds of weapons and tools, as well as jewelry. They made bows, arrows, lances, and clubs out of wood and necklaces from the fiber of trees that were strung with dried beets or nuts. They wore precious objects around their necks or in their hair: a wild boar's tooth, a tiger's claw, a parrot's feathers, shells from mussels. A large river flowed through the endless forest, but the forest dwellers did not dare tread on its banks except in the dark of night, and many had never seen it. Sometimes the more courageous ones crept out of the thickets at night, fearful and on the lookout. Then, in the faint glimmer of dusk, they would watch the elephants bathing and look through the treetops above them and observe the glittering stars with dread as they appeared to hang in the manifold interlaced branches of the mangrove trees. They never saw the sun, and it was considered extremely dangerous to see its reflection in the summer.

A young man by the name of Kubu belonged to the tribe of forest dwellers headed by the blind Mata Dalam, and he was the leader and spokesman for the dissatisfied young people. In fact, ever since Mata Dalam had grown older and become more tyrannical, the malcontents had made their voices heard in the tribe. Until then it had been the blind man's uncontested right to be provided with food by the other members of the tribe. In addition, they came to him for advice and sang his forest song. Gradually, however, he had introduced all sorts of new and burdensome customs that were revealed to him, so he said, in a dream by the divine spirit of the forest. But several skeptical young men asserted that the old man was a swindler and was concerned only with advancing his own interests.

The most recent custom Mata Dalarn had introduced was a moon celebration in which he sat in the middle of a circle and beat a drum made of leather. Meanwhile the other forest dwellers had to dance in the circle and sing the song "Gulo Elah" until they were exhausted and collapsed on their knees. Then all the men had to pierce their left ears with a thorn, and the young women were led to the priest, who pierced each of their ears with a thorn.

Kubu and some other young men had shunned this ritual and had endeavored to convince the young women to resist as well. One time it appeared that they had a good chance to triumph over the priest and break his power. It was when the old man was conducting the new moon ceremony and piercing the left ear of a woman. A bold young man let out a terrible scream while this was happening, and the blind man chanced to stick the thorn into the woman's eye, which fell out of its socket. Now the young woman screamed in such despair that everyone ran over to her, and when they saw what had happened, they were stunned and speechless. Immediately the young men intervened with triumphant smiles on their faces, and when Kubu dared to grab the priest by his shoulders, the old man stood up in front of his drum and uttered such a horrible curse, in such a squealing scornful voice, that everyone retreated in terror. Even the young man was petrified. Though nobody could understand the exact meaning of the old priest's words, his curse had a wild and awful tone and reminded everyone of the dreadful holy words of the religious ceremonies. Mata Dalam cursed the young man's eyes, which he granted to the vultures as food, and he cursed his intestines, which he prophesied would roast in the sun one day on the open fields. Then the priest, who at this moment had more power than ever before, ordered the young woman to be brought to him again, and he stuck out her other eye with the thorn. Everyone looked on with horror, and no one dared to breathe.

"You will die outside!" the old man cursed Kubu, and from the moment of this pronouncement, the other forest dwellers avoided the young man as hopeless. "Outside"—that meant outside the homeland, outside the dusky forest. "Outside"—that meant horror, sunburn, and glowing deadly emptiness.

Terrified, Kubu fled, and when he saw that everyone retreated from him, he hid himself far away in a hollow tree trunk and gave himself up for lost. Days and nights he lay there, wavering between mortal terror and spite, uncertain whether the people of his tribe would come to kill him or whether the sun itself would break through the forest, besiege him, flush him out, and slay him. But the arrows and lances did not come; nor did the sun or lightning. Nothing came except great languishment and the growling voice of hunger.

So Kubu stood up once again and crawled out of the tree, sober and with a feeling almost of disappointment. "The priest's curse was nothing," he thought in surprise, and then he looked for food. When he had eaten and felt life circulating through his limbs once more, pride and hate surged up in his soul. He did not want to return to his people anymore. All he wanted now was to be solitary and remain expelled. He wanted to be known as the one who had been hated and had resisted the feeble curses of the priest, that blind cow. He wanted to be alone and remain alone, but he also wanted to take revenge.

So he walked around the forest and pondered his situation. He reflected about everything that had ever aroused his doubts and seemed questionable, especially the priest's drum and his rituals. And the more he thought and the longer he was alone, the clearer he could see. Yes, it was all deceit. Everything had been nothing but lies and deceit. And since he had already come so far in his thinking, he began drawing conclusions. Quick to distrust, he examined everything that was considered true and holy. For instance, he questioned whether there was a divine spirit in the forest or a holy forest song. Oh, all that too was nothing. It too was a swindle. And as he managed to overcome his awful horror, he sang the forest song in a scornful voice and distorted all the words. And he called out the name of the divine spirit of the forest, whom nobody had been allowed to name on the pain of death—and everything remained quiet. No storm exploded. No lightning struck him down!

Isolated, Kubu wandered for many days and weeks with a furrowed brow and a piercing look. He went to the banks of the river at full moon, something that nobody had ever dared to do. There he looked long and bravely, first at the moon's reflection and then at the full moon itself and all the stars, right in their eyes, and nothing happened to him. He sat on the riverbank for entire moonlit nights, reveling in the forbidden delirium of light, and nursed his thoughts. Many bold and terrible plans arose in his mind. "The moon is my friend," he thought, "and the star is my friend, but the blind old man is my enemy. Therefore, the 'outside' is perhaps better than *our* inside, and perhaps the entire holiness of the forest is also just talk!" And one night, generations before any other human being, Kubu conceived the daring and fabulous plan of binding some branches together with fiber, placing himself on the branches, and floating down the river. His eyes glistened, and his heart pounded with all its might. But this plan came to naught, for the river was full of crocodiles.

Consequently, there was no way into the future but to leave the forest by way of its edge—if there even was an edge to the forest at all—and to entrust himself to the glowing emptiness, the evil "outside." That monster, the sun, had to be sought out and endured, for—who knew?—in the end maybe even the ancient lore about the terror of the sun was just a lie!

This thought, the last in a bold, feverishly wild chain of reflections, made Kubu tremble. Never in the whole of history had a forest dweller dared to leave the forest of his own free will and expose himself to the horrible sun. And once more he walked around for days carrying these thoughts with him until he finally summoned his courage. Trembling, on a bright day at noon, he crept toward the river, cautiously approached the glittering bank, and anxiously looked for the image of the sun in the water. The glare was extremely painful to his dazzled eyes, and he quickly shut them. But after a while he dared to open them once more and then again and again, until he succeeded in keeping them open. It was possible. It was endurable. And it even made him happy and courageous. Kubu had learned to trust the sun. He loved it, even if it was supposed to kill him, and he hated the old, dark, lazy forest, where the priest croaked and where the young courageous man had been outlawed and expelled.

Now he made his decision, and he picked his deed like a piece of ripe sweet fruit. He made a full hammer out of ironwood and gave it a very thin and light handle. Then, early the next morning, he went looking for Mata Dalam. After discovering his footprints, he found him, hit him on the head with the hammer, and watched the old man's soul depart through his crooked mouth. Kubu placed his weapon on the priest's chest so that the people would know who had killed him, and using a mussel shell, he carved a sign on the flat surface of the hammer. It was a circle with many straight rays—the image of the sun.

Bravely he now began his trip to the distant "outside." He walked straight ahead from morning till night. He slept nights in the branches of trees and continued his wandering early each morning over brooks and black swamps and eventually over hills and moss-covered banks of stone that he had never seen before. As they became steeper he was slowed down because of the gorges, but he managed to climb the mountains on his way through the infinite forest, so that he ultimately became doubtful and sad and worried that perhaps some god had prohibited the creatures of the forest from leaving their homeland.

And then one evening, after he had been climbing for a long time and had reached some higher altitude where the air was much drier and lighter, he came to the edge without realizing it. The forest stopped—but with it the ground stopped, too. The forest plunged down into the emptiness of the air as if the world had broken in two at this spot. There was nothing to see but a distant, faint red glow and above, some stars, for the night had already commenced.

Kubu sat down at the edge of the world and tied himself tightly to some climbing plants so that he would not fall over. He spent the night cowering in dread and was so wildly aroused that he could not shut his eyes. At the first hint of dawn, he jumped impatiently to his feet, bent over the emptiness, and waited for the day to appear.

Yellow stripes of beautiful light glimmered in the distance, and the sky seemed to tremble in anticipation, just as Kubu trembled, for he had never seen the beginning of the day in the wide space of air. Yellow bundles of light flamed up, and suddenly the sun emerged in the sky beyond the immense cleft of the world, large and red. It sprang up from an endless gray nothingness that soon became blue and black—the sea.

And the "outside" appeared before the trembling forest dweller. Before his feet the mountain plunged down into the indiscernible smoking depths, and across from him some rose-tinted cliffs glistened like jewels. To the side lay the dark sea, immense and vast, and around it the coast ran white and foamy, with small nodding trees. And above all of this, above these thousand new, strange mighty forms, the sun was rising, casting a glowing stream of light over the world that burst into flames of laughing colors.

Kubu was unable to look the sun in its face. But he saw its light stream in colorful floods over the mountains and rocks and coasts and distant blue islands, and he sank to the ground and bent his face to the earth before the gods of this radiant world. Ah, who was he, Kubu? He was a small dirty animal who had spent his entire dull life in the misty swamp hole of the dense forest, fearful, morose, and submitting to the rule of the vile, crooked gods. But here was the world, and its highest god was the sun, and the long, disgraceful dream of his forest life lay behind him and was already being extinguished in his soul, just as the image of the dead priest was fading. Kubu crawled down the steep abyss on his hands and feet and moved toward the light and the sea. And over his soul in fleeting waves of happiness, the dream-like presentiment of a bright earth ruled by the sun began to flicker, an earth on which bright, liberated creatures lived in lightness and were subservient to no one but the sun.

RED MAGIC (1921)*

Heywood Broun

Everybody said it was a great opportunity for Hans. The pay was small, to be sure, but the hours were short and the chance for advancement prodigious. Already the boy could take a pair of rabbits out of a high hat, or change a bunch of carrots into a bowl of goldfish. Unfortunately, the Dutchmen of Rothdam were vegetarians, and Hans was not yet learned enough in magic to turn goldfish back to carrots. Many times he had asked his master, Kahnale, for instruction in the big tricks. He longed to go in for advanced magic, such as typhoons, volcanic eruptions, and earthquakes. He even aspired to juggle planets and keep three stars in the air at once.

Kahnale only smiled and spoke of the importance of rudiments. He pointed out that as long as inexperience made mistakes possible, it would be better to mar a carrot or two than the solar system.

Not all the boy's projects were vast. It seemed as if there was as much enthusiasm in his voice when he asked about love philters as when he spoke of earthquakes. His casual inquiry as to the formula for making a rival disappear into thin air betrayed an eagerness not present in his planetary researches.

But to every question Kahnale replied, "Wait." The magician intimated that a bachelor of black arts might play pranks with the winds, the mountains, and the stars forbidden to a freshman. True love, he declared, would be the merest trifle for one who knew all the lore. Hans found surprisingly small comfort in these promises. He had seen the sixteen-foot shelf of magic in the back room where the skeletons swung in white arcs through the violet haze. Millions of words stood between him and Gretchen, and she was already seventeen and he had turned twenty. It irked him that he should be forced to learn Arabic, Chaldean, and a little Phœnician to win a Dutch girl. Sometimes he imagined she cared for him in spite of a seeming disdain and he hoped that he might win her without recourse to magic, but then she grew coy again.

* Heywood Brown, *Seeing Things at Night* (New York: Harcourt, Brace, 1921).

Anyway, Kahnale had told him that only postgraduate students should seek to read the heart of a woman.

And so Hans polished the high hats, fed the rabbits, read the prescribed pieces in Volume One and learned a little day by day. He yearned more. It seemed as if there must be a shortcut to the knowledge which he wanted, and this belief was strengthened one day when he discovered a thin and ever so aged volume hidden behind the books of the sixteen-foot shelf. Before he had a chance to open the little book Kahnale rushed into the room and cried out to him in a great and terrible voice to drop the volume. Carefully, the magician returned the book to its hiding place and he warned Hans never to touch it again upon pain of the most extensive and prodigious penalties. He not only intimated that disobedience would be dangerous to Hans, but to his family, to the town of Rothdam, to Holland, and to the world.

Six months passed, and Hans had striven to remember so many things since the day of the warning that he had all but forgotten the words of Kahnale. Lying atop the dike, Hans gave the magician never a thought. The boy drew pictures in the loose sand with the toe of his sabot and brushed them away one after the other. At last he completed a design which struck his fancy and he ceased work to admire it. He had drawn a large heart, and exactly in the center he had written "Gretchen."

It may have been a charm or a coincidence, but he looked up from the sand design just in time to see her passing along the road which ran parallel to the dike. He shouted after her, but it was a capricious day with Gretchen, and she went along about her business without once looking back, under the pretense that she had not heard the greeting.

Hans raged and made as if to demolish the heart, and Gretchen, and indeed the whole dike, but then he thought of something better. He got up and entering the house of Kahnale, went into the back room without even stopping to rattle the skeletons. The room was empty, and Hans rummaged behind the long row of magic books until he found the old volume, which he felt sure would give him some of the needful secrets which had been withheld from him. Opening the book, he blew away a thick topsoil of ancient dust and was chagrined to find that whatever knowledge lay before him was concealed in some language so ancient that he could not understand a single word.

"Perhaps," he thought to himself, "this is a charm I can set to ticking even if I can't understand it." Fearing that Kahnale might come upon him, he hid the book under his coat and carried it out to his retreat on top of the dike. In a low voice he began to read the strange and fearsome sentences in the book. Although they meant nothing to him, they possessed a fine rolling cadence which captured his fancy, and more boldly and more loudly Hans went on with his reading.

While Hans meddled with the book of magic, Kahnale was in consultation with the mayor of Rothdam, who sought some charm or potion which would ensure him reelection. He had been a thoroughly inefficient mayor, but the magician dealt with clients as impartially as a lawyer or doctor, and he agreed to weave the necessary spells. He stipulated only that the mayor should accompany him to the house on the dike, where there was a more propitious atmosphere for black art than in the town hall. After some little fuss and fume about the price and the long walk and his dignity, the mayor consented, and the two men descended the great stairway of the town hall. No sooner had they reached the street than Kahnale looked at the sky in amazement. The day had been the most stolid and fair of days when he entered the mayor's office, but now the western sky was filled with tier upon tier of angry black clouds, and as he looked there was a fearsome flash of fire broad as a canal and a roll of thunder that shook the ground beneath their feet.

"Quick!" cried Kahnale, and seizing the mayor by the arm he rushed him down the road which led to the sea. As they ran a rising wind with a salt tang smote their faces. The clouds were growing blacker and heavier. It almost seemed as if they might topple. There was another flash bright as the light which blinded Saul. The mayor crossed himself and prayed. Kahnale cursed. They were within a hundred feet of the sea when a second flare of fire outlined a figure on the dike. It swayed to and fro and moaned above the growing roar of the wind.

In a sudden hush between the gusts the figure turned, and they could hear the voice distinctly enough, though it seemed to be the voice of some one a long way off. "Eb dewollah," said the voice, and Kahnale clapped his hands to his head in horror.

"It is the end," cried the wizard. "There is no hope. This is the final charm. The Lord's Prayer is last of all."

"I do not hear the Lord's Prayer. What is it?" pleaded the Mayor.

"You would not understand," explained Kahnale. "The prayer is said backward, as in all charms. He has reached 'Eb Dewollah,' and that is 'Hallowed Be!' The prayer is the last of the charm."

"Charm? What charm?" said the mayor querulously, clinging dose to Kahnale.

"The master charm," said the magician. "This is the spell which when said aloud summons all the forces of the devil and brings the destruction of the world."

"The world!" interrupted the Mayor in amazement. "Then Rothdam will be destroyed," and he began to weep.

Kahnale paid no heed. "It can't be stopped," he muttered. "It must go on. He has the book and there is no power strong enough to stop the spell."

"If I only had my policemen and my priest," moaned the Mayor.

"Is that all?" said Kahnale. "I have enough magic for that."

The magician spoke three words and made two passes in the air before he turned and pointed to Rothdam. Instantly the bell in the town hall which called all villagers to the dike tolled wildly. The wind was rising and shrilling louder and louder, and the sky was now of midnight blackness. The mayor looked up in wretched terror at the figure on the dike and started to rush at him as if to pitch him into the sea. Kahnale held him back.

"Wait," he said. "If you touched the devil servant you would die."

Above the shriek of the wind rose the voice from the dike. "Nevaeh ni," said the voice. "In heaven," muttered Kahnale. "It is almost done."

Down the road in the teeth of the gale came the villagers of Rothdam. In the van were the mayor's police in red coats. They carried clubs and blunderbusses, and one, more hurriedly summoned than his companions, held a poker.

"There," cried the Mayor, "shoot that man on the dike!" And with the first flash of light the foremost guard ran halfway up the steep embankment and leveled his blunderbuss. He fired. The roar of the gun was answered by a crash of thunder. A fang of fire darted from the center of the clouds and the guard rolled down the dike and lay still at the bottom.

"Tra ohw," came the voice from the dike. The priest, not daunted by the fate of the guard, hurried close to the side of the swaying figure and sprinkled him with holy water, but no sooner had the water left his hands than each drop changed to a tiny tongue of fire, leaping and dancing on the shoulder of the devil servant. The priest drew back in horror, and the mayor, with a cry of fear, threw himself at the foot of the dike and buried his face in the long grasses. High above the booming of the gale and the crash of the waves against the barrier came the voice from the dike, "Rehtaf."

"Father," said Kahnale, "I come, master devil!" he cried with one hand raised.

The sea, which had almost reached the top of the dike, suddenly receded. Back and back it went and bared a deep and slimy floor. On that floor were many unswept things of horror. The earth trembled. The black clouds were banks of floating flame. The villagers turned to run from the dike, for now the sea was returning. It rushed toward the dike in a wave a hundred feet high.

Out of the crowd one ran forward and not back. It was a girl with flaxen hair and red ribbons. She ran straight to the figure on the dike.

"It's Gretchen," she called. "Save me, Hans, save me." She threw her arms around the boy's neck and kissed him. The wall of water hung on the edge of the dike like a violin string drawn tight. Then it surged forward and swallowed up both boy and girl.

Some folk in Rothdam say that Hans dropped the book of black magic and kissed Gretchen before the water swept over them, but the villagers are not sure about this trifle, since at that moment they were watching the rebirth of a lost world.

The wave of water a hundred feet high dwindled until it was no wave, but only a few tall grasses swaying gently in the dying land breeze. The clouds of fire faded to mist, pink tinted by the setting sun. Somewhere about were roses.

The villagers rushed to the top of the dike. A policeman who had muddied his uniform as if by a fall rose to his feet and followed them, rubbing his head. Far below the dike lay a calm sea. On the horizon were ships.

"Rothdam and its brave citizens are saved," said the mayor. "To-night I will burn two hundred candles in honor of our patron saint, who has this day delivered us and enabled us to continue a happy existence under the best municipal government Rothdam has ever known." There were cheers.

That night Kahnale walked on the dike alone. Everybody else was in the cathedral. That is, everybody but one policeman, who pleaded a severe head-ache. The magician listened to the bells of the cathedral and then he shook his head. "It was not the saint who saved us," he muttered. "There are no miracles. Somewhere there is a rational magical explanation for all this." But he had to shake his head again. "It is not in the books," he muttered.

Just then the moon came from behind a cloud and silvered some marks in the path of Kahnale. The magician stooped and looked. There on the top of the wave-swept dike, drawn in the loose sand, was a large heart, and in the center of it was written "Gretchen."

THE MYSTERIOUS BOOK (1921)*

Dean Fansler

Once upon a time there lived a poor father and a poor son. The father was very old, and was named Pedro. The son's name was Juan. Although they were very poor, Juan was afraid of work.

One day the two did not have a single grain of rice in the house to eat. Juan now realized that he would have to find some work, or he and his father would starve. So he went to a neighboring town to seek a master. He at last found one in the person of Don Luzano, a fine gentleman of fortune.

Don Luzano treated Juan like a son. As time went on, Don Luzano became so confident in Juan's honesty that he began to entrust him with the most precious valuables in the house. One morning, Don Luzano went out hunting. He let Juan alone in the house, as usual. While Juan was sweeping and cleaning his master's room he caught sight of a highly polished box lying behind the post in the corner. Curious to find out what was inside, he opened the box. There appeared another box. He opened this box, and another box was still disclosed. One box appeared after another until Juan came to the seventh. This last one contained a small triangular-shaped book in gold and decorated with diamonds and other precious gems. Disregarding the consequences that might follow Juan picked up the book and opened it. Lo! At once Juan was carried by the book up into the air. And when he looked back, whom did he see? No other than Don Luzano pursuing him, with eyes full of rage. He had an enormous deadly looking bolo[†] in his hand.

As Don Luzano was a big man, he could fly faster than little Juan. Soon the boy was but a few yards in front of his antagonist. It should also be known that the book had the wonderful power of changing anybody who had laid his hands on it, or who had learned by heart one of its chapters, into whatever form that person wished to assume. Juan soon found this fact out. In an instant Juan had disappeared, and in his place was a little steed galloping as fast as he could down the street. Again, there was Don Luzano after him in the form of a big fast mule, with bubbling and foaming mouth, and eyes flashing with hate. The mule ran so fast that every minute seemed to be bring Juan nearer the grave.

---

* *Filipino Popular Tales* (Lancaster, PA: American Folk-Lore Society, 1921).

† A long, heavy single-edged machete.

Seeing this danger Juan changed himself into a bird—a pretty little bird. No sooner had he done so that he saw Don Luzano in the form of a big hawk about to swoop down on him. Then Juan suddenly leaped into a well he was flying over, and there became a little fish. Don Luzano assumed the form of a big fish and kept up the chase, but the little fish entered a small crack in the wall of the well, where the big fish could not pursue him farther. So Don Luzano had to give up and go home in great disappointment.

The well in which Juan found himself belonged to three beautiful princesses. One morning, while they were looking into the water, they saw the little fish with its seven-colored scales, moving gracefully through the water. The eldest of the maidens lowered her bait, but the fish would not see it. The second sister tried her skill. The fish bit the bait, but just as it was being drawn out of the water, it suddenly released its hold. Now the youngest sister's turn came. The fish allowed itself to be caught and held in the tender hands of this beautiful girl, who placed the little fish in a golden basin of water and took it to her room, where she cared for it very tenderly.

Several months later the king issued a proclamation throughout his realm and other neighboring kingdoms, saying that the youngest princess was sick.

"To any one who can cure her," he said, "I promise to give one-half of my kingdom."

The most skillful doctors had already done the best they could, but all their efforts were in vain. The princess seemed to grow worse and worse every day.

"Ay, what foolishness!" exclaimed Don Luzano when he heard the news of the sick princess. "The sickness! Pshaw! That's no sickness, never in the wide world!"

The following morning there was Don Luzano speaking with the king. "I promise to cure her," said Don Luzano. "I have already cured many similar cases."

"And your remedy will do her no harm?" asked the king after some hesitation.

"No harm, sir. Rely on my honor."

"Very well. And you shall have half my kingdom if you are successful."

"No, I thank you, your Majesty. I, being a faithful subject, need no payment whatever for any of my poor services. As a token from you, however, I should like to have the fish that the princess keeps in her room."

"O my faithful subject!" exclaimed the king in joy. "How good you are! Will you have nothing except a poor worthless fish?"

"No more. That's enough."

"Well, then," returned the king, "prepare your remedy, and on the third day we shall apply it to the princess. You can go home now, and you may be sure that you shall have the fish."

Don Luzano took his leave of the king, and then went home. On the third day this daring magician came back to the palace to apply his remedy to the princess. Before he began any part of the treatment, however, he requested that the fish be given to him. The king consented to his request, but as he was about to dip his hand into the basin, the princess stopped him. She pretended to be angry on the ground that Don Luzano would soil with his hands the golden basin of the monarch. She told him to hold out his hands, and she would pour the fish into them. Don Luzano did as he was told, but before the fish could reach his hands, the pretty creature jumped out. No fish could be seen, but in its stead was a beautiful gold ring adorning the finger of the princess. Don Luzano tried to snatch the ring, but as the princess jerked her hand back, the ring fell to the floor, and in its place were countless little mungo* seeds scattered about the room.

Don Luzano instantly took the form of a greedy crow, devouring the seeds with extraordinary speed. Juan, who was contained in one of the seeds that had rolled beneath the feet of the princess, suddenly became a cat, and rushing out, attacked the bird. As soon as you could wink your eyes or snap your fingers, the crow was dead, miserably torn to pieces. In place of the cat stood Juan in an embroidered suit, looking like a gay young prince.

"This is my beloved," confessed the princess to her father as she pointed to Juan.

The king forgave his daughter for concealing from him the real condition of her life, and he gladly welcomed his new son-in-law. Prince Juan, as we shall now call our friend, was destined to a life of peace and joy. He was rid of his formidable antagonist, he had a beautiful princess (who was no longer sick), and he had an excellent chance of inheriting the throne. There is no more.

Narrated by Leopoldo Uichanco, a Tagalog from Calamba, La Laguna.

---

* A small legume about the size and shape of a lentil. Same as mongo.

THE BATTLE OF THE ENCHANTERS (1923)*

Elsie Clews Parsons

There were a man and a woman. They had a very lazy son. One day his father sent him to go open the store. His father mounted him on a donkey. He went to the store. When he reached the door of the store, the donkey stopped. He said, "Now, lazy as I am, I am not going to get off to open the door."

He stayed there till night. People came to do business, but he did not get off to sell anything. At night, when he came home, his father asked him what he sold. He said he sold nothing.

"Did people not come to buy?"

"They came, but I did not open the door. They went away."

His father jeered at him.

His mother said, "Don't jeer at my son!"

Next day he asked his father to make him a line and hook. He was going fishing. His father said, "Good-for-nothing! You want to be a fisherman! I sent you to the store, but you did not like it. Now you want to go fishing!"

His mother said, "Go arrange a line and hook for him to go fishing!"

Then his father arranged a line and hook. He went to the sea to fish. He took three days to get to the sea. When he arrived, he lay down behind a stone. Then he saw some men coming on horseback. When they arrived, they made the rock open, and they entered. The next day they came out. They went away. He saw all they did. After his father found that he was late returning, he went to find him. When he arrived where his son was, those men returned, and he said to them, "I want you to teach my son for me."

The men were seven robbers. They said, "Yes, but on condition that you come to take your son at the end of seven years."

The father agreed. The captain gave him a receipt to bring in seven years and fetch his son. He went home and told his wife that he had put their son in school, to go get him in seven years. "There is the receipt to fetch him when the seven years are over."

He dug a hole at the foot of his bed. He buried the receipt seven arms deep.

---

* *Folk-Lore from the Cape Verde Islands* (New York: G. E. Stechert, 1923).

Every day the robbers went out and left the boy in the house, and the captain said to him, "You may go everywhere but into that room there. Do not touch anything in it."

When the captain left, the boy went into that room and took all the books that were there. He studied until he knew all they knew. Well, one day the sergeant said to the captain, "You better take care with that boy, because he is smart."

The captain answered, "Oh, he knows nothing."

The sergeant said, "Well, you know it all."

At this point the boy knew every place where they stole. Then one day he asked the captain for permission to go and see his father. That very day they stole a sack of money from his father that his father had marked. So the boy took this sack of money and went out to see his father. When he reached home, he asked his father, "Where's the sack of money you had in such a place?"

His father looked, but he did not find it. He said he lost it.

Then his son said to his father, "Here is the sack with your money."

His father opened the sack, looked in, and saw that it was his sack of money.

Then his son asked his father, "Where do you keep that receipt? You see that on the day my time is up, if you lose that receipt, you lose me."

His father looked for the receipt but did not find it.

His son said, "Dig deeper, seven arms deep, you will find it."

The father dug seven arms deep until he found it.

His son said, "Good! On the day my time is up, when you come to get me, the captain will not want to give me up to you, but he will give you three doves in a cage for you to choose from. Of these three doves, take the poorest and ugliest of all. He will ask you, 'Why do you not take the prettiest?' You're to say to him that you like the one you chose. That one is me. If you take any other, you will lose me."

Then the son said, "Good-bye!" He went.

Well, when the time was up, the father went to get his son. He arrived and said, "Good-day, captain!—Good-day, friends! I come to get my son."

He delivered the receipt to the captain. The captain gave him a cage with three doves to choose one. The father took the ugliest of all. The captain said to him, "Why don't you take the prettiest?"

"This pleases me."

The sergeant said to the captain, "You see, now, what I told you?"

Then after that the captain delivered his son to him. They went home.

When they reached home, a day came when he said to his father, "Today is the day the captain is going to ride to a certain place where there are birds of gold. We will get up early, we will go there, we will arrive there before him, and we will take the birds."

So they went and took the birds. When they took the birds, he said to his father, "I will become a donkey. Put these birds upon it, and pass by the door of the king. He will want to buy them and offer you fifty thousand reis for each one. You are to refuse and tell him only if he will give you one hundred thousand reis for each one will you sell them. But when you sell them, donkey and all, take only the cord which is on the neck of the donkey, because that cord is me."

The father passed by. The king offered to buy. The father sold them as his son told him, but he was entranced with so much money, and he forgot to take off the cord. He went home.

When the son saw that his father had forgotten, he was confused. The king sent the birds to the room of the princess. Well, when the princess lay down and went to sleep, the birds turned into the boy. He took the princess by the nose. The princess was frightened and cried for her father. She said that someone was inside her room. The king said to her, "You are crazy; where did anyone come out from here?"

She cried out again. The king came and looked everywhere, but he found nothing. He said to her, "If you cry for me again, I will come here. I will settle you."

Well the king went and lay down. Again the boy caught the princess by the nose. The princess started to cry, but she did not cry for fear of the king. The boy said to her, "I am a person. See! Your father has been sick for some time and has been treated by all the doctors there are, but he does not get better. On a certain day a doctor will come who will cure him of his sickness, but he will not want to receive any money, except this ring that I give you. Your father will not want to give it, but don't you mind! Tell him that you will give him the ring, but when you give him the ring, take the ring off your finger with your left hand as you reach out."

Now the boy went out to the house of his father. When he reached the house, he said to his father, "What did you do? You forgot what I said. You were in such a hurry, but still it is all right. Tomorrow is the day for a horse-race in the city. We will go there. My master will be there. I shall win from him because he is old, and I am younger than he. He will come on a very pretty black horse. I will change into a little white horse all harnessed. You will ride it. I will run and will pass him. He will offer to buy your horse. You tell him yes, if he gives you five hundred thousand reis, you will sell him the horse, but you will take off the bridle. If you do not take off the bridle, you will lose me."

They went to the races. He passed the other horse. As soon as he passed, the captain proposed to the father to buy. He sold him just as his son told him to do, but he was entranced with so much money, he forgot to take off the bridle.

When the boy saw that he had forgotten and that he was in the hands of the captain, he made the captain have diarrhea. The captain turned to a man nearby and said, "Take this horse for me. I am going to the little house, but don't take off the bridle."

There stood a tank of water. All the great men of the city were there. The horse began to pull to drink in the tank. The man began to pull him, he did not want to let him drink. The governor of the city said to him, "You slouch! A horse like that you keep from drinking! Let him drink!"

When the captain knew he was drinking, he came out from the little house, coming with his trousers in his hand. The man took the bridle off the horse to drink. The captain arrived in a hurry to take it. When he reached out his hand to take it, the boy turned into a taínha.* He jumped inside the tank of water. The captain turned into a shark. He jumped inside the water after him. He made off. Now he could not see where he was. He ran after him. The taínha came to the top of the water, the shark after him. He changed into a dove of gold and flew into the sky. The captain changed into a falcon and flew after him. He flew until he arrived over the house of the king. He came down and entered the window of the king. Then he alighted on the lap of the princess. The princess said, "O father! See how yesterday you brought me a golden bird. Today God sends me a little golden dove!"

The king said, "Some falcon is after him."

The king took his gun, went out on the verandah, saw the falcon spying, and started to fire at him. The falcon flew away.

* A mullet.

Early the next day a doctor came to the door of the king with all his cures. He knocked at the door. They asked him what he wanted. He said that he came to cure the king of an ailment that he had had for many years. They had him come in. He treated the king and cured him. The king asked him what it cost. He said that he would charge him nothing, he desired only a ring which the princess had on her finger. The king said, "No, I have money to pay you what you ask, not the ring of my daughter."

The princess answered, "What is a ring?"

The princess pulled off the ring with her left hand and held it out. When he started to take it, the princess let the ring fall on the ground. It changed into a quarta of corn. The doctor turned into a falcon. He started to gather up the corn and swallowed it. A grain rolled and thrust itself under the foot of the princess. The falcon ate all the corn until only that grain was left. He turned his neck to take it under the foot of the princess. The corn changed into a razor and cut the neck of the falcon. Just here was the end of the captain.

Then the king married the young man to the princess. He sent for his father and mother. They all came to live at the palace. Only yesterday I passed by there, and they were all sitting on the verandah.

The informant for this tale was Gregorio Teixeira da Silva of Fogo.

THE SORCERER'S APPRENTICE (1926)*

Romuald Pramberger

A poor widow had a son, and when he turned fourteen years old, he began an apprenticeship with a carpenter. Within a short time he was using a plane, hammer, and saw as if he had always been accustomed to working with them. In his spare time, especially on Sundays, he nosed around in all kinds of books, and this is how he also learned to read and write very well.

After he finished his apprenticeship, he began to wander about looking for work. One day he came upon a forest, and after entering it, he kept walking until late at night but could not find a way out. Therefore, he climbed a tree to see if he could gain a clearer view of the surroundings, and he noticed a small light in the distance. So he made a beeline straight to the small light

* Romuald Pramberger, "Der Zauberlehrling," *Deutsche Märchen aus dem Donaulande*, ed. Paul Zaunert (Jena: Eugen Diederichs, 1926).

and soon reached a little cottage in the middle of the forest. You can't imagine how happy he was to find a place where he might have a roof over his head, at least for a few hours. After he rapped at the window a couple of times an old man appeared at the door and asked him what he wanted.

"I'd like a place to stay for the night," the young carpenter answered. "And if you have some leftovers from supper in a bowl, I'd appreciate if I might have them."

Then the man led him into the living room, pulled down a little table from the wall, and said: "Little table, set yourself!" And suddenly the choicest dishes imaginable stood on the table.

Of course the young man did not hesitate to begin eating, for he had never eaten such good food, and he did not forget to thank the old master for everything. In turn the man smiled and said: "Tell me, can you read?"

"Just a little," responded the carpenter.

"Good," laughed the old man. "Then I'll hire you, and all you'll actually have to do is to dust the books, page by page."

Upon saying this he led his new servant into a room where books upon books were piled and filled the space. Soon afterward the master went on a journey and stayed away for three years. During this time, however, the young man studied the books and became extremely knowledgeable about all kinds of sorcery, for these books dealt only with sorcery. So now whenever he wanted to eat he took down the little table from the wall and said: "Little table, set yourself!" And all at once he had everything that he wanted.

Now, when the master returned home, he was satisfied with the dusting that the carpenter had done, and as soon as the young man asked him for his wages, he gave him plenty of money. Afterward the carpenter left for his home and began living with his old mother for some time without any problems. After he had spent all his money, however, he said to his mother: "I'm going to change myself into a dog, and you're to bring me to the marketplace and sell me for forty gilder."

And this is just the way it happened. His mother soon found a buyer for the handsome brute of a dog. It was a butcher who used the dog to herd his cattle and was very satisfied because the dog served him very well for a few days. But one day the dog suddenly vanished, and the young man went cheerfully back to his home.

Later when the young carpenter spent the forty gilder, he transformed himself into a horse and told his mother to take him to the marketplace and demand four hundred gilder for him. After the sale she was to take the halter back with her; otherwise, if she didn't, it would be his misfortune.

Meanwhile the sorcerer had noticed that many pages in his books on sorcery were missing, and he concluded that his former servant had learned how to do magic. So the sorcerer went searching for him, and when he came to the marketplace in the city, he immediately recognized his former servant in the form of a white horse.

So he went over to the mother and soon negotiated a deal to buy the white horse, but as she was about to take the halter with her, the sorcerer refused and told her that it was not customary for the seller to take off the halter from the horse. No matter how much the woman argued, it didn't help. She had to go home without the halter. Meanwhile the sorcerer led the horse to the stable of a nearby tavern and then went inside to drink some booze, for he was very happy about his good catch.

Unknown to him the white horse began to calling out to the stable boy in a low voice, and when the amazed boy went over to him, the horse asked him to take off the halter. Just as the groom was doing this, the sorcerer entered the stable and angrily tore the horse out of the stall, causing the old halter to turn into the buckle of a strap so that the sorcerer was left empty-handed without the halter. Then a bird quickly flew out of the stable, and the sorcerer reacted by transforming himself into a vulture and pursued the bird as swiftly as the wind. He was just about to pounce on the bird in the air when the two flew over the king's castle, where the king's wonderfully beautiful daughter was sitting in the front garden.

In a flash the bird transformed himself into a little golden ring and dropped down into the princess's lap. She was completely astonished and immediately tried on the ring, which fit as if it were made for her. Consequently the sorcerer had to abandon his pursuit for the time being, but he didn't give up the chase.

It so happened at this time that the princess's old father was sick, and all the doctors in his realm had sought to heal him in vain. By chance, a few days after the princess had obtained the ring, a highly experienced doctor arrived, examined the king, and healed him. Everyone in the realm was very happy about this.

"Take half of my kingdom as a reward for your services," the king said to the doctor.

"Oh no," replied the modest doctor. "I only want a small gift, and it's the tiny ring on the princess's finger. Otherwise, there's nothing else I want."

Indeed, the doctor was the sorcerer.

However, the young man had already transformed himself from ring to human the previous night and had appeared before the princess. Well, it did not take long for them to become united and to spend a beautiful night together. During this time the young man had asked the princess to let the little ring fall to the ground if he were ever to be in danger. So now as the doctor extended his hand to take the ring she let it unexpectedly drop, and it changed into a tiny grain of wheat barely visible and rolled into a crack in the floorboard.

Quickly, however, the doctor transformed himself into a hen right before the eyes of the king and his royal household. Then the little grain of wheat swiftly changed itself into a fox, and the fox grabbed the hen by its neck and bit it in two.

Once the young man assumed his natural shape again, he asked the king to allow him to wed the princess. And so afterward there was a merry wedding.

THE MISTRESS OF MAGIC (1926)*

Seumas MacManus

Once upon a time, and a good time it was, there was a man in the mountains of Donegal who had one son, named Manus, who was growing up a fine, brave, nice boy entirely and a help and comfort to his father. But on a night doesn't there arrive at this man's house a prince from the East with eleven of his followers, and he asked to be put up for the night, and Manus's father put him up and welcome. After supper the prince from the East began putting his followers and himself through a lot of wonderful magical tricks which astonished Manus's father very, very much indeed. And he said he wished his son Manus could work tricks like that.

Said the prince of the East, "How would you like it if I took your son Manus with me and I taught him magic, too?"

"I would like it very well indeed," said Manus's father. "Only I am very fond of Manus, and I wouldn't like to spare him long."

"Would a year and a day be too long?" said the prince of the East.

* *The Donegal Wonder Book* (New York: Frederick A. Stokes, 1926).

"It would not," said Manus's father. "And if you'll promise to teach Manus your magical tricks and have him here again in a year and a day from now, you'll be doing me a great favor, and I'll willingly let you have him."

"Very well and good," said the prince from the East, agreeing to that. "I will take Manus with me, and verse him so well and soundly in magical tricks that when I bring him back to you in a year and a day, I promise that he'll astonish you."

The father was as well pleased at this as Manus, and Manus was as well pleased as the father. Next morning Manus bade the father farewell and set off and away with the prince of the East and his eleven followers.

The father, though he felt lonesome enough without his Manus, wrought hard and tried to be happy. Still he couldn't help counting the time. And every day was a week to him, and every week was seven, till the year and a day were around, and he looked for his brave Manus again.

Right enough, on the very day when the year and a day were up, late in the evening, the prince of the East arrived and Manus with him, and eleven other followers. And I tell you that was a glad meeting between Manus and his father. Manus was grown a bigger and a stouter and braver and a finer fellow far than when he went away, and his father was proud of him. But if he was proud of him when he first saw him, he was double as proud when, after supper, the prince of the East began to put Manus through his magical tricks, astonishing and priding the father at the wonderful things Manus could do.

"Ay," said the prince of the East, "he is very good, surely for his time; but if the boy had only time enough it's a wonderful magician he would make. Wait till you see what these eleven and myself can do."

And then he began to put his other eleven followers and himself through their tricks. If Manus's tricks had been great and fine, the tricks that the prince himself and his eleven followers now went through astounded Manus's father out and out, and far surpassed anything Manus could do.

"Well, well, I wish and I wish," said the father, "that Manus had the ability of you twelve."

"And that he could have," said the prince of the East, "if you only leave him long enough in his apprenticeship."

"How much longer do you want him?" said the father.

"Let us say a year and a day," said the prince from the East. Although the father was grieved at the notion of parting with poor Manus again, still the temptation was great. So he agreed with the prince that he should have Manus for another year and a day, provided he would fetch him back there to the same spot again at the end of that time, more perfect in magic.

On the very next morning the father had to part with poor Manus again, and a sad parting you may be sure it was. But the father said, "Manus, dear, keep up your heart and the year and a day will pass like a week—till you are with me again."

And off the prince of the East and Manus and his other eleven followers set. And the father turned to his work and tried to be happy whilst the time went round, but every day was a week to him, and every week was seven, looking forward to Manus's coming again.

But the longest tale must have a finish, and the lonesomest year an ending, so at long and at last, the year and a day passed, and on the very last evening of the time, the prince of the East with Manus and his other eleven followers, they arrived at Manus's father's in Donegal. And great and great as was the joy of Manus's father at the meeting, just every bit as great was the joy of Manus, and a happy pair they were that night.

The father laid down a royal supper for all of them; and, when they had eaten and drunk to their heart's content, the prince of the East put Manus on the floor and began putting him through his tricks, for the father's delight. And if Manus had been clever the first time, he was double as clever now. And the father, delighted, said the like of Manus for cleverness he had never seen before, and that he'd now be as proud as a prince for Manus all the days of his life.

Said the prince of the East, "Manus is good, and very good—for his time. But if I had only long enough of him, I would make him the most wonderful magician in the world again. Just wait till you see," said he, "what these other eleven followers of mine can do."

And he began putting the other eleven followers and himself through magical tricks. And if Manus's tricks had opened his father's eyes, the tricks he now saw opened them far wider surely.

And said he, "My son, Manus is good and very good, as you say—but I only wish he was as good as that."

"Will you let me have him for another year and a day?" said the prince of the East, "'till you see what I will make of him?"

"And a thousand welcomes," agreed the father.

Next morning sad enough was the parting; and Manus again set out with the prince of the East and the other eleven followers. And the father he turned and went to his work and tried to feel happy. But every day was a week to him, and every week seven, till at long and at last the year and a day were round. But at the end of the time neither prince nor Manus appeared. For, unfortunately, when the last agreement was made, Manus's father forgot to put into it that he would have to bring Manus back at the time's end. But if Manus's father and Manus himself had overlooked this point, the prince of the East hadn't been blind to it—for he was a right cunning knave.

As restless as a hen on a hot griddle was the poor father all the dreary day, waiting and watching. But no prince came, and alas! no Manus, although all the day he watched and waited, and all the night, and all the next day, too. With his heart nigh breaking he got up early on the morning of the third day, and he took with him a cake of hard bread well-buttered, and set out to find the castle of the prince of the East and fetch his Manus home. On and on before him he traveled till the sun was high, and himself hungry and tired as well. Then at midday he sat down, under a rowan tree, to eat his cake and rest himself. And a gray hawk came flying and alit on the rowan tree.

"Hungry, hungry I am," said the hawk. "Little old man, won't you divide your dinner with me?"

"It's little enough is it for myself," said Manus's father, "but I can't bear to see any of God's creatures go wanting."

So he divided his cake with the hawk.

"You'll not lose by this," said the hawk. "There's only one creature in all the world knows where that prince's castle is, and it's I only who have that knowledge," said the hawk. "I once put the prince under an obligation to me—and once I went to his castle, but never went there again, for it's almost beyond the world and a seven year's journey to travel there. But I'm so sorry for you that if you like to follow me, I'll lead you there. By reason of the obligation I put the prince under I can get you entrance to his castle. But I cannot tell you how you'll fare when you get there."

"Thank you," said Manus's father. "And I'll follow you if it was ten times as far."

Accordingly off they set with the hawk leading, and flying ahead of Manus's father. When be would be on the hill the hawk would be in the hollow, and when he would be in the hollow the hawk would be on the hill. And so it fared, and so he followed, while the days grew to weeks, and the weeks to months and the months to years—and the years grew to seven. And on the night before the last day of the seventh year the hawk told him they were now within a day's journey of the prince's castle, and that when he reached it, he was to demand entrance and possession of his son in the name of the Gray Hawk of Knowledge—"which," the hawk said, "is my name. He'll have to give you both admittance and the chance of picking out your son among his twelve followers," said the hawk. "Only, when he puts the twelve before you to pick from, he'll be at liberty to have them in any shape he likes. No man will he able to tell one from another of them, so much alike will they be. And yet you'll have only one choice and must abide by it. It's heartily sorry I'll be if you fail. But may God bless you," said the hawk, "and send that you don't fail."

Right heartily Manus's father thanked the hawk and said, "Well, if I fail it won't be your fault anyway. You have surely done your best, now. And," he said sorrowfully, "the best can do no more."

Well and good. Toward evening of the next day he came in sight of a gorgeous castle of many towers—seated on a mountain-top and surrounded by great trees. And on the top of the highest tower alighted the Gray Hawk of Knowledge.

Manus's father now knew he had reached his journey's end. So climbing up to the great castle he knocked on the gates. And it was the prince of the East himself who appeared.

"What is it you're wanting?" said he.

"I demand admission and search for my son," he replied, "in the name of the Gray Hawk of Knowledge."

The prince of the East looked black when he heard this. But there was nothing for it but to open the gates and let him in. And the prince said, "In the morning you'll be given chance of finding your son."

Manus's father got his supper and was shown to bed in one of the towers. But just as he was about to fall asleep he was aroused by a tapping on the window pane. He got up and saw perched outside a pigeon that was doing the tapping. He opened the window to the pigeon—and when it flew in it turned into a young woman, the most beautiful, he thought, he had ever seen.

She said, "I'm the daughter of the prince of the East. And I must confess that I have fallen in love with your son, young Manus from Ireland. And it grieves me that my father has held him here under spells. And I now have come to help you to find him. Though I must warn you that even if you find him, you'll still find it the hardest task in the world to get him entirely free of my father. In the morning my father will take you out into the courtyard, and when he blows a whistle, twelve blackbirds will sit upon a tree and begin to sing, and you'll be asked to take your choice of the twelve. They are my father's twelve followers, and your son is one of them. The way you'll know your son is by his singing the saddest song. Heaven send that you choose wisely. But, even then, your trouble will only have begun."

Then she turned into a pigeon again, and flew out among the trees that surrounded the castle. In the morning the prince of the East took Manus's father into the courtyard. And he blew a whistle, and twelve blackbirds appeared and perched upon a tree, and all twelve began to sing.

Said the prince, "Out of those twelve choose your son."

One of the blackbirds sitting on the topmost branch sang a song that was sad and very sad, and forlorn entirely.

"I choose," said he, "that blackbird perched on the topmost branch of the tree."

The prince of the East looked as black as thunder. But there wasn't anything for it but to turn the blackbird into the shape of a man again. And it was Manus. And he and his father embraced and cried for very joy.

With little delay they set out for home—on the very next morning. As they went along, the son said, "Dear Father, the prince of the East doesn't mean to part with me easily. He'll surely come after us and try to get me from you by some trick or other. You are a poor man, Father," said Manus, "and if you manage well, I, by virtue of my magical knowledge, can get for you a good penny from the villain."

"How is that?" said the father.

Said Manus, "I'll turn myself into a sheep with a tether to me. You'll lead me along; and at twelve o'clock today you'll be met by a sheep buyer and eleven boys. He'll ask you what you'll take for the sheep. You say that this is a particular sheep, and you cannot part with it under a hundred pounds. He'll quickly close the bargain and pay you the money. Let him have the sheep, but on the peril of your life don't let away the tether. Then all will be well."

To this the father agreed, and into a sheep Manus turned himself, with his father driving him along with the end of the tether in his hold. And just at noon what should he meet up with but a sheep buyer, and eleven boys, who asked if he would sell the sheep.

"Yes," said Manus's father. "But as this is a particular sheep, I'll not part with it under a hundred pounds."

"You'll get your price," said the sheep buyer. And down he paid him a hundred pounds in gold, and took the sheep with him, Manus's father keeping the tether.

Then the sheep buyer pushed on his way with his eleven boys and his sheep, and Manus's father followed his way. And Manus's father wasn't three hours traveling, when who but his son overtook him. And both of them rejoiced.

Next morning said Manus to his father, "My master doesn't mean to part with me as easily as you think. But if you do right today we'll get some more money out of the villain."

"How do you mean?" asked the father.

Said Manus, "I'll turn myself into a goat with a tether to it. You'll drive me before you, and at twelve o'clock you'll be met up by a goat buyer and eleven boys. He'll ask you to sell him the goat. Then you must say that this is a particular goat, and you wouldn't think of parting with it for less than two hundred pounds. He'll give you that, but you must be sure on the peril of your life not to part with the tether."

"All right," said the father.

So turn himself into a goat Manus did, and his father drove him before him, the end of the tether in his hand. And at twelve o'clock, sure enough, what does he meet but a goat buyer and eleven boys.

And said the goat buyer, says he, "Will you sell the goat?"

"I'll do that," said Manus's father. "But as this is a particular goat, I wouldn't think of parting with it under two hundred pounds."

"I'll give you that," said the goat buyer. And he did. He paid down to Manus's father two hundred golden pounds, and took away the goat before him—Manus's father slipping the tether off and keeping it.

On then went Manus's father, and he wasn't three hours traveling when up to him came Manus again. And both of them rejoiced.

"We're doing well, Father," said Manus, "in punishing the villain. That's three hundred pounds you've got, and tomorrow if you act well, you'll have three hundred more."

"How is that?" asked his father.

"Tomorrow," said Manus, "I'll turn myself into a horse with a bridle. At twelve o'clock in the day, you'll meet an army captain with eleven dragoons, all armed with cutlasses, and the army captain will say that he is in want of a horse and will ask you to sell him yours. You must say that this is a particular horse and you won't part with him under three hundred pounds. He'll buy me, but you be sure on the peril of your life not to let me away without first slipping off and keeping the bridle."

His father promised to do this. Next day Manus turned himself into a horse. And at twelve o'clock, right enough, up meeting them comes an army captain and eleven dragoons, every one of them armed with a cutlass. And the captain halted Manus's father and told him he was in need of a horse. "I like the looks of that one you're leading," said he. "Will you sell him?"

"I'll sell him," said Manus's father. "But as he's a very particular horse, I wouldn't think of parting with him under three hundred pounds."

"I'll give you that," said the army captain. "But come," said he, "to this inn till I pay you the money, and we've a drink over it."

To the inn with them, unfortunately, went Manus's father, who got his three hundred golden pounds paid there and had a drink with them over it. That drink led to a second, and the second to a third, till in the end poor Manus's father forgot about the bridle. Off went the captain, and his eleven dragoons, taking with them the horse and the bridle also. And although Manus's father waited three days and three nights his son never came. And off he set to seek his son again.

Now the prince of the East rode Manus home, for of course it was he who was the army captain. With his followers there he held a council, and it was decided Manus should be punished by being roasted to death in a mill-kiln.

So on the very next day they put Manus into the mill-kiln, from which there was no escape, and they built the grate under.

Now the beautiful princess, who loved him, was in sore distress when she found they were burning her lover in the mill-kiln. Calling up all her magical power, she turned the millrace into the kiln, leaving it then to Manus's own powers to extricate himself.

The minute the water flowed in on top of him, Manus turned himself into an eel, and in the flow of water swam out into the river.

Then the prince of the East and his eleven followers turned themselves into twelve otters and dived into the river after him. Manus curled himself under the deepest stone in the river. But the otters searched every stone till they came to the right one.

When he found himself discovered, Manus turned himself into a white pigeon, and flew to the woods. But into twelve hawks turned the prince and his followers, and away after Manus.

Swift and very swift was their flight, and close and very close the chase till at long and at last the white pigeon tired and weakened and must soon give up. And the hawks were fast closing on it. A castle was near at hand toward which the white pigeon, in extremity, flew. Just as it came to the castle, the ballroom window was thrown open, and a beautiful lady appeared at it and waved on the white pigeon to come that way. And this beautiful lady was none other than the princess herself who had flown there before him. For this was the castle of her mother's brother.

In through the window flew the white pigeon, turned itself into a ring, and went upon the princess's finger. In this great room was a party of ladies and gentlemen dancing and feasting. The twelve hawks, when they arrived, changed themselves into six fiddlers and six pipers, came under the ball-room window, and began to play the most enchanting airs ever heard so that all the assembled lords and ladies flocked to the window to look and to listen. And when they had finished playing, the king of the castle was so grateful to them that he bade them ask any reward they wished, and they should have it.

"We only ask," said the leader of them, "the ring upon that fair young lady's finger."

"You shall surely have that," said the king.

But the princess took the ring from her finger and threw it into the heart of the blazing fire.

That minute the musicians turned themselves into six bellows and six bellows blowers and blew till they blew the ring out upon the floor. Into six blacksmiths and six sledges they then transformed themselves and began to batter and beat at the ring. The ring went up in a burst of sparks, and the sparks fell over the room in a shower of wheat. And into twelve geese they then changed, and began to eat the wheat—when the wheat turned into a fox, and took the heads off the twelve geese.

Then the fox changed itself into Manus in his own form again. And he and the princess embraced and kissed each other. And when the king and the lords and ladies heard the whole story it is surprised and delighted they were.

It was agreed that they should be married within a week. All who were there were bidden to the wedding—and ten who weren't, there for the one that was. Manus sent for his father to Donegal, and brought him there. Their wedding lasted nine days and nine nights—and the last day and night was better and merrier than the first.

After the wedding the three of them went to the castle of the prince of the East, which Manus and his wife now owned, and there they lived happy ever after.

THE TWO MAGICIANS (1937)*

Joseph Médard Carrière

It's good to tell you that there was once an old man and a woman. They had a large number of children, and then they had another child whom they wanted to baptize. However, they couldn't find anyone to become his godfather. Then an old magician passed by, and they asked him whether he'd be their son's godfather.

"Yes," he said, "but you must give him to me when he begins to think at the age of seven, and he is to stay with me until he turns sixteen. I'll give him a place in my school," he said, "and you must recognize him at the end of this time if you want him back."

This was done when the boy reached the age of seven. Then his father took him to the godfather, who placed him in his school. When the boy was almost finished with the school, he concealed a secret from his godfather that he had learned almost as much about magic as his godfather knew. Three months before he was to be discharged from the school, he left secretly and went to his father. Once he was there, Pierre said to his father, "In three months you must come to fetch me. On the day that you come to fetch me, there will be others assembled before you. All of us will be pigeons," he said. "The one that you take, you must keep whether it's your son or not. It doesn't make any difference. You must keep it. But I am going to tell you what you have to do. I'll be an old sickly pigeon," he said. "Then, when you begin to choose among the boys, I'll lay down on my side and begin to raise my wing," he said. "You'll recognize me as this pigeon. That will be me."

The time came for all the fathers to fetch their sons whom they had sent to the school. They had left their sons at the school as boys and expected to recognize them as humans. Indeed, they would have been able to recognize them as such. But the young men had all been changed into pigeons and were

---

* "Les deux Magiciens," *Tales from the French Folklore of Missouri*, Joseph Médard Carrière (Evanston, IL: Northwestern University Press, 1937), pp. 91–96.

gathered there in such a way that their sons appeared as strangers. Pierre's father's turn came, and he advanced to the place where the pigeons were kept and looked around him. There was only one that was sickly and raised one of its wings. It appeared as though it had lived there a long time. "If that doesn't turn out to be my son, I'll be troubled for a long time."

When the old man chose Pierre, the godfather cried out: "Hey! Pierre, you'll pay for this one day! You'll see!"

That didn't matter. Pierre was in a good place. He was with his father. The godfather was in a bad mood when Pierre was about to leave.

"Pierre," he said, "you have learned many things that I have never shown to anyone else."

"But I've learned them," Pierre said to his godfather. "I've learned them from you."

Now Pierre departed with his father, and he asked him whether he had any money.

"No, my son," he said, "I don't have any money."

"Would you like to make a hundred dollars on our way?"

"Very well, Pierre," he said. "I'd certainly be proud to have a hundred dollars."

"I'm going to change myself into a dog," Pierre said, "and I'm going to hunt for all sorts of things, rabbits and squirrels. I'm going to look for all kinds of wild animals," he said. "Then, you're to sell me for a hundred dollars to the first men that you meet."

"What!" his father replied. "You can change yourself into a dog, just like that?"

"Ah, yes!" he said. "I can change myself into a dog. It's because of this that my godfather is so angry with me. I secretly learned all his magic."

So Pierre changed himself into a dog and began to run through the woods to catch some rabbits and squirrels. He caught so much that his father could hardly carry them. Then Pierre stopped hunting and followed behind his father, who soon encountered two men.

"Good day!" one of them said to him. "Where did you get all this wild game?"

"Ah!" the father said. "I got these animals with my dog. It was my dog," he said, "that caught them."

"Oh!" the man said. "But I don't believe that your dog can catch so much wild game like that."

"Ah!" the father responded. "Very well. If you don't believe me, sit down awhile, and then I'll send my dog hunting for wild game again." He said to his dog: "Go and hunt for a rabbit or a squirrel again."

Pierre departed, and he didn't leave his father much time to chat before he returned carrying a little rabbit. Then the two men asked the old father, "Is it necessary for you yourself to go hunt and catch the animals with the dog?"

"Ah! Not at all," he said. "The dog catches them and then brings them to me."

"Are you willing to sell your dog?" they said.

"Ah!" he said. "That would cost me a lot to sell my dog. I'm too poor to buy meat," he said.

"Very well," said one of the men. "I'll tell you what I'll do. If you sell me your dog, I'll pay you a hundred dollars."

"All right," the old man said. "I don't like to give away my dog, but I'll take a hundred dollars."

"Do you have anything to tie to your dog to lead it away?" one man asked.

"You don't need anything to attach to the dog," he said. "You just have to tell it to follow you, and then the dog will just follow you."

So he sold the dog, and then the men paid him a hundred dollars, and then he said to the dog, "From now on, you're to leave me, and you're to go with those men there."

Pierre went over to his father and licked his hands as if he wanted to say good-bye. Then he departed with the two men. Once they went into the woods, he caught squirrels, rabbits, wood rats, and quails. It didn't take him very long before he had hunted everything that they believed the dog could find on the ground After all this the two men said to one another that they should have paid three hundred dollars for the dog. And Pierre picked himself up while the men were talking on a trail, and then he moved away until he no longer heard them chatting. Soon he went and rejoined his father. When he arrived at his father's place, he transformed himself back into a young man. Later the two men realized that the dog was missing. They turned back to go and see the old man, believing that they dog was with him. Once they caught up with the old man and were very near his home, they asked whether he had seen the dog.

"No," he said. "I haven't seen your dog. I haven't seen anything. I have nothing but my little son who has come to join me at my little house in the country," he said. "I think that your dog is lost. It'll return to you as soon as you go back into the woods unless something has happened to it."

The two men went back into the woods to look for the dog while the old man went to his home with his son. The two men kept looking for the dog but never found it.

The father and son did this many times, and one day there were some races. Pierre said to his father that he was going to transform himself into a horse, and he said: "I'm going to change myself into a horse that's very thin, and I'll assume the air of a sick horse not capable of racing, but don't worry if I run behind the other horses. I am going to win the race and pass all the other horses."

So he went to the races and won. Everyone had laughed at the old horse and thought that it would never win the race. The old man won nine hundred dollars as well as the crown because his horse had won the race. Then Pierre said to his father: "My godfather will be coming to buy me. Sell me for about nine hundred dollars but make sure to keep the bridle."

The godfather came and bought the horse, but he kept the bridle and led the horse away to his stable. Once there the servants gave him water and hay, but the horse didn't eat or drink. The stable boys said: "That's strange, a good horse like that which doesn't eat or drink!"

They returned the next day, but it was just the same. Once again the horse didn't eat or drink anything. One of the stable boys said to another: "You know what, I am going to take the horse to the fountain. Perhaps it will drink outside."

The other said: "I don't know whether we should do this, but we could try."

So they led the horse to the fountain, where it began to dance about and clatter, but it didn't want to drink. Then one of the servants said; "Perhaps if we take off the bridle it will drink."

The other responded: "You can take it off, okay, but you know, our master said that we are never to remove the bridle."

"I know," the other said, "but we must try. We can't let the horse die of thirst and hunger."

When they removed the bridle to let the horse drink it transformed itself into a little fish. Just then the godfather came, and he, too, changed himself into a fish. But he couldn't catch the boy even though he changed himself into two fishes. When the boy saw this, he changed himself into a pigeon and flew into the air. Then, when the godfather looked, he transformed himself into an eagle and pursued the pigeon. When the pigeon saw his godfather coming after him, he turned himself into a man and landed near a door to a palace and cried out to the princess: "Hello!" and asked whether he might spend some days there. The princess let him enter.

The eagle changed himself into a man and then he, too, went to the entrance of the palace after causing the old king to fall sick. Then he cried out: "Hello!"

The princess went out, and the godfather asked her whether he could rest and sleep there that night. She replied that she didn't know whether he, a stranger, could stay, because her father had fallen ill. Then he asked whether he could enter and examine her father. Perhaps he could cure him. Having said that he was allowed to enter. When the pigeon saw this, he changed himself into a ring on the princess's finger. She was quite surprised and could do nothing but look at the ring on her finger. Then the godfather turned to her side and said, "If you give me the ring that you have on your finger, I'll cure your father."

She replied that she would give him the ring if he cured her father. Then, since he was a magician, he began to work and revive the old king. After nine hours, the old king was revived and said, "I'm very well now and am going to bed."

The princess went to her room to prepare to go to sleep. She had hardly got into bed when she found a man in the bed with her. Just as she was about to cry out, the man told her to be quiet and to look at her finger to see if the ring was still there. Once she looked, she could not find the ring. Then he said: "It was me who was on your finger. Now I'd like you to do the following," he said. "When the time comes for you to give up the ring, he will extend his hand. Then you are to let the ring fall on the ground as soon as you can. When you do this, let it slip from your hand to the side," he said. "It will break into tiny pieces. I ask you," he said, "to put your foot on the largest piece. When he comes to pick up the pieces, he won't be able to do all that quickly. So, he'll turn himself into a cock to gather them. When he comes to you as a cock," he said, "lift your foot, and I'll transform myself into a fox and eat him."

The next morning the godfather came and asked the princess for the ring. He extended his hand to take it. As the princess reached out to give him the ring, she let it slip from her hand onto the floor, and it broke into pieces. When the godfather saw this, he transformed himself into a cock and went to lift her foot. As soon as he did this, the piece changed itself into a fox, and then he ate his godfather.

Told by Frank Bourisaw in Old Mines, Missouri.

THE HIGH SHERIFF AND HIS SERVANT (1958)*

John Mason Brewer

Oncet dere was a Nigguh what wucked for a white high sheriff dat hab de knowledge to turn hisse'f into diffunt kinds of animals, sich ez birds, fishes, an' rabbits, an' lots of othuh things.

Attuh wuckin' for de high sheriff 'bout two years, de Nigguh done come to learn all de tricks de sheriff knowed an' gits him 'nothuh job, but he yit lib in de same town what de sheriff lib. De sheriff don' hab de information dat de Nigguh done learnt all his tricks, but he yit don' lack hit 'bout de Nigguh quittin' wuckn' for 'im. So one day when he run 'cross de Nigguh downtown, he lights into cussin' im out an' callin' im all kinds of dirty names, an' de Nigguh hauls off an' slaps de sheriff slap-dab in de face, an' staa'ts to runnin' wid de sheriff rat at his heels, gainin' on 'im all de time. But when de sheriff gits in han's rech of de Nigguh, de Nigguh turnt hisse'f into a frog an' say, "Sheriff, Ah'm a frog on de groun'!"

Den when he talk in dis wisse, de sheriff turnt hisse'f into a snake an' say, "Ah'm a snake on de groun' rat attuh you, Nigguh!"

Den when de snake done jes' bout ketched up wid de frog, de Nigguh turnt hisse'f into a bird an' say, "Sheriff, Ah'm a bird in de air."

Den de Sheriff turnt hisse'f into a hawk an' say, "Ah'm a hawk in de air rat attuh you, Nigguh!"

An' jes' bout de time de hawk done almos' ketch wird de bird, de Nigguh turnt hisse'f into a fish an' say, "Ah'm a fish in de wadduh, sheriff!"

Den de sheriff turnt hisse'f into a shark an say, "Ah'm a shark in de wadduh rat attuh you, Nigguh!"

An' when de shark done jes' 'bout rech de fish, an' done open his mouf to swallow 'im, de Nigguh turnt hisse'f into a rabbit an' say, "Ah'm a rabbit on de groun', sheriff!"

Den der sheriff turnt hisse'f back into a human bein' an say, "You go ahaid on den, Nigguh, 'caze Ah sho ain't gonna be no dawg."

De pint am dis: a white man willin' to be anything 'cep'n a dawg to git de uppers on a Nigguh.

* *Dog Ghosts and Other Texas Negro Folk Tales*, J. Mason Brewer (Austin: University of Texas Press, 1958), pp. 20–21. Copyright © 1958, renewed 1986.

THE MAN AND HIS SON (1962)*

Corinne Saucier

Once upon a time a man had an only child, who was very bright. The devil taught school about a mile from the home of this old man. The little boy attended this school. He was so bright that he could become anything he wanted. He had learned this art from the devil. The boy told his father that the devil wanted him because he realized how bright he was, even brighter than his teacher. He said to his father: "If you just listen to me, I can make a lot of money for you, but you must do what I say." He continued: "The demon schoolteacher has a horse that has never been beaten in a race. I am going to become a horse. You wager with him. He will put up two thousand dollars. He will want to buy me. He will offer you five thousand dollars for me. I shall beat his horse. Then sell me, but do not sell the bridle. I shall be 'blowed up' if you do."

So the old man went to see the devil about the race. They came to an agreement, and when the day set for it came, the boy turned into the most beautiful horse that had ever been seen; then he went to the starting point of the race. The race started, and he won by more than a hundred feet. After the race the devil-schoolteacher said to the old man: "You must sell me your horse."

The teacher knew that the winning horse was in reality the little boy who had assumed the shape of a beautiful horse. He said: "I will give you five thousand dollars for your horse if you will just let me have it."

The old man was so poverty-stricken, he thought awhile and then said: "I will sell you the horse, but not the bridle."

The old teacher then said: "I will give you five thousand dollars for the bridle."

"Well," answered the old man, "take it."

The old man now had ten thousand dollars. The old teacher took the horse to his servant and told him never to remove the horse's bridle, but did not explain why. The little boy, now a horse, would not drink. It was the same thing about food, he would not eat. One day, the servant said: "I am going to take that horse to the river and remove his bridle to see if he will drink. He is going to die anyway."

---

* *Folk Tales from Louisiana* (Baton Rouge, LA: Claitor's Publisher, 1962).

When the bridle was removed, the horse turned into a fish (patassa). He jumped into the river. The teacher turned into a larger fish (garfish), and leaped after him. The little boy came out of the water and turned into a beautiful ring and dropped in front of a young lady, who was rocking in a rocking chair on the gallery. The old devil turned into a hawk and kept going beyond the place where the ring was. Then he returned.

The young lady was sick, very sick. She was worried. The teacher advertised himself as a doctor who could cure any human ailment. The young lady's father saw the advertisement and went to see the doctor. The doctor told him he would take the case under one condition: if he gave him the ring in payment, and it must not be handed to him, but thrown on the floor. So he started treating the young lady, and when she was well, he said: "I shall come for my pay tomorrow."

The next day he returned. He sat down and said: "Throw it on the floor."

It turned into a grain of corn and the devil turned into a rooster. Then the little boy turned into a wild cat (pichou) and ate the devil. That is why there is no devil today.

THE MAGICIAN AND HIS DISCIPLE (1997)*

A. K. Ramanujan

A childless king did penance (*tapas*) and prayed to Siva. By His grace, he had two sons. The king and queen fondly doted on these children of their late years. Enemy kings took advantage of his being very old and his children being very young. They laid siege to his kingdom. The king could not withstand the attack. Vanquished, he left the palace with his wife and children while it was still honorable to do so. He went to a faraway kingdom and lived there as a beggar. The hardships of his life did not bother him, but he did worry about his children. They were already seven and eight, and he was anxious about their education. One day he went to a learned guru and pleaded with him: "You must take my children under your wing and give them a proper

* *A Flowering Tree and Other Oral Tales from India*, A. K. Ramanujan, with a Preface by Stuart Blackburn and Alan Dundes (Berkeley: University of California Press, 1997). Copyright © 1997 by the Regents of the University of California.

education. I am poor. I cannot offer you money. But I can give you one of my children as repayment."

The guru agreed and kept the children with him. The old king returned to his beggar's life. The guru was good to the boys. He sent the older boy to graze cows and taught him little skills like counting. The younger boy was very smart. When the guru showed him one thing, he learned ten things. He learned the eighteen mythologies, the six sciences, and the four Vedas. Besides, he became expert in the arts of magic—sorcery, legerdemain, especially in metempsychosis, the subtle art of entering other bodies. Very soon he was better than his guru.

One day the younger son sat in a corner and looked into the far distance with his inner eye to see what his parents were doing. He was grieved by their hardships. His heart melted for them. They had not one but two sons. Yet their old age was empty; they had nothing but trouble. He also learned about his father's promise. As repayment for his sons' education, his father was going to give away one of them. But the clever guru had taught his elder brother only to be a cowherd, and had educated only him, the younger of the two. There must be some trick, some treachery in this arrangement.

The young man got up, thinking, "If I don't do something about this right now, my parents will lose me and die in poverty."

He changed at once into a bird, flew to his parents' place, and changed back into himself before he entered their hut. As their son touched their feet respectfully, the old king and queen were full of joy. They touched his hair, fondled his face, held his hand, and blessed him.

"Son, what brought you here? Is everything well? Tell us," they asked.

The son said, "Father, ever since you left us in the care of our guru, my brother and I have done everything to please him. The guru has taught me everything, but he has neglected my brother. He sends him out everyday with the cows. I know you've promised to give one of us to him. When the time comes, offer to give the guru my brother and ask for me. He will tell you all sorts of things—how wonderful my brother is, how much smarter and better educated he is. But you must be stubborn, insist that you want only the younger boy. I'll take care of the rest. I came here only to tell you this."

Then he touched their feet again, changed into a bird, and flew away. His old father waited for the right day, chose an auspicious hour, and went to the guru. When the guru learned of the father's visit, he dressed the older brother in silk, brought him to the schoolroom, made him sit in front as if

he were a top-ranking number-one student, and spread big books in front of him. In his conversation he named him several times. As for the younger brother he was dressed in rags and made to sit with the stupidest pupils. When the old father arrived the guru showed him both his sons and said, "Look, of your two sons, the older boy is brilliant. He learns everything before you even mention it. He has become a great scholar. But the younger fellow listens to nothing I say. Nothing enters his head. He doesn't want to do anything. He grazes cattle. You can have one of these two. Tell me which one you want."

The old king remembered what his young son had told him when he came as a bird. He replied, "Wise sir, you've taught at least one of them some good sense. You've taken a lot of trouble over them. That's a great thing. Whatever happens to me now, you shouldn't be harmed or cheated. So I'll give you the smart fellow, the older brother. You keep him. I'll take the stupid one. The older fellow is too smart for us; when he sees how poor we are, he'll leave us one day in search of better things. The younger fellow will adjust to our poverty better."

The guru thought, "I gave him a finger. He took the whole hand."

In spite of all his persuasions, the old king insisted on taking the younger son, and finally did so. When they reached home, the son was hungry and wanted food. As the father had spent all day in travel, he had not gone out that day to beg. So there was no food at home. The parents told him how they lived, showed him how little they had. That night they all drank water and went to bed.

Early next morning, the son heard a town crier beat his tom-tom and make an announcement: "A reward, a reward for anyone who will bring a rooster to fight the palace rooster!"

The young man woke up his father at once and said, "Father, let's make some money. I'll become a rooster. Take me to the palace and sell me for a thousand rupees."

And he changed into a big fat rooster. Somewhat fearfully, the father held the rooster under his arm and took it to the palace. The local king was thrilled with it. He gave the old man a thousand rupees as a reward and also a new turban as a special gift. The servants brought an iron coop and covered the rooster with it. As soon as they disappeared, the rooster turned into a bandicoot, burrowed a hole in the ground, and returned to his parents as their beloved prince.

That evening the palace was ready for the cockfight. When they picked up the iron coop, the cock was gone. There was only a big rat hole in the ground. The servants ran to the king and told him that a bandicoot had eaten up the rooster. He couldn't believe it, so he too came and looked. In his dismay, he said: "It's a shame that in such a solid palace as ours there are bandicoots and rats that make burrows. I'm ashamed to live in such a palace. Break it down and build a stronger palace!"

Work began that very day. The thousand rupees the parents got for the rooster didn't last very long.

"What next?" asked the old man.

The son said, "Father, in this town there's a merchant named Ratnakara. He fancies horses. I'll change into a rare breed of horse. You can sell it to him for a thousand rupees."

Then he changed into a rare breed of horse called *Pancakalyani,* "the breed of five virtues." The old king took the horse to the merchant Ratnakara. The merchant looked at it and knew at once what a splendid horse it was. He said, "This looks like a valuable horse. But we must get its quality, the condition of its teeth and the whorls on its body, examined by experts."

Then he sent for the guru who had taught him much about horses. The guru came down and carefully examined the horse's mouth and teeth and every inch of its body all the way down to the tip of its tail. It didn't take him long to discover that the horse was no other than his own pupil, who was now playing tricks on people. He was still hurting from having to give him up. He knew he had been outwitted then by his own prize pupil. He felt he couldn't let it happen again. He couldn't let the young fellow get too strong and do his master in. So he made plans to destroy him. He told the merchant, "O surely, this is a rare breed. No doubt about it. But there are things wrong with its quality, the whorls aren't right. The science of horses says that only a *sanyasi* can ride it safely. So I'll buy it. Why don't you give me a gift of a thousand rupees? Giving a Brahmin such a gift will earn you merit."

The merchant Ratnakara gave him the money. The guru gave the bewildered old king the thousand rupees and bought the horse. Then the guru mounted the horse and rode it roughshod. He rode it into pits and craters, onto boulders and craggy places, till the horse was dying of fatigue and thirst, and then he took it to a creek with a tiny trickle of water. The pupil who was the horse knew his guru's treacherous plans and made his own calculations. As soon as he touched water, he changed into a fish and glided away in the water. The guru saw what was happening and at once called his disciples. He asked them to pour poison into the water. They ran to the hermitage to get the poison.

The prince, who was now a fish, knew he would be killed if he stayed in the water. He looked around. He saw an untouchable whetting his knife, getting ready to cut up a dead buffalo. The prince quickly left his fish form and entered the carcass of the dead buffalo. When the untouchable turned around, he saw the dead buffalo get up and walk away. He started running, panic-stricken, screaming that a demon had entered the dead beast. The watchful guru knew at once that this was another of his star pupil's tricks. He stopped the untouchable and told him, "Look here. If you run like this, the demon buffalo will destroy you. You must kill it now. I'll help you."

They quickly captured the fleeing animal and forcibly tied it to a tree. The guru told the untouchable, "Strike now with your knife."

The prince didn't know what to do and was about to give up when he saw a many-colored parrot lying dead in the hole of that very tree. Just as the untouchable was swinging his knife at him, the prince entered the parrot's body and flew up into the sky. The guru took the form of a brahmany-kite and gave him chase. But after all, the pupil was young, the guru was old. Though the kite had large wings, he couldn't move them fast enough. The parrot flew farther and farther away. As he flew over a palace, he saw a princess on the terrace, shaking out and drying her long hair in the sunshine after a bath. She was exquisitely beautiful. The parrot flew down and perched right on the back of her hand. She was amazed. Who wouldn't be glad if a lovely parrot came all on its own and perched on one's hand? She caressed it, kissed it, and talked to it. She was beside herself with delight when she found that the parrot could also talk.

When the kite saw her take the bird in, he knew his enemy had eluded him. He was downcast, but he flew on, hatching new plots. The princess loved the many-colored parrot and took great care of it, never letting it out of her sight. She would bathe, eat, and sleep in the company of the parrot in the cage. After several days, the prince who was now a parrot waited one night till the princess was asleep and came out of the cage. He changed into his human form, gently undressed the princess, fondled her all over, and returned to the cage as a parrot.

In the morning, when the princess woke up, her sari was in disarray. Her body still remembered the touch of a man. Was it a dream, or had someone come into her bedroom? All the doors of her chamber were shut. The sentinels outside were still there. Not even a fly could have come in past the wakeful sentinels and the bustling maids. Who could have entered her bedroom and done these things to her? If he (she was sure it was a man) came once, he would come again. She would catch him next time, she decided, and settled her disheveled clothes.

That night she didn't play long with the parrot. She went to bed early and lay there pretending to be asleep. At midnight, the parrot came out of the cage and turned into a prince. He came to her bed and started doing what he had done the previous night. The princess got up suddenly, caught his hands, and asked him, "Who the devil are you? How did you get here? You were a parrot. How did you become a man?"

The prince, caught in the act, had to tell her the truth. He told her his whole life. He confessed: "It's true what I did was wrong. But I couldn't control myself when I saw you lying there in all your beauty. You must become mine. Or else, I'll be heartbroken."

As he blurted out his love, the princess too loved him. "Who in the world has your looks, your magical powers? You are my husband from this moment. I'll help you in any way I can," she promised.

The prince used his magical inner eye again and learned of his guru's plots even as he sat there on her bed. Then he said to her, "Princess, tomorrow my guru will come to this palace in the guise of an acrobat. He wants to kill me. He will please your father with his marvelous acrobatic feats and ask for a reward. When your father offers him gold and silver, he'll refuse it and ask for the parrot in the princess's bedroom. Your father will send maids to get the parrot. You must refuse. He will send maids again and again, many times. Then you get into a rage and break the neck of the parrot in front of them all. But my guru will not stop there. He'll ask for the necklace of pearls round your neck. At that point, you tear off the pearl necklace and throw it down. I'll do the rest."

After this talk he made love to the princess most tenderly and went back to the cage as a parrot. Next day, just as the prince had foretold, the guru did come in the guise of an acrobat. He showed the king and the court various kinds of fabulous tricks. They all shouted happily, "Great! Terrific!" The delighted king held out to him a handful of gold coins. But the acrobat would have none of it. He said, "Your Highness, your daughter has a many-colored parrot. That's what I'd like to have. Give it to me if you wish. I want nothing else."

The king sent maids to the balcony, where the princess sat watching. She refused to yield the parrot two or three times. When the king insisted, she came down, threw a tantrum, and twisted the parrot's neck, killing it then and there.

The acrobat now asked for the pearl necklace that had appeared magically around her neck. In her rage, she pulled it off and spilled the pearls on the court floor. The pearls turned into little worms. The acrobat ran towards them, quickly changed into a hen, and began to peck at them and devour them. At once the prince, who was now the worms on the floor, abruptly changed into a tomcat, leaped on the hen, and held it by its neck.

The guru cried out from within the hen, "*Ayyo*, I'm defeated. I surrender. Let me go now. Remember, you were once my disciple."

The disciple screamed from within the cat, "No, you're full of lies. I'm going to kill you this time, so that you won't bother me or anyone else again."

All the people who were standing around were astonished at the turn of events. Cats and hens talking like human beings! Can such things be? The king, who had recovered his poise sooner than others, raised his voice: "Who are you? What's with all these shapes?" he asked.

The hen squeaked, "Ask the cat."

The cat explained, beginning with, "This is my guru. I was his disciple," and went on to tell the whole story: how his father had lost his kingdom, how he had sent his two sons to the guru, how the guru had tried to cheat his father, how he had himself escaped all the villainous plots, right up to the present moment. The king heard the story and said, "A guru shouldn't be killed. Let him go. He will not bother you anymore."

The prince was now confident of his powers. He could counter whatever the guru did, escape every snare. So he showed mercy and let the guru go. Both of them gave up their animal forms, as cat and hen, and became human again.

The king married his daughter to the young prince and gave him half his kingdom as dowry. The prince brought home to the palace his elder brother from the guru's place, and sent palanquins to his parents, who had seen life at its worst, a king and a queen who had lived as beggars. He waged war against his father's old enemies and won back his father's kingdom for him.

Everyone was happy. Even the guru.

PART III

Krabat
Tales

ABOUT AN EVIL MAN IN GROSS-SÄRCHEN (1837)*

Joachim Leopold Haupt

There once was a very evil man in Groß-Särchen close to Hoyerswerda, and he dug up a nearby brook and made it flow in another direction. He did all this because he couldn't bring the Polish ox that he had harnessed under control. As a result, the brook flowed in a very crooked course that can still be seen today. This same man often drove to Dresden in a miraculously short time. He himself was the one who guided the horses and commanded the stable boy to lay down and go to sleep in the back of the wagon. However, the stable boy woke up once, and when he looked around, he perceived that they were not traveling on the ground but flying through the air. At first he was horrified, screamed loudly, and wanted to stand up. But his master threatened him sternly and ordered him to lay down again; otherwise they could both have an unfortunate accident. Because of their conversation they were already in real danger. The master had not paid enough attention to the horses, and they had not been able to keep flying high enough so that the wagon crashed into the top of the Kamenzer steeple, which is still bent and crooked to this very day.

From time to time this man also put black oats into a glazed cooking pot and spoke some words. Immediately thereafter soldiers, not much bigger than the kernels of the oats, came out of the pot, and they rapidly grew and eventually became like other men. Then they assembled themselves in the castle courtyard and marched back and forth, commanded by the master. When he then spoke some more words, they became smaller and smaller and went back into the cooking pot. Afterward, if one looked inside the pot, there was nothing to see except black oats. One time the stable boy overheard his master and made note of his words. Then, when his master was in the fields, he, too, tried to perform the trick. Indeed, he succeeded perfectly, but when he wanted to bring the soldiers back into the cooking pot, he couldn't remember the words, and the soldiers attacked and beat him, and he was in danger of losing his life. The noise that they made was so great that the master, who was in the fields, heard them. So he ran quickly to the spot, freed the inquisitive stable boy, ordered the wild soldiers to return to the cooking pot, and changed them back into black oats.

* "Von einem bösen Herrn in Groß-Särchen," *Neues Lausitzisches Magazin* 15.2 (1837): 203–4.

KRABAT: A LEGEND FROM FOLKLORE (1858)*

Michael Hornig

Once there was a certain Krabat, who came to Leipzig for the first time and attended the "black" school, where the "Black One" taught various kinds of sorcery before numerous and special onlookers. He did not demand any money for this except for one soul every year. After a year passed, all the spectators had to gather before the Black One, who had them seated in a row on a bench and transformed them into ravens. Then the mother of each one of the onlookers had to come and guess who her son was among the ravens. In case she did not succeed, her son's soul was almost certain to be taken by the Black One. There was only one single hope for salvation. Those sons whose mothers were unlucky in guessing played dice, and whoever rolled the lowest number became the Black One's eternal victim.

Such a menacing day also awaited our Krabat. But the clever young man knew how to overcome the danger. At the right time he wrote all about this to his mother and told her that she was to come to him, and when the Black One was to ask her to recognize him, he would be the raven that scratched itself on its right wing. Everything turned out as planned. The mother guessed correctly and soon saved her son and drove happily with him to their home. Later, Krabat knew how to make good use of his time and to win friends. When the prince, who was the ruler of Saxony at that time, needed soldiers, Krabat fulfilled this request by shaking some chaff inside a cooking pot. Then he said a magic spell, and all at once there was a hue and cry! Fully dressed soldiers came out of the pot. For this and other help that he received from Krabat, the prince thanked him by making the former Krabat the lord of the estate Groß-Särchen. From there Krabat often flew through the air within an hour to Dresden, where he was always well-received and seen. When he crashed into the steeple of the church in Kamenz one time because he had fallen asleep, the coachman cried out to him: "We're stuck and can't move!"

Upon hearing this Krabat jumped out of the coach, set the coach free, and it continued flying. Ever since this time the highest tip of the Kamenz steeple is somewhat bent.

Krabat was very charitable and generous toward his underlings and others so that God would be merciful to him and would not let him die through sorcery. He even went to the church in Wittichenau, where he was buried

---

* "Krabat: Powejestka z ludu," *Serbse Nowiny* (Bautzen: Mesačny Přidawk, 1858): 22.

when he died. Since he had never married, the prince of Saxony reclaimed Krabat's estate.

KRABAT (1865)*

Georg Gustav Kubasch

Once upon a time there was a poor man who had only one son, and since he was the poorest man in the village, the people elected him as herdsman. At first his little son looked after the pigs and calves with his father. However, he was soon released from this work.

In those days there were so-called black schools, which were controlled by the devil. There were always twelve boys who attended such a school, and at the end of each year, the devil took one away never to be seen again. At that time there were only eleven attending the school, and therefore, they went looking for a twelfth. They came to the field, where the poor man, who called himself Krabat, was herding some animals with his son.

"Send this boy with us to the school," they cried out to the herdsman. "Can't you herd these animals by yourself?"

At first the father felt uneasy about this, but once the eleven boys promised him that his son would learn a great deal, he agreed to let him go. Indeed, even the young Krabat looked forward to learning something. For a long time he had been bored by herding the animals. So they immediately gave him all the things that had belonged to the twelfth pupil, and Krabat said good-bye to his father and went away. Now the boy had a large writing board and the sixth and seventh book of Moses for learning the various arts that the devil taught them. Krabat was very diligent and learned everything in a short time so that he excelled in all the sciences and was better than all his companions. His superiority irritated the others very much because each thought that he would be the one whom the devil would keep alive. Generally, the devil never took away the best pupil. Some years passed, and eventually Krabat left the school to demonstrate his skills to the people in the region.

At that time he lived in Groß-Särchen, where he had a beautiful castle. Moreover, the Saxon prince, who considered him to be a great artistic

---

* "Krabat," in *Lužičan. Časopis zu Zabawu a Poweučenje*, ed. J. E. Smoler, vol. 6, part II (Bautzen: 1865): 168–71.

magician, was fond of him, and each holiday Krabat drove to visit him in Dresden. It took Krabat an hour for him to fly from Groß-Särchen to Dresden. It's said that one time when the coachman was flying over Kamenz to Dresden, he bumped into the church steeple. The coachman, not aware they were flying, wanted to get off and lift the coach, but Krabat saw this in the nick of time and grabbed hold of the coachman. Otherwise, he would have fallen to the ground. Then Krabat himself lifted the coach away from the church steeple, which was bent and has remained bent up to the present day.

Krabat also went often to lunch in the parish of Wittichenau. After lunch the minister began to ask: "Well, Krabat, show us something!"

Upon this request Krabat demanded a bunch of oats and spilled them into a puddle, while reading the seventh book of Moses. All of a sudden numerous soldiers sprang out of the puddle—the same amount of oats that he had spilled into it. They sang and made a racket until Krabat read another verse from the same book. Then the soldiers fled and jumped back into the puddle, and suddenly there were as many ducks in it as there had been oats. Krabat's servant had observed all this, and after stealing Krabat's book, he tried to read the same verses and to pour the oats into a cooking pot. All at once a large number of soldiers came out of the pot. They demanded some work to do; otherwise they were going to beat him. So, at first, the coachman ordered them to carry away the dung heaps from the courtyard, and they quickly did this.

"What now?" they began to ask.

"Sweep up the sand into a pile!"

They were able to do this just as quickly, and even today there is a hill near Särchen where they piled all the sand.

When Krabat, who was in the fields just at that time, saw the soldiers, be began to curse the servant and went home. When he arrived inside, the soldiers were beating the servant because he didn't know what orders for work he was to give them. Krabat rescued him, and the servant had to promise him that he wouldn't use his book any more.

At that time the Turks and the Saxons had begun a quarrel that erupted into a war. The Saxon prince was captured and laid in chains in a Turkish fortress. Krabat, who, as is known, was the prince's best friend, was also among the prisoners. So the prince crawled over to him in the night and asked him with a quiet whisper whether he could rescue him.

"I'll gladly do this favor for you," Krabat answered.

The next day Krabat changed the prince into a barley corn and changed himself and the prince's servant into flies. Then he pushed both of them through a keyhole, and he himself fled as the last one through the keyhole. They flew over the Black Sea to Dresden. While they were flying over the sea, the servant noticed a swallow up high, and someone was riding on it. He immediately told this to his master Krabat, who quickly tore off a button from the prince's vest and shot it directly at the rider on the back of the swallow. Soon the rider fell to the ground, and Krabat realized that he had just shot his best friend. However, he couldn't do anything about it because his friend had been sent out by the Turkish sultan to kill the prince.

Now Krabat was already quite old and took to his bed deadly ill. Since he did not know the day and hour of his death he called his servant to him and said, "Here, take this book, and go and throw it into the river."

However, the servant wanted to keep the book very much. Therefore, he stood outside for a while, hid the book, and then returned.

"Did you throw the book into the river?" Krabat asked.

"Yes," answered the servant.

"Didn't something miraculous appear?"

"No."

"Well you didn't throw the book into the river!" Krabat cried out.

So he sent the servant back to the river one more time. When the servant returned Krabat asked him again whether he had thrown the book into the river. And once again the servant said that he hadn't noticed anything miraculous because he hadn't thrown the book into the river.

"If," Krabat began, "you don't throw the book for me into the river this instant, you yourself will be flung into the water!"

In fear for his life the servant carried the book to the river, and the water began to cook and roll, and the bushes along the side of the river began to burn. The servant returned to Krabat and told him what had happened.

"This is what had to happen," Krabat said and died.

THE SORCERER'S APPRENTICE, I (1880)*

Edmund Veckenstedt

A farmer had a son who was very smart. His friends advised him to have his son learn something respectable. When the boy had grown up, his father

* "Der Zauberlehrling," I, *Wendische Sagen, Märchen und abergläubische Gebräuche* (Graz: Leuschner und Lubensky, 1880).

apprenticed him to a sorcerer in the city. He reached an agreement with the sorcerer to have him study for three years. So the sorcerer was ready to accept the apprentice and to release him after three years if the farmer would be able to recognize his son after this time had passed, no matter what shape or form the boy was in. The farmer agreed to all this. Upon his departure his son whispered to his father that he would scratch himself behind his ears when the sorcerer brought him to his father.

The three years passed. The young farmer used the time of the apprenticeship so cleverly that he became smarter than his master.

One day, at the appropriate time, the sorcerer brought the farmer three pigeons in a cage. The dark sorcerer challenged him to search for his son among the pigeons. Now one of the pigeons scratched its head without the sorcerer noticing it, and so the farmer knew which pigeon his son was. Consequently, he chose the right pigeon and regained his son.

One day the father complained to his son that he didn't have any money. His son said that he would soon get some for him by changing himself into a horse. Then his father could readily sell him at the marketplace, but he had to remove the bridle and keep it; otherwise his son would be under the power of whoever bought the horse. After agreeing to this the father left for the market with the horse. Soon a gentleman met him and bought the horse. Then the farmer wanted to take off the bridle. When the gentleman saw this, he offered the exact same amount of money that he had paid for the horse. Although the father recalled his son's ban, he thought: "Money is money. If your son is smart, he'll find a way to get out of this." So he sold the bridle.

Now the gentleman, who was none other than the wicked sorcerer of black art, was happy, and as he went to put the bridle on the horse, it suddenly transformed itself into a dove. The wicked sorcerer immediately changed into a raven and flew after it. After the birds circled each other in the sky for a while, the dove spied an open window. So it immediately flew into a room where a maiden was sitting. Then the dove transformed itself into a ring and put itself on the maiden's finger. Right after this, a man stood before her and asked for the ring. But before the maiden could take off the ring it fell to the ground as a barley corn. Quickly the man transformed himself into a hen and wanted to peck and eat the barley corn. But the maiden noticed that something was wrong here. So she grabbed the hen and slit off its head. This was then the end of the sorcerer.

Soon thereafter the barley corn changed itself into the young farmer. He glanced at the maiden and found that she was the same maiden whom he had very much liked before he had been apprenticed to the sorcerer. Since she had saved him from the power of the sorcerer, he decided to marry her. This is, indeed, what happened, and from then on the young couple lived contently and happily.

Collected in Branitz. Recorded by Hendrich Jordan.

THE SORCERER'S APPRENTICE, II (1880)*

Edmund Veckenstedt

A father had a son, and one day he spoke to him, "I don't want you to learn a trade. Instead, you're to learn the black art."

This is why the father apprenticed him to one of the most powerful sorcerers in the land. He was to stay with him for four years and then return to the father. Well, when the time arrived for the son's return, the father wanted to fetch his son from the sorcerer, and before he left his home, he received a secret message from his son telling him to do the following: "The sorcerer will not let me go free just like that. He wants a huge payment for his services. When you come to the sorcerer, he'll show you a large room full of young ravens sitting on tall poles. I'll be the twelfth in the row, and I'll rub my right leg with my beak. You are to demand this raven and rush away with it."

So the father went to the sorcerer and asked him for his son.

"Yes," the sorcerer said, "you can have him, but you must point him out to me. If you can't do that, then he is mine."

Upon saying this he led the father into a room where the ravens were perched. Then the father correctly asked for the raven that was rubbing its right leg with its beak. Quickly, he took the young raven and rushed home. Along the way the father said: "Be my son," and immediately the raven became a handsome young man.

While they were on their way home, they came to a small city where horse trading was taking place at a market. So the son said: "Father, we can make

---

* "Der Zauberlehrling," II, *Wendische Sagen, Märchen und abergläubische Gebräuche* (Graz: Leuschner und Lubensky, 1880).

some good money here. I'll transform myself into a horse, and then you can sell me at the market. But make sure that you keep the halter."

No sooner had he said all this than the son transformed himself into a black stallion. Then the father led the horse to the marketplace in the city and soon sold it. Afterward the old man stuck the halter in his pocket and went on his way. He had barely reached the property of his home when he found his son standing before him again. They laughed about their good earnings and how they had swindled money from the buyer.

From this point on they kept visiting all the markets in the region for many years, and the father swindled a good amount of money from many people. Finally, however, the hour struck for the son. There was a market for horse traders in a large city, and the father and son went there. Just before they entered the city, the son transformed himself into a horse, and the old man led him to the city gate. It did not take long before a fat livestock dealer came and made a deal for the horse. The father sold it, but before he could remove the halter and take it with him, the dealer had already gone away. "Well," thought the famer, "my son will certainly find his way home."

But the dealer led the horse quickly to the nearest blacksmith to have him put horseshoes on the horse. While he was there, he tied the horse to a post. Then he went into a tavern to drink a glass of beer. Meanwhile, many children gathered around the blacksmith's shop to look at the handsome horse. Then the horse suddenly spoke to one of the young boys who was standing nearby. "Take the halter off me."

Then the young boy said to the other children: "Just listen to this. The horse can talk!" And the frightened boy moved away from the horse.

But then the horse spoke again: "Take the halter off me."

So finally, one of the other boys approached the horse and removed the halter and whoosh!—the horse ran into the field.

Just then the dealer came out of the tavern and saw the horse transform itself into a dove, and so he became a hawk. For a long time the two of them circled in the sky, when all of a sudden the hawk attacked the dove. But the dove quickly changed itself into a mouse, and the hawk immediately became a cat. So the mouse ran into a hole, and the cat sat down in front of it.

Finally the little mouse stuck its head out of the hole, and just look!— One, two three, the cat caught the little mouse and gobbled it up. So, finally, Satan managed to get the son.

Told near Vetschau. Recorded by Alexander von Rabenau.

THE STORY ABOUT KRABAT (1885)*

Johann Goltsch

Once upon a time there was a swineherd by the name of Krabat. He had a book of magic that enabled him to understand various kinds of black arts. For example he taught the pigs to stand at attention on their hind legs whenever he wanted to honor someone who was passing by. This is how he honored the king one time when he was in the field and his majesty drove by in his coach. The king was very delighted about this and ordered Krabat to appear before him. The king thanked him for the honor that Krabat had shown him by having his pigs stand at attention, and he gave him the estate of Groß-Särchen as a gesture to express also his great appreciation for Krabat's show. But Krabat had to drive every day at noon to Dresden to lunch with the king. Of course, this was not difficult for Krabat, who had a great understanding of magic. So he drove with his servant through the sky to the royal city and dined at the royal table. One time, however, he was delayed at home so that he departed Groß-Särchen later than usual. Consequently, he ordered his coachman to drive the horses in a rush so that they would arrive punctually in Dresden. The coachman whipped the horses, and the coach flew whistling through the air. Unfortunately, the coach banged into the church steeple of Kamenz along the way and bent it so that it remains crooked even today. The coachman wanted to get off the coach and lift the wagon, but Krabat warned him, "For God's sake, don't you dare! You could slip and fall."

So Krabat himself got out of the coach and lifted the coach. Then off they rushed so that they really arrived on time at the royal castle.

This was how Krabat made life easy for himself using his magic art for a long time. People tell all sorts of stories about his magic. For instance, whenever he read from front to back in his magic book and poured oats into his cooking pot, soldiers would come out of it. Then whenever he read from back to front the soldiers would return into the pot. One time when Krabat went to mass his servant wanted to try his luck with the soldiers. And indeed one soldier after the other climbed out of the cooking pot. The room soon filled with more and more with soldiers, and the servant wanted them to go back into the pot. However, he had forgotten how to achieve this. His whole body trembled and shook because he didn't know what to do. Meanwhile,

* "Bajka wo Krabaće," *Lužica*, vol. 4 (Bautzen: 1885): 90–91.

the number of soldiers increased without stopping, and the pot never seemed to become empty. At this time Krabat was still at mass, and suddenly he noticed that something was happening in his house. He quickly gathered himself together and rushed home. As soon as he caught sight of the huge crowd of soldiers, he swiftly grabbed his book of magic and read from back to front, causing the soldiers to jump back into the cooking pot. Then he gave the inquisitive servant a great scolding and told him that if he had arrived a second later, he wouldn't have had any more power over the soldiers, and they wouldn't have returned into the cooking pot.

As the years passed Krabat began to age. Soon he fell sick, and he called his servant to him on his sickbed. Then he gave him his book of magic and commanded: "Throw this book into the pond behind the village, and don't tell anyone where you've thrown it."

However, the servant hoped to make use of the book for his advantage after Krabat's death. So when he departed from Krabat, he hid the book behind a bush and then returned home. But Krabat called the servant to him and said: "You didn't toss the book into the pond as I ordered you to do. I cannot die until you throw the book into the pond. Turn around immediately and carry out my order so I can die in peace."

Since the servant didn't know what else to do, he threw the book into the pond. When the book was in the pond, the water began cooking and became so hot that the servant was scared and rushed home. After he arrived, he saw that his master had died.

It is no longer known where Krabat's castle stood in Groß-Särchen. But people still tell stories about Krabat, and the bent steeple of the church in Kamenz provides evidence of his trips through the air.

THE WENDISH FAUST LEGEND (1900)*

Georg Pilk

Centuries ago there lived a poor herdsman in the village of Eutrich near Königswartha. Due to the extremely miserable conditions that prevailed in his hut, his stepson, the young Krabat, had to try to earn some money early each day by looking after some geese, and sometimes, whenever the bread was

---

* "Die wendische Faust-Sage," *Bunte Bilder aus dem Sachsenlande* 3 (1900): 191–201.

too meager, he was also compelled to go begging at the doors of strangers. Indeed, the young man, who was, by the way, healthy and very handsome, went about for weeks and even months looking for alms. During one of his wanderings, he arrived at the village of Schwarz-Collm, the first time he had ever been there, and it was there that he encountered a man living in the so-called satan's mill. This miller was notorious for miles around because he practiced black magic, and consequently, he was feared and avoided by all the pious people. The miller took an exceptional liking to young Krabat and asked him: "Do you have any desire to stay with me? You'd have a good life, and I could teach you many things!"

The young man agreed and decided to stay in satan's mill. His teacher was indeed a sorcerer and teacher of black magic. He always had twelve mill workers at his place, but in reality they studied sorcery, and the miller maintained that there always had to be twelve apprentices. When the year of teaching and testing ended, one of the workers would soon be gone. A large wheel would be turned and reveal the unfortunate worker who had been doomed to his fate. At this particular time there were now only eleven pupils, and Krabat was supposed to fill the gap that had just arisen. The young man, who was very bright and talented, quickly absorbed and mastered all the eerie knowledge of his master. During this time he also had to conclude the customary pact with the devil, even though he was well aware of the danger hovering around him. But once he was under the power of the evil miller and dependent on him, he could not openly withdraw from the sorcerer. Fearing greatly for his life—for his year as an apprentice was about to end—he thought about some trick to gain his freedom. So he requested a leave to visit his parents, and the miller granted it. The joy of the reunion after such a long separation soon succumbed to the most profound sadness when Krabat's mother realized that her son had fallen into the hands of a sorcerer and that he was learning black magic. The young man wept bitter tears because he did not want his parents to share the fate of someone lost.

"Mother, only you can save me. If you want to do this, come to Schwarz-Collm and demand that the miller set me free. He'll do this but only under the condition that you recognize me among my other eleven companions. So I'll tell you now how you'll be able to recognize me. We'll all be transformed into black ravens and will be sitting in a room and scraping and scratching ourselves with our beaks as birds do. All my comrades will have turned their necks toward the left side, but I'll pluck at something under the right wing.

So you must pay attention because this is the only possible sign of recognition that I'll be able to give you. Once you recognize me, you're to state firmly: 'This is my son!' Then the miller must let you have me because in a situation like this no sorcerer can resist a mother."

What mother would not have been moved by such an urgent plea! After his mother agreed to do what he wished, Krabat could rest assured and return to the master of the mill. Then after a few days had passed, his mother set out for Schwarz-Collm, and everything turned out there just as her son had indicated. When she requested to take her son home with her, she was led into a very dark room in which twelve ravens were sitting on a bar. Then the miller instructed her to point out her son, and thanks to the prearranged signal, she was able to do this. She guessed correctly. Full of inner fury, the sorcerer touched the one raven that had scratched itself under the right wing with a little wand, and the bird was transformed into the young Krabat. Then, as quickly as possible, he rushed from there with his mother but not without taking a book of magic, his master's most important one. It was because of this theft that the miller was to pursue him with bitter hostility.

Once Krabat arrived home, he found that there was still a shortage of food and poverty. There was no money at hand, and since he had been somewhat spoiled, he did not take pleasure in eating dry bread. Consequently, he soon went to his stepfather and said: "Father, we can't go on like this. We must have money, and since you don't have any, I'll obtain some for you."

"Now, how do you think you'll go about that?" the father asked.

"Soon the cattle market will take place in Wittichenau. I'll change myself into a fat ox. Then you'll take me there and sell me. But I don't want you to sell me to any of the honest commoners but to one of the tricky Kamenzer cattle dealers! Also I want you to demand a high price, and you'll get it. No matter what a buyer may offer you, don't let him have the bridle. Otherwise, it will be my unlucky day because I won't be able to regain my human form, and I'll end up under a butcher's cleaver. Once you have the money, leave the marketplace as fast as you can and go home. I'll follow you soon thereafter. Then you won't have to put up with such a wretched life."

This is what Krabat said and went off without paying attention to his father's objections. Soon the old man heard the mumbling of an ox outside his hut, and when he looked closer, he saw that it was one of the most magnificent kind of oxen he had ever seen. When the day of the cattle market in Wittichenau arrived, the father drove the ox to the market, which was heavily attended. No sooner did the dealers glimpse the glorious animal than they began arguing and bidding for it earnestly. Soon the ox was sold for a tidy sum. The father took the bridle with him, while the cattle dealer led the ox in the direction of Kamenz. Along the way the dealer stopped at a tavern with other dealers. The ox was put into a stall in the stable, and his owner caroused and rejoiced with his friends about what everyone thought to be a profitable purchase. As he was doing this, he ordered the stable maid to go and give the ox some fodder. When she did this, the animal said to her in a human voice: "I don't like hay and straw. I'd prefer some nice roast meat!"

The maid was extremely horrified and rushed back into the tavern and told everyone that the ox could speak and rejected hay and straw. Instead it wanted roast meat. The cattle dealers laughed and shook their heads. Just one of them went with her to see what had happened in the stall. No sooner did he open the door to the stall, however, than a swallow whizzed outside, for Krabat had taken on the form of a bird. The ox had disappeared, and the young sorcerer arrived in the parental home in Eutrich sooner than his father.

Some time passed, and the money they had obtained was coming to an end. So they planned a new similar trick. Krabat said to his stepfather: "This time I'd like you to take me to the market as a horse. But don't ever sell the halter and the bridle with the horse. Take both of them home, otherwise it will be my unlucky day!"

Immediately thereafter Krabat transformed himself into a splendid young steed. The father mounted the horse and rode to Wittichenau. The handsome horse drew the attention of all the experts, and an elderly man with a white beard joined the crowd. He made the highest offer, and the deal was soon completed. After the white-bearded man had paid, the buyer refused, however, to hand over the halter and the bridle to the father. All of the father's efforts to acquire them were in vain. The white-haired man swung himself onto the horse and galloped away. It was Krabat's teacher, the miller from Schwarz-Collm, who had heard about the first accomplishment of his former apprentice and had come filled with anger in order to punish Krabat for the theft of his book of magic and, if possible, to ruin his life. For the moment he let Krabat feel his power. He dug his spurs into the horse's sides and used his whip to force the steed to run wildly through the woods and fields, over bushes and thorns. After a long mad ride, he arrived at a blacksmith's workshop, where he stopped and requested the smith to put four red-hot shoes on the horse's hoofs because the young horse had not yet been shod. This request seemed somewhat strange to the blacksmith. So he invited the rider into his shop to choose the iron shoes himself. While the two of them entered the shop, the blacksmith's young helper was placed in charge of the horse, which was tied to a post and dripping with sweat. All at once the horse whispered into his ear: "Quick! Pull the bridle off my left ear."

The helper was ready to do this, and no sooner did he lift the bridle, the horse disappeared, and Krabat soared singing into the air in the form of a lark. But it didn't take long for the sorcerer to come flying as a hawk in pursuit of him. When the lark saw that the hawk was faster and it could not escape the predator, it plunged toward the ground, jumped into an open fountain, and became a fish. A virtuous maiden approached the fountain to fetch some water, and miraculously, the fish that she had glimpsed became a gold ring and slid itself onto one of her fingers. Overcome by joy she wanted to rush home, but suddenly a white-bearded man, who was the sorcerer, stood before her and asked her to sell him the ring. He made all kinds of conceivable efforts and offered her a fabulous price for the ring. But she steadfastly refused and kept the gem. The evil sorcerer had no power over the innocent maiden. But he remained near her parents' farmstead. Soon thereafter the maiden came again with an apron full of barley that she scattered among the chickens. As she did this, the ring slid off her finger and changed itself into a barley corn. While the chickens pecked up the fodder, a strange rooster strutted up to them and wanted to eat the barley corns with them. All at once Krabat transformed himself from a barley corn into a fox, grabbed the rooster like lightning, and tore the bird to pieces. That was the end of his master, who was overtaken by death as he pursued the practice of black magic.

After his return to his home village Eutrich, Krabat made the acquaintance of the ruler of the country. He was just taking care of a herd of pigs when August the Strong drove by there in a carriage. As if they had heard a command, all of the pigs suddenly stood up on their hind feet in attention and paraded straight as candles before the king. Because of this little show, the Wendish Eumaeus* drew the king's attention, and the monarch took him to Dresden, where he was employed in the royal kitchen. But the royal chef did not take a liking to the young man, who was curious and always sniffing things. As the cook was slicing noodles one time, and Krabat inconveniently got in his way, the irritated cook boxed his ears. Soon thereafter Krabat took

* Eumaeus was Odysseus's swineherd and friend in the *Odyssey*.

his revenge. After the dinner plates were carried out, the highly esteemed ladies and gentlemen noticed with horror that instead of noodles, there were live worms on their plates, and instead of roasted chicken, there were frisky frogs that hopped out of the soup bowls. The cook fell out of favor and was to be released. But because he declared his innocence so faithfully, the king quickly guessed who the actual instigator of the prank was. As punishment for this practical joke, Krabat was dismissed from the royal kitchen and sent packing.

He returned once again to the home of his parents and grew to become a mature, handsome man. Then, as was their custom at that time, the Saxon recruiters appeared unexpectedly one night. They surrounded the little villages in the region and dragged all the suitable young men by force to serve in the army. Even Krabat was to experience this fate. He was given a place in a Dresden infantry regiment. In the meantime the war with Turkey had erupted, and Krabat took part as a musketeer in the campaign. During this war, the king was captured by the Turks. The imperial and Saxon generals came together and worriedly conferred about how to free the king. Then Krabat stepped forward, reported to the commanders, and said that he knew all about their embarrassing situation, and he maintained that nobody was more capable to bring back the king alive than he was. Though they all shrugged their shoulders in disbelief, the generals did not stop him. So Krabat cried: "Give me a saddled horse, and make it quick! I only have an hour's time to save the king!"

The horse was brought, and at first Krabat rode straight ahead. Then suddenly he swung himself and the horse into the air so that he eventually could be seen only as a tiny speck in the sky. Once he arrived in the Turkish camp, which was fairly far away, he was invisible and could only be seen by the king, who recognized his former cook's assistant Krabat as the infantryman dressed in a uniform with long tails and with a longer musket.

"Where did you come from, and how did you get here?" he asked.

"I've come to rescue you, your majesty! Quick, grab hold of the tails of my uniform and don't worry about whatever may happen!"

The king complied with his request, and away they flew through the sky. When the Turks realized that their highly prized prisoner had disappeared, something that could only have happened through unnatural forces, they recalled that they, too, had a sorcerer who was serving in their army. So they commanded him without delay to get ready and follow the fugitives. After a while Krabat, who never looked behind him, asked whether anyone was following them. The answer came: "Yes, a great black bird is coming after us, and it's coming nearer and nearer."

Then Krabat conjured up a dark cloud behind them and asked the king again whether anyone was following them without looking back at the pursuer. The answer was that the bird was still flying closer. So now Krabat conjured up a tremendous high wall. But even this did not present an insurmountable obstacle. The bird easily swung itself over the wall.

"Is it still there?" Krabat asked.

"Yes, it's right on our heels," the king replied.

"Tear off a golden button from your jacket and give it to me!" Krabat cried.

Krabat loaded the button into his weapon and shot over his shoulder without aiming and looking backward. Now the bird had finally disappeared, and as it was falling through the air and dying, it uttered a shrill scream repeatedly. Krabat winced and began to weep.

"What's grieving you?" the king asked.

"Your majesty should know that I've just shot my best friend. I recognized him by his mournful cry. At one time we were apprentices to the same master. Oh, that it had to be me that sent my companion to his eternal death! It's him for sure. His life has ended with his use of black magic. If I had known, I would have chosen some other way to help us."

It was under these laments that the eerie ride through the sky continued.

When they happily returned to the army, the king ordered that his rescuer be given a lavish reward. After the campaign ended, the king wanted to pay his debt in a proper way. But first he wanted to make use once more of Krabat's art of magic. Still vested in the interests of a fortunate and successful war, he desired to discover the secret plans of the Turkish commanders. The sorcerer Krabat helped him accomplish this and changed himself and the king into two flies so that they could overhear the sultan's conversations in his headquarters. Krabat warned the king not to land on a silver spoon. While Krabat had assumed the shape of an insect and constantly ran around the rim of the sultan's plate, the royal fly mistakenly touched a silver spoon while whirring about. All at once a huge dog that had been lying under the table began to growl. Since the two spies were now transformed back into their human shapes and could be seen by the Turks, they had to escape as quickly as possible. There was one Turkish soldier who tried to prevent them, and Krabat threw an iron wheel over his head that immediately turned into a knotted tie around his neck. This was how they escaped.

After the war had ended and the king had retuned home to his residence, he gratefully thanked his young savior by offering him large sums of money. However, Krabat modestly refused the money. Only when the king pressured him to voice some kind of favor that he wanted, Krabat expressed his desire to own the estate of Groß-Särchen near Hoyerswerda.

"Just as long as you don't wish to include the large duck pond in Groß-Särchen," the king said, "then this estate is yours forever."

From then on a friendly relationship developed between the king and Krabat, who became the landlord of an estate. The former musketeer declined the positions offered to him to serve the state. However, he remained the private counselor and supporter of the gracious king for the rest of his life. As private counselor he had permission to dine at the royal table any time he wished, even without an appointment, and he often made use of this. At eleven o'clock in the morning he drove away from Groß-Särchen with his tableware, and at exactly twelve noon he was in the royal castle in Dresden. The wild drive through the sky went over Kamenz and Königsbrück. In the course of time the king's favorite, who was considered to be more influential than the prime minister, was envied by various people. Among them there were twelve dignitaries who felt especially degraded. However, their resentment was directed more toward the king himself than against his harmless favorite. They conspired to kill him by poisoning his tea. After killing him, they wanted so spread the rumor that the king had died suddenly from a heart attack. In his home in Groß-Särchen Krabat perceived the highly treacherous plans, as well as the particular names of the conspirators and the arranged time of the crime. Everything had been revealed to him by his magic mirror made of bronze. It was necessary to act with speed because the king's murder was to happen that very evening. So he quickly had the horses harnessed.

"This time I myself shall drive," he indicated to the coachman. "Sit down inside the carriage! I must be by the king's side in half an hour!"

So they took off like an arrow shot into the dark autumn night. Before they reached the village, the rattle of the wheels were suddenly not to be heard. Without making a sound, the horse and wagon rose up into the sky. The coachman had nothing to do, and as he was unaccustomed to sitting on the soft cushion, he soon fell asleep and only awakened as the flight was interrupted by a powerful jolt. Troubled, he cried out: "We've certainly hit a large stone curb," and he wanted to step out of the carriage to straighten out the tableware. However, Krabat ordered him to remain seated. He freed the carriage by himself from the steeple on the Kamenzer Church, where it had been hanging after crashing into it. (Ever since this accident the iron weather vane of the church in Kamenz is said to have remained bent.) Right before the decisive moment Krabat landed in the courtyard of the Dresden castle. The dinner had already begun. The king held the cup with the poison inside in his hand. Krabat rushed inside and urgently implored the king not to drink. The cupbearer was to taste the tea before the king drank it. The king accepted this proposal, and the cupbearer had to obey the king's command. Then the cupbearer immediately fell lifeless to the ground. The conspirators were then all exposed and sentenced to death. For the execution Krabat called a man he knew, the executioner Bunderman from Lissahora near Neschwitz, and he came to Dresden. This was the man who carried out the sentence.

There are many of Krabat's miraculous deeds recounted by the Wendish people. However, the list would take up too much of the reader's time. Therefore, I shall now conclude the legend, and it ends harmoniously. Krabat became a friend and benefactor of the village and the entire region. In his old age he used his magic art only to increase the chief provision of food for his subjects, improved their payments for plowing the fields, cleared away overnight the swamps that caused sickness and fever, watered the withered seedlings, and transformed the cascading hailstorm by himself that devastated the region and beyond its borders to fluttering down feathers that caused no damage. He worked tirelessly for his people who were without means, and since he did not have any heirs, he eventually bequeathed to them in his will his entire hereditary property that was divided into forty parcels of land. Only those farmers who already owned property were not included in his will, and the pond on his property of Groß-Särchen, which the king had reserved for himself, was granted to his majesty. Shortly before his death Krabat had his book of magic thrown into the large pond. The servant who was supposed to carry out this task refused to do this at first. He wanted to keep the secret writings for himself. When he returned to the house, Krabat asked him: "Did you throw the book into the water?"

He answered: "Yes, my lord. It's lying in the water."

Krabat looked at him with a stern face and said: "What did the water say?"

Now the servant had no idea how to respond. He had to return once again to the pond, and this time he really sank the book near a post in the dark water that sizzled, bubbled, and roared as it rose up as high as a man. (Later a monster was seen at this spot, and even in winter, as terrifying rumor has it, the monster was seen to break through the ice covering the pond.) Krabat's last sickbed was set up in the Groß-Särchen inn. The friendly innkeepers made a great effort to care for him. He said to his loyal friends around the bed that they should pay attention to his life after death. He told them that when his spirit separated itself from the earthly shell of his body, and if it were to become a black raven sitting on the chimney of the house in which he died, then he would be eternally lost. If, however, one could see a white swan on top of the chimney, it would mean that he had found a blessed end. All the underlings of his estate gathered in the hour of their beloved master's death in front of the house. They awaited the news about his death in the most profound and earnest silence. Soon he no longer suffered. Just then the Wendish mourning song could be heard in the room in which he died. Then everyone looked up above. There, on top of the ridge of the roof, the white feathers of a swan were gleaming.

KRABAT (1959)*

Jerzy Slizinski

HOW THE MOTHER LIBERATED HER SON FROM THE SORCERER

Yes, I've heard that Krabat was born in Eutrich. His father was a worker there and had many children and was poor. When Krabat left school and finished his schooling, his mother brought him to the mill in Schwarzkollm so that he could learn all about working in a mill. But the young man didn't like it there. And one time, after he had returned home for a brief time, he told his mother that he didn't like being at the master's place and that he had to change himself into a raven there. And he said that there were more young boys there as apprentices, and they, too, had to change themselves into ravens and then go to sleep in a dark chamber, and the next day they had to change themselves back into humans and go to work again. And there could only be twelve boys at a time, and each year the miller took away one of the boys, and this boy would disappear. And nobody knew which boy would be the next one that the miller would take. This is why Krabat wanted his mother to come to him. The master of the mill would lead his mother into a dark

* *Sorbische Volkserzählungen*, edited by Jerzy Slizinski (Berlin: Akademie-Verlag, 1964), pp. 45–50. Copyright © DeGruyter.

chamber, and twelve black ravens would be sitting on a long bar. And eleven would be holding their beaks under their left wings. And one would hold his beak under the right wing, and the mother was to ask for the raven holding its beak under the right wing.

So the mother went to the master and asked for her son. At first the master refused to give her the boy. However, she persisted, and so the master led her to the dark chamber and said to her: "Choose the one who's your son."

"That one," she said, "the one that has its beak under its right wing."

And then the master replied, "The devil taught you what to do!"

And this is how she had regained her son.

HOW THE FATHER SOLD KRABAT AS AN OX

The mother and her son returned home, and Krabat became a herdsman. But there was still poverty in his parents' home.

Krabat had secretly taken the magic books from the mill with him and knew himself how to do magic. And he could change himself into animals and into seeds. One time, when the poverty had become very great, he said to his father that he would transform himself into an ox, and then his father was to take him to the Wittichenau fair and to sell him.

At first his father refused to do this, but then later, he agreed.

On the day of the fair Krabat transformed himself into an ox, and his father drove him to the fair, where he sold him for a very good price. Then the father went home with the money, and the buyer drove the ox to his house.

On his way home, the buyer stopped at a tavern and tied the ox in a stable and said to the stable maid: "Give the ox a little clover."

When the maid brought the clover to the ox, it said to the maiden: "Take off the rope from my neck," and she did as she was told.

Then the maid went into the tavern and said to the buyer that the ox could speak. So the buyer went to the stall, and the ox had already vanished. Krabat had changed itself into a swallow and had flown through a window and had arrived home sooner than his father.

HOW KRABAT'S FATHER SOLD HIM AS A HORSE

Now the family's distress came to an end, and once again the parents and children had enough to eat. They lived for a long time without worries.

When the money was used up, however, the family was once again impoverished. Consequently Krabat said to this father: "I'm going to change myself now into a horse, and you'll drive me and sell me again at the Wittichenau Fair."

The master of the Schwarzkollm mill heard that Krabat had changed himself into an ox, and thereafter, he constantly attended the markets in Wittichenau, and on the day that Krabat's father drove the horse to Wittichenau, the miller bought it. Then he got on the horse and rode it to the nearest blacksmith and told the smith that he wanted shoes put on the horse's feet. The horse put up a fight, and the smith's apprentice had to keep the horse in check by holding the bridle. And then the horse said to the apprentice: "Remove the bridle from my head."

The apprentice was afraid, but he took the bridle from the horse's head. Immediately thereafter the horse transformed itself into a swallow and flew away through a window. And immediately the mill master transformed himself into a hawk and flew after the swallow. However, the swallow was faster than the hawk and reached home before the hawk could catch it. When the swallow was under the roof of the house, the hawk no longer had any power over the swallow.

KRABAT AS A FLY AT THE KING'S COURT

Krabat had bought an estate in Groß-Särchen. From there he drove to Dresden to the king's court and took part in the royal dinners as a fly. But the dogs became restless when Krabat was there as a fly. Finally, the servants became aware of this and that the flies were also fidgety. So they shut the windows and struck the flies to death. Meanwhile, Krabat as fly hid in a corner of the room. When the servants eventually opened the windows, he flew out of the hall. Then he returned to his home with his coachman.

One time, when he was on the way to Dresden with his coachman flying through the air, the coachman bumped into the church steeple at Pulsnitz. The coachman wanted to continue flying with the coach, but Krabat said: "I'll take over. You're not driving high enough."

Then Krabat shoved him to the side, and they continued flying.

Ever since that time when the servants sought to beat Krabat as a fly to death, he no longer drove to Dresden.

KRABAT'S DISOBEDIENT SERVANT

Krabat was the benefactor of the common folk and supported the people wherever he could, and all the villagers held him in high esteem.

When he was in church one time his coachman opened the magic books and began reading them. He read that one should pour oats into a pot on the oven. Then he continued reading, and all at once soldiers burst from the pot. Soon the entire courtyard was filled with soldiers. So now the coachman was scared, but Krabat, who had suddenly become restless in the church, came home in the nick of time and saw numerous soldiers in the courtyard. So he went inside to the kitchen, scolded the coachman, took the books and read them backward. All at once the soldiers returned into the pot.

HOW KRABAT DIED

Krabat became old. He divided parcels of his estate among the farmers and workers. And when he was lying on his deathbed, he gave his magic books to his coachman and told him that he was to throw them all into the pond.

After the coachman returned to him Krabat asked him what the water had done, and the coachman said: "Nothing!"

Then Krabat asserted that the coachman hadn't thrown the books into the pond and ordered him to go back there and to throw them into the pond. When the coachman returned, Krabat asked him what the water had done, and the servant answered that the water bubbled. Thereupon, Krabat replied that the coachman had really thrown the books into the pond this time.

After this, Krabat's health took a turn for the worse, and so he said: "When I die, either a raven or a swan will be sitting on the top of my house. If it is a raven, then I'll be damned, and if it is a swan, then I shall be blessed."

When Krabat died, a white swan sat on top of the roof, and the people knew then that Krabat had been blessed.

Told by Hermann Bjenada, a tailor (born 1889 in Komorow, Bautzen).
Recorded on October 24, 1959, Komorow, Bautzen.

Biographies of Authors, Editors, Collectors, and Translators

'Attār, Farīd al-Dīn (ca. 1110–ca. 1221), a famous Persian Muslim poet and Sufi hagiographer, was also an expert pharmacist. His works were discovered in the fifteenth century, when he became widely celebrated as a gifted mystical poet. Many of Attar's prose and poetical works deal with the soul's search for itself or pantheistic quest for god. Attar's stories were part of his teachings, and his short tale "The Magician's Apprentice" (ca. 1220) appeared in Hellmut Ritter's *The Ocean of the Soul* (1955), a compilation of Attar's four epic works, *Asrārnāma, Ilāhīnāma, Mantiq al-tayr*, and the *Musībatnāma*, and other writings. The ending of "The Magician's Apprentice," when the apprentice learns from the fairy who tells him that he has always been seeking himself and that "all the world is you," reflects Attar's Sufi philosophy.

Barbeau, C. Marius (1883–1969), Canadian folklorist and anthropologist, is considered one of the founders of Canadian folklore and anthropology. After studying at the University of Laval and at Oxford University, he took a position in 1911 at the National Museum of Canada, where he worked for the rest of his life. He did extensive work on indigenous and French-Canadian folklore and edited numerous collections of tales, legends, and songs. Among his notable works are "Contes Populaires Canadiens," *Journal of American Folklore* 29.51 (January–March 1916); *Folksongs of French Canada* (1925); *Grand'mère raconte* (Grandmother Tells Tales, 1935); *Il était une fois* (Once Upon a Time, 1935); *L'Arbre des rèves* (*The Tree of Dreams*, 1947); *The Golden Phoenix and Other Fairy Tales from Quebec* (1958); "Huron-Wyandot Traditional Narratives" (1960) in *Translations and Native Texts*; and *Tsimsyan Myths* (1961).

Baring-Gould, Sabine (1834–1924), a British Anglican priest, novelist, folklorist, and prolific writer on various subjects, published more than 1,000 articles and books during his lifetime. His major achievement in folklore is considered to be his two collections of folk songs, *Songs and Ballads of the West* (1889–91) and *A Garland of Country Songs* (1895), with Henry Fleetwood Sheppard. Baring-Gould had a strong proclivity for the gothic and uncanny and published such interesting collections of tales as *The Book of Were-Wolves* (1865); *Curious Myths of the Middle Ages* (1866); *Curiosities of Olden Times* (1896); and *A Book of Ghosts* (1904). His tale "The Master and His Pupil" was part of an appendix on *Household Stories* in William Henderson's *Notes on the Folklore of the Northern Counties of England and the Borders* (1866).

Bechstein, Ludwig (1801–60), a German writer and collector of fairy tales, to a certain extent rivaled the Brothers Grimm in popularity in the nineteenth century. He studied at universities in Leipzig and Munich and eventually became a librarian at the court of the duke of Saxony and Meiningen in 1831. This position, which he held until he died, enabled him to devote a good deal of his time to writing and collecting folk tales. His most important works are *Thüringische Volksmärchen* (Folk Tales of Thuringia, 1823); *Deutsches Märchenbuch* (*German Fairy-Tale Book*, 1845); *Neues Deutsches Märchenbuch* (*New German Fairy-Tale Book*, 1856); and *Thüringer Sagenbuch* (*Thuringia Book of Legends*, 1858).

Blackburn, Stuart (n.d.), is a Senior Research Fellow at the School of Oriental and African Studies in London. He has written several books on folklore in India. His two most recent books are *Moral Fictions: Tamil Folktales from Oral Tradition* (2001) and *Print, Folklore and Nationalism in Colonial South India* (2003). His main research interests are the study of texts in performance, oral genres, oral histories, and material culture. His current project is a long-term collaborative study of cultural change in the tribal state of Arunachal Pradesh, India.

Bladé, Jean-François (1827–1900), a French magistrate and writer, studied law at universities in Toulouse and Paris and eventually became a judge. He also maintained a great passion for literature and wrote novels and stories while gathering folk tales in the region of Gascogne. His major work is the three-volume collection *Contes populaires de Gascogne* (1886).

Bompas, Cecil Henry (n.d.), a member of the Indian Civil Service, was the translator of *Folklore of the Santal Parganas* (1909), a collection of more than 100 stories of the Munda tribe, located at that time in the district of Santal Parganas about 150 miles north of Calcutta. The stories he translated were gathered first by the Reverend Paul Olaf in the Santali language, and he also added some tales of the Hos of Singhbhum, a tribe closely related to the Santals.

Brewer, John Mason (1896–1975), a poet, essayist, and historian, was among the first major African American folklorists. He taught at many different colleges and universities in Texas and North Carolina and was responsible for publishing the first collection of slave folk tales in *Juneteenth* in 1932. After this publication he dedicated a good deal of his work to the study of African American folklore, often collecting the tales in dialect. He published three major collections of black Texas folklore: *The Word on the Brazos: Negro Preacher Tales from the Brazos Bottoms of Texas* (1953); *Aunt Dicy Tales: Snuff-Dipping Tales of the Texas Negro* (1956); and *Dog Ghosts and Other Texas Negro Folk Tales* (1958).

Brězan, Jurij (1916–2006), was a renowned Sorbian writer of novels and stories for young people and a translator who made the "Krabat" tales famous in Central Europe. He wrote more than thirty books, which included autobiographical works and essays. In 1954 he translated Martin Nowak-Neumann's important children's book, *Master Krabat* (*Meister Krabat*, 1954), from Upper Sorbian into German. In the following years he wrote three different versions of the Krabat hybrid fairy tale, *The Black Mill* (*Die schwarze Mühle*, 1968); *Krabat, or The Transformation of the World* (*Krabat, oder, Die Verwandlung der Welt*, 1976); and *Krabat, or the Preservation of the World* (*Krabat oder die Bewahrung der Welt*, 1995); each from a different political perspective. In 1975, Celino Bleiweiß directed a television film based on Brězan's *The Black Mill*, which was widely disseminated in the German Democratic Republic (East Germany).

Broun, Heywood (1888–1939), was an American journalist, author, and one of the founders of the American Newspaper Guild. After attending Harvard he worked for several New York newspapers, including the *New York Tribune*, the *New York World*, and the *New York Telegram*. In addition to his journalistic and literary endeavors (he wrote several books and edited a literary weekly), Broun was also active in politics as a socialist. He wrote two important fairy-tale works, *The 51rst Dragon* (1919) and *Gandle Follows His Nose* (1926). "Red Magic" appeared in *Seeing Things at Night* (1921), a collection of his stories and newspaper columns.

Buchan, Peter (1790–1854), a Scottish writer, editor, folklorist, and printer, is best known as a collector of ballads. He published several important collections, including *Scarce Ancient Ballads* (1819); *Gleanings of Scarce Old Ballads* (1825); *Ancient Ballads and Songs of the North of Scotland* (1828); and *Scottish Traditional Versions of Ancient Ballads* (1845). Buchan also gathered Scottish folk tales, but they were not published during his lifetime. In 1908 John Fairley edited and published them in *Ancient Scottish Tales*.

Burton, Sir Richard Francis (1821–1890) was a gifted linguist, explorer, prolific author, and one of the most flamboyant celebrities of his day. Forced to leave Oxford University for unruly behavior, he joined the British army in India, where he gained a remarkable knowledge of Arabic, Hindustani, and Persian and eventually became fluent in twenty-nine languages and many dialects. During his lifetime Burton translated unexpurgated versions of many Oriental texts, including *Vikram & the Vampire; or Tales of Hindu Devilry* (1870); *Kama Sutra* (1883); and *Arabian Nights* (1885–88), which is perhaps his most celebrated achievement.

Busk, Rachel (1831–1907), a British pioneer folklorist, spent a good part of her life traveling in Europe and recording folk tales. From 1862 onward she made Rome her home and collected tales there from maids, servants, and others from the lower classes. Her major publication is *The Folk-Lore of Rome, Collected by Word of Mouth from the People* (1874). Other important works are *Sagas from the Far East: Kalmouk and Mongol Tales* (1873); *Patrañas, or Spanish Stories, Legendary and Traditional* (1870); and *Household Tales from the Land of Hofer, or Popular Myths of Tirol* (1871).

Campbell, John Gregorson (1836–90), a Scottish folklorist, studied at the University of Glasgow and practiced law until 1858, when he became a Presbyterian minister. He developed an interest in Scottish folklore and began collecting all types of folk tales in the late 1850s and 1860s, often publishing them in such journals as *Celtic Review*, *Transactions of the Inverness Gaelic Society*, and *Celtic Magazine*. The majority of his collected tales, however, were published posthumously in *Clan Traditions and Popular Tales of the Western Highlands and Islands* (1895); *Superstitions of the Highlands and Islands of Scotland* (1900); and *Witchcraft and Second Sight in the Highlands and Islands of Scotland* (1902).

Campbell of Islay, John Francis (1822–85), a Scottish folklorist, writer, and lawyer, studied at Eton and Oxford and later became the foremost authority on Celtic folklore and the Gaelic people. He did meticulous field research in the Scottish islands, West Scotland, Ireland, Scandinavia, London, and on the Isle of Man. The result was his *Popular Tales of the*

West Highlands: Orally Collected Translated, published in four volumes, which contains folk tales, heroic poems, proverbs, songs, children's stories, myths, and essays.

Carrière, Joseph Médard (1902–70), a French-Canadian scholar and folklorist, taught French literature for many years at the University of Virginia. He specialized in the study of French folklore in Missouri and Michigan, and produced two important books based on his fieldwork in those states: *Tales from the French Folk-Lore of Missouri* (1937) and *Les contes du Detroit* (*The Tales of Detroit*), published posthumously in 2005.

Comparetti, Domenico (1835–1927), an Italian professor of Greek classics, taught at various universities and became one of the foremost scholars of folklore in Italy. Comparetti's prolific work covered all aspects of European literature and folklore, from ancient Greece through nineteenth-century Europe. Among his important books on folklore are *Virgilio nel Medio Evo*, 2 volumes (1872); *Novelline popolari italiane* (1875); and *Il Kalevala o la poesia tradizionale dei Finni* (1891).

Cosquin, Emmanuel (1841–1919), a French folklorist, devoted most of his life to the study of European folklore and its origins. Between 1877 and 1881 he collected numerous tales from the region of Champagne, which he published in the journal *Romania*. Each tale was fully annotated and demonstrated Cosquin's comprehensive knowledge of folk and fairy tales. As a result of this work, he published *Contes populaires de Lorraine* (1886), which compared the folk tales in this collection with other French and European tales.

Courlander, Harold (1908–96), an American, folklorist, anthropologist, and novelist, focused on African, Caribbean, Native American, and African American folklore, including oral traditions, folk tales, music, and dance. Courlander did extensive fieldwork in Africa, Haiti, and the American Southwest among the Hopi Indians. He also worked as a journalist and a broadcaster for Voice of America. Among his most significant works are *The Fire on the Mountain and Other Ethiopian Stories* (1950); *Terrapin's Pot of Sense* (1957); *The Cow-Tail Switch and Other West African Stories*, with George Herzog (1959); *The Drum and the Hoe: Life and Lore of the Haitian People* (1960); and *People of the Short Blue Corn: Tales and Legends of the Hopi Indians* (1970).

Curtin, Jerome (1835–1906), an American folklorist, translator, and ethnologist, traveled to Russia after his graduation from Harvard in 1863. He remained there thirteen years and became a specialist in Slavic languages. When he returned to America, he published books about his travels, translations of Polish novels, and several anthologies of folk and fairy tales. Among his most interesting collections are *Myths and Folk-lore of Ireland* (1890); *Myths and Folk-tales of the Russians, Western Slavs, and Magyars* (1890); and *Tales of the Fairies and of the Ghost World* (1895).

Dasent, Sir George Webbe (1817–1896), an English scholar, journalist, and folklorist, studied at King's College London and Oxford University, and upon graduation was appointed to a diplomatic post in Stockholm, Sweden. There he met Jacob Grimm, who encouraged him to learn Scandinavian languages and folklore. Dasent remained in Stockholm until 1845, when he returned to London to work for the *Times*. In 1853 he was appointed professor of English at King's College London, but his real interest was Scandinavian culture, and he published numerous essays and translations of Scandinavian folk and fairy tales. His most important translations are *Popular Tales from the Norse* (1850) by Peter Christen Asbjørnsen and Jørgen Moe; another edition of *Popular Tales from the Norse* (1888); and *East O' the Sun and West O' the Moon* (1888).

Denton, William (1815–88), a British priest and folklorist, was active in causes to help the poor and persecuted people in Eastern Europe and Turkey. Aside from writing numerous pamphlets and commentaries on the Bible, he took a great interest in Serbian folklore and edited *Serbian Folk-lore: Popular Tales* (1874).

Dorson, Richard (1916–81), a renowned American folklorist, directed the Folklore Institute at the University of Indiana. As one of the pioneers of folklore in the United States, Dorson wrote numerous books on all aspects of folklore from a sociohistorical perspective. He was credited with coining the terms "fakelore," which covered pseudo-representations of authentic folklore, and "urban legends," which consisted of stories about city life that were not true. Not only did he write theoretical and historical books and edit numerous anthologies of folk tales, but he also did fieldwork in Michigan, and in 1956 he produced one of the most important books about African American tales, *Negro Tales in Michigan*.

Fansler, Dean (1885–1945), an American professor and editor, was one of the early teachers of English in the Philippines. He published an anthology of folk tales, *Filipino Popular Tales*, in 1921, which included tales Fansler collected in English from 1908 to 1914. In his preface he stated, "Only in very rare cases was there any modification of the original version by the teller, as a concession to Occidental standards. Whatever substitutions I have been able to detect I have removed. In practically every case, not only to show that these are bona fide native stories, but also to indicate their geographical distribution, I have given the name of the narrator, his native town, and his province. In many cases I have given, in addition, the source of his information. I am firmly convinced that all the tales recorded here represent genuine Filipino tradition so far as the narrators are concerned, and that nothing has been 'manufactured' consciously."

Fryer, Alfred Cooper (n.d.), is the author of the *Book of English Fairy Tales from the North-Country* (1884) and *Tales from the Harz Mountains* (1908).

Gardner, Fletcher (1869–n.d.), an American folklorist, was among the first scholars to focus on the Tagalogs, and published several tales in the *Journal of American Folklore* in 1906 and 1907. He also published articles on Philippine beliefs and superstitions.

Goethe, Johann Wolfgang von (1749–1832), a German poet, dramatist, novelist, and civil servant, is regarded as Germany's greatest classical writer. Among his famous works are *Die Leiden des jungen Werthers* (*The Sorrows of Young Werther*, 1774); *Das Märchen* (*The Fairy Tale*, 1795); *Wilhelm Meisters Lehrjahre* (*Wilhelm Meister's Apprenticeship*, 1796); *Faust Part One* (1808); *Die Wahlverwandtschaften* (*Elective Affinities*, 1809); *Aus Meinem Leben: Dichtung und Wahrheit* (*From My Life: Poetry and Truth*, 1811–30); *Wilhelm Meisters Wanderjahre, oder Die Entsagenden* (*Wilhelm Meister's Journeyman Years, or the Renunciants/Wilhelm Meister's Travels*, 1821); and *Faust Part Two* (1832). Many of these works contain fairy-tale elements. Early in his career, Goethe wrote "Der Zauberlehrling" ("The Sorcerer's Apprentice," 1797), a poem, which was later the basis of a symphonic scherzo by Paul Dukas, which in turn was animated by Disney in *Fantasia*.

Goltsch, Johann (1864–1916), a Sorbian folklorist and pastor, published "Bajka wo Krabaće" ("The Story about Krabat," 1885) in the magazine *Lužica*.

Görres, Guido (1805–52), a German historian and poet, wrote various studies about German Catholicism and also edited the first illustrated magazine for children. In addition he was regarded as one of the finest German Catholic poets of the nineteenth century and edited two volumes of Clemens Brentano's fairy tales in 1846. His important collection of stories and ballads, *Altrheinländische Mährlein und Liedlein*, appeared in 1843 and contained numerous songs from the oral tradition.

Grimm, Jacob (1785–1863), and Wilhelm Grimm (1786–1859), German librarians and philologists, published seven editions of their pioneer collection *Kinder- und Hausmärchen* (*Children's and Household Tales*) from 1812 to 1857. This work, along with their other scholarship dealing with ancient and medieval literature, had a profound influence on the development of folklore studies and collections in the nineteenth century. From 1806 to 1810, when the brothers had become librarians and begun writing scholarly articles about medieval literature, they started systematically to gather folk tales and other materials related to folklore. By 1840, when both brothers moved to Berlin and became professors at the University of Berlin, they focused their attention on the *German Dictionary*, one of the most ambitious lexicographical undertakings of the nineteenth century. For the rest of their lives the Grimms devoted themselves to teaching, research, completing the monumental *German Dictionary*, and working on the different editions of the *Kinder- und Hausmärchen*.

Hahn, Johann Georg von (1811–69), an Austrian folklorist, philologist, and diplomat, spent many years in Albania and Greece and eventually became the Austrian consul-general in Athens. He is considered the founder of Albanian studies in Europe and published essays and studies of both Albanian and Greek folklore. His most significant work is the two-volume collection *Griechische und albanesische Märchen* (1864), first published in German.

Haupt, Joachim Leopold (1797–1883), a German Protestant minister and Sorbian folklorist, took a great interest in Sorbian folk songs, legends, and fairy tales. He published tales written in Wendish, Upper Sorbian, and German in many different newspapers and journals and helped initiate the tradition of Krabat stories with the publication of a short legend about an evil squire in Groß-Särchen in *Neues Lausitzisches Magazin*. He also published an important collection of folk songs, *Volkslieder der Wenden in der Ober und Niederlausitz* (1841–44), in two volumes.

Hesse, Hermann (1877–1962), a German writer, poet, and essayist, mixed Western and Eastern elements in his unusual fairy tales. Born in Calw, Germany, Hesse ran away from his private school and in 1895 became a bookseller in Tübingen. During this time he began writing poetry. He moved to Basel, Switzerland, in 1899 and published his first novel, *Peter Camenzind*, in 1909. Thereafter, he remained in Switzerland and dedicated himself to writing. Hesse had a strong lifelong interest in fairy tales and edited collections of tales by the German Romantics. He published his own collection, *Märchen (Fairy Tales)*, in 1919. Almost all his best-known works—such as *Demian* (1919): *Siddhartha* (1922); and *Das Glasperlenspiel* (*The Glass Bead Game*, 1942)—are modeled in some way after fairy tales.

Hodgetts, Edith (d. 1902), a British writer of fairy tales and children's books, translated Russian fairy tales in her collection *Tales and Legends from the Land of the Tzar* (1890).

Hornig, Michael/Michal Hórnik (1833–94), a Sorbian folklorist, published a version of the Krabat story "Krabat. Powěstka z ludu" ("Krabat: A Story from the Folk") in his book *Serbske Nowiny* (1858).

Jahn, Ulrich (1861–1900), a German teacher and folklorist, specialized in the folklore of Pomerania. His major works are *Hexenwesen und Zauberei in Pommern* (1886); *Schwänke und Schnurren aus Bauernmund* (1889); and *Volksmärchen aus Pommern und Rügen* (1891).

Jordan, Hendrich (1841–1910), a Sorbian teacher, writer, and folklorist, is regarded as one of the most dedicated researchers of Lower Sorbian folklore. He published a variety of tales in Lower and Upper Sorbian and in German as well as many folk songs and tales in the journal *Časopis Maćicy Serbskeje* (*ČMS*) from 1872 to 1902. In 1860 he published a collection of Sorbian tales under the title *Najrjeňše ludowe bajki* (*The Most Beautiful Folk Tales*).

Jülg, Bernhard (1825–96), a German philologist, specialized in comparative linguistics and was an expert in Sanskrit and Eastern Asian languages. He is particularly known for his translation of the Mongolian Siddhi-Kür folk tales in 1866.

Kubasch, Georg Gustav (1845–1924), a Sorbian pastor, editor, and journalist, published numerous articles and folk tales in the Catholic magazine *Katolski Posol* and the Sorbian magazine *Nowiny Serbske*. A dedicated Sorbian patriot, Kubasch was editor of the magazine *Serbski hospodar*. He was known to be a dedicated Sorbian patriot and helped establish the Sorbian Peasant Association in 1888.

Lucian of Samosata (125–180 CE), Greek satirist and rhetorician, was known for his great wit. He wrote more than seventy works of fiction, including comic dialogues and essays. His *Philopseudes* (Lover of Lies or Cheater, ca. 170) is a frame story that includes the dialogue about "Eucrates and Pancrates," which served as the basis of the "Humiliated Apprentice" tradition and Goethe's poem "The Sorcerer's Apprentice."

Luzel, François-Marie (1821–95), a French folklorist, was one of the foremost
    collectors of Breton folk tales. He held various positions as instructor, his-
    torian, and journalist and also wrote poetry. Early in his life he developed a
    great interest in folk tales and published such collections as *Contes Bretons*
    (1870). Many of his collections consisted of tales in Breton dialect with
    translations into French along with historical data. In the 1880s he secured
    a position of curator in the Archives at Quimper, a position that enabled
    him to do research on Breton folk tales that resulted in the collections
    Veillées bretonnes (1879); *Légendes chrétiennes* (1882); and *Contes populaires
    de Basse-Bretagne* (1887). At the same time he contributed a vast number
    of tales to folklore journals in France.
MacManus, Seumas (1869–1960), an Irish storyteller, dramatist, and folk-
    lorist, adapted traditional stories and songs to preserve them for future
    generations. During his time in Ireland he collected hundreds of tales and
    published them while living in Dublin and later in New York. Among his
    notable books are *In Chimney Corners: Merry Tales of Irish Folklore* (1899);
    Donegal Fairy Stories (1900); *Tales That Were Told* (1920); *The Donegal
    Wonder Book* (1926); and *Tales from Ireland* (1949).
Mardrus, Joseph Charles (1868–1949), a French doctor and translator, was
    born in Cairo and worked as a physician in Northern Africa. His expertise
    in Arabic led him to publish his version of *The Thousand and One Nights*
    (*Le livre des mille et une nuits*, 1898–1904) in sixteen volumes, which were
    translated into English by Powys Mathers in 1923. Mardrus's translation
    of the *Nights* is not entirely authentic or based on Arabic manuscripts.
    He invented some of the tales or took them from other collections. In the
    case of "The Twelfth Captain's Tale," which is related to the "Sorcerer's
    Apprentice" tradition, it is clear that he adapted his version from Guil-
    laume Spitta-Bey's "The Story of Clever Mohammed" in *Contes arabes
    modernes* (1883).
McKay, John G. (n.d.), a Scottish author and translator, edited and translated
    Gille A'Bhuidseir: The Wizard's Gillie and Other Tales from the magnificent
    Manuscript Collections of the late J. F. Campbell of Islay. McKay also
    edited *More West Highland Tales* (1940).
Naaké, John Theophilus (1837–1906), a folklorist and translator, worked in
    the British Museum and translated *Slavonic Fairy Tales* (1874).
Nesbit, Edith (1858–1924), was a prolific and popular English writer of chil-
    dren's books, poetry, fantasy, and realistic novels. Many of her fantasies,

such as *The Phoenix and the Carpet* (1904) and *The Story of the Amulet* (1906), rely on fairy-tale elements but cannot strictly speaking be called fairy-tale novels. However, Nesbit did publish numerous fairy tales in the *Strand Magazine* and later collected them in books: *The Book of Dragons* (1900); *Nine Unlikely Tales* (1901); and *The Magic World* (1912). Most of these delightful tales featured protagonists snared in absurd situations and often parodied traditional tales. "The Magician's Heart," which was published in *The Magic World*, is a good example of Nesbit's gentle humor and subtle manner of dealing with the conflict between magician and apprentice.

Nowak-Neumann, Martin (1900–1990), was a Sorbian painter, writer, and journalist whose name was Měrćin Nowak-Njechorński until 1958, when he changed it to German. During the 1920s, while studying art in Leipzig and Dresden, Nowak-Neumann became fascinated by Sorbian folklore, and from that time onward, he devoted himself to editing newspapers and journals, writing articles and stories, and creating art in the region of Bautzen. In 1954 he published *Mišter Krabat* (*Master Krabat*) in Sorbian, a book for young readers, which he also illustrated. It was translated into German by Jurij Brězan that same year and had a strong influence on future Krabat stories published in the German Democratic Republic (East Germany).

Ovid (Publius Ovidius Naso (43 BCE–17/18 CE), the renowned Roman poet, wrote the *Metamorphoses* (8 CE), an imaginative interpretation of classical myth, composed in epic meter, and considered one of the most important source books of mythology. Trained as a lawyer, Ovid held various judicial positions in Rome until he decided to devote himself entirely to poetry. He wrote two noteworthy books of love poetry: *Amores* (The Loves) and *Ars Amatoria* (The Art of Love). However, his poetry disturbed the emperor Augustus, who banished him to a small fishing village of Tomi in 8 CE, where he spent the rest of his life. His poetry continued to have a major influence on European poets up through the Renaissance.

Parsons, Elsie Clews (1875–1941), an American anthropologist, sociologist, and folklorist, played a prominent role in the American Folklore Society by serving as associate editor of the *Journal of American Folklore* (1918–41) and as president of the Society (1919–20). Her major interest was the study of Native American tribes (the Tewa, Pueblo, and Hopi) in the Southwest; she also collected tales on the Cape Verde Islands and Antilles.

Among her notable collections are *Folk-Lore from the Cape Verde Islands* (1923); *Folk-Lore of the Sea Islands, S.C.* (1924); and *Folk-Lore of the Antilles, French and English*, 3 volumes (1933–43).

Pétis de la Croix, François (1653–1713), a French orientalist and writer, became the Arabic interpreter at the French royal court in 1695 after having studied Arabic, Persian, and Turkish and spending many years in Syria, Persia, and Turkey. Among his notable books dealing with folk and fairy tales are *Histoire de la Sultane de Perse et des Visirs. Contes Turcs* (1707), which was translated as *The Persian and the Turkish Tales, Compleat* by William King in 1714; and *Les mille et un jours* (*A Thousand and One Days*, 1710–12). *The Persian and the Turkish Tales* included "The Story of the Brahmin Padmanaba and the Young Hassan," a version of "The Humiliated Apprentice." His *Thousand and One Days* was to some extent conceived in competition to *The Thousand and One Nights*. The main source of inspiration for his collection was a fifteenth-century Ottoman Turkish compilation, and he adapted a selection of these tales.

Pilk, Jurij (Georg) (1858–1926), a Sorbian historian, folklorist, composer, and teacher, published several important books on Sorbian history. He is best known for the publication of "Der wendische Faust" (1896) in the German magazine *Sächsischer Erzähler*. This story was also translated into Sorbian and published the same year as *Serbki Faust*, in the magazine *Łužica*, and republished as *Die wendische Faust-Sage* (1900) in *Bunte Bilder aus dem Sachsenlande* in Leipzig. It was Pilk's Krabat story that brought together most of the important plot and thematic elements from different tales that had circulated in the region of Upper and Lower Sorbia and in Germany. His version was to have a lasting influence in the twentieth century.

Pitrè, Giuseppe (1841–1916), a Sicilian doctor, folklorist, and ethnographer, played a major role in fostering the study of popular traditions in Italy. He developed an anthropological and historical approach in his voluminous essays and collections of Sicilian and Italian tales. In addition, he edited the significant journal of folklore, *Archivio per lo studio delle tradizioni popolari* (*Archive for the Study of Popular Traditions*, 1882–1909), corresponded with major folklorists throughout the world, and founded a museum of folklore in Palermo. Among Pitrè's most significant works are *Biblioteca delle tradizioni popolari siciliane* (*Library of Popular Sicilian Traditions*, 1870–1913); *Fiabe, novelle e racconti popolari siciliani* (*Fairy Tales, Novellas, and Popular Tales of Sicily*, 1875); *Novelle Popolari Toscane* (*Popular Tuscan*

Novellas, 1885); and *Curiositá popolari tradizionali* (*Curiosities of Popular Traditions*, 1894).

Pramberger, Romuald (1877–1967), an Austrian Benedict monk, folklorist, and writer, studied religion and law at the universities of Vienna, Innsbruck, and Rome. After 1905, while living as a priest at various cloisters in Styria, he began collecting articles, costumes, utensils, and tales as an amateur folklorist. Gradually, he learned to do thorough research about the customs, beliefs, and stories of the people in the region of Styria and often recited the tales on radio. Some of his stories were published in anthologies or journals; his major work was *Märchen aus Steiermark* (1935).

Preußler, Otfried (1923–2013) was a German teacher and author of children's books. During his years as a school teacher in Bavaria, Preussler wrote a series of popular children's books using traditional fairy-tale characters and motifs, including *Der kleine Wassermann* (*The Little Water Sprite*, 1956); *Die kleine Hexe* (*The Little Witch*, 1957); *Der Räuber Hotzenplotz* (*The Robber Hotzenplotz*, 1962); and *Das kleine Gespenst* (*The Little Ghost*, 1966). His books had great success in Germany because he depicted robbers, ghosts, and witches more as zany and comical than dangerous, and he parodied traditional fairy-tale themes and plots. His major accomplishment, however, was a more serious work, namely *Krabat* (1971), translated into English as *The Satanic Mill*. This novel was based on the Sorbian legend about Krabat closely tied to the tradition of "The Sorcerer's Apprentice." It was adapted for the cinema by the Czech animator, Karel Zeman, in 1978 and as a German live-action film with the title *Krabat* in 2008.

Rabenau, Alexander von (1845–1923), a Sorbian folklorist, collected numerous Sorbian folk tales published in 1889. He donated his large collection to the Märkisches Museum in Berlin, but they were lost in 1945 due to the bombing of the museum.

Ramanujan, Attipate Krishnaswami (1929–93), was an Indian poet, philologist, folklorist, and playwright whose scholarly work spanned several disciplines. In his study of folklore he was interested in cultural ideologies and the contextual relationship between oral and literary tales. Two of his most important contributions to Indian folklore are *The Interior Landscape: Love Poems from a Classical Tamil Anthology* (1967) and *Folktales from India, Oral Tales from Twenty Indian Languages* (1991). In 1997 Stuart Blackburn and Alan Dundes published a posthumous collection of tales collected by Ramanujan under the title *A Flowering Tree and Other Oral Tales from India.*

Ritter, Hellmut (1892–1971), a prominent German orientalist, was an expert in Persian, Arabic, and Turkish culture and also in Sufi beliefs and rituals. He edited an important analytical compilation of stories written by the Iranian poet Farīd-al-Dīn's in *Das Meer der Seele. Mensch, Welt und Gott in den Geschichten des Farīduddīn ʿAttār* (1955), translated as *The Ocean of the Soul: Men, the World and God in the Stories of Farid Al-Din ʿAttar* (2003).

Ryder, Arthur William (1877–1938), was an American folklorist and professor of Sanskrit at the University of California, Berkeley. A gifted translator of numerous Sanskrit works, he published two major translations of the *Panchatantra* (1925) and *The Bhagavad-gita* (1929). In addition he translated a significant frame narrative, *Twenty-two Goblins* (1917), from Somadeva's *Kathasaritsagara* (*The Ocean of Story*), which dates to the eleventh century.

Schott, Arthur (1814–75), and Albert Schott (1809–47), German folklorists from Swabia, published the first important collection of Rumanian folk tales, *Walachische Märchen* (1845), in German.

Scott, Sir Walter (1771–1832), a Scottish writer, poet, and playwright, was famous for his historical novels. Among his notable works are *Waverley* (1814); *Rob Roy* (1817); *Ivanhoe* (1819); *The Bride of Lammermoor* (1819); and *Kenilworth* (1821). Scott had a strong interest in folk and fairy tales and often incorporated them into his novels and collections. His short tale "The Last Exorciser," based on the tradition of "The Sorcerer's Apprentice," was published in 1838.

Sheykh-Zāda (n.d.) was the author of *The History of the Forty Vezirs or the Story of the Forty Forns and Eves* (Contes turcs [Qyrq wezīr ḥikājesi], written in Turkish by Sheykh-Zāda [Šaiḫzāda] and translated into English by Elias John Wilkinson Gibb in 1886).

Slizinski, Jerzy (1920–88), a Czech writer and folklorist, specialized in the study of Slavic folklore. He taught literature and languages at the University of Prague and published an important collection of Sorbian folk tales, *Sorbische Volkserzählungen* (1964), in German. In addition he edited the publication of *Bracia Grimm i folklor narodów slowianskichmaterialy z miedzynarodowej konferencji* (*The Brothers Grimm and the Folklore of the Slavic Peoples*, 1989), based on a conference held in Warsaw in 1985.

Somadeva (flourished in the latter part of the eleventh century), a Hindu poet, was a Kashmiri Brahmin of the Saliva sect and Sanskrit writer, responsible for preserving some of the most significant tales of ancient India. His major work, written about 1070, was the *Kathasaritsagara*, generally translated as *The Ocean of Story*, which often featured master/pupil conflicts. The complete translation of Somadeva's *Karthasaritsagara* was first accomplished by Charles Henry Tawney in two volumes published in 1880 and 1884. Later his translation was expanded to ten volumes with notes and other stories by Norman Penzer in 1924–28.

Southey, Robert (1774–1843), a British poet, essayist, historian, and biographer, was regarded as one of the famous romantic Lake poets. A prolific writer, he is also credited with writing the first English version of "The Three Bears." Among his notable early poetic and prose works are *Poems* (1797–99); *St. Patrick's Purgatory* (1798); *After Blenheim* (1798); *The Devil's Thoughts* (1799); *English Eclogues* (1799); *The Old Man's Comforts and How He Gained Them* (1799); and *Thalaba the Destroyer* (1801).

Straparola, Giovan Francesco (ca. 1480–1558), an Italian writer, was born in Cavaggio and later moved to Venice. He left few documents about his life. Aside from a small volume of poems, his major work is *Le piacevoli notti* (1550–53), translated variously as *The Facetious Nights, The Delectable Nights,* or *The Pleasant Nights*. The seventy-three stories in Straparola's work include "Maestro Lattanzio," which was the first literary model of "The Rebellious Sorcerer Tale" and influenced many writers. Straparola's collection has a framework similar to Boccaccio's *Decameron*. The tales are told on thirteen consecutive nights by a group of ladies and gentlemen gathered at the Venetian palace of Ottaviano Maria Sforza, former bishop of Lodi and ruler of Milan, who has fled with his widowed daughter Lucretia to avoid persecution by his political enemies. The framework and many of the tales were imitated by other European writers.

Swynnerton, Charles (1877–1938), a British missionary in India, was the author of *The Adventures of the Panjáb Hero Rájá Rasálu and Other Folk-tales of the Panjáb* (1884); *The Afghan War* (1880); *Indian Nights' Entertainment; or, Folk-tales from the Upper Indus* (1892); and *Romantic Tales from the Panjáb* (1903).

Tawney, Charles Henry (1837–1922), an English scholar and translator, taught briefly at Cambridge University and then moved to India in 1864 for health reasons to assume the position of professor at Presidency College in Calcutta. In India he acquired fluent knowledge of Sanskrit, Hindi, Urdu, and Persian and became an accomplished translator. His major achievement was the publication of the multivolume *The Ocean of Story* (Somadeva's *Kathā Sarti Sāgara*, 1880–84). He also published an important collection of Jain stories in *Kathākoça* (1895).

Veckenstedt, Edmund (1840–1903), a German folklorist and educator, collected and wrote mainly about Sorbian tales and founded the important journal *Zeitschrift für Volkskunde* in 1889. Among his more notable books that focused on Sorbian and Central European stories are *Wendische Sagen, Märchen und abergläubische Gebräuche* (1880); *Die Mythen, Sagen und Legenden der Žamaiten* (1883); and *Pumphut, ein Kulturdämon der Deutschen, Wenden, Litauer und Žamaiten* (1885).

Wiener, Leo (1862–1939), American historian, linguist, and translator, was born in Russia and came to America very early in his childhood. By 1896 he attained a position as professor of Slavic literature and was famous for translating twenty-four volumes of Leo Tolstoy's works into English. Among his other significant publications was *The History of Yiddish Literature in the Nineteenth Century* (1899). Wiener also collected and published Yiddish folk tales in various European journals such as the *Mitteilungen der Gesellschaft für jüdische Volkskunde*.

Woycicki, Kazimierz Wladyslaw (1807–79), Polish author, historian, and journalist, was one of the most prolific Polish writers of the nineteenth century. He wrote about diverse topics, and one of his great interests was Polish folklore. During the 1830s Woycicki often traveled about Poland and collected proverbs and folk tales, which he published in Polish and German. He eventually became one of the most notable historians of Warsaw.

Filmography

The Wizard's Apprentice (1930)
USA, black and white, 10 minutes
Director: Sidney Levee
Music: Paul Dukas
Producer: William Cameron Menzies

Fantasia (1940)
USA, color, animation, 125 minutes
Director: Norman Ferguson, James Algar
Screenplay: Joe Grant, Dick Huemer
Music: Paul Dukas

The Sorcerer's Apprentice (1955)
Germany, color, ballet, 13 minutes
Director: Michael Powell
Screenplay: Dennis Arundell, based on Johann Wolfgang von Goethe's
     poem "The Sorcerer's Apprentice"
Music: Walter Braunfels

The Sorcerer's Apprentice (1962)
USA, black and white, TV film, 30 minutes
Director: Joseph Lejtes
Screenplay: Robert Bloch
Producer: Alfred Hitchcock

Die schwarze Mühle (*The Black Mill*, 1975)
East Germany, color, 80 minutes
Director: Celino Bleiweiß
Screenplay: Celino Bleiweiß and Jurij Brězan's novel
Music: Andrzej Korzynski

Krabat or The Sorcerer's Apprentice (*Carodejuv ucen*, 1978)
Czechoslovakia/West Germany, color, animation, 73 minutes
Director: Karel Zeman
Screenplay: Jirí Gold, based on the novel by Otfried Preußler
Music: Frantisek Belfin

The Sorcerer's Apprentice (1980)
Canada, color, animation, 26 minutes
Director: Peter Sander
Narrator: Vincent Price

Fantasia 2000 (1999)
USA, color, animation, 75 minutes
Director and Screenplay: Jessica Ambinder-Rojas, Lois Freeman-Fox,
    Julia Gray, Craig Paulsen, and Gregory Plotts
Music: James Levine

The Sorcerer's Apprentice (2002)
South Africa, color, 86 minutes
Director: David Lister
Screenplay: Brett Morris
Music: Paul Dukas, Mark Thomas

Earthsea (2004)
USA, color, TV mini-series, 172 minutes
Director: Rob Lieberman
Screenplay: Gavin Scott, based on novels by Ursula Le Guin
Music: Jeff Roma

Merlin's Apprentice (2006)
USA, color, TV mini-series, 176 minutes
Director: David Wu
Screenplay: Roger Soffer, Christian Ford
Music: Lawrence Shragge

Tales from Earthsea (2006)
Japan, color, animation, 115 minutes
Director: Gorō Miyazaki
Screenplay: Gorō Miyazaki, Keiko Niwa
Music: Tamiya Terashima

Krabat or *Krabat and the Legend of the Satanic Mill* (2008)
Germany, color, 120 minutes
Director: Marco Kreuzpaintner
Screenplay: Michael Gutmann, Marco Kreuzpaintner, based on the novel
    by Otfried Preußler
Music: Annette Focks

The Sorcerer's Apprentice (2010)
USA, color, 109 minutes
Director: Jon Turtletaub
Screenplay: Lawrence Konner, Mark Rosenthal
Music: Trevor Rabin

The Boy and the Beast (*Bakemono no ko*, 2015)
Japan, color, animation, 119 minutes
Director: Mamoru Hosada
Co-director: Ryo Horibe
Screenplay: Mamoru Hosada
Music: Masakatsu Takagi

Bibliography

LITERATURE

Armin, Robert. *The Collected Works of Robert Armin*. Intro J. P. Feather. 2 vols. London: Pavier, 1609. Reprint New York: Johnson, 1972.

Arnason, Jón. *Icelandic Legends*. Trans. George Powell and Eiríkur Magnússon. London: Richard Bentley, 1864.

Augiéras, François. *L'apprenti sorcier*. Paris: Éditions Julliard, 1964.

———. *The Sorcerer's Apprentice*. Trans. Sue Dyson. London: Pushkin Press, 2001.

Baader, Bernhard. *Neugesammelte Volkssagen aus dem Lande Baden und den angrenzenden Gegenden*. Karlsruhe: Verlag der Herder'schen Buchhandlung, 1859.

———. *Volkssagen aus dem Lande Baden und den angrenzenden Gegenden*. Karlsruhe: Verlag der Herder'schen Buchhandlung, 1851.

Bain, Robert Nisbet, ed. *Cossack Fairy Tales*. Illustr. E. W. Mitchell. London: Lawrence & Bullen, 1894.

Barbeau, C. Marius. *Il était une fois . . .* Illustr. Phoebé Thomson. Montreal: Éditions Beauchemin, 1935.

———. Special Issue dedicated to *Contes Populaires Canadiens, Journal of American Folklore* 29.51 (January–March 1916): 1–137.

———. *The Tree of Dreams*. Illustr. Arthur Price. Toronto: Oxford University Press, 1955.

Barbeau, Marius, and Michael Hornyansky. *The Golden Phoenix and Other French-Canadian Fairy Tales*. Illustr. Arthur Price. New York: Henry Z. Walck, 1958.

Bartens, Hans-Hermann, ed. *Märchen aus Lappland*. Munich: Hugendubel, 2003.

Bavis, Cyril. *The Sorcerer's Apprentice*. Franklin, TN: Flowerpot Press, 2014.

Bechstein, Ludwig. *Deutsches Märchenbuch*. Leipzig: Linschmann, 1845.

———. *Deutsches Märchenbuch*. Leipzig: Hartleben, 1857.

———. *Neues Deutsches Märchenbuch*. Leipzig: Hartleben, 1856.

———. *Sämtliche Märchen*. Ed. Walter Scherf. Darmstadt: Wissenschaftliche Buchgesellschaft, 1970.

Begin, Mary Jane. *The Sorcerer's Apprentice*. Boston: Little Brown, 2005.

Blackburn, Stuart. *Moral Fictions: Tamil Folktales from Oral Tradition*. Helsinki: Academica Scientiarum Fennica, 2001.

Bladé, Jean-François. *Contes populaires de la Gascogne*. 3 vols. Paris: Maisonneuve frères et Ch. Leclerc, 1886.

———. *Poésies Populaires de la Gascogne*. 2 vols. Paris: Maisonneuve et Ch. Leclerc, 1882.

Booss, Claire, ed. *Scandinavian Folk & Fairy Tales: Tales from Norway, Sweden, Denmark, Finland, and Iceland.* New York: Avenel Books, 1984.

Bošković-Stulli, Maja. *Kroatische Volksmärchen.* Trans. Wolfgang Eschker and Vladimir Milak. Cologne: Diederichs Verlag, 1975.

Bowman, James Cloyd, and Margery Bianco, eds. *Tales from a Finnish Tupa.* Trans. Aili Kolehmainen. Illustr. Laura Bannon. Chicago: Albert Whitman, 1958.

Bowring, Edgar Alfred. *The Poems of Goethe.* 2nd ed. New York: Hurst, 1874.

Brendle, Thomas, and William Troxell, eds. *Pennsylvania German Folk Tales, Legends, Once-Upon-a-Time Stories, Maxims, and Sayings.* Norristown, PA: Pennsylvania German Society, 1944.

Brewer, John Mason. *Dog Ghosts and Other Texas Negro Folk Tales.* Austin: University of Texas Press, 1958.

Brězan, Jurij. *Die schwarze Mühle.* Illustr. Werner Klemke. Berlin: Verlag Neues Leben, 1968.

———. *Krabat oder die Bewahrung der Welt.* Bautzen: Dornowina-Verlag, 1995.

———. *Krabat, oder, Die Verwandlung der Welt.* Berlin: Verlag Neues Leben, 1976.

Briggs, Katharine, ed. *A Dictionary of British Folk-Tales in the English Language,* 4 vols. London: Routledge and Kegan Paul, 1970.

Broun, Heywood. *Seeing Things at Night.* New York: Harcourt, Brace, 1921.

Buchan, Peter. *Ancient Ballads and Songs of the North of Scotland.* 2 vols. Edinburgh: William Paterson, 1875.

———. *Ancient Scottish Tales.* Intro. John Fairley. Peterhead, UK: 1908.

Burton, Richard F. *The Book of the Thousand Nights and a Night: A Plain and Literal Translation of the Arabian Nights Entertainment.* 10 vols. Stoke Newington, UK: Kamashastra Society, 1885–86.

———. *Supplemental Nights to the Book of the Thousand Nights and a Night, with Notes Anthropological and Explanatory.* 6 vols. Stoke Newington, UK: Kamashastra Society, 1886.

———. *Vikram & the Vampire: or Tales of Hindu Devilry.* London: Longmans, Green, 1870.

Bushnaq, Inea, trans. and ed. *Arab Folk Tales.* New York: Pantheon, 1986.

Busk, Rachel Harriette, ed. *Sagas from the Far East; or, Kalmouk and Mongolian Traditionary Tales.* London: Griffith and Farran, 1873.

Campbell, Marie. *Tales from the Cloud Walking Country.* Bloomington: Indiana University Press, 1958.

Campbell of Islay, John Francis. *Gille A'Bhuidseir. The Wizard's Gillie and Other Tales.* Ed. J. G. McKay. London: Saint Catherine Press, 1914.

———. *Popular Tales of the West Highlands.* 3 vols. Edinburgh: Edmonston and Douglas, 1862.

Canavan, Trudy. *The Magician's Apprentice.* New York: Hachette, 2009.

Carrière, Joseph Médard. *Contes du Détroit.* Ed. Marcel Bénéteau and Donald Deschênes. Sudbury, Canada: Éditions Prise de parole, 2005.

———. *Tales from the French Folk-Lore of Missouri.* Evanston, IL: Northwestern University Studies 1937.

Child, Francis James, ed. *The English and Scottish Popular Ballads.* 5 vols. New York: Houghton, Mifflin, 1882–98.

———. *The English and Scottish Popular Ballads.* Reprint of nineteenth-century edition. New York: Dover, 1965.

Christiansen, Reidar, ed. *Folktales of Norway*. Trans. Pat Shaw Iverson. Chicago: University of Chicago Press, 1964.

Clarke, Susanna. *Jonathan Strange & Mr. Norrell*. Illustr. Portia Rosenberg. London: Bloomsbury, 2004.

Clarkson, Atelia, and Gilbert Cross. *World Folktales*. Charles Scribner's Sons, 1980.

Coelho, Adolpho Francisco. *Contos Populares Portuguezes*. Lisbon: Plantier, 1879.

———. *Tales of Old Lusitania, from the Folklore of Portugal*. Trans. Henriette Monteiro. London: Sonnenschein Ywan, 1885.

Comparetti, Domenico. *Novelline popolari italiene*. Bologna: Forni, 1875.

Cooper, Paul Fenimore. *Tricks of Women & Other Albanian Tales*. New York: William Morrow, 1928.

Courlander, Harold. *Terrapin's Pot of Sense*. New York: Henry Holt and Company, 1957.

———. *A Treasury of Afro-American Folklore*. New York: Crown, 1976.

Coxwell, C. Fillingham. *Siberian and Other Folk-Tales*. London: C. W. Daniel, 1925.

Crane, Thomas Frederick. *Chansons Populaires de la France: A Selection from Popular Ballads*. New York: G. P. Putnam's Sons, 1885.

Curtin, Jerome. *Myth and Folk-Lore of Ireland*. Boston: Little, Brown, 1890.

Dann, Jack, and Gardner Dozois, eds. *Sorcerers*. New York: Ace, 1986.

———. *Wizards*. New York: Berkley, 2007.

Dawkins, R. M. *Modern Greek in Asia Minor*. Cambridge: Cambridge University Press, 1916.

Dewan, Ted. *The Sorcerer's Apprentice*. New York: Doubleday, 1998.

Disney, Walt. *The Sorcerer's Apprentice*. New York: Random House, 1973.

———. *The Sorcerer's Apprentice: From Walt Disney's Fantasia*. New York: Grosset & Dunlap, 1940.

Dorson, Richard, ed. *Buying the Wind*. Chicago: University of Chicago Press, 1964.

———. *Negro Folktales in Michigan*. Cambridge, MA: Harvard University Press, 1956.

Douglas, Sheila, ed. *The King of the Black Art and Other Folk Tales*. Aberdeen: Aberdeen University Press, 1987.

Duane, Diane. *So You Want to Be a Wizard*. New York: Delacorte, 1983.

Dunsany, Lord (Edward Plunkett). *The Charwoman's Shadow*. New York: G. P. Putnam and Sons, 1926.

Ehrentreich, Alfred. *Englische Volksmärchen*. Jena: Eugen Diederichs Verlag, 1938.

El-Shamy, Hasan, ed. and trans. *Folktales of Egypt*. Chicago: University of Chicago Press, 1980.

Ewers, Hanns Heinz. *Der Zauberlehrling, oder die Teufelsjäger*. Munich: Müller, 1910.

———. *The Sorcerer's Apprentice*. Trans. Ludwig Lewisohn. New York: John Day, 1927.

Fansler, Dean, ed. *Filipino Popular Tales*. Lancaster, PA: American Folklore Society, 1921.

Feist, Raymond. *Magician: Apprentice*. New York: Doubleday, 1982.

———. *Magician: Master*. New York: Doubleday, 1986.

Flanagan, John. *The Ruins of Gorlan*. Melbourne, Australia: Random House, 2004. The first novel in the *Rangers Apprentice* series, which consists of 12 novels.

Flisar, Evald. *The Sorcerer's Apprentice*. Norman, OK: Texture Press, 2012.

Ford, Patrick. *The Mabinogi and Other Medieval Welsh Tales*. Berkeley: University of California Press, 1977.

Francis, H. T. *Jātaka Tales*. Cambridge: Cambridge University Press, 1916.

Fryer, Alfred. *Book of English Fairy Tales from the North-Country*. London: W. Swan Sonnenschein, 1884.

Gág, Wanda. *The Sorcerer's Apprentice*. Illustr. Margot Tomes. New York: Coward, McCann & Geoghegan, 1979.

Gale, James, ed. and trans. *Korean Folk Tales: Imps, Ghosts and Fairies*. London: J. M. Dent, 1913.

Galland, Eugène, ed. *Recueil de Chansons Populaires*. 6 vols. Paris: Maisonneuve, 1883.

Gardner, Fletcher, "Tagalog Folk-Tales. II." *Journal of American Folklore* 20.79 (October–December 1907): 300–310.

Garnett, Lucy. *Greek Folk Poesy*. London: David Nutt, 1896.

Gmelch, George, and Ben Kroup. *To Shorten the Road*. Dublin: O'Brien Press, 1978.

Goltsch, Johann. "Bajka wo Krabaće." *Lužica* 4 (1885): 90–91.

Görres, Guido, ed. *Altrheinländische Märlein und Liedlein*. Coblenz: 1843.

Goyert, Georg. ed. *Vlämische Märchen*. Jena: Eugen Diederichs, 1925.

Gray, Nicholas Stuart. *The Sorcerer's Apprentices*. New York: St. Martin's Press, 1965.

———. *The Sorcerer's Apprentices*. Reprint. Illustr. Martin Springett. New York: St. Martin's Press, 1987.

Greenberg, Martin, and Russell Davis. *Apprentice Fantastic*. New York: DAW, 2002.

Griffith, F. L. *Stories of the High Priests of Memphis: The Sethon of Herodotus and the Demotic Tales of Khamuas*. Oxford: Clarendon Press, 1900.

Grossman, Lev. *The Magician King*. New York: Viking/Penguin, 2011.

———. *The Magicians*. New York: Viking/Penguin, 2009.

———. *The Magician's Land*. New York: Viking/Penguin, 2014.

Hahn, Johann Georg von. *Griechische und albanesische Märchen*. 2 vols. Leipzig: W. Engelmann, 1864.

Halpert, Herbert, and J.D.A. Widdowson, eds. *Folktales of Newfoundland: The Resilience of the Oral Tradition*. New York: Garland, 1996.

Haltrich, Josef. *Deutsche Volksmärchen aus dem Sachsenlande in Siebenbürgen*. Vienna: Carl Graser, 1882.

Hansen, William. "Apprentice and Ghost: Eukrates and the Automaton." In *Ariadne's Thread: A Guide to International Tales Found in Classical Literature*. Ithaca, NY: Cornell University Press, 2002. 35–38.

Haupt, Joachim Leopold. "Von einem bösen Herrn in Groß-Särchen." *Neues Lausitzisches Magazin* 15.2 (1837): 203–4.

Hazen, Barbara. *The Sorcerer's Apprentice*. Illustr. Tomi Ungerer. New York: Lancelot Press, 1969.

Hearn, Michael Patrick. *The Porcelain Cat*. Illustr. Leo and Diane Dillon. New York: Milk & Cookies Press, 2004.

Henderson, William. *Notes on the Folklore of the Northern Counties of England and the Borders*. London: Longmans, Green, 1866. With an appendix on *Household Stories* by Sabine Baring-Gould.

Hodgetts, Edith. *Tales and Legends from the Land of the Tzar: Collection of Russian Stories*. London: Griffith Farran, 1890.

Holt, Tom. *The Outsorcerer's Apprentice: A Novel of Overlords, Underlings, and Inhuman Resources.* New York: Orbit, 2014.

Hornig, Michael. *Serbse Nowiny.* Bautzen: Mesačny Přidawk, 1858.

Hosoda, Mamoru. *The Boy and the Beast.* Trans. Sawa Matsueda Savage. New York: Hachette, 2016.

———. *The Boy and the Beast.* Trans. ZephyrRZ. Illustr. Renji Asai. Tokyo: Kadokawa Corporation, 2016.

Houghton, Louise Seymour. *The Russian Grandmother's Wonder Tales.* London: Bickers and Son, 1906.

Jewett, Sophie, ed. and trans. *Folk-Ballads of Southern Europe.* New York: G. P. Putnam's Sons, 1913.

Johnson, Charles. *The Sorcerer's Apprentice.* New York: Atheneum, 1986.

Jones, Diana Wynne. *House of Many Ways.* New York: Greenwillow Books, 2008.

Jülg, Bernhard, ed. *Kalmükische Märchen: Die Märchen des Siddhi-Kür oder Erzählungen eines verzauberten Todten.* Leipzig: F. A. Brockhaus, 1866.

Kallas, Oskar. *80 Märchen der Ljutziner Esten.* Dorpat: 1900.

Karadschitsch, Wuk Stephanowitsch. *Volksmärchen der Serben.* Trans. Wilhelmine Karadschitsch. Berlin: Georg Reimer, 1854.

Karlinger, Felix, ed. *Märchen griechischer Inseln.* Cologne: Eugen Diederichs Verlag, 1979.

Kaye, Marvin. *The Penguin Book of Witches & Warlocks: Tales of Black Magic, Old and New.* New York: Penguin Books, 1989.

Khatchatrianz, Iakov. *Armenian Folk Tales.* Trans. N. W. Orloff. Illustr. Martyros Saryan. Philadelphia: Colonial House, 1946.

Kingscote, Georgiana, and S. M. Natesa Sastri, eds. *Tales of the Sun or Folklore of Southern India.* London: W. H. Allen, 1890.

Kooi, Jurjen, and Theo Schuster. *Der Großherzog und die Marktfrau: Märchen und Schwänke aus dem Oldenburger Land.* Leer: Schuster, 1994.

Krauss, Friedrich Salomon. *Sagen und Märchen der Sudslaven.* Leipzig: W. Friedrich, 1884.

Kreutzwald, Friedrich. *Ehstnische Märchen.* Ed. Amton Schiefner and Reinhold Köhler. Trans. F. Löwe. Halle: Verlag der Buchhandlung des Waisenhauses, 1869.

Kropej, Monika, Zmago Šmitek, and Roberto Dapit, eds. *A Treasury of Slovenian Folklore.* Trans. Barbara Kerr and Joan Meade. Radvovljica: Didakta, 2010.

Kubasch, Georg Gustav. "Krabat." In *Lužičan. Časopis zu Zabawu a Poweučenje.* Ed. J. E. Smoler. Vol. 6, part 11. Bautzen: 1865. 168–71.

Kúnos, Ignácz. *Forty-four Turkish Fairy Tales.* Illustr. Willy Pogány. London: Harrap, 1913.

Kurti, Alfred. *Persian Folktales.* London: G. Bell & Sons, 1971.

Langstaff, John. *The Two Magicians.* Illustr. Fritz Eichenberg. New York: Atheneum, 1973.

Lebermann, Norbert. *Blaue Blumen.* Nuremberg: Süddeutsche Verlags Akt, 1927.

———. *New German Fairy Tales.* Trans. Frieda Bachmann. Illustr. Margaret Freeman, 1930.

Le Guin, Ursula. *The Earthsea Trilogy.* New York: Penguin Books, 1982.

———. *The Farthest Shore.* New York: Atheneum, 1972.

———. *The Other Wind.* New York: Harcourt, 2001.

———. *Tehanu.* New York: Atheneum, 1990.

———. *The Tombs of Atuan*. New York: Atheneum, 1971.

———. *A Wizard of Earthsea*. Illustr. Ruth Robbins. Berkeley, CA: Parnassus Press, 1968.

Lewis, Matthew G. *Tales of Wonder*. 2 vols. London: Bulmer & Co., 1801.

Lichtheim, Miriam. *Ancient Egyptian Literature: A Book of Readings*. 3 vols. Berkeley: University of California Press, 1980.

Little, Denise, ed. *The Sorcerer's Academy*. New York: DAW, 2003.

Lucian of Samosata, *The Works of Lucian*. Trans. A. M. Harmon, vol. 3. London: William Heinemann, 1921.

Luzel, François-Marie. *Contes Inédits*. Ed. Françoise Morvan. Vol. 1. Rennes: Presses Universitaires de Rennes, 1995.

Macfie, J. M. *Myths and Legends of India: An Introduction to the Study of Hinduism*. Edinburgh: E. & T. Clark, 1924.

MacManus, Seumas. *The Donegal Wonder Book*. New York: Frederick A. Stokes, 1926.

Mahy, Margaret. *The Magician of Hoad*. New York: HarperCollins, 2008.

Mardrus, Joseph Charles. *Le livre des mille nuits et une nuit*. 16 vols. Paris: Éditions de la Revue Blanche, 1889–1904.

Mardrus, Joseph Charles, and E. Powys Mathers, eds. *The Book of the Thousand and One Nights*. 4 vols. London: Casonova Society, 1923.

———. *The Book of the Thousand and One Nights*. Illustr. Roderick McRae. 8 vols. New York: Dingwall-Rock, 1930.

Maspero, Gaston. *Les contes populaires de l'Égypte ancienne*. Paris: Maisonneuve, 1882.

———. *Popular Stories of Ancient Egypt*. London: H. Grevel, 1915.

———. *Popular Stories of Ancient Egypt*. Ed. Hasan El-Shamy. Santa Barbara, CA: ABC-CLIO, 2002.

Mayer, Marianna. *The Sorcerer's Apprentice: A Greek Fable*. Illustr. David Wiesner. New York: Bantam, 1989.

Mažuranić, Ivana Brlić. *The Brave Adventures of a Shoemaker's Boy*. English version by Lorna Wood. Trans. Theresa Mravintz and Branko Brusar. London: J. M. Dent & Sons, 1971.

Mbiti, John. *Akamba Stories*. Oxford: Clarendon Press, 1966.

McCaffrey, Anne, ed. *Alchemy and Academe*. New York: Doubleday, 1970.

McHugh, Maura. *Twisted Fairy Tales*. Illustr. Jane Laurie. London: Quantum Publishing, 2012.

McKay, John G., ed. and trans. *Gille A'Bhuidseir. The Wizard's Gillie and Other Tales*. London: Saint Catherine Press, 1914.

———, ed. *More West Highland Tales*. 2 vols. Edinburgh: Oliver & Boyd/Scottish Anthropological and Folklore Society, 1940.

Mijatovich, Elodie Lawton. *Serbian Folk-Lore*. Ed. Rev. W. Denton. London: W. Isbister, 1874.

Millien, Achille. *Contes de Bourgogne*. Ed. Françoise Morvan. Rennes: Éditions Ouest-France, 2008.

Millien, Achille, and Paul Delarue. *Contes du Nivernais et du Morvan*. Illustr. Arsène Lecoq. Paris: Éditions Érasme, 1953.

Moore, Inga. *The Sorcerer's Apprentice*. New York: Atheneum, 1989.

Morrow, James. *The Philosopher's Apprentice*. New York: William Morrow, 2008.

Naaké, John. *Slavonic Fairy Tales: Collected and translated from the Russian, Polish, Serbian, and Bohemian.* London: Henry S. King and Company, 1874.

Nicoloff, Assen, ed. *Bulgarian Folktales.* Cleveland: A. Nicoloff, 1979.

Nigra, Constantino, ed. *Canti popolari del Piemonte.* Turin: E. Loescher, 1888.

Nowak-Neumann, Martin. *Meister Krabat der gute sorbische Zauberer.* Trans. Jurij Brězan. Illustr. Měrćin Nowak-Neumann. Afterword by Paul Nedo. Berlin: Kinderbuchverlag, 1954.

Noy, Dov, ed. *Folktales of Israel.* Trans. Gene Baharav. Chicago: University of Chicago Press, 1969.

Oakley, E. S., and Tara Dutt Gairola. *Himalayan Folklore. Kumaon and West Nepal.* New Delhi: Cosmo Publications, 1935.

Orain, Adolphe. *Contes de l'Ille et Vilaine.* Paris: Maisonneuve, 1901.

Ouyang, Wen-chin, and Paulo Lemos Horta, eds. *The Arabian Nights: An Anthology.* London: Everyman's Library, 2014.

Ovid. *Metamorphoses.* Trans. Brookes Moore. Boston: Cornhill Publishing, 1922.

Ovid. *Metamorphoses.* Trans. Stanley Lombardo. Intro. W. R. Johnson. Indianapolis/Cambridge: Hackett, 2010.

Papashvily, George, and Helen Papashvily. *Yes and No Stories: A Book of Georgian Folk Tales.* Illustr. Simon Lissim. New York: Harper & Brothers, 1946.

Parker, Henry, ed. and trans. *Village Folk-Tales of Ceylon.* 3 vols. New Delhi: Asian Educational Services, 1997. First published in London: Luzac, 1910–14.

Parsons, Elsie Clews. *Folklore from the Cape Verde Islands.* Cambridge, MA: George Stechert & Co., 1923.

———. *Folk-Lore of the Antilles, French and English: Part III.* New York: American Folk-Lore Society, 1943.

Pétis de la Croix, François. *Histoire de la Sultane de Perse et des Visirs. Contes Turcs.* Paris: 1707.

———. *Histoire de la Sultane de Perse et des Vizirs.* Ed. Raymonde Robert. Paris: Honoré Champion, 2006.

———. *The Persian and the Turkish Tales, Compleat.* Trans. William King. 2 vols. London: W. Mears and J. Browne, 1714. Reprint edited by Malcom Bosse. 2 vols. New York: Garland, 1972.

Petitôt, Emile. *Traditions Indiennes du Canada Nord-Ouest.* Paris: Maisonneuve Frères et C. Leclerc, 1886.

Philip, Neil, ed. *The Penguin Book of Scottish Folktales.* London: Penguin Books, 1991.

Pilk, Georg. "Die wendische Faust-Sage." *Bunte Bilder aus dem Sachsenlande,* 3 (1900): 191–201.

Ponti, James. *The Sorcerer's Apprentice.* New York: Disney Press, 2010.

Pourrat, Henri. *Le diable et ses diableries.* Ed. Claire Pourrat. Paris: Gallimard, 1977.

Pramberger, Romuald. *Märchen aus Steiermark.* Sekau: Verlag der Benediktinerabtei, 1935.

Preußler, Otfried. *Die kleine Hexe.* Stuttgart: Thienemann, 1952.

———. *Krabat.* Würzburg: Arena, 1971. Translated by Anthea Bell as *The Satanic Mill.* London: Abelard-Schuman, 1972.

Prineas, Sarah. *The Magic Thief.* Illustr. Antonio Javier Caparo. New York: HarperCollins, 2008.

———. *The Magic Thief Found.* Illustr. Antonio Javier Caparo. New York: HarperCollins, 2010.

———. *The Magic Thief Lost*. Illustr. Antonio Javier Caparo. New York: HarperCollins, 2009.

Radlov, Wilhelm. *Proben der Volksliteratur der türkischen Stämme Süd-Sibiriens*. St. Petersburg: 1868.

Ramanujan, A. K. *A Flowering Tree and Other Oral Tales from India*. With a preface by Stuart Blackburn and Alan Dundes. Berkeley: University of California Press, 1997.

Ransome, Arthur. *Old Peter's Russian Tales*. New York: Frederick A. Stokes, 1916.

Ritter, Hellmut, ed. *Das Meer der Seele. Mensch, Welt und Gott in den Geschichten des Farīduddīn 'Attār*. Leiden: Brill, 1955.

———. *The Ocean of the Soul: Man, the World and God in the Stories of Farīd al-Dīn 'Attār*. Trans. John O'Kane with Bernd Ratke. Leiden: Brill, 2003.

Rolland, Eugène, ed. *Recueil de Chansons Populaires*. 6 vols. Paris: Maisonneuve, 1883.

Rose, Elizabeth. *The Sorcerer's Apprentice*. Illustr. Gerald Rose. New York: Walker, 1966.

Rostron, Richard. *The Sorcerer's Apprentice*. Illustr. Frank Lieberman. New York: William Morrow, 1941.

Ryder, Arthur, ed. and trans. *The Panchatantra*. Chicago: University of Chicago Press, 1956.

———. *Twenty-two Goblins*. London: J. M. Dent & Sons, 1917.

Sastri, Pandit Sangendhi Mahalingam Natesa. *The Dravidian Nights Entertainments: Being a Translation of Madanakamarajankadai*. Madras, India: Excelsior Press, 1886.

———. *Folklore in Southern India*. I. Bombay: Education Society's Press, Byculla, 1884.

Saucier, Corinne, ed. *Folk Tales from French Louisiana*. Baton Rouge, LA: Claitor's Publishing Division, 1962.

Schiefner, Franz Anton von. *Tibetan Tales Derived from Indian Sources*. Trans. W.R.S. Ralston. London: Trübner, 1882.

Schönwerth, Franz Xaver von. *The Turnip Princess and Other Newly Discovered Fairy Tales*. Ed. Erika Eichenseer. Trans. Maria Tatar. New York: Penguin, 2015.

Schott, Arthur, and Albert Schott. *Walachische Märchen*. Stuttgart: J. G. Cotta, 1845.

Schreiber, Charlotte (Lady Charlotte Guest). *The Mabinogion*. London: Quaritch, 1877.

Schullerus, Pauline. *Rumänische Volksmärchen aus dem mittleren Harbachthat*. Hermannstadt: 1907.

Scott, Sir Walter. *The Poetical Works of Sir Walter Scott; containing Minstrelsy of the Scottish Border, Sir Tristrem, and Dramatic Pieces*. Paris: Baudry's European Library, 1838.

Seki, Keigo, ed. *Folktales of Japan*. Trans. Robert Adams. Chicago: University of Chicago Press, 1963.

Shafak, Elif. *The Architect's Apprentice*. London: Viking, 2014.

Shah, Tahir. *Sorcerer's Apprentice: To the Heart of Magical India*. London: Weidenfeld & Nicholson, 1998.

Sheykh-Zāda, *The History of the Forty Vezirs, or The Story of the Forty Morns and Eves*. Trans. Elias John Wilkinson Gibb. London: George Redway, 1886.

Sian-tek, Lim. *Folk Tales from China*. Illustr. William Arthur Smith. New York: John Day, 1944.

Simpson, William Kelly, ed. *The Literature of Ancient Egypt: An Anthology of Stories, Instructions, Stelae, Autobiographies, and Poetry*. New Haven, CT: Yale University Press, 2003.

Slizinski, Jerzy, ed. *Sorbische Volkserzählungen*. Berlin: Akademie-Verlag, 1964.

Somadeva, *Tales from the Kathāsaritsāgara*. Trans. Ashia Sattar. Foreword by Wendy Doniger. London: Penguin, 1994.

Spitta-Bey, Guillaume. *Contes arabes modernes*. Leiden: E. J. Brill, 1883.

Steel, Flora Annie. *Tales of the Punjab: Told by the People*. Illustr. J. Lockwood Kipling. London: Macmillan, 1894.

Stevermer, Caroline. *A Scholar of Magics*. New York: TOR, 1994.

Straparola, Giovan Francesco. *The Pleasant Nights*. Ed. Donald Beecher. 2 vols. Toronto: Donald Beecher, 2012.

Swynnerton, Charles. *The Adventures of the Panjáb Hero Rájá Rasálu and Other Folk-tales of the Panjáb*. Calcutta: W. Newman, 1884.

———. *Indian Nights' Entertainment, or, Folk-Tales from the Upper Indus*. London: Elliot Stock, 1892.

———. *Romantic Tales from the Panjáb*. Westminster: A. Constable, 1903.

Tawney, Charles Henry, ed. and trans. *The Kathákoca; or, Treasury of Stories*. London: Royal Asiatic Society, 1895.

Tawney, Charles Henry, trans. *The Ocean of Story* (Somadeva's *Kathā Sarti Sāgara*). Bengal: Asiatic Society of Bengal, 1880–84.

———. *The Ocean of Story*. Ed. N. M. Penzer. 10 vols. London: Chas. J. Sawyer, 1924.

Thomas, Rosemary Hyde, ed. *It's Good to Tell You: French Folktales from Missouri*. Illustr. Ronald Thomas. Columbia: University of Missouri Press, 1981.

Thorpe, Benjamin, ed. *Yule-Tide Stories: A Collection of Scandinavian and North German Popular Tales and Traditions*. London: Henry G. Bohn, 1853.

Tibbitts, Charles John, ed. *Folk-Lore and Legends: Oriental*. London and New York: White and Allen, 1892.

———. *Russian and Polish Folk-Lore and Legends*. London: W. W. Gibbings, 1890.

Tremearne, A.J.N. "Fifty Hausa Folk-Tales (Concluded). *Folklore* 22.4 (December 31, 1911): 457–73.

Ursu, Anne. *The Real Boy*. New York: HarperCollins, 2013.

Van Buitenen, Johannes Adrianus Bernardus. *Tales of Ancient India*. Chicago: University of Chicago Press, 1959.

Veckenstedt, Edmund. *Wendische Sagen, Märchen und abergläubische Gebräuche*. Graz: Leuschner und Lubensky, 1880.

Wardrop, Marjory. *Georgian Folk Tales*. London: David Nutt, 1894.

Weinreich, Beatrice Silverman, ed. *Yiddish Folktales*. Trans. Leonard Wolf. New York: Pantheon, 1988.

Wheeler, Howard. *Tales from Jalisco Mexico*. Philadelphia: American Folk-Lore Society, 1943.

White, T. H. *The Sword in the Stone*. London: Collins, 1938.

Wiedemann, Alfred. *Altägyptische Sagen und Märchen*. Leipzig: Deutsche Verlagsactiengesellschaft, 1906.

Wiener, Leo. "Di Majnse vin dem Pojps." *Mitteilungen der Gesellschaft für jüdische Volkskunde* 9.2 (1902): 104–7.

Willard, Nancy. *The Sorcerer's Apprentice*. Illustr. Leo and Diane Dillon. New York: Scholastic, 1993.

Williams, Michael. *A Sorcerer's Apprentice*. New York: Warner Books, 1990.

Winkler, Karl, ed. *Oberpfälzische Sagen, Legenden, Märchen und Schwänke*. Kallmünz: Michael Laßleben, 1935.

Wilson, Epiphanius, ed. *Turkish Literature*. Rev. ed. London: Colonial Press, 1901.

Woycicki, Kazimierz Wladyslaw. *Polnische Volkssagen und Märchen*. Trans. Friedrich Heinrich Lewestam. Berlin: Schlefinger'sche Buch- und Musikhandlung, 1839.

Zaunert, Paul, ed. *Deutsche Märchen aus dem Donaulande*. Jena: Eugen Diederichs, 1926.

Zipes, Jack, ed. and trans. *The Complete Fairy Tales of the Brothers Grimm*. New York: Bantam, 1987. Rev. 3rd ed. New York: Bantam, 2003.

———, ed. and trans. *Fairy Tales and Fables from Weimar Days*. Hanover, NH: University Press of New England, 1989.

———, ed. and trans. *The Original Folk and Fairy Tales of the Brothers Grimm: The Complete First Edition*. Princeton, NJ: Princeton University Press, 2014.

Zông, In-Sôb. *Folk Tales from Korea*. London: Routledge & Kegan Paul, 1952.

Zunser, Helen. "A New Mexican Village." *Journal of American Folklore* 18.188 (April–June 1935): 125–78.

CRITICISM

Anatol, Giselle Liza, ed. *Reading Harry Potter: Critical Essays*. Westport, CT: Praeger, 2003.

———. *Reading Harry Potter Again: New Critical Essays*. Santa Barbara, CA: ABC-CLIO, 2009.

Anderson, Graham. "Magicians and Their Allies." In *Fairytale in the Ancient World*. London: Routledge, 2000. 103–11.

Ankarloo, Bengt, and Stuart Clark, eds. *Witchcraft and Magic in Europe: Ancient Greece, and Rome*. Philadelphia: University of Pennsylvania Press, 1999.

Anttonen, Pertti. "Oral Traditions and the Making of the Finnish Nation." In *Folklore and Nationalism in Europe during the Long Nineteenth Century*. Ed. Timothy Baycroft and David Hopkin. Leiden: Brill, 2012. 325–50.

Ashliman, D. L. *A Guide to Folktales in the English Language: Based on the Aarne-Thompson Classification System*. Westport, CT: Greenwood Press, 1987.

Assmann, Aleida. *Cultural Memory and Western Civilization: Functions, Media, Archives*. Cambridge: Cambridge University Press, 2011.

Assmann, Jan. *Cultural Memory and Early Civilization: Writing, Remembrance, and Political Imagination*. Cambridge: Cambridge University Press, 2011.

Azzouni, Safia, and Uwe Wirth, eds. *Dilettanismus als Beruf*. Berlin: Kulturverlag Kadmos, 2010.

Baycroft, Timothy, and David Hopkin, eds. *Folklore and Nationalism in Europe during the Long Nineteenth Century*. Leiden: Brill, 2012.

Beavers, Herman. "The Pedagogy of Discomfort in *The Sorcerer's Apprentice*." In *Charles Johnson: The Novelist as Philosopher*. Ed. Marc Conner and William Nash. Jackson: University of Mississippi, 2007. 40–56.

Blackburn, Stuart. *Print, Folklore, and Nationalism in Colonial South India*. Delhi: Permanent Black, 2003.

Blécourt, Willem de. "Der Zauberer und sein Schüler: Die Erzählung und sein historischer Ursprung." In *Faszination des Okkulten: Diskurse zum Übersinnlichen*. Ed. Wolfgang Müller-Funk and Christa Agnes Tuczay. Tübingen: Francke, 2008. 43–72.

———. "Zauberer und Schüler." In *Enzyklopädie des Märchens*. Ed. Rolf Wilhelm Brednich. Vol. 14. Berlin: De Gruyter, 2014. 1165–68.

Bloch, Ernst. *The Utopian Function of Art and Literature: Selected Essays*. Trans. Jack Zipes and Frank Mecklenburg. Boston: MIT Press, 1988.

Bolte, Johannes, and Georg Polivka, eds. *Anmerkungen zu den Kinder- und Hausmärchen der Brüder Grimm*. Vol. II. Leipzig: Dieterische Verlagsbuchhandlung, 1915.

Boschung, Dietrich, and Jan Bremmer, eds. *The Materiality of Magic*. Paderborn: Wilhelm Fink, 2015.

Bowie, Andrew. *Adorno and the Ends of Philosophy*. London: Polity, 2013.

Briggs, Katharine, ed. *A Dictionary of British Folk-Tales in the English Language Incorporating the F. J. Norton Collection*. London: Routledge & Kegan Paul, 1970.

Bülow, Christopher von. "Mem." *Enzyklopädie Philosophie und Wissenschaftstheorie*. Ed. Jürgen Mittelstraß. 2nd ed. Vol. 5. Stuttgart: Metzler, 2013. 318–24.

Burke, Peter. *Languages and Communities in Early Modern Europe*. Cambridge: Cambridge University Press, 2004.

———. *Popular Culture in Early Modern Europe*. New York: Harper & Row, 1978.

Burkert, Walter. "Itinerant Diviners and Magicians: A Neglected Element in Cultural Contacts." In *The Greek Renaissance of the Eighth Century B.C.: Tradition and Innovation*. Ed. Robin Hägg. Stockholm: Paul Åströms Förlag, 1983. 115–19.

Cadonna, Alfredo, ed. *India, Tibet, China: Genesis and Aspects of Traditional Narrative*. Florence: Leo Olschki, 1999.

Catarella, Teresa. "The Study of the Orally Transmitted Ballad: Past Paradigms and a New Poetics." *Oral Tradition* 9.2 (1994): 468–78.

Christiansen, Reidar Th. *The Migratory Legends: A Proposed List of Types with a Systematic Catalogue of the Norwegian Variants*. FFCommunications 175. Helsinki: Suomalainen Tiedeakatemia, 1958.

Cloud, Daniel. *The Domestication of Language: Cultural Evolution and the Uniqueness of the Human Animal*. New York: Columbia University Press, 2015.

Collingwood, Robin George. *The Philosophy of Enchantment: Studies in Folktale, Cultural Criticism, and Anthropology*. Ed. David Boucher, Wendy James, and Philip Smallwood. Oxford: Clarendon Press, 2005.

Conner, Marc, and William Nash, eds. *Charles Johnson: The Novelist as Philosopher*. Jackson: University of Mississippi, 2007.

Copenhaver, Brian. *Magic in Western Culture: From Antiquity to the Enlightenment*. Cambridge: Cambridge University Press, 2015.

Cosquin, Emmanuel. "Les Mongols et leur pretendu rôle dans la transmission des contes indiens vers l'occident européen: étude de folk-lore comparé sur l'introduction du 'Siddhi-kur' et le conte du 'Magicien et son apprenti.'" *Revue des traditions Populaire* 27 (1912): 336–73, 393–430, 497–526, 545–66.

Coyle, Lauren. "Retracing Hegel in Adorno's *Negative Dialectics* and Related Lectures." *Telos* 155 (Summer 2011): 39–60.

Culhane, John. "The Sorcerer's Apprentice." In *Walt Disney's Fantasia*. New York: Harry Abrams, 1983. 78–105.

Cutolo, Raffaele. *Into the Woods of Wicked Wonderland: Musicals Revise Fairy Tales*. Heidelberg: Universitätsverlag Winter, 2014.

Debruge, Peter. "Film Review: 'The Boy and the Beast.'" *Variety*, 2015. http://variety.com/2015 /film/reviews/the-boy-and-the-beast-film-review-1201601172/.

Defrance, Anne, and Jean-François Perrin, eds. *Le conte en ses paroles: La figuration de l'oralité dans le conte merveilleux du Classicisme aux Lumières*. Paris: Éditions Desjonquères, 2007.

Delbanco, Andrew. *College: What It Was, Is, and Should Be*. Princeton, NJ: Princeton University Press, 2012.

———. "Our Universities: The Outrageous Reality." *New York Review of Books* (July 9, 2015): 38–41.

Dennett, Daniel. "The Cultural Evolution of Words and Other Thinking Tools." In *Cold Spring Harbor Symposia on Quantitative Biology*. Vol. 74. Woodbury, NY: Cold Spring Laboratory Press, 2010. 435–41. symposium.chip.org.

———. *Intuition Pumps and Other Tools for Thinking*, New York: Norton, 2013.

———. "The New Replicators." In *The Encyclopedia of Evolution*. Ed. Mark Pagel. Oxford: Oxford University Press, 2002. 169–92.

Deresiewicz, William. "The Neoliberal Arts: How College Sold Its Soul to the Market." *Harper's Magazine* (September 2015): 25–32.

Drout, Michael. *Of Sorcerers and Men: Tolkien and the Roots of Modern Fantasy Literature*. New York: Barnes & Noble, 2006.

During, Simon. *Modern Enchantments: The Cultural Power of Secular Magic*. Cambridge, MA: Harvard University Press, 2004.

Ehrhardt, Marie-Luise. *Die Krabat-Sage: Quellenkundliche Untersuchung zur Überlieferung und Wirkung eines literarischen Stoffes aus der Lausitz*. Marburg: N. G. Elwert, 1982.

Erll, Astrid. *Memory in Culture*. Trans. Sara Young. New York: Palgrave, 2011.

Erll, Astrid, and Ansgar Nünning, eds. *A Companion to Memory Studies*. Berlin: DeGruyter, 2010.

Fantham, Elaine. "Sunt quibus in plures ius est transire figuras: Ovid's Self-Transformers in the 'Metamorphoses.'" *Classical World* 87.2 (November–December 1993): 21–36.

Farr, James. *Artisans in Europe, 1300–1914*. Cambridge: Cambridge University Press, 2000.

Flint, Valerie. *The Rise of Magic in Early Medieval Europe*. Princeton, NJ: Princeton University Press, 1991.

Forsdyke, Sara. *Slaves Tell Tales and Other Episodes in the Politics of Popular Culture*. Princeton, NJ: Princeton University Press, 2012.

Frangoulidis, Stavros. *Witches, Isis and Narrative: Approaches to Magic in Apuleius' Metamorphosis*. Berlin: Walter de Gruyter, 2008.

Freund, Winfried, and Walburga Freund-Spork. *Otfried Preußler: Krabat*. Stuttgart: Philipp Reclam, 2012.

Gabler, Neal. *Walt Disney: The Triumph of the American Imagination*. New York: Random House, 2006.

Gallardo-C., Ximena, and C. Jason Smith, "Cinderfella: J. K. Rowling's Wily Web of Gender." In *Reading Harry Potter: Critical Essays*. Ed. Giselle Liza Anatol. Westport, CT: Praeger, 2003. 191–205.

Graf, Fritz. *Magic in the Ancient World*. Trans. Franklin Philip. Cambridge, MA: Harvard University Press, 1997.

Hägg, Robin, ed. *The Greek Renaissance of the Eighth Century B.C.: Tradition and Innovation*. Stockholm: Paul Åströms Förlag, 1983.

Halliday, W. R. "The Force of Initiative in Magical Conflict." *Folklore* 21.2 (June 1910): 147–67.

———. *Indo-European Folk-Tales and Greek Legend*. Cambridge: Cambridge University Press, 1933.

Hansen, William. "Apprentice and Ghost: Eukrates and the Automaton." *Ariadne's Thread: A Guide to International Tales Found in Classical Literature*. Ithaca, NY: Cornell University Press, 2002. 35–38.

Hegel, Georg Wilhelm Friedrich. *Phenomenology of Spirit*. Foreword by J. N. Findlay. Trans. A. V. Miller. Oxford: Oxford University Press, 1977.

———. *Sämtliche Werke*. Ed. Hermann Glockner. Vol. 7, *Grundlinien der Philosophie des Rechts*. Stuttgart: Fromann, 1917.

Heylighen, Francis, and Klaas Chielens. "Evolution of Culture, Memetics." In *Encyclopedia of Complexity and Systems Science*. Ed. Robert Meyers. New York: Springer, 2009. 3205–20.

His, Maria. "Die magische Flucht und das Wettverwandeln." *Archives Suisses des Traditions populaires* 30.1 (1930): 107–29.

Holden, Stephen. "New Tricks." *New York Times* (December 31, 1999). http://www.nytimes.com/movie/review?res=9802E0D81538F932A05751C1A96F958260.

Hopkins, Lisa. "Harry Potter and the Acquisition of Knowledge." In *Reading Harry Potter: Critical Essays*. Ed. Giselle Liza Anatol. Westport, CT: Praeger, 2003. 25–34.

Hose, Susanne. *Erzählen über Krabat: Märchen, Mythos und Magie*. Bautzen: Lusatia Verlag, 2013.

———. "Krabat und die Erzählforschung. Eine Diskursbetrachtung." In *Krabat—Aspekte einer sorbischen Sage*. Ed. Martin Neumann. Potsdam: Zentrum für Lehrerausbildung an der Universität Potsdam, 2008. 47–59.

Howe, Katherine, ed. *The Penguin Book of Witches*. New York: Penguin Books, 2014.

Irving, Paul C. Forbes. *Metamorphosis in Greek Mythology*. Oxford: Oxford University Press, 1990.

Irwin, Robert. *The Arabian Nights: A Companion*. London: Allan Lane, 1994.

———. "Night Classics." *Times Literary Supplement* (April 17, 2015): 12–13.

James, Wendy. "A Fieldworker's Philosopher: Perspectives from Anthropology." In Robin George Collingwood, *The Philosophy of Enchantment: Studies in Folktale, Criticism, and Anthropology*. Ed. David Boucher, Wendy James, and Philip Smallwood. Oxford: Clarendon Press, 2005. lvi–xci.

Jenkins, Henry. "'It's Not a Fairy Tale Anymore': Gender, Genre, *Beauty and the Beast*." In *Textual Pachers: Television Fans & Participatory Culture*. New York: Routledge, 1992. 120–51.

Kalitan, Damian. "In Search of The Sorcerer's Apprentice: Between Lucian and Walt Disney." *Journal of Education, Culture and Society* 1 (2012): 94–101.

Kaschewsky, Rudolf. "Siddhi Kür." In *Enzyklopädie des Märchens*. Ed. Rolf Wilhelm Brednich. Vol. 12. Berlin: Walter de Gruyter, 2007. 638–42.

Kline, George. "The Existentialist Rediscovery of Hegel and Marx." In *Phenomenology and Existentialism*. Ed. Edward Lee and Maurice Mandelbaum. Baltimore, MD: Johns Hopkins University Press, 1967. 113–38.

Kojève, Alexandre. *Introduction to the Reading of Hegel: Lectures on* The Phenomenology of Spirit. Ed. Allan Bloom. Trans. James Nichols Jr. New York: Basic Books, 1969.

Kroll-Zaidi, Rafil. "New Movies." *Harper's Magazine* (January 2016): 83–88.

Labbie, Erin Felicia. "The Sorcerer's Apprentice: Animation and Alchemy in Disney's Medievalism." In *The Disney Middle Ages: A Fairy-Tale and Fantasy Past*. Ed. Tison Pugh and Susan Lynn Aronstein. New York: Palgrave Macmillan, 2012. 97–115.

Landa, Ishay. *The Apprentice's Sorcerer: Liberal Tradition and Fascism*. Leiden: Brill, 2010.

Landy, Joshua, and Michael Saler, eds. *The Re-Enchantment of the World: Secular Magic in a Rational Age*. Stanford, CA: Stanford University Press, 2009.

Lawson, John Cuthbert. *Modern Greek Folklore and Ancient Greek Religion*. Cambridge: University of Cambridge Press, 1910.

Lee, Edward, and Maurice Mandelbaum, eds. *Phenomenology and Existentialism*. Baltimore, MD: Johns Hopkins University Press, 1967.

Le Guin, Ursula. "Gedo Senki. A First Response." (August 15, 2006). http://www.ursulakleguin .com/GedoSenkiResponse.html.

———. "A Whitewashed Earthsea." *Slate* (December 16, 2004). http://www.slate.com/articles /arts/culturebox/2004/12/a_whitewashed_earthsea.html.

Levi, Eliphas. *The History of Magic* [1860]. Trans. A. E. Waite. Glastonbury, UK: Lost Library, 1999.

Lindow, John. *Trolls: An Unnatural History*. London: Reaktion Books, 2014.

Lörincz, L. "Les 'Contes du cadavre ensorcelé (Ro-Scrun) dans la littérature et le folklore tibétains." *Acta Orientalia Academiae Scientarum Hungaricae* 18 (1965): 305–16.

Luck, George. *Arcania Mundi: Magic and the Occult in the Greek and Roman Worlds*. Baltimore, MD: Johns Hopkins University Press, 1985.

———. "Witches and Sorcerers in Classical Literature." In *Witchcraft and Magic in Europe: Ancient Greece and Rome*. Ed. Bengt Ankarloo and Stuart Clark. Philadelphia: University of Pennsylvania Press, 1999. 91–159.

Maggi, Armando. *Preserving the Spell: Basile's "The Tale of Tales" and Its Afterlife in the Fairy-Tale Tradition*. Chicago: University of Chicago Press, 2015.

Martino, Ernesto de. *Magic: A Theory from the South*. Trans. Dorothy Louise Zinn. Chicago: Hau Books, 2015.

———. *Primitive Magic: The Psychic Powers of Shamans and Sorcerers*. Bridport, Dorset: Prism Press, 1988.

Marzolph, Ulrich, and Richard van Leeuwen, eds. *The Arabian Nights Encyclopedia*. 2 vols. Santa Barbara, CA: ABC-CLIO, 2004.

———. "The Good, the Bad and the Beautiful: The Survival of Ancient Iranian Ethical Concepts in Persian Popular Narratives of the Islamic Period." In *Early Islamic Iran*. Ed. Edmund Herzig and Sarah Stewart. London: I. B. Tauris, 2012. 16–29.

Mauss, Marcel. *A General Theory of Magic*. Trans. Robert Brain. London: Routledge & Kegan Paul, 1972.

"Memetics." From Wikipedia, the free encyclopedia, https://en.wikipedia.org/wiki/Memetics.

Mettler, Suzanne. *Degrees of Inequality: How the Politics of Higher Education Sabotaged the American Dream*. New York: Basic Books, 2014.

Müller-Funk, Wolfgang, and Christa Agnes Tuczay, eds. *Faszination des Okkulten: Diskurse zum Übersinnlichen*. Tübingen: Francke, 2008.

Nedo, Paul. "Krabat: Zur Entstehung einer sorbischen Volkserzählung." *Deutsches Jahrbuch für Volkskunde* 2 (1956): 33–50.

Neumann, Martin, ed. *Krabat—Aspekte einer sorbischen Sage*. Potsdam: Zentrum für Lehrerausbildung an der Universität Potsdam, 2008.

Nikolajeva, Maria. "Do We Feel Sorry for the Older Brothers? Exploring Empathy and Ethics in Fairy Tales through Cognitive Poetics." In *Cambridge Companion to Fairy Tales*. Ed. Maria Tatar. Cambridge: Cambridge University Press, 2015. 134–49.

Ogden, Daniel. "Eucrates and Demainete: Lucian, 'Philopseudes.'" *Classical Quarterly* 54.2 (2004): 484–93.

———. *In Search of the Sorcerer's Apprentice: The Traditional Tales of Lucian's Lover of Lies*. Swansea: Classical Press of Wales, 2007.

Ormand, Kirk. "Marriage, Identity, and the Tale of Mestra in the Hesiodic Catalogue of Women." *American Journal of Philology* 125.3 (Autumn 2004): 303–38.

Osmond, Andrew. "The Sorcerer's Apprentice." Review of *The Sorcerer's Apprentice*, directed by Jon Turteltaub. *Sight and Sound* 20.10 (2010): 72.

Ostry, Elaine. "Accepting Mudbloods: The Ambivalent Social Vision of J. K. Rowling's Fairy Tales." In *Reading Harry Potter: Critical Essays*. Ed. Giselle Liza Anatol. Westport, CT: Praeger, 2003. 89–102.

Otto, Bernd-Christian. *Magie: Rezeptions- und diskursgeschichtliche Analysen von der Antike bis zur Neuzeit*. Berlin: De Gruyter, 2011.

Otto, Bernd-Christian, and Michael Stausberg, eds. *Defining Magic: A Reader*. Sheffield, UK: Equinox Publishing, 2013.

Oziewicz, Marek. *Justice in Young Adult Speculative Fiction: A Cognitive Reading*. New York: Routledge, 2015.

Phelps, Edmund. "What Is Wrong with the West's Economies?" *New York Review of Books* (August 13, 2015): 54–56.

Pugh, Tison, and Susan Aronstein, eds. *The Disney Middle Ages: A Fairy-Tale and Fantasy Past*. New York: Palgrave Macmillan, 2012.

Purkis, Diane. "Enchanting." *Times Literary Supplement* (February 12, 2016): 5.

Rangwala, Shama. "A Marxist Inquiry into J. K. Rowling's Harry Potter Series." In *Reading Harry Potter Again: New Critical Essays*. Ed. Giselle Liza Anatol. Santa Barbara, CA: Praeger, 2009. 127–42.

Ranke, Kurt, and Rolf Wilhelm Brednich, eds. *Enzyklopädie des Märchens*. 14 vols. Berlin: De Gruyter, 1975–2014.

Richter, Karin, and Bärbel Schwenk-Kories. *Krabat und die Schwarze Mühle: Die sorbische Sage im literarischen, ethnischen, historischen und medialien Kontext*. Baltmannsweiler: Schneider Verlag, 2010.

Riva, Raffaella. "The Tales of the Bewitched Corpse: A Literary Journey from India to China." In *India, Tibet, China: Genesis and Aspects of Traditional Narrative*. Ed. Alfredo Cadonna. Florence: Leo Olschki, 1999. 229–56.

Robert, Raymonde. "Le Contes et la Rhétorique Judiciaire: L'Histoire de la Sultane de Perse et des Vizirs de Pétis de la Croix (1707)." In *Le conte en ses paroles: La figuration de l'oralité dans le conte merveilleux du Classicisme aux Lumières*. Ed. Anne De France and Jean-François Perrin. Paris: Éditions Desjonquères, 2007. 122–37.

Robertson, Noel. "The Ritual Background of the Erysichthon Story." *American Journal of Philology* 105.4 (Winter 1984): 369–408.

Roth, Michael. *Knowing and History: Appropriations of Hegel in Twentieth-Century France*. Ithaca, NY: Cornell University Press, 1988.

Rubini, Luisa. "Italy: A History between Translations, Chapbooks and Fairy Tales." *Fabula* 44.1/2 (2003): 25–54.

Salzberg, Rosa. *Ephemeral City: Cheap Print and Urban Culture in Renaissance Venice*. Manchester, UK: University of Manchester Press, 2014.

———. "In the Mouths of Charlatans: Street Performers and the Dissemination of Pamphlets in Renaissance Italy." *Renaissance Studies* 24.5 (2010): 638–53.

Salzberg, Rosa, and Massimo Rospocher. "Street Singers in Italian Renaissance Urban Culture and Communication." *Cultural and Social History* 9.1 (2012): 9–26.

Sammond, Nicholas. *Babes in Tomorrowland: Walt Disney and the Making of the American Child, 1930–1960*. Durham, NC: Duke University Press, 2005.

Sandel, Tony. "Strong at the Heart: The Sexual Abuse of Boys in Literature." http://www.strongattheheart.com/the-sexual-abuse-of-boys-in-literature-by-tonysandel/.

Šarakšinova, Nadežda. "Les Contes du cadavre ensorcelé chez les Bouriates." *Acta Orientalia Academia Scientiarum Hungaricae* 16 (1963): 45–54.

Sharp, Cyril. *English Folk Songs*. London: Novello, 1920.

———. *English Folk Songs from the Southern Appalachian*. New York and London: G. P. Putnam's Sons, 1917.

———. *One Hundred English Folksongs*. Philadelphia: Oliver Ditson, 1916.

Shen, Qina. *The Politics of Magic: DEFA Fairy-Tale Films*. Detroit: Wayne State University Press, 2015.

Shifman, Limor. *Memes in Digital Culture*. Cambridge, MA: MIT Press, 2014.

Shuster, Martin. *Austonomy after Auschwitz: Adorno, German Idealism, and Modernity*. Chicago: University of Chicago Press, 2014.

Sircar, Sanjay. "E. Nesbit's 'The Magician's Heart,' New Comedy and the Burlesque Kunstmächen." *Merveilles & Contes* 9.1 (1995): 5–25.

———. "One Tale for Four and New Morals for Old: The Construction and Themes of E. Nesbit's 'The Magician's Heart.'" *Folklore* 22 (2002): 7–32.

Smallwood, Philip. "The Re-Enactment of Self: Perspectives from Literature, Criticism, and Culture." In Robin George Collingwood, *The Philosophy of Enchantment: Studies in Folktale, Cultural Criticism, and Anthropology.* Ed. David Boucher, Wendy James, and Philip Smallwood. Oxford: Clarendon Press, 2005. xxii–lv.

Stone, Linda, and Paul Lurquin. *Genes, Culture, and Human Evolution: A Synthesis.* Intro. Luigi Luca Cavalli-Sforza. Oxford: Blackwell, 2007.

Styers, Randall. "Magic." In *Vocabulary for the Study of Religion.* Ed. Robert Segal and Koku von Stuckrad. Leiden: Brill, 2015. http://referenceworks.brillonline.com/entries/vocabulary-for-the-study-of religion/magic-COM_00000154.

———. "Magic and the Play of Power." In *Defining Magic: A Reader.* Ed. Bernd-Christian Otto and Michael Stausberg. Sheffield, UK: Equinox Publishing, 2013. 255–62.

———. *Making Magic: Religion, Magic, and Science in the Modern World.* Oxford: Oxford University Press, 2004.

Thomas, Keith. *Religion and the Decline of Magic: Studies in Popular Beliefs in Sixteenth and Seventeenth Century England.* London: Weidenfeld and Nicolson, 1971.

Thompson, Stith. *The Folktale.* New York: Holt, Rinehart and Winston, 1946.

Timbers, Frances. *Magic and Masculinity: Ritual Magic and Gender in the Early Modern Era.* London: I. B. Tauris, 2014.

Uther, Hans-Jörg. "The Magician and His Pupil" (ATU 325). In *The Types of International Folktales: A Classification and Bibliography.* Vol. 1. Helsinki: Academia Scientiarum Fennica, 2004. 207–9.

Warner, Marina. *Phantasmagoria: Spirit Visions, Metaphors, and Media into the Twenty-first Century.* Oxford: Oxford University Press, 2006.

———. *Stranger Magic: Charmed States and the Arabian Nights.* Cambridge, MA: Harvard University Press, 2012.

Watts, Steven. *The Magic Kingdom: Walt Disney and the American Way of Life.* Boston: Houghton Mifflin, 1997.

Wirth, Uwe. "Dilettantische Konjekturen." In *Dilettanismus als Beruf.* Ed. Sofia Azzouni and Uwe Wirth. Berlin: Kulturverlag Kadmos, 2010. 11–30.

Würzbach, Natascha. *The Rise of the English Street Ballad, 1550–1650.* Trans. Gayna Walls. Cambridge: Cambridge University Press, 1990.

Young-Bruehl, Elisabeth. *Childism: Confronting Prejudice against Children.* New Haven, CT: Yale University Press, 2012.

Zipes, Jack. *Grimm Legacies: The Magic Power of the Grimms' Folk and Fairy Tales.* Princeton, NJ: Princeton University Press, 2014.

———. *The Irresistible Fairy Tale: The Cultural and Social Evolution of a Genre.* Princeton, NJ: Princeton University Press, 2012.

———. *Why Fairy Tales Stick: The Evolution and Relevance of a Genre.* New York: Routledge, 2006.

Zumeta, William, David Breneman, Patrick Callan, and Joni Finney. *Financing American Higher Education in the Era of Globalization.* Cambridge, MA: Harvard Education Press, 2012.

Zvelebil, Kamil Veith. "Drawidisches Erzählgut." In *Enzyklopädie des Märchens.* Ed. Kurt Ranke. Vol. 3. Berlin: Walter de Gruyter, 1999. 842–51.

Selected and Chronological List of Sorcerer's Apprentice Tales

This extensive list includes works in this volume and others that, due to space, could not be included. The number of tales is even greater than indicated here.

Ovid, "Erysichthon and Mestra" (8 CE)
Metamorphoses. Trans. Brookes Moore. Boston: Cornhill Publishing, 1922.

Gaston Maspero, "The Veritable History of Satni-Khamois and His Son Senosiris" (46–47 CE)
"L'Histoire véritable de Satni-Khamois e son fils Senosiiris." In *Les contes populaires de l'Égypte ancienne*. Paris: Maisonneuve, 1882.
Popular Stories of Ancient Egypt. London: H. Grevel, 1915.
Popular Stories of Ancient Egypt. Ed. Hasan El-Shamy, Santa Barbara, CA: ABC-CLIO, 2002.

Lucian of Samosata, "Eucrates and Pancrates" (ca. 170 CE)
The Lover of Lies, or The Doubter. In *The Works of Lucian*. Trans. A. M. Harmon. Vol. 3. London: William Heinemann, 1921.

Somadeva, "The Youth Who Went through the Proper Ceremonies. Why Did He Fail to Win the Magic Spell?" (ca. 11th century CE)
Arthur W. Ryder, trans. *The Twenty-Two Goblins*. London. J. M. Dent & Sons, 1917.

Somadeva, "The Story of Nischayadatta" (ca. 1070)
Charles Henry Tawney, trans. *The Ocean of Story* (Somadeva's *Kathā Sarti Sāgara*). Bengal: Asiatic Society of Bengal, 1880–84.

Farīd al-Dīn 'Attār, "The Magician's Apprentice" (ca. 1220)
Hellmut Ritter. *The Ocean of the Soul: Man, the World and God in the Stories of Farīd al-Dīn 'Attār*. Trans. John O'Kane with Bernd Ratke. Leiden: Brill, 2003.

François Pétis de la Croix, "The Story of the Brahmin Padmanaba and the Young Hassan" (1707)
"Histoire du Brachmane Padmanaba et du jeune Fyquaï." *Histoire de la Sultane de Perse et des Visirs. Contes Turcs*. Paris: 1707.

Giovan Francesco Straparola, "Maestro Lattanzio" (1553)
"Maestro Lattanzio sarto ammaestra Dionigi suo scolare; ed egli poco impara l'arte che gl'insegna, ma ben quella' sarto teneva ascosa. Nasce odio tra loro, e finalmente Dionigi

lo divora, e Violante figliuola del re per moglie prende." In *Le Piacevoli Notti*. 2 vols. Venice: Comin da Trino, 1550/53.

Eustache Le Noble, "The Apprentice Magician" (1700)
"L'Apprenti magicien." In *Le Gage touché, histoires galantes*. Amsterdam: Jacques Desbordes, 1700.

Johann Wolfgang von Goethe, "The Pupil in Magic" (1798); also known as "The Sorcerer's Apprentice"
"Der Zauberlehrling." In *Musen-Almanach für das Jahr 1798*. Ed. Friedrich Schiller. Tübingen: J. G. Cotta, 1798.

Robert Southey, "Cornelius Agrippa's Bloody Book" (1801)
Matthew G. Lewis, ed. *Tales of Wonder*. Vol. 1. London: Bulmer, 1801.

Jacob and Wilhelm Grimm, "The Nimble Thief and His Master" (1819)
"De Gaudeif an sien Meester," *Kinder- und Haus-Märchen. Gesammelt durch die Brüder Grimm*. 2 vols. Berlin: G. Reimer, 1819.

Sir Walter Scott, "The Last Exorciser" (1838)
The Poetical Works of Sir Walter Scott; containing Minstrelsy of the Scottish Border, Sir Tristrem, and Dramatic Pieces. Paris: Baudry's European Library, 1838.

Kazimierz Wladyslaw Woycicki, "The Sorcerer and His Pupil" (1839)
"Der Hexenmeister und sein Lehrling." *Polnische Volkssagen und Märchen*. Trans. Friedrich Heinrich Lewestam. Berlin: Schlefinger'sche Buch- und Musikhandlung, 1839.

Arthur and Albert Schott, "The Devil and His Pupil" (1845)
"Der Teufel und sein Schüler." *Walachische Märchen*. Stuttgart: J. G. Cotta, 1845.

Bernhard Baader, "Magic Book" (1851)
"Zauberbuch." *Volkssagen aus dem Lande Baden und den angrenzenden Gegenden*. Karlsruhe: Verlag der Herder'schen Buchhandlung, 1851.

Benjamin Thorpe, "The Magician's Pupil" (1853)
Yule-Tide Stories: A Collection of Scandinavian and North German Popular Tales and Traditions from the Swedish, German, and Danish. London: Henry G. Bohn, 1853.

Heinrich Pröhle, "The Magic Combat" (1854)
"Zauber-Wettkampf." *Märchen für die Jugend*. Halle: Verlag der Buchhandlung des Waisenhauses, 1854.

Wuk Stephanowitsche Karadschitsch, "Der Teufel und sein Lehrjunge" (1854)
Volksmärchen der Serben. Trans. Wilhelmine Karadschitsch. Berlin: Georg Reimer, 1854.

Ludwig Bechstein, "The Magic Combat" (1857)
"Der Zauber-Wettkampf." *Deutsches Märchenbuch*. Leipzig: Linschmann, 1845.

John F. Campbell, "The Master and His Man" (1862) and "The Master and His Pupil" (1862)
Popular Tales of the West Highlands. Vol. 3. Edinburgh: Edmonston and Douglas, 1862.

Matija Ravnikar, "The Wizard's Apprentice" (1860)
Monika Kropej, Zmago Šmitek, and Roberto Dapit, eds. *A Treasury of Slovenian Folklore.* Trans. Barbara Kerr and Joan Meade. Radvovljica: Didakta, 2010.

Jón Arnason, "The Black School" (1864)
Icelandic Legends. Trans. George Powell and Eiríkur Magnússon. London: Richard Bentley, 1864.

Johann Georg von Hahn, "The Teacher and His Pupil" (1864)
"Der Lehrer und sein Schüler." *Griechische und albanesische Märchen.* Vol. 2. Leipzig: W. Engelmann, 1864.

Sabine Baring-Gould, "The Master and His Pupil" (1866)
William Henderson. *Notes on the Folklore of the Northern Counties of England and the Borders.* London: Longmans, Green, 1866. With an appendix on *Household Stories* by Sabine Baring-Gould.

Rachel Harriette Busk, "The Saga of the Well-and-Wise-Walking Khan" (1873)
Sagas from the Far East; or, Kalmouk and Mongolian Traditionary Tales. London: Griffith and Farran, 1873.

Csedomille Mijatovies, "The Bitter Bit" (1874)
Serbian Folk-Lore. Ed. Rev. W. Denton, London: W. Isbister, 1874.

John Naaké, "The Book of Magic" (1874)
Slavonic Fairy Tales: Collected and Translated from the Russian, Polish, Serbian, and Bohemian. London: Henry S. King, 1874.

Domenico Comparetti, " Oh, Relief!" (1875)
"Bene mio." *Novelline popolari italiene.* Bologna: Forni, 1875.

Giuseppe Pitrè, "The Tuft of Wild Beet" (1875)
"La troffa di la razza." *Fiabe, novelle e racconti popolari siciliani.* 4 vols. Palermo: Lauriel, 1875.

Charlotte Schreiber, "Taliesin" (1877)
Charlotte Schreiber (Lady Charlotte Guest). *The Mabinogion.* London: Quaritch, 1877.

Edmund Veckenstedt, "The Sorcerer's Apprentice I" and "The Sorcerer's Apprentice II" (1880)
"Der Zauberlehrling I" and "Der Zauberlehrliung II." *Wendische Sagen, Märchen und Abergläubische Gebräuche.* Graz: Leuschner und Luebensky, 1880.

Josef Haltrich, "The Arch-Sorcerer and His Servant" (1882)
"Der Erzzauberer und sein Diener." *Deutsche Volksmärchen aus dem Sachsenlande in Siebenbürgen.* Vienna: Carl Graser, 1882.

Gaston Maspero, "The Veritable History of Satni-Khamois and His Son Senosiris" (1882)
"L'Histoire véritable de Satni-Khamois et son fils Senosiris." *Les contes populaires de l'Égypte ancienne.* Paris: Maisonneuve, 1882.

Franz Anton von Schiefner, "The Magician's Pupil" (1882)
Tibetan Tales Derived from Indian Sources. Trans. W.R.S. Ralston. London: Trübner, 1882.

Guillaume Spitta-Bey, "The Story of Clever Mohammed" (1883)
"Histoire de Mohammed l'Avisé." *Contes arabes modernes.* Leiden: E. J. Brill, 1883.

Alfred Cooper Fryer, "The Master and His Pupil; or, The Magic Book" (1884)
Book of English Fairy Tales from the North-Country. London: W. Swan Sonnenschein, 1884.

Adolpho Francisco Coelho, "The Magician's Servant" (1885)
Tales of Old Lusitania, from the Folklore of Portugal. Trans. Henriette Monteiro. London: Sonnenschein Ywan, 1885.

François-Marie Luzel, "The Magician and His Servant" (1885)
"Le magicien et son valet." *Bulletin de la Societé Archéologique du Finistère* (1885).

Richard Burton, "The Second Kalendar's Story" (1885–86)
The Book of the Thousand Nights and a Night: A Plain and Literal Translation of the Arabian Nights Entertainment. 10 vols. Stoke Newington, UK: Kamashastra Society, 1885–86.

S. M. Natesa Sastri, "The Deceiver Shall Be Deceived" (1886)
Pandit S. M. Natesa Sastri. *The Dravidian Nights Entertainments: Being a Translation of Madanakamarajankadai.* Madras, India: Excelsior Press, 1886.

Sheykh-Zāda, "The Lady's Fifth Story" (1886)
Sheykh-Zāda. *The History of the Forty Vezirs, or The Story of the Forty Morns and Eves.* Trans. Elias John Wilkinson Gibb. London: George Redway, 1886.

Franz Xaver von Schönwerth, "The Sorcerer's Apprentice" (ca. 1886)
"Der Zauberlehrling." *Oberpfälzische Sagen, Legenden, Märchen und Schwänke.* Ed. Karl Winkler. Kallmünz: Michael Laßleben, 1935.

George Webbe Dasent, "Farmer Weathersky" (1888)
Popular Tales from the Norse. Edinburgh: David Douglas, 1888.

Edith Hodgetts, "The Blacksmith and the Devil" (1890)
Tales and Legends from the Land of the Tzar: Collection of Russian Stories. London: Griffith Farran, 1890.

Edith Hodgetts, "The Wonderful Trade" (1890)
Tales and Legends from the Land of the Tzar: Collection of Russian Stories. London: Griffith Farran, 1890.

Charles Swynnerton, "The Story of the Merchant and the Brahmin" (1892)
Indian Nights' Entertainment, or, Folk-Tales from the Upper Indus. London: Elliot Stock, 1892.

Robert Nisbet Bain, "Oh: The Tsar of the Forest" (1894)
Cossack Fairy Tales. Illustr. C. W. Mitchell. London: Lawrence & Bullen, 1894.

Flora Annie Steel, "Sir Buzz" (1894)
Tales of the Punjab: Told by the People. Illustr. J. Lockwood Kipling. London: Macmillan, 1894.

Marjory Wardrop, "Master and Pupil, or The Devil Outwitted" (1894)
Georgian Folk Tales. London: David Nutt, 1894.

Lucy Garnett, "The Negro; or, The Red Water" (1896)
Greek Folk Poesy. London: David Nutt, 1896.

Adolphe Orain, "The Transformations" (1901)
"Les Metamorphoses." *Contes de L'ille-et-Vilaine.* Paris: G. P. Maisonneuve & Larose, 1901.

Leo Wiener, "The Story about the Sorcerer" (1902)
"Di Majnse vin dem Pojps." *Mitteilungen der Gesellschaft für jüdische Volkskunde* 9.2 (1902): 104–7. See the translation "The Sorcerer's Apprentice." In *Yiddish Folktales.* Ed. Beatrice Silverman Weinreich. Trans. Leonard Wolf. New York: Pantheon, 1988.

Joseph Charles Mardrus, "The Twelfth Captain's Tale" (ca. 1904)
"Le conte deuxième du capitaine." *Le Livre des mille nuits et une nuit.* Vol. 16. Paris: Éditions de la Revue Blanche, 1889–1904.

Fletcher Gardner, "The Battle of the Enchanters" (1907)
"Tagalog Folk-Tales. II." *Journal of American Folklore.* 20.79 (October–December 1907): 300–310.

Peter Buchan, "The Black King of Morocco" (1908)
Ancient Scottish Tales. Intro. John Fairley. Peterhead, UK: 1908.

Cecil Henry Bompas, "The Boy Who Learnt Magic" (1909)
Folklore of the Santal Parganas. London: David Nutt, 1909.

Achille Millien, "The Magician's Apprentice" (1909)
"L'Apprenti Magicien." *Paris-Centre* (January 29, 1909).

Henry Parker, "The Teacher and His Pupil" (1910)
Henry Parker, ed. and trans. *Village Folk-Tales of Ceylon.* 3 vols. London: Luzac, 1910. See vol. 2.

A.J.N. Tremearne, "How the Hunter Was Hunted" (1911)
"Fifty Hausa Folk-Tales (Concluded)." *Folklore* 22.4 (December 31, 1911): 457–58.

Ignácz Kúnos, "The Wizard and His Pupil" (1913)
Forty-four Turkish Fairy Tales. Illustr. Willy Pogány. London: Harrap, 1913.

John Francis Campbell of Islay, "The Wizard's Gillie" (1914)
Gille A'Bhuidseir: The Wizard's Gillie and Other Tales. Ed. and trans. John G. McKay. London: Saint Catherine Press, 1914. From the magnificent Manuscript Collections of the late J. F. Campbell of Islay.

H. T. Francis, "The Rash Magician" (1916)
Jātaka Tales. Cambridge: Cambridge University Press, 1916.

Claude-Marius Barbeau, "The Two Magicians" (1916)
"Les deux Magiciens." *Journal of American Folklore* 29.61 (January–March 1916): 87–99.

Sokratis Stephanu Kiomurzoghlu, "Master and Pupil" (1916)
R. M. Dawkins. *Modern Greek in Asia Minor*. Cambridge: Cambridge University Press, 1916. 365–69.

Hermann Hesse, "The Forest Dweller" (1917)
"Der Waldmensch." First published as "Kubu" in *Simplicissimus* (1917).

Johann Georg von Hahn, "The Teacher and His Pupil" (1918)
"Der Lehrer und sein Schüler." *Griechische und albanesische Märchen*. Vol. 2. Leipzig: W. Engelmann, 1864.

Adolf Dirr, "The Master and His Pupils" (1920)
Caucasian Folk-Tales. Trans. Lucy Menzies. London: Dent, 1925. First published in *Kaukasische Märchen*. Jena: Diederichs, 1920.

Heywood Broun, "Red Magic" (1921)
Seeing Things at Night. New York: Harcourt, Brace, 1921.

Dean Fansler, "The Mysterious Book" (1921)
Filipino Popular Tales. Lancaster, PA: American Folklore Society, 1921.

Elsie Clews Parsons, "The Battle of the Enchanters" (1923)
Folk-Lore from the Cape Verde Islands. New York: George Stechert, 1923.

Georg Goyert, "Jan the Sorcerer" (1924)
"Jan der Zauberer." *Vlämische Märchen*. Jena: Eugen Diederichs, 1925.

C. Fillingham Coxwell, "The Frame-Story to Siddhi-Kur" (1925)
Siberian and Other Folk-Tales. London: C. W. Daniel, 1925.

Seumas MacManus, "The Mistress of Magic" (1926)
The Donegal Wonder Book. New York: Frederick A. Stokes, 1926.

Romuald Pramberger, "The Sorcerer's Apprentice" (1926)
"Der Zauberlehrling." *Deutsche Märchen aus dem Donaulande*. Ed. Paul Zaunert. Jena: Eugen Diederichs, 1926.

Norbert Lebermann, "The Magician's Apprentice" (1927)
"Der Zauberlehrling." *Blaue Blumen*. Nuremberg: Süddeutsche Verlags Akt, 1927. Trans. Frieda Bachmann. Illustr. Margaret Freeman. New York: Alfred Knopf, 1930.

Paul Fenimore Cooper, "The Devils Duped" (1928)
Tricks of Women & Other Albanian Tales. New York: William Morrow, 1928.

Ben Kroup, "Horse, Hound, and Hawk" (1930–32)
Told by John Power.
George Gmelch and Ben Kroup. *To Shorten the Road*. Dublin: O'Brien Press, 1978.

E. S. Oakley and Tara Dutt Gairola, "A Magical Contest" (1935)
Himalayan Folklore. Kumaon and West Nepal. New Dehli: Cosmo Publications, 1935.

Helen Zunser, "The Two Witches" (1935)
Told by Antonio.
"A New Mexican Village." *Journal of American Folklore* 18.188 (April–June 1935): 125–78.

Joseph Médard Carrière, "The Two Magicians" (1937)
"Les deux Magiciens." *Tales from the French-Folklore of Missouri.* Evanston, IL: Northwestern
    University Studies, 1937.

Alfred Ehrentreich, "Meister und Schüler" (1938)
Englische Volksmärchen. Jena: Eugen Diederichs Verlag, 1938.

Richard Rostron, "The Sorcerer's Apprentice" (1941)
The Sorcerer's Apprentice. Illustr. Frank Lieberman. New York: William Morrow, 1941.

Elsie Clews Parsons, "The Battle of the Enchanters" (1943)
Folk-Lore of the Antilles, French and English: Part III. New York: American Folk-Lore Society,
    1943.

Howard Wheeler, "Los Dos Hermanos" (1943)
Tales from Jalisco Mexico. Philadelphia: American Folk-Lore Society, 1943.

Thomas Brendel and William Troxell, "The Magician" (1944)
Pennsyvania German Folk Tales, Legends, Once-Upon-a-Time Stories, Maxism, and Sayings.
    Norristown, PA: Pennsylvania German Society, 1944.

Iakov Khatchatrianz, "Okhik" (1946)
Armenian Folk Tales. Trans. N. W. Orloff. Illustr. Martyros Saryan. Philadelphia: Colonial
    House, 1946.

George and Helen Papashvily, "Mywhat" (1946)
Yes and No Stories: A Book of Georgian Folk Tales. Illustr. Simon Lissim. New York: Harper
    & Brothers, 1946.

In-Sôb Zông, "The Legend of Zôn U-Czi" (1952)
Folk Tales from Korea. London: Routledge & Kegan Paul, 1952.

Katharine Briggs, "Auld Scairie and the Black Cat" (1955)
Told by Robert Stewart.
British Folk-Tales. Part B. Vol. 2. London: Routledge & Kegan Paul, 1971.

Richard Dorson, "The Mojo" (1956)
Told by Abraham Taylor.
Negro Folktales in Michigan. Cambridge, MA: Harvard University Press, 1956.

Harold Courlander, "The Do-All Ax" (1957)
Terrapin's Pot of Sense. New York: Henry Holt, 1957.

James Cloyd Bowman and Margery Bianco, "Nilo and the Wizard" (1958)
Tales from a Finnish Tupa. Trans. Aili Kolehmainen. Illustr. Laura Bannon. Chicago: Albert
   Whitman, 1958.

John Mason Brewer, "The High Sheriff and His Servant" (1958)
Dog Ghosts and Other Texas Negro Folk Tales. Austin: University of Texas Press, 1958.

Marie Campbell, "The Boy That Was Trained to Be a Thief" (1958)
Tales from the Cloud Walking Country. Bloomington: Indiana University Press, 1958.

Corinne Saucier, "The Man and His Son" (1962)
Folk Tales from French Louisiana. Baton Rouge, LA: Claitor's Publishing Division, 1962.

Keigo Seki, "The Good Fortune Kettle" (1963)
Folktales of Japan. Trans. Robert Adams. Chicago: University of Chicago Press, 1963.

Richard Dorson, "Two Witches" (1964)
Buying the Wind: Regional Folklore in the United States. Chicago: University of Chicago Press, 1964.

Nicholas Stuart Gray, "The Sorcerer's Apprentices" (1965)
The Sorcerer's Apprentices. New York: St. Martin's Press, 1965.

John Mbiti, "A Man Who Could Transform Himself" (1966)
Akamba Stories. Oxford: Clarendon Press, 1966.

Dov Noy, "The Pupil Who Excelled His Master" (1969)
Folktales of Israel. Trans. Gene Baharav. Chicago: University of Chicago Press, 1969.

Katharine Briggs, "The Black King of Morocco" (1970)
A Dictionary of British Folk-Tales in the English Language. Vol. 1. London: Routledge & Kegan
   Paul, 1970.

Alfred Kurti, "The Bald Herdsman" (1971)
Persian Folktales. London: G. Bell & Sons, 1971.

John Langstaff, "The Two Magicians" (1973)
The Two Magicians. Illustr. Fritz Eichenberg. New York: Atheneum, 1973.

Maja Bošković-Stulli, "The Devil and His Pupil" (1975)
"Der Teufel und sein Schüler." *Kroatische Volksmärchen*. Trans. Wolfgang Eschker and Vladimir
   Milak. Cologne: Diederichs Verlag, 1975.

Günter Petschel, "How a Boy Escaped the Devil" (1975)
"Wie ein Knabe dem Teufel entrissen ward." *Niedersächsische Sagen*. Göttingen: Otto Schwartz,
   1975.

Neil Philip, "The Black Laird" (1975)
Narrated by Betsy Whyte and recorded by Peter Cooke and Linda Headlee.
The Penguin Book of Scottish Folktales. London: Penguin Books, 1991.

Jacqueline Simpson, "Schoolboys Raise the Devil" and "The Wizard of Abergavenny" (1976)
The Folklore of the Welsh Border. London: B. T. Batsford, 1976.

Patrick Ford, "The Tale of Gwion Bach" (1977)
The Mabinogi and Other Medieval Welsh Tales. Berkeley: University of California Press, 1977.

Henri Pourrat, "The Little Grey Bird or the Apprentice Who Ate the Master" (1977)
"Le petit oiseau gris ou l'apprenti qui mangea le maître." *Le diable et ses diableries*. Ed. Claire
    Pourrat. Paris: Gallimard, 1977. 355–65.

Felix Karlinger, "The Art That Nobody Can Do" (1979)
"Die Kunst, die keiner kann." *Märchen griechischer Inseln*. Cologne: Eugen Diederichs Verlag,
    1979.

Assen Nicoloff, "The Devil and His Disciple" (1979)
Bulgarian Folktales. Cleveland: A. Nicoloff, 1979.

Claire Booss, "The Pupil Who Excelled His Master" (1984)
Scandinavian Folk and Fairy Tales: From Norway, Sweden, Denmark, Finland, Iceland. New
    York: Avenel Books, 1984.

Inea Bushnaq, "The Boy Magician" (1986)
Arab Folk Tales. New York; Pantheon, 1986.

Jurjen Kooi and Theo Schuster, "Hans Bär" (1994)
Der Großherzog und die Marktfrau: Märchen und Schwänke aus dem Oldenburger Land. Leer:
    Schuster, 1994.

Herbert Halpert and J.D.A. Widdowson, "Master Arch" (1996)
Folktales of New Foundland: The Resilience of the Oral Tradition. Vol. 1. St. John's, New
    Foundland: Breakwater Books, 1996.

A. K. Ramanujan, "The Guru and His Disciple" (1997)
A Flowering Tree and Other Oral Tales from India. Preface by Stuart Blackburn and Alan
    Dundes. Berkeley: University of California Press, 1997.

Stuart Blackburn, "The Guru and His Disciple" (2001)
Fictions: Tamil Folktales from Oral Tradition. Helsinki: Academica Scientiarum Fennica, 2001.

Hans-Hermann Bartens, "The Alcoholic Shoemaker" (2003)
"Der trunksüchtige Schuster." *Märchen aus Lappland*. Munich: Hugendubel, 2003.

Maura McHugh, "The Master and His Apprentice" (2012)
Twisted Fairy Tales. Illustr. Jane Laurie. London: Quantum Publishing, 2012. London: Asiatic
    Society of Bengal, 1880–84.

ndex

NOTE: *n* following a page number indicates an end- or footnote.